Joy

Joy

Book 2 of Heavensgate

Leo Kane

Copyright (C) 2015 Leo Kane
Layout design and Copyright (C) 2021 by Next Chapter
Published 2021 by Next Chapter
Cover art by Griffith Designs
This book is a work of fiction. Names, characters, places, and incidents are the product of the author's imagination or are used fictitiously. Any resemblance to actual events, locales, or persons, living or dead, is purely coincidental.
All rights reserved. No part of this book may be reproduced or transmitted in any form or by any means, electronic or mechanical, including photocopying, recording, or by any information storage and retrieval system, without the author's permission.

To Cheryl, Faye and Rachael, my beloved daughters, I experienced the true meaning of joy the first time I held you in my arms. In this life and the next the joy of you will never leave me.

Did you discover wonderment inside a yearning?
A change in your atmosphere
Was there an ease inside your hurting?
when you found joy inside a fear
Throw a hate into the pond…
throw a wish to sink it down
You had an affair with the beyond
without ever making a sound
Found love with the eclipse
A fear with a half moon
can you touch a stranger with a kiss?
To hatred you become immune
I wish to let us imitate reality
chase the dragons from our dreams
Show me your gift of immortality
walk the stars so we may trap the beams
Naomi S Porch, 2015

'Some of you say,
"Joy is greater than sorrow," and others say, "Nay, sorrow is the greater."
But I say unto you they are inseparable.
Together they come, and when one sits with you at your board, remember that the other is asleep upon your bed.'
Khalil Gilbran, The Prophet

'Spes anchora vitae'
'Hope is the anchor of my life.'
Joy

Chapter One

-THE END OF THE BEGINNING-

Jacob fought for every agonising breath as the anguished voice of his alter-ego, Jake, screamed in his head,

Listen to me, Jacob. Go to sleep, let me out and I will save us. Let me the fuck out man.

Jacob clutched his chest, pleading with the beautiful apparition, 'No please, don't. I don't want to see it; please don't make me look.'

Stop begging and fight her man, fight her. For sweet fuck's sake let me out, Jacob.

Relentless, cruel time, counted down the slow thud of Jacob's heart as he collapsed to the floor. His last seconds marched into eternity as he suffered crushing overwhelming pain.

Give us our fucking heart back, bitch.

Merciless needles travelled down Jacob's left arm, stitching him into oblivion.

This fuckin' hurts man; it's fuckin' killing us. Let me out.

She stood over Jacob, long silver hair flowing around her body as if she floated underwater; her arms stretched out to him with her bony white hands cupped open revealing her treasure. Jacob lay gasping like a fish on a cruel hook, tears streaming from his eyes. He knew it was over.

Heavensgate: Joy

Don't you dare fuckin' look in her hands, Jacob, or I swear on Satan's shit I will kill you myself.

Jacob saw it, nestling and beating in her palms, a misshapen, brown, wet, muddy heart, initialed with a childish 'J'.

The vision spoke, her words resonating in his mind like gently chiming bells ringing out his soul, 'See you soon, sweetie. I have your heart in my hands.'

Hope. Oh fuck. Jacob, it's Hope. Don't leave me, Jacob. Nooooooooo.

Chapter Two

-THE GATE-

Heavensgate glowed like an oasis in the firmament. To human eyes it might appear as a bright, delicate, candle flame burning inside a snow globe, but no living human would ever pass this way. Profound darkness surrounded the Gate and the silent universe swept over it on a tsunami of stars. It had been an age since the Angels were summoned here and Heavensgate's combination of eternal and earthly beauty dazzled them. Even so, they would rather be far away from this place.

Death had commanded the immortals to attend a special passing.

The Angel Redemption waited with Hope in angry silence. Gabriel balked at the last moment and turned to flee, reluctant to enter the Realm of Inbetween, until his Lord took his hand and, as all must do when touched by Death, the Angel became serene.

In the Lodge at Heavensgate, the immortals congregated around Jacob Andersen's almost, but not quite, empty body.

Hope threw Death a petulant glance. She floated back and forth as if blown by an invisible breeze, tapping her sharp little teeth with translucent finger nails. Hidden inside her robe, she wore a fine silver chain from which hung a small, withered, black heart. Her icy tears fell onto the corpse as her voice rang out in sorrow saying, 'I have played my part in this vile event. What is the delay?'

Death declined to reply, drilling into her spirit with eyes that spun galaxies until she added, 'I beg your indulgence, my Lord.'

Redemption bowed in deference to Lord Death and nodded a greeting at Gabriel. The fiery Angel waited, pretending patience, dressed in her faded, red cloak. It was an item of clothing Gabriel thought belonged in the Middle Ages. The pale Angel stared at Jacob's body, his expression mournful, biting pink manicured nails. Together, the four Guardians of the Gate bore witness as they waited for the life story to conclude.

Louise knelt by her husband's cooling body. She pinched his nose and breathed living air between his indigo lips, repeatedly pressing hard on his still chest. She prayed, 'Please God don't take him from me. Jacob, my love, breathe for me, baby. Oh God, no no nooooo.'

Death glanced at his pocket watch as the melody 'Que Sera, Sera' drifted into the air, the notes discordant and tinny.

-What a lot fuss. If I could I would plug my ears from this cacophony of anguish.-

Hope cursed him under her breath.

Inexorable as the tide Death moved toward the mortals. Hope wept, comforted by Gabriel, who fought to control an embarrassing nervous tic as he wrapped his silken opaque wings around her. Redemption glanced at them and sighed in annoyance before disappearing further into the cloak's soft folds to watch Death's starlit hand assist the departure of Jacob's spirit.

Hope sobbed louder and the melancholy knell of funeral bells clanged and crashed in the air around them. The noise broke Redemption's fragile tolerance and she snapped, 'Hope, give it up. You had your chance with this mortal. Maybe if you had kept your rampant libido in check this wouldn't be happening.'

Hope broke away from Gabriel's hug and turned on Redemption, her eyes flashing ice. She choked back her retort as the immortals witnessed a second spirit that rose like oily smoke from the cooling cadaver's mouth.

Gabriel fluttered long, jewel-studded lashes at Death, a question in his eyes. Death shrugged. The appearance of the demon was of no immediate interest. His duty was to lead Jacob's soul through the Gate.

The shade took form as Gabriel asked Hope, 'Did you know there were two spirits in there?'

Flashing across the short space between them the apparition towered in a black funnel in front of Hope, cutting off her reply and wrapping her in the stench of burning flesh. Gabriel ran to hide behind Redemption who sneered at him mouthing, 'Coward.' He didn't care, his aura quivered in warning.

Hope stopped weeping. She watched, intrigued as the apparition spun and coalesced until it took the form of a man. In a jangling voice she said, 'Jake, is that you?'

The spirit screamed in terrible pain and anguish and, employing the menace of Hell to give it voice, shouted,

WHAT THE FUCK JUST HAPPENED HERE?

Something akin to human pity flitted across Hope's ancient gray eyes as she said, 'What just happened here, Jake, is **I** saved **him** from **you**.'

Fuck you Hope, bring Jacob back.

'It's not in my power, Jake.'

Hope, either bring Jacob back or fuckin' take me away from this hell. I can't survive without the stupid bastard; you gotta take us both together.

Redemption threw back her cloak and exploded in a blaze of freezing red light, blinding Jake who flinched, passing an arm before his eyes like a shield. Gabriel admired Redemption's magnificence from a distance, awestruck.

Jake threw his shade on top of Jacob's body in an attempt to re-enter it and fell through the cooling flesh to disappear under the floor. He returned confused and discouraged, to face Redemption who asked,

'Jake, are you ready to repent?'

Repent? What the fuck for?

'Then the Gate refuses entry to you and your fragments, Demon.'

I am not a demon. I have no fragments. My name is Jake Andersen and that thing on the floor is my body, which I need. So put me and Jacob back in it or take me with him.

-We refuse you, Demon. You may not pass through the Gate without our blessing.-

Jake whined, *You can't do this to me.*

Redemption took pity. 'Jake, I invite you to repent the murders, the rapes, the lies and the illusions which you used Jacob's mind and body for.'

Jake stamped his feet crying, *I did it all so he wouldn't have to. He wanted me to do those things, he was a yellow-bellied coward. He used me.*

Death's voice crashed through Jake's spirit like thunder.

-No, you unrepentant, misbegotten son of the Devil, you used Jacob to commit evil. You will not cross the Gate. The honour must be earned. Demon, you have much soul work to do if you wish to leave here.-

Jake moaned, *It isn't fair. Why won't you help me?*

Hope turned her lovely face away from the tortured ghost.

The fragment known as Jake tipped its head to one side as if listening to a voice only he could hear. He clicked his fingers and grinned at Death who snarled and shielded his immortals behind him. The Guardians watched, helpless as Jake's shadow grew vibrant, attaining the appearance of a healthy man in his prime. Jake flexed muscular shoulders, punched the air and shouted, *Thank you, my Lord.*

No longer afraid or pleading he smiled and taking Hope's hands in his, said,

My Lord has spoken and now I understand. I'm free of that streak of chicken shit yellow bellied sonofabitch. I am free of Saint fuckin' Jacob. Join me, Hope.

Hope stretched her lips and ran her tongue over her teeth. Her voice clanged like broken bells as, staring unflinching into Jake's astounding jade eyes, she said, 'Your soul is free to seek Redemption. Don't waste any more time.'

Jake embraced her. *Stay with me, Hope. I love you. It was always me who loved you. Jacob was never man enough. Stay and help me to learn how to repent. Hope, I need you.*

She struggled out of his arms to reply, 'You are not a man. You belong to your dark lord, the Beast. You lost me long ago.'

Jake bowed low, mocking her, then straightening up he spat in her face and shouted, *Well fuck you too, my Lady, you prick-teasing bitch.*

A sly look crept across his handsome face as he strutted over to Death and stared with unflinching insolence into his star filled eyes. Gabriel moaned and grabbed hold of Redemption, who stood glaring at Hope with disgust distorting her striking features.

Jake crowed like a lunatic.

So, all powerful Reaper, tell me, as Jacob has gone, am I right in thinking that Heavensgate, the Lodge, Lake Disregard, the town, everything, all of this is mine?

He spread his arms wide and spun around on the spot leaving smoke rings in his wake.

Death was bored with the game.

-Demon, this Realm exists for every soul granted the misfortune or opportunity to pass through. Kneel and thank the Creator for your place at Heavensgate. Don't waste your remarkable good fortune.-

Oh I won't. Thanks for the advice, fucker.

-Do no more harm. I wish you remorse, repentance and redemption.-

Why does that sound like a curse?

-It will be what you make it.-

Wait. Listen, please. The twins, Nancy and Sam, they died, but I swear that when they were in their coffins they looked at me. Hope, they looked at me as if they hated me. It wasn't my fault, the fire… it was not my fault!

With reluctant compassion Hope replied, 'The fire was your doing, Jake, however, it is understood there was no intent to do harm. Have faith in the truth and start from there. I will know when you are ready. Look.'

Fuck off, I saw what you just did to Jacob. I won't look. No.

-I command you, Demon, to look at my Lady.-

Jake's eyes refused to close as his head turned of its own accord forcing his gaze to fix on Hope.

She reached into her gown, pulling out the chain to reveal the blackened and misshapen heart that hung there. It was weak, it was damaged, but it was beating. Hope's voice rang sharp in his head as she said, 'We will meet again, Jake. Your heart will tell me when you are ready.'

Chapter Three

-HOME COMING-

The Guardian opened the Gate releasing delicate light that illuminated the immortal gathering. Death beckoned to a waiting female spirit whose love for the dead man shone bright as a newly forged sword.

-Come, Annie, reclaim your son.-

She stepped forward, excited and smiling until Jake dropped to the floor and crawled toward her. A sick mewling sound issued from his throat as he attempted to kiss her feet. Sounding as sincere as the devil he said, *Mom, I love you.*

Annie's spirit wavered as she cried out, 'You are *not* my son. You are a child of fire and hate, a parasite on this place and on Jacob's soul. I command you, Demon, to leave him now.'

Jake leaped to his feet screaming, *Well fuck you too, you old cumbag.*

Annie raised her hand as if to strike him, but let it fall to her side and said, 'I forgive you.'

Jake opened his mouth to reply when they heard a child's sweet voice ask, 'Momma? Have you come for me, Momma?'

Annie and Jake fell to their knees before Jacob's soul which had assumed his seven year old form. Jake held out his arms to the boy and begged,

Jacky. Please don't leave me. We are the same person. Stay with me.

Heavensgate: Joy

Fighting tears of joy, Annie spoke to her beloved son, saying, 'Look, Daddy's here, sweetheart. Come to momma, it's time to leave.'

Jon Andersen, once again a young husband and father, bent to tickle his son under the chin and, in a voice gruff with emotion, said, 'Jacky, you're safe now. You want to climb up, eh?'

The child laughed with excitement as Jon raised him onto his broad shoulders. With Annie at his side, they ignored Jake's screams and wails and walked back through the Gate. As they passed over Jon jiggled his hips from side to side, singing, *'I'm your Boogie Man'* creating fits of giggles in Jacky who wrapped small fingers into his father's hair, his eyes wide with wonder as he spotted his brother and sister playing on the other side.

Jake crawled over to Jacob's cooling corpse to sit beside the silently weeping, oblivious and recently widowed Louise. He snarled at her saying,

I preferred Susie to you, you cold hearted bitch. Why aren't you dead? Where's Tommy? What is going on here? I hate this fuckin' hell hole.

Louise shivered as Jake's invisible rage washed over her raising goosebumps on her flesh. Realising it was time to call 911 she rose on stiff legs to end the heartbroken vigil over her husband's body. Jake glared at her retreating back.

That's right, fuck off and leave us, we don't need you.

Holding Jacob's hand he rocked and keened.

It's not fair, Jacob, I want to go with you. Come back for me.

Sometime later, the paramedics comforted Louise and collected Jacob's body. Darkness enveloped Jake's anguish transporting him into the Nothing where the Beast welcomed him home with great celebration and affection.

The empty Lodge settled down to wait.

Death placed an elegant arm across Gabriel's shoulders. Hugging him to his side and kissing the top of his dark head, he said,

-Close the Gate, my Angel. In a multi-verse of astounding events this has to be one of my personal favourites.-

Gabriel's wings and eyelashes fluttered under Death's rare praise. He clasped his hands and began the chant that would seal the Gate. It clashed closed with the sound of a million cymbals, sparking thunder and lightning. The cacophony rode a sound wave that birthed an avalanche high in the Sierra's majestic peaks. A tsunami of snow pushed the wind before it, blasting the slender tops of thousands of pine trees that bent their heads as if in prayer or mourning. The same almighty force pressed Lake Disregard's water back from the shore, revealing emptiness darker than the vacuum of space. Redemption applauded. Death called out,

-Bravo, Gabriel. Magnificent as ever.-

Hope waited for the spectacle to end and drew closer to Death. Her seductive voice chimed as she asked, 'My Lord, is the demon, Jake, to be denied passage through the Gate for all eternity?'

-I am not privy to the Creator's plans for such abominations. However,-

Death loomed over Hope, his soft voice holding a thinly concealed threat as he said, **there is a matter of greater import that I must discuss with you, my Lady.-**

Hope glanced at Redemption, who threw her a sarcastic smile while Gabriel chewed his finger nails.

-**The stalemate between Joy and I must come to an end. Hope, you will return her heart and bring her spirit to me without question or argument. You are not to rescue Joy from her destiny. Be the nothingness; be without substance; be without influence. Do not interfere again. No more excuses. Obey my command.-**

Hope's voice chimed uncertainly as she said, 'My Lord, what if I cannot return her heart and, therefore, cannot obey your command?'

Death sighed and replied,

-All souls choose their path and if they stray it is our immortal duty to guide them home. It is your duty, Hope, to play your part. Return Joy's heart or suffer the consequences.-

Redemption wrapped herself tightly in her cloak, nodding in solemn agreement and amusement as Gabriel pretended not to hear the exchange and busied himself preening his feathers.

As is her nature, Hope could not let the matter rest. She pressed Death further, asking, 'What will Joy have left if I refuse to give her my gift of hope, my Lord?'

Death's voice thickened the atmosphere with menace as he said,

-You test my patience, Lady. Joy is not mortal, you know this. She chose this reincarnation to remind her spirit of human despair and sorrow. Her purpose was to gain empathy in order that she may help multitudes of souls to appreciate the fleeting euphoria of happiness.-

Hope huffed saying, 'That is torture.'

Exasperated, Death grasped Hope by her shoulders and, controlling his temper, said,

-Joy chose her path. This is the last time I will remind you, Lady Hope, to stop meddling in her journey. She strayed once before, and she is ripe and ready to stray again.-

Hope gazed into his eyes and said, 'Sweet Lord, she was a child.'

Death thrust her away from him. Redemption snorted with derision as Hope stumbled.

-Enough! Joy *was* a child, she is one no longer. She must fulfill her destiny, as must every soul. You, Lady Hope, will cease to question the Creator's plans.-

'I will, in a moment.' Hope recovered her composure and flashed a rare smile Death's way as she pressed on asking, 'What is the Creator planning for Jake?'

Death stood clenching and unclenching his fists. Frustrated and bewitched in equal measure, he struggled to deny Hope an answer.

-Jake is of the Demon kind. He was a mere fragment of Jacob Andersen's human life. The personality cannot be considered

alive in the human sense. It is damaged, irretrievably wounded. Nothing good can survive it.-

Hope shone icy blue as she told him, 'My Lord, I witnessed their suffering. Jacob is free but the Beast's sickness feeds on Jake's fragmented soul like cancer. He is weary beyond endurance and...'

-*And* what insignificant scrap of 'humanity' and life remains in the demon is fortunate that you, Hope, stole its black heart.-

Hope rallied and retorted, 'I am not to blame for this. When I *collected* Jacob's heart I could not have known the demon had him. I fulfilled my duty to bring hope to a child whose heart was intent on killing him with grief. My Lord.'

-Irrelevant. You interfered with destiny and you continue to meddle.-

Gabriel found his courage and purred, 'Where there is life there is Hope and vice versa. Isn't that so, my Lord?'

Death scoffed at him.

-Believe what you will, Gabriel. My Lady will obey me.-

Redemption scowled in disbelief as Hope bowed her head before her Lord saying, 'Please forgive my impertinence, my Lord. I adore you.'

-I do not require adoration. I demand obedience. Leave this place. We have work to do.-

Chapter Four

-ENGLAND, 1983-

In the living room of a stone-built cottage at the English seaside, brown and yellow floral curtains were pulled tight across the leaded window to hide the occupants from prying eyes.

Joy sat ramrod straight on the wreck of a stained sagging sofa, afraid to make the slightest noise and chewing her fingernails until they bled. The child was forced to keep her place and face forward; she was their audience.

Eight year old Joy knew her dad wasn't the real danger, her mother, Glenda, known in the village as Madonna, was the greater threat, the parent to be most feared and best avoided. Glenda was the one who relished reminding Joy that she was forced upon her; the one who ensured her daughter understood that she was unwanted, unloved and useless. This was the woman who gathered Joy on her lap for 'story time', held her close and made her look up the word 'abortion' in the dictionary.

The adults fought and Joy watched. Glenda and Ken faced each other in the cramped room, their bodies leaning forward, bouncing on their toes like boxers. Their features distorted with hate, reminding Joy of the gargoyles that decorated the church, as they hurled abuse and threats like poison darts intended to wound and disable the strongest of loves and their love didn't come close.

Ken grabbed Glenda by her skinny throat, his spittle flying in her eyes as he screamed, 'Don't fight me, Madonna. Don't you fucking move, bitch. I'm warning you, if you want to see tomorrow, don't…even…breathe.'

Seeing compliance in her eyes, he released his grip and stood before his wife with his hands rested on his knees, panting as if he had run a marathon. Glenda, her neck branded where the fingers of the man she chose to love, honour and cherish had throttled her, stood immobile as a royal guard on sentry duty. Ken picked up a bottle of vodka, took a swig and wiped his mouth with the back of his hand before slapping his wife across her vacant face and shouting, 'Do you even care how your Virgin Mary act makes me feel, eh? Do you?'

Having no more nails to go at, Joy sucked a loose strand of hair as she witnessed a short cessation of hostilities while her parents gathered strength for round two. This was a routine the three of them knew well and each one played their part to perfection.

Ken was ready to go again. He snarled, 'Let's see what a bloody Holy Virgin looks like.' A flush of shame rose unchecked from Joy's chest to her cheeks as her father struggled with Glenda's clothes, fighting reluctant zips, hooks and sleeves. He spewed foul, spiteful curses as seams ripped and buttons flew. Her mother moved only to raise her arms and legs to facilitate the brutal stripping. She didn't protest or make any attempt to resist. Joy wanted her Mum to fight back; she never did. Glenda saved her pain and anger for her small daughter.

Joy stared at a stain on the wall, every muscle tense and aching as she waited for this latest episode of marital madness to escalate. Ken loomed over her shouting, 'Look girl. See what happens to whores that parade themselves as pure. Take a bloody good look and never, ever forget this.'

He bundled up his wife's clothes and flung them into the open fire where hungry flames licked and tasted the meal before devouring it whole. Glenda waited naked, gaunt and albino-white apart from the multi-coloured bruises on her torso. Ken's wiry body shook with self-righteous fury as he prodded the burning rags with an iron poker then left it to rest in the fire. Joy's stomach clenched and tears began to fall as she watched him wait for the moment that it would glow red hot.

Ken looked at his small daughter who struggled to control her shakes and said, 'I'm doing this for you, Joy. It's my job to protect you. Your pure virginal mummy should keep her mouth shut. The lying bitch will get you crucified one day.'

The poker glowed amongst the coals. It was time. Glenda shuddered. Joy accidentally caught her mother's eye as she heard the trickle of urine running onto the carpet. Glenda threw her a vicious smile and Joy dragged her eyes away, trembling inside and out. She needed to get away and hide before she was made to pay in hair and skin for her 'lack of respect.'

She risked closing her stinging eyes as Ken raised the poker in front of her mother's exquisite face. His voice relaxed and gentle, he said, 'You choose the spot, Madonna, or I must.'

Joy held her breath; her heart beat like a trapped bird behind her ribs. Anticipation made her retch. Glenda held out her left forearm, supporting her elbow on the palm of her right hand. She steeled herself as the man she had loved and trusted with her life carefully positioned the searing hot metal across an unhealed wound.

The smell of burning flesh filled the cottage, followed by a sickening crack as Glenda's head hit the tiled hearth. Scarlet blood trickled to join the urine on the carpet. Brandishing the poker, Ken turned his attention on Joy snarling, 'Get upstairs, you little bitch, while I take care of your poor sick mother.'

She sidled past him on weak legs, head down and arms crossed protectively in front of her frail body. Out of his reach, she pelted up the steep narrow stairs as if pursued by the hounds of hell. She crashed into her bedroom and shot under the bed where she lay, trembling like a sapling in a storm.

Downstairs, her father, sweating booze and choking on his crocodile tears, dropped the poker and used his bare hands to bat out the flame that licked at Glenda's hair. He picked up his wife and carried her naked violated body to the couch where he sobbed out his self-pity saying, 'Why do you make me do this, Glenda? Why? You know how much I love you, lass.' Then he unzipped his jeans and pissed on her face.

Chapter Five

-SPES ANCHORA VITAE-

Joy waited long enough to be confident that her father had passed out drunk before daring to leave the flimsy shelter of her hiding place. She stared at her reflection in the tall mirror; had an idea and walked toward it with her skinny arms stretched out before her. Rare tears streaked down her face as she begged, 'Please let me in magic mirror, please, please let me in.' Her tiny fingers knocked against the unrelenting glass.

Joy wasn't surprised when the mirror didn't help her. After all, it was the same one her mother would stand Joy in front of, naked, and say, 'Mirror, mirror on the wall who is the ugliest girl of all?' Glenda would pretend to listen as the mirror answered her before saying in an offended tone, 'You are right mirror. It is Joy, *she* is the ugliest of them all.' Glenda would then take her time to point out her shamed daughter's ugliness in the mirror, inch by inch.

The humiliation would only end when Joy forced out the hated words, 'I'm sorry I ruined your life, Mother. I'm sorry I offend you and the mirror.' Satisfied, Glenda would say, 'Stay here and think about how your badness and ugliness hurt me.' Sometimes she would spit on Joy as she left. Other times she would nurse her and sing 'There Once Was an Ugly Duckling' while she rocked Joy on her knees and stroked her hair. Those times were the most terrifying of all.

For as long as Joy could remember, life had been frightening. She lived in dread that her alcoholic father would find her in one of her secret hidey holes or, worse still, that her mother would beat him to it.

She was habitually locked in the cellar 'for your own good', where she huddled trembling in the coal dust, listening in clinging darkness to foul words fly like knives across the room above her head. She never cried. She refused to cry, even when her mother beat her black and blue, even when she tore chunks out of her hair, screaming, 'You vain little whore.'

When Glenda nipped the tender skin behind Joy's knees and at her inner thigh, the pain made the child heave and retch, but she never allowed a single tear to fall.

After Joy was forced to spend sleepless hours on the cold, earthen, cellar floor Glenda would shake her awake as weak sunlight crept through the coal grate overhead. On those mornings, Joy was dragged by her hair up the worn stone steps and into the kitchen. Her mother made the exhausted child stand naked in a plastic bowl full of tepid water where she was scrubbed red raw until her father said, 'That's enough Glenda, the little whore looks all shiny and new. You can dress her now'.

'There you are, my ugly duckling, all fresh out of the packet,' Glenda would say after brushing Joy's long blonde hair one hundred times while her father polished her school shoes with his spit, singing and whistling Monty Python's, *Always Look on the Bright Side of Life,* the muscles in arms flexing as he worked out the 'bloody scuffs and scratches'. By the time Joy was ready, any one glancing through the kitchen window would have smiled at the scene of familial bliss.

Usually late, she would be dropped off at the local school's big iron gates and ordered by her father to, 'Get out of the bloody car and say not a word to anyone or you'll get what's coming to you, my lass.' Entering the huge, red brick building, tired and full of dread, she would frequently receive the stinging slap of a wooden ruler across her palm for 'telling wicked lies about why you are late'. She was brave and, despite her parents' threats, when punishment was meted out for lateness or for sleeping in class, she told her teachers the truth, but if they believed her they never said so. Her last school report read:

'Joy has such a vivid imagination; she should aim to be either a novelist or a politician.'

The unloved child was losing weight and losing hope. At night, even in the cellar, she knelt on grazed scabby knees and prayed silently to baby Jesus that Glenda and Ken would disappear. She prayed for rescue that never came.

Joy was withdrawn and unnaturally tidy in appearance so, children, being cruel as only they can be, ensured school was a ritual of bullying. She endured taunts and lonely playtimes spent trying to blend into the background or hide in the toilet block; which is where she was when a small cold hand pressed something into her palm.

A small girl, with long silver hair and a dress made of violet flowers, stood before her. She tipped her head to one side and smiled, then rushed to embrace Joy before disappearing through the back of the cubicle.

Joy squealed in shock as she felt a sharp pain in her right hand and the warm slickness of scarlet blood that trickled between her fingers. She ran to the row of small sinks and held her palm under freezing water until the throbbing subsided. Drying her hand on her skirt she stared wide eyed at violet lettering that moved like veins beneath her pale skin, it read:

spes anchora vitae

She bit her lip and clenched her hand tight, dashing from cubicle to cubicle, throwing open the wooden doors. She was alone. Her knees shook and tears pricked the back of her eyes as she whispered, 'Where are you girl? What have you done? Madonna will kill me when she sees this.' There was no answer. As the bell for lessons rang in the yard, Joy opened her fist to find her skin clear and unmarked.

Chapter Six

-PAPER HEARTS-

One winter's day, Joy's life changed forever.

It was the last day of term before Christmas and the Bay wore sunny, but frosty weather. The North Sea shimmered like blue silk, while greedy gulls cried, turning lazy circles across the cloudless sky.

Joy, exhausted after spending another night in the cellar, had fallen asleep at her battered school desk. Hearing the gentle tinkle of Christmas bells she roused herself to see a woman facing the class. The stranger's white hair flowed down to her ankles; her dress was embroidered with violets that seemed to leap off the material to spread their scent around the room as she moved flashing rainbow lights from silver rings and bangles. The class was awestruck, even Jimmy was quiet, his big, hazel eyes staring through a messy ginger fringe.

The woman spoke in a sing-song voice. 'Hello, my sweets. I am Hope. Today we will make your hearts sparkle.' In her hands she held a branch of Silver Birch, bare of leaves and fixed in a pot covered in Christmas paper. Her coral tinged lips smiled, flashing perfect teeth, as she said, 'This is going to be our Friendship Tree.'

Hope raised a red velvet cloth on the teacher's desk to reveal gold and silver pens, every colour of glitter, feathers in fluorescent pinks and greens, tiny stick-on mirrors, shiny gold and silver stars and new sticks of glue. At the side was a pile of plain paper hearts, one for each child. She knelt beside them, encouraging creativity and tickling their ears to make them giggle. As the paper hearts grew brighter and shinier, the scent of Parma violet candy filled the room clinging to the children like smoke.

Joy threw herself into the task. She used every type of decoration until satisfied that her paper heart was beautiful. Hope threaded each heart on an individual loop of satin ribbon. As she tied the knots and hung the hearts on the silver branch she sang 'Jingle Bells' while the children danced around her brimming with hope that Santa would bring them the special gift off their lists.

When the Friendship Tree was finished the class applauded with sticky, glitter and ink smeared hands. The tree sparkled as its display of heart-shaped leaves spun in a slight breeze firing shards of dazzling light across the room.

Multi-coloured glitter adorned the children's faces, clothes and hair. Jimmy wore a head dress of pink feathers; his rowdy friends shrieked with laughter and chased him around, trying to knock it off his head.

While the rest of the class ran wild, Joy sat quietly admiring the tree so only she saw Hope disappear like a genie at the pantomime. She fell off her small wooden chair clutching at her throat, tears filling her eyes as her empty stomach hurled burning bile into her mouth.

Joy wasn't the only one to suffer from Hope's departure. Jimmy's cohorts viciously fought each other. Some children screamed and cried or curled up in the foetal position; others sat sucking their thumbs staring into space and rocking back and forth. When dusk fell, no-one turned on the lights.

When it was time to go home, Joy's heart was missing.

Chapter Seven

-THERE ONCE WAS AN UGLY DUCKLING-

Joy wasn't the same after she lost her heart. Her thoughts began to turn in on themselves as pain became a solid and malformed presence which followed her around, impersonating her shadow. She knew her home life was grim. She understood that she carried a dangerous dark, bad secret. It was too much for a child to bear.

In a bid to escape her warring parents, she spent hours playing on the beach, often risking the rapid tides as she stretched out her stolen moments of peace.

On Christmas Eve, 1983, ferocious North Sea waves battered the Bay heralding the approach of one of the worst storms in living memory. Despite the weather, Joy attempted to jump over the foam before the next wall of icy water crashed onto the sand. She wore her school uniform and spit polished shoes because everything else was either too small or too dirty. Shivering and wet through, she knew the state of her clothes would invite a severe beating. She didn't care. Her small stomach quivered as she thought, 'That bitch, Madonna, isn't going to lay a finger on me ever again.'

The eight year old was angry about being bullied at school, angry about the domestic violence, the shouting and beatings at home. She was sick of being thrown in the old bath full of cold water and distressed beyond measure because this morning, after the ritual painful brushing, her mother had cut off Joy's beautiful blonde hair. Glenda attacked her daughter's head with blunt kitchen scissors simply because she couldn't find a hair tie. There were bleeding cuts on her scalp where the scissors had dug in and part of one ear lobe was sliced open. Her hair looked like it belonged on a broken doll that had been attacked by a toddler. It had been a tough day for a little girl.

Joy cried out her pain to the open sea, screaming at the top of her voice,

'You don't love me. You'll be sorry when they see what you do to me. I hate you. I wish I was dead.'

She fell silent; she had spotted the unmistakable outline of her father walking along the beach toward her. Her heart leapt, Daddy was coming to save her. Mum wouldn't miss her if she disappeared, but maybe, just maybe, Dad might.

For a moment, father and daughter locked eyes across the short distance between life and death. Joy wished he would run across the stormy beach and hug her tight; if she was to live she wanted it to be because her Daddy loved her. If he loved her then perhaps she could bear the rest.

Her small heart filled with hope as she jumped up and down waving an excited two handed hello. Ken saw her, thrust his hands deeper into his pockets and shrugged his shoulders. Then he turned and walked away from the tiny daughter he and Glenda had starved of affection and abused.

Joy shivered with sorrow as hungry waves crashed down on the beach. Her last hope trudged across the sand toward the concrete slip way. Ken headed for drinks at the Bay Inn which clung, on ancient bricks and mortar, to the rocks at the foot of the village.

A sudden squall broke, pelting pain over the lonely child crying on the exposed beach. Joy felt sick and afraid, she wanted to be a cloud going home to the sea. Hot tears stung her cold cheeks; she hugged herself tight, turning in frantic circles on the sand not knowing what to do. Ken had made his choice and by the time eight year old Joy had controlled her sorrow, she had made hers.

Sea water had filled the hated school shoes drenching Joy's feet. The weather and sea spray took care of the rest of her. The bedraggled child turned her back on the village and, with her crushed heart pounding an alarm in her bony chest, she ran into the sea to face the next big wave that crashed over her head. Her feet swept from under her as she was picked up like driftwood and spun upside down. Shocked by the rush of cold, Joy swallowed freezing, salty water. Fighting her instincts she welcomed the killer into her lungs, thinking only of her parents' reaction when they found her body.
She panicked, thrashing her limbs as she was dragged out to sea on the raging, retreating tide. She was a hair's breadth away from a large rock. Hope surged in her. Her small arms reached for safety. Her vision blurred. Her small lungs overflowed and her chest exploded.

Something travelled in the deep, accompanying Joy's body as it was swept away by the current that dragged beneath, rushing to obey the pull of the moon. Death also followed, ready to hold her hand as she passed from the Mortal Realm. But, for a split second before the murderous sea swallowed her, Joy had experienced hope, and now her soul wasn't willing to be easily parted from this life.
Bemused by her persistence Death tapped at his pocket watch. He tapped a second time and the fingers continued to move forward. No irritating tune issued forth, although, for a split second, he heard the distant chime of bells. He snapped the ancient timepiece closed. This was unusual, but all things are possible and mistakes are made. He would wait.
No-one had seen Joy's father abandon his little girl to the cruel sea. No-one that is, except Joy, whose self-appointed mission was to fracture his soul and destroy her mother in the process.

Chapter Eight

-DADDY'S GIRL-

Tossed on churning black water by the storm, the crew of a small fishing boat had watched, helpless, as the little girl ran into the waves and disappeared in the tumult. There was nothing the fishermen could do. Joy was dragged out to sea as thunder crashed over the Bay and lightning struck the tall chimneys of the red roofed village. The clamour was followed by hailstones beating on land and sea. The boat's Captain raised the alarm with the Coast Guard and the search for a body began.

The weather worsened, impeding all attempts to find and recover Joy's body. Darkness fell and air rescue pilots bounced their helicopters on dangerous winds to spread searchlights over the tumult until ordered to put their own safety first. The lifeboat was forced to return to base. The despairing and exhausted crew joined the group of people who had weathered the storm to gather on the slipway and spread the news. The child was lost, there was no hope, she had drowned. The local vicar was there, waiting to see if he was needed. He met Ken's eyes across the crowd and was about to approach him when Joy's father ran back to the bar to drink himself into guilty oblivion.

The lifeboat crew, led by Skipper Solomon, made their silent, slow way up the Bay's steep and narrow lanes headed for Oakleaf Cottage. People followed behind making a somber procession as the wind blasted against their backs as if to hurry them forward. They reached the door of Joy's home. The Skipper knocked, calling for her mother, 'Madonna, open up! Madonna!' The door flew open, revealing Glenda, drunk and disheveled, dressed in a flimsy silk nightie and holding a drink. She clutched the glass to her bosom, spilling whisky onto her hand and licking it off before registering the crowd and shouting, 'We don't need the Social. What are you bunch of bloody do-gooders doing here? Piss off!'

Hailstones battered the crowd who stared at her with mixed expressions of pity and disgust on their numb faces. The Skipper twisted his soaked woollen hat in his hands. He shouted to be heard above the wind that whipped around the small square of cottages like a banshee, saying, 'Glenda, you don't understand. We aren't from the Social. It's me, Solomon. Where's your Ken?' Glenda looked the Skipper up and down with complete disinterest and burped, pouring a nimbus of alcohol fumes into the frigid night. Solomon moved closer, flinching as the wind changed direction flinging bullets of ice at his face and neck, the crowd pressed in behind him like emotional vampires. He shouted, 'Glenda lass, please focus. Where's Joy's dad? We need to find him.'

Glenda appeared oblivious to the cold as she wobbled in the doorway and said, 'Ken's not the little bastard's dad. Who knows which one of those virgin hunting rapists he was? Anyhow, what's the drunken bastard done this time, eh? No. Don't tell me. I don't bloody care.' Glenda moved to close the door.

The Skipper pushed a booted foot in the way and said, 'It's your Joy, I'm sorry lass, it looks like she's drowned.'

Joy had thought she was ready for the impact her death would have. She had been anticipating the punishment inflicted on her parents. What had Madonna said about her father? Surely Ken was her real dad? Had she suffered him for no good reason? A raging fire lit her soul. Her angry spirit roared, her energy sending tiles skittering from nearby roofs to crash onto the cobbles startling the people below. Joy relished her revenge as her mother pushed past Solomon and stumbled barefoot into the street. The newborn spirit hovered overhead, uncaring as the crowd muttered about the bastard Joy's possible father and stared at Glenda's needle tracked, burnt and bruised arms. She sank to her knees on the mossy, rain slicked pavement. Revenge burned in Joy like a righteous flame to be snuffed out when her mother screamed at the leaden sky, 'Nooo. You can't take my baby! You can't take my duckling!'

Chapter Nine

-THE GHOST-

The search for Joy's body continued for three stormy days and nights until it became too dangerous to continue. On New Year's Eve, the police visited Glenda and Ken and showed them a plastic evidence bag containing a single school shoe that had washed up ten miles down the coast. When the coppers left Ken cracked open another bottle of vodka and, for the first time in their nine years together, he shared it with Glenda.

The local newspaper headline proclaimed:

CHILD OF VIRGIN DROWNED AT CHRISTMAS

After that the national media hounded Joy's parents causing them to barricade themselves in the cottage with the phone torn from its wall socket and the television smashed against the wall.

On January $8^{th.}$ 1984, Glenda woke nursing her usual hangover and needing a fix. Stumbling bleary eyed into the kitchen to put the kettle on the hob she was emptying the coins out of her purse and swearing at the lack of ready money for her habits when she was distracted by the sound of a foot kicking the table leg. She spun around and, forgetting that her child was dead, automatically reached out to crack Joy on the back of the head. Her hand flew through thin air. The momentum threw her against the edge of the table, bruising her thighs. Joy continued to kick the table leg with one, wet shoe while her mother screamed for Ken. Joy vanished as he ran into the room and a trembling Glenda struggled to explain what she had seen. Ken shook his hysterical wife by the shoulders then he slapped her hard across the face saying, 'You're imagining things, you stupid junkie cow. Your little bitch has gone.'

Glenda pointed a shaking finger beneath the table. Seeking more ammunition to use against her, Ken crouched down. He threw her a sarcastic look, lifted the edge of the greasy tablecloth and stared into the milky eyes of the drowned child who sat there with her hands protectively covering the top of her head. He saw their dead Joy wearing one shoe, her school uniform wet through, her skin mottled and bloated, and he didn't say a word. Feeling calmer than he had ever been in his life, Ken picked up his car keys, grabbed his sobbing wife and ran out into the rain where he pushed her into the car and locked the doors before firing up the ignition and racing toward Ravenshill.

Ken's last thought before he drove his car over the cliff was that Joy could not be there, even though he could clearly see her in the rear view mirror. When the morning tide receded, a pair of shocked dog walkers found two bodies on the rocks below, crushed in the vehicle's wreckage.

That day in 1984, while rescue services battled the weather to retrieve Glenda and Ken's shattered remains and deliver them to the morgue, the heavens raged over the Bay, creating incredibly high tides. Throughout the morning, furious gale force winds tore miles of shoreline away, tossing it into the North Sea where it was devoured. By midafternoon tourists and cliff top dwellers alike fled to safety as coastal houses and caravans were flung like God's pillow fight into the sea and swept away by towering waves that rode the backs of frenzied currents. Sky hit land and water with the crash of a drunken orchestra as silver lightning arced across the Bay. Black storm clouds roiled and fought an almighty battle in the sky, concealing the place where Heaven and Earth met.

As the worst storm in a century wreaked devastation across England's North East coast, Joy lay in a mossy green hollow, unmoving, unharmed and impervious to the chaos that surrounded her.

While every living creature for miles sought safety and shelter, swirling clouds rippled on the cliff top like a summer mirage to reveal an ageless, handsome man dressed like a children's party act. Under a squashed yellow top hat, his black curls hung in a ponytail down his back. Death's eyes were darker than hell, his lips clamped tight in a thin line. This was the second time he had called to collect this tiny soul. He crouched down beside Joy's body, stroking her cold cheek and whispered,

-Come on baby, I won't hurt you.-

Death pressed his mouth to hers and rested a star sheathed hand over her heart. The child remained as still as the tomb.

-Joy, it's time to come home, my love.-

He reached inside his coat pocket and sprung open the silver pocket watch. The tiny music box notes of Jingle Bells drifted above the storm as Joy slumbered on. Death glanced at the dial, his brow creasing as he checked the time. His eyes narrowed into angry slits and he bit his bottom lip hard enough to make it bleed, which he could not. Leaving Joy to sleep, Death stood tall and casting off his disguise flung his arms out wide, turned his immortal face to the churning sky and roared into the storm,

-Hope!-

Death exploded away from Joy's body in fury, shooting like a comet between the Bay's red-roofed cottages; resisting the temptation to seize a replacement soul at random. His roars of rage reached Hope sending her fleeing to the Nothing where she waited and tried to prepare herself for Death's arrival. She didn't have to wait long.

'My Lord.' Hope knelt before her master, her eyes downcast as Death loomed over her flinging his furious words into her sensitive ears.

-You ignored my warnings. You interfered with Joy's heart. I know it was you, I see your cursed mark. I would have taken her home. Her immortal soul would have been cleansed, healed and reincarnated to fulfill its destiny. You have disobeyed your Lord. What is your defence?-

'I am Hope. I did my duty. I saved my sister.'

Death reached down and gently helped Hope to her feet, then, as she smiled with relief, he laughed in her face. Hope snapped, 'You find me amusing, my Lord Death?'

-I do. You saved Joy for a fate far worse than my kiss, and you, my Lady, will put it right. You will return her heart and I will collect her soul. Do not fail me.-

Hope lowered her eyes to hide her exasperation. Cold lips swept her cheek in farewell and she looked around the Nothing, whispering thanks to the Great Creator that she was alone and unharmed.

Chapter Ten

-RESURRECTION-

Joy woke in the mossy hollow, sheltered from the wind and stared up at the blue sky, hypnotised by a triple arced rainbow. She still wore her school uniform, but one shoe was missing.

Doctor Mark Timpson's spaniel snuffled at her bare foot with his wet nose, making her giggle and attracting his owner's attention. Looking down at her, Mark's voice trembled with recognition. 'Joy. Goodness me. Is that really you child?'

'I think so,' she croaked, her tongue swollen and heavy in her mouth.

The Doctor carried Joy the two miles from Ravenshill Cliff to his Victorian house in the Bay. She was content to leave with the stranger and his sweet dog. It never occurred to her to question her situation even though the village, the cars and the people all looked very different to when she last saw them.

When Mark walked into the house with Joy in his arms his wife, Angie, fell to her knees, wrapping the girl in her embrace as if she had expected her. Taking in the child's bedraggled appearance, she said, 'I bet you'd like a hot bath, clean clothes and something to eat. Am I right or am I right?'

'You are right, missis.' Joy coughed dirt onto the hall carpet and spat out a pearly sea shell.

Mark said, 'I'll clean this up love; why don't you take Joy for that bath?'

Keeping up a nervous stream of chatter, Angie ran warm water into the tub while Joy undressed in the steam filled bathroom, keeping her eyes lowered to the blue tiled floor.

When she saw the bruises covering the child's skinny torso Angie fought to hold back her tears and the questions that nipped at the end of her tongue, desperate to escape her mouth. The fists and feet that had delivered such cruel and vicious pain had been positioned with precision where injuries wouldn't be easily seen. Angie reached out, longing to soothe the small rib cage that bore a multi-coloured print made by a stomping boot, then, knowing it was too soon, she withdrew her hand. Her heart ached at the sight of the small, tortured body, but her soul stood in awe and admiration, cheering the miracle that was Joy.

Joy's excited voice interrupted her thoughts, saying, 'I only ever get a cold bath or a stand up wash in a bowl. Mum scrubs me 'til my skin is shiny red and new.' Angie drew in a shuddering breath and, with a forced smile, pointed at the foaming bath tub. Keeping her raging emotions in check, she said, 'Jump right in and have a good old soak.'

Joy sat surrounded by rainbow filled bubbles that refracted the light, holding them up to her nose she blew, her eyes wide as they floated and popped around her.

Unable to contain herself, Angie asked, 'Why were you on the cliff top, love?'

Joy lowered her sea green eyes and, with great care and concentration poured streams of bubbles from one thin hand to the other. Angie risked pressing her. 'Please tell me, I can keep a secret.'

'If I do, you'll tell me to bloody shut-up.'

Angie immediately regretted her impatience and threw her hands in the air saying, 'Good grief child. No, I wouldn't. Not ever.'

Joy continued to teem and ladle bath water from hand to hand, slowly beginning to relax in the steamy heat. Angie twisted her wedding ring, trying not to appear too eager for the girl's explanation and failing miserably.

Ten minutes of silence later, as the water cooled and the bubbles died, Joy put her trust in the woman who would become the mother she'd prayed for long before her own was driven to her death. When she spoke, relief flooded through Angie like a balm.

'On Christmas day Mum and Dad did lots of drinking and snoozing. Mum kept picking parcels from under the broken tree and putting them back. The Police lady came and Mum cried.' Joy glanced at Angie checking her expression before she continued, 'When she left, Dad blew tunes on empty beer bottles. Mum took off her clothes and danced in front of the fire and dad whistled at her. Mum cried again and so did he.'

'What did you do, Joy?'

'I sat on the couch. They ignored me all day. I speak when I am spoken to.'

Joy splashed the bath water so hard so that it spilled over the tub, drenching the floor. She flinched and retreated to the far end of the tub until Angie laughed, throwing a yellow duck into the water and asked, 'What happened next, love?'

Joy held the plastic toy as if it was treasure and raced through her story, afraid of interruption.

'I can't remember much. Mum came in the kitchen to put the kettle on and screamed, so I hid under the table and put my hands on my head. Then Dad came in and told her I was dead or something. He was cross and I was scared. Mum must have given me away 'cause he bent down and looked straight at me. He didn't shout. He picked up the car keys and they didn't even put their coats on over their pajamas. They went outside in bare feet and I ran after them. They got in the car and I sneaked onto the back seat.'

'Where did you go?'

'To the cliffs, of course. Can I get out now?'

Joy sat wrapped in a fluffy towel on Angie's ample lap. As Angie dried Joy's oddly chopped hair, she said, 'I have a secret, Missis.'

'Well, I can keep it if you want to tell me.'

Joy lowered her eyes and decided to risk disbelief. 'Santa came to school and the teacher told Mum that I asked him for new parents. When we got home she slapped my face and sent me to bed. Dad was at work. I fell asleep, but she woke me up.'

Joy swallowed a strangled sob and Angie said, 'It's OK, sweetheart, you don't have to tell me unless you want to.'

'Will you believe me?'

'I already do.'

Joy's small body sagged against Angie like dead weight. As her words, empty of any emotion, dropped into Angie ears the woman's heart beat in fury.

'Mum pulled me out of bed by my hair and punched me here.' Joy placed her hands over her stomach. 'She swung me about and smacked my bottom. She shouted, 'You won't sit down for a month of Sundays after I've finished with you, you little bitch.' She threw me in a cold bath, pushed me under and held me down. I kept my eyes open. I saw her red face wobbling through the water. I held my breath, it really, really hurt.' Joy shook on Angie's lap, but no tears fell as she recalled the last traumatic abuse of her short life. Angie squeezed her tight and said, 'I promise you, Joy, that no-one will ever hurt you again.'

As the sun set over the Bay, The Timpsons sat with Joy, sipping mugs of hot cocoa. Mark ruffled her hair; his kind face shone as he said, 'I'm wondering why you were asleep on the cliff top today.'

Joy moved away from his touch, saying, 'Promise you won't be cross?'

Mark reminded himself to go slowly, saying, 'We could never be cross with you, love.'

Joy mumbled, 'I was bad. Dad drove to Ravenshill. Mum was talking to our Lord in Heaven, Hello is his name. The car went faster and faster. Dad said, 'Glenda shut the *rude word* up with your praying. The little runt's dead. Everyone blames us. I can't live like this. It ends today.' Dad saw me in the mirror. I waved at him, he was crying. Mum screamed and slapped his hands. She tried to get the steering wheel off him, but he punched her in the face. I couldn't help her. I could never help her, and she hated me.'

Mark swallowed the lump in his throat and asked, 'Did Daddy stop the car and let you out?'

'No. I opened the door and jumped.'

Angie's hands flew to her face. Joy saw her distress and spilled out her story's end.

'It didn't hurt. I rolled over and over into the long grass. I saw Dad's car fly off the cliff. A rainbow came down and collected me. I went to sleep in the clouds and I woke up in the sunshine.'

Angie said, 'There's an old toy box in the corner, why don't you see what you can find? There might be a lonely teddy waiting for you.'

With Joy out of earshot, Mark, his face flushed and his eyes bright, exclaimed, 'Angie, you know what this means don't you, love?'

That night, Joy slept in the room which was to become her sanctuary, with the spaniel, Charlie, curled up on her bed. Angie and Mark sat downstairs, sipping wine. After two glasses of Rioja, Angie found the courage to raise the subject they had been skirting around and whispered, 'Is it her, Mark? Is she the one?'

Her husband's deep voice trembled as he replied, 'The facts fit, Angie. The child, Joy, drowned on Christmas Eve, 1983. Her father committed suicide, killing her mother in the process in January, 1984 when he drove his car off Ravenshill.'

Angie's brow creased. 'Mark, that was ten years ago, how can we be certain?' Mark put down his glass and rummaged in the writing desk until he found a yellowed newspaper showing a school photograph of a girl who could be the twin of the one asleep upstairs. He passed it to his wife. 'Angie, look at her face. Look, the blazer and school badge in the photo are the same as our girl's. And, if that's not enough to convince you then take a look at this...' Mark turned the page to a photo of Joy's parents and passed the article to his wife. Angie had read the story at the time, but now it held fresh meaning.

Heavensgate: Joy

Mark began to pace. His voice trembling with excitement, he said, 'After Glenda and Ken's bodies were recovered from the wreckage the press began to dig into their backgrounds. Do you remember Ken and Glenda?'

'Yes, love, and I remember the gossip in the village when Joy was born. People said that Glenda, poor lass, she was only fourteen when she gave birth to Joy, wouldn't name the father. She insisted she'd been gang raped, poor thing. But she also claimed that her virginity was intact. People nicknamed her Madonna and the name stuck.' Mark shrugged and said, 'Every time Ken got drunk he'd tell anyone who cared to listen that, whenever they had sex, Glenda's hymen 'grew back'.'

Angie sighed. 'The man wasn't well, love.'

'No, and if Glenda was to be believed, he wasn't Joy's father either.'

Angie raised an eyebrow saying, 'This is too important to be settled by an old newspaper and gossip. I'm as excited as you, but we can't make the facts fit just because we're tired of waiting.'

Mark took the paper and replaced it in the drawer. He drew up a chair opposite his wife of thirty-five years, held her hand and said, 'Angie, Joy's body was lost at sea. The search found nothing except a school shoe, washed up miles along the coast. Today, when Charlie and I found Joy at Ravenshill, wearing that tattered school uniform, she only had one shoe so I had to carry her home.'

He jumped to his feet, unable to contain himself. His eyes shone with fervour and his voice was full of wonder as he said, 'Ken and Glenda's graves are in the Bay's churchyard. Their missing, presumed drowned child is asleep in our house, and she is still only eight years old. This is the day we have waited so long for.'

Angie leaned into her husband's warmth, wrapping him in her embrace. Her tears fell onto his shoulder as she said, 'It's settled then, this is both our duty and our blessing. It is our fate and our honour to protect Joy, always.'

Mark, his own voice choked with tears replied, 'I agree, Angie, and if anyone asks we'll tell them Joy is our foster child.'

The question as to Joy's origins never arose because nobody else could hold onto the memory of her for more than a minute.

Joy was home schooled. She had no friends except the ever loyal spaniel, Charlie and their neighbours' foster children, Ruby and Gabi, who by some miracle were the only other people in the village able to recall her from one day to the next.

Happy and loved, Joy forgot her life before the Timpsons, however, Death, the Creator and the Immortals did not.

Chapter Eleven

-LIFE AFTER DEATH-

As she grew older, Joy put her feelings of emptiness down to terminal loneliness; she was wrong. Joy felt empty because, at least in the mortal sense of the word, she was dead. She didn't know about her status for a long time and, when she began to suspect the truth, she put her head in the ostrich position, leaving her rear exposed.

Because Joy refused to accept Death, she carried on living. Given a choice she would have preferred to spend her days reading fortunes in a striped tent on the seafront. However, bills had to be paid, so she worked hard to make a success of the café she had inherited in her twenties. For the next decade, she served popular homemade diet busting cakes, a wide variety of beverages and hundreds of tatty British seaside souvenirs to tourists with cash to splash.

In high season, Joy indulged her not so secret gypsy ambitions by luring nervous customers to the back room where she would read their palms or terrify them with the tarot. She would happily read the bumps on your head if you paid her enough.

Her favourite means of divination had been a gift from her foster mother, Angie; Joy loved the spectacular crystal ball, despite it only ever having shown her one boring scene of a vast lake ringed by mountains and pine forest. The weather inside the crystal was slightly more interesting as it changed constantly. In the vision place, summer and winter, and day and night didn't follow any known clock. Inside the globe, it could be night time with a sky that boiled with starlight one moment and the next it could be a sunny afternoon, so hot that the glass felt warm to the touch. Now and again an empty row boat, full of crisp, colourful, autumn leaves floated into view. Joy once saw a black motorbike cross the vista, ridden by a long shadow accompanied by a pillion passenger whose silver hair streamed behind her. Other than those few events the crystal's image remained steady, even on the occasions Joy whipped the velvet cloth off the ball in a desperate attempt to catch it by surprise.

Joy loved her café and was good with the customers, always remembering the small details of their lives from previous holiday maker chats. In return for her attention and grace, not one of the hundreds of people passing through the café's doors each year remembered her for more than a fleeting moment. When Joy spoke with them, they were happy, but the moment they were distracted by a chocolate éclair or a steaming mug of English tea, she faded from their memory and a sense that life was bleak and futile temporarily overwhelmed them. The more delicate souls never recovered and fell into clinical depression that could only be eased by lifelong medication or by fulfilling an unreasonable longing to actually live in Joy's café. A particularly sensitive few resolved their despair by committing suicide. Joy had no idea she was responsible for so much heartache. She didn't realise the impact her presence and her absence both had on people. It hurt her that, with rare exceptions, she didn't exist in their memories.

Joy lived in hope that one day, maybe one special person, like her friends Ruby and Gabi, would remember her for longer than a conversation. She wished for someone to love and to be loved in return. Unfortunately for Joy, wishes do come true.

Despite being statuesque, blonde and enviably slim despite the cream cakes, Joy believed she was an unattractive and unremarkable woman. She took it for granted that if she was wet, cold, and desperate enough to comment on it, the weather appeared to obey her and she never noticed how, when her feet ached after a long day at the café making her dread the walk home, space and time would change to accommodate her. She could open locks with the slightest touch and, sometimes, she attracted attention from entities not normally associated with the British seaside, especially not in Yorkshire.

As Joy's powers grew, thrill seeking customers more and more frequently threw money at her Gypsy persona. But recently some had begun to run weeping from the back room making Joy doubt the value of her psychic abilities. Therefore, after a particularly distressing tarot reading, with a man who recited the Lord's Prayer as he backed away making the sign of the cross, Joy wrapped her cards in silk and placed them reverently in a box decorated with a silver pentagram. The china phrenology bust and pretty, but obviously malfunctioning, crystal ball were both confined to the back of a wardrobe.

Joy foreswore all things supernatural. Unfortunately, the supernatural could not so easily turn its back on Joy.

Hidden in the darkness, the Nothing swirled in the ball's crystal depths parting to reveal a tall, bare-chested man outside a large log cabin by the lake. He held an axe and, testing the blade's sharpness, the man smiled as it cut him. He squeezed the pad of his thumb to encourage his blood to drip freely onto the ground where it sizzled before sinking into the earth. Smiling, he knelt, and pressed his right index and middle fingers to his lips in a kiss before thrusting them deep into the wet soil. With his free hand, he swept a bloody cross over his heart, which, for the first time in a long time, pounded against his ribs. The rush of blood that flashed through his veins aroused him, making him shiver with anticipation.

Snow began to fall, each flake touched by moonlight to shine like diamonds. The sparkling ice hissed against his body, cloaking him in curling tendrils of steam. Satisfied with his work, the man turned his handsome face to the starless sky and shouted into the void,

Joy!

Chapter Twelve

-THE BAY, ENGLAND-

A gale force wind burst open the doors to Joy's Café and blasted its furious way inside where it flew, screaming round the tables like an angry toddler. Sachets of sugar, vinegar and ketchup were scattered in every direction as plastic chairs flew away from their tables. Gabi fought his way across the floor and threw himself at the double doors that banged in the frame as if possessed.

'Why you no help me, lardy arse?' Gabi's voice was shrill as he tried to close the café against the storm raging war across the Bay.
'Because you're bloody rude.' Ruby shouted above the screaming wind, as she crouched down behind the cake display fridge, which acted as a marvellous windbreak.

Close to tears; Gabi used all his strength and his skinny, narrow back to try and force at least one door shut. He battled the spiteful wind, which blew sand into his streaming eyes and exfoliated his skin.
'Help! We blow away!'
Ruby popped her head above the counter. She ducked down again, horrified as plastic chairs skittered across the floor, creating modern art against the walls and table legs.
'Shut up, you sodding drama queen! What kind of a man are you anyway? Why can't you be more like Zorro?'

'Ruby, Zorro is Mexicano. Help me, *por favor.*'

Sulking, Ruby dragged herself away from the shelter of the éclairs, scones and jam puffs and crossed the café at a snail's pace. The wind whipped her hair around her head like flames as she threw her considerable weight against a door knocking Gabi outside, where he was instantly blown back in as if he weighed nothing at all. Working together they managed to secure and lock both doors before collapsing onto the rain slicked floor. The wind howled outside, buffeting the café's structure, tearing at its roof and battering the windows, furious at being denied entry. Gabi sat with pointy elbows resting on bony knees. He held his ponytailed head in his hands. A single sob escaped him and echoed in the wrecked mess of the café, whilst Ruby made a futile attempt to escape from the tangle of her long, copper curls.

'I hate you,' Gabi sniffed.

'Put it in writing to the bloody management,' retorted Ruby.

A third voice rang across the café, 'If you have quite finished, may I have tea and carrot cake now?'

The miserable combatants looked up at the impeccably dressed woman. Her silver hair was piled in an elegant chignon on the side of her head, her body was slim and her features ageless. As she moved her hands a dozen diamond rings flashed rainbows across the walls and ceiling. She looked at Gabi and Ruby with a knowing expression on her exquisite face. They sat dumbstruck where they had dropped, staring at her.

Gabi was the first to break saying, 'We closed. How you get past us?'

The woman ignored his question and said, 'I have a seven o'clock appointment with Joy. It grows dark and she is late.'

Ruby spoke through clenched teeth, 'Gabi, she looks different, but we know this old soul.'

'Then we wait and see if *she* know we know her. Be safer,' whispered Gabi behind one hand, wiggling the fingers of the other at the woman who observed them with one raised eyebrow and a deliberate smirk on her coral pink lips.

Ruby's temper sparked into flame. She battled to hold it in check as she stared at the woman and said, 'It *is* her, Gabi. She's in disguise, but I can smell her. What if Death sent her? What should we do?'

'I not know, no panic, sssh.'

Gabi sprung his gangly frame off the terracotta tiled floor and pranced, dodging fallen chairs and the rest of the wind created mess, over to an impressive display of tea. Winking at their customer, he said, 'I choose for you the Earl of Gray, he magnificent.' He kicked the juke box and Roxy Music's 'Angel Eyes' dropped onto the turntable and blasted out of the speakers.

The customer sighed, and in a voice dripping ice said, 'Stop acting the fool, Gabi, and Ruby, make sure no-one enters the café.'

Ruby raised herself up to her full five foot nothing and, puffing out her considerable assets, said, 'Good evening, *my Lady* Hope. Pardon the question. Do you have a gun or any magical devices on your person?'

Hope's ancient eyes sparkled at Ruby like frost on dead grass as she replied, 'Thank you for your respectful salutation. I am unarmed.'

'Good, so don't be ordering us around, we are human in this place, as are you, Madam.'

'If you say so. Ah, good, here comes Joy.'

'Your order, my Lady.' Gabi set tea and a slice of cake on the table, bowing low enough to touch his toes as he backed away and fell squealing over an upturned chair.

Ruby shouted, 'Gabi, will you please stop being so bloody servile. Get up and clean up before Joy gets here, *please.*'

She used her sleeve to rub condensation from the window and, peering through the rain splattered panes, watched her friend and employer stomp up the cliff path. Joy's chest heaved with the effort of fighting the strong gusts that threatened to force her back the way she had come. She stopped walking and Ruby saw her exasperated expression as she appeared to mutter a few words to herself. The tempest coughed, as if embarrassed for the trouble it had caused her, and veered away, taking a north easterly route up the coast.

Ruby smiled to herself as she turned to Hope asking, 'Why are you here, Madam?'

Gabi, who was busy rearranging the fallen chairs, clung firmly onto the back of one, his eyes wide as he mouthed, 'What?' His pale skin turned ash gray as if he might pass out at any moment.

'My business is with Joy, not with you. Unlock the door and let your Mistress in.'

'*Mistress?* This isn't bloody Downton Abbey. This is a shitty café in a Godforsaken corner of England.'

'Don't blaspheme and please don't shout; your regular voice is sufficiently annoying to get my attention.'

Ruby ran pudgy hands through her already crazy hair and glared at Hope with flashing eyes. Gabi trembled and pretended not to notice the confrontation as he collected dozens of condiment sachets from the floor.

Hope gave Ruby a reluctant smile. 'Peace, sister, please?'

'Peace you say? Huh. I can guess why you're here. I will not allow you to harm Joy. I demand you leave, *sister,* or feel my wrath.'

'I cannot leave. I have my duty as you have yours.'

Ruby picked up the nearest plate and threw it against the wall. Gabi scurried into the back room and hid shivering behind the coats.

Reaching the café, Joy pressed the tip of one finger against the double doors, the lock, obedient to her touch, clicked and opened. As she stepped inside, no-one commented that she hadn't any keys. She stood, rooted to the spot, staring at the ethereal woman. More than two decades had passed since that day in the classroom when Hope stole Joy's heart. Her soul knew this spirit and leapt in horror and recognition that made her throat constrict. She could neither breathe nor swallow.

Sensing her distress Gabi bravely left his refuge and dashed to Joy's side. He squeezed her shoulder, saying, 'Are you OK, my Mistress?'

Joy dragged in a ragged breath, almost toppling forward. Ruby rushed to support her, noting with concern the film of sweat hidden behind Joy's rain spattered face.

'It's OK, Ruby, Gabi, thank you, I'm OK. You may go home, your 'Mistress' will close up the café tonight.' Gabi rushed to collect their belongings.

'I am *not* leaving you alone with her. You can't trust her, she's not, well, she isn't *natural*,' Ruby hissed, making an exaggerated sign of the evil eye in Hope's direction.

Joy took one of Ruby's hands in her own and said, 'Don't be silly Ruby. I'm a big girl. I know what I'm doing. If I need you I am pretty sure that you will know it. Gabi is waiting. See? He has your rag of a cloak and that suitcase you call a handbag.' Gabi helped his angry colleague into her moth eaten old cloak before strutting his skinny stuff into a white leather jacket with pink silk lining.

Ruby sang 'Pretty in Pink' under her breath. Gabi relaxed a little and threw his arm across Ruby's shoulders to hug her small round frame to his long lanky one, he kissed the tip of her nose then whispered in her ear, 'This meeting has to happen and, somehow, Joy understands that. Come, it's time for us to leave, mi Amor, and gracias for the song.'

Throwing Hope a stern look Gabi turned the 'Open' sign to 'Closed' and they left their friend at the stranger's mercy. Neither one looked back as they walked arm in arm down the steep, wet, cobbled road, their emotions in turmoil and their faces as blank as a freshly plastered wall.

Ruby's stomach sank as she considered the implications of Hope's, not entirely unforeseen, visit. She wondered if she should return to the café and try, somehow, to change the course of fate. Hearing her thoughts, Gabi hugged her arm tighter in his saying, 'Mi amor, you may just as well try to turn the tide in the Bay.'

Ruby stared up into his sorrowful eyes and exclaimed, 'Oh, Gabi, I wasn't expecting Hope to return so soon. We must do something. Tell me what we should do?'

The minutes ticked by as Gabi stood, still as a statue, thinking of the impenetrable plans which turn the universe, before, in a voice full of sorrow, he said, 'Ruby, we will do what we always do, we shall carry out our duty with love, which is all we are allowed.'

Ruby sniffed and said, 'What happened to your accent, Casanova?'

Despite the events set in motion that night, the Bay's residents and tourists carried on as usual, oblivious to the Creator turning the wheel of destiny in their midst. In the eyes of everyone they passed Ruby and Gabi appeared to be two ordinary villagers on their way home from work. People on the street smiled and said 'Good evening.' The odd car honked a greeting as it sped past them.

Taking a few seconds to ensure they were unobserved Ruby and Gabi stepped into the shelter of the Bay's only bus stop and vanished into thin air. Anyone looking may have seen two dragonflies, one ruby red and the other opalescent as they flitted into the darkness, with moonlight glinting off their gossamer wings.

On the cliff top road, the café's windows flashed with blinding blue light before turning as opaque as black ice on a lake.

Chapter Thirteen

-THE MEDDLER-

With caution, as one might approach a venomous snake, Joy pulled out a red plastic chair and, resting her hands palm down on the table, faced the being whose skin glowed with a cold violet light. The air carried an electric charge that danced along her skin. The women sat motionless under the eye watering glare of fluorescent tubes, each considering the potential desires and strengths of the other.

In the empty café, the everyday noise of humming fridges and the drip, drip, drip of a leaky tap sounded excessively loud. Joy was the first to speak, 'Is it really you? You look different. So much time has passed. I had forgotten all about you. How could I do that?'

Hope's voice rang like a blade on ice as she said, 'Hello, Joy, we need to talk.' She sipped her Earl Gray tea with one pinkie finger crooked out and pushed the plate of uneaten carrot cake to one side saying, 'I prefer angel cake, do you have any?'

Joy ignored the question and asked, 'Hope, it is you isn't it? What brings you back to the Bay?'

'Unfinished business, dear, and a favour owed to an old friend. Also, my sweet, I want to see how you are.'

'I am my usual dull self with nothing interesting to report. Do you plan to stay long?' Joy sat on her hands to hide the tremors beginning to rattle their way through her bones.

'Well, it depends on whether or not the locals take me into their hearts.'

Hope locked eyes with Joy, assessing the impact of her words; she got no satisfaction; Joy had closed down all expression in order to concentrate on not screaming.

Hope raised one eyebrow and observed, 'You have grown strong, Joy, that's good. Did you know that I opened 'Ye Olde Gifte Shoppe' in the village? I know, it's a terrible name, but the tourists simply love it. I intend to read the Tarot there, for free. You don't mind, do you?'

Hope leant back in the chair and stared at her with a smile playing across her lips while Joy's legs twitched as stinging electric shocks ploughed up and down her spine. The table top became malleable; nothing in the café held its impression of reality. Joy risked another look into Hope's icy eyes and took a deep breath before responding, 'That beautiful shop is yours? I noticed the *decorations*. I've never seen so many hearts held hostage. All appear unique and, with few exceptions, beautiful; and so vivid that they almost seem alive.' Hope refused to rise to the bait replying, 'Sadly, my sweet, it is often the exceptions which make the rule, don't you agree?'

Joy struggled not to slump her shoulders as the air grew claustrophobic and heavy around her. The café became insubstantial as empty space. Her heart beat faster; as the old stone walls faded to gray, shimmering as they pulsated in and out of existence. She fought to control her breathing and conceal her anxiety, but fresh sweat raised the hairs at the nape of her neck and pricked jewels of moisture along her brow. She licked her lips, as much to check they were still there as to moisten them.

'Why are you afraid of me, Joy?' Hope's voice was hard and sharp as diamonds.

Joy swallowed, dry-mouthed and said, 'I am not.' Her trembling body betrayed her and an unusual feeling of hopelessness made her reckless. She suddenly felt that she had nothing to lose so, she cleared her throat, sat up straight and said, 'No more games, Hope. I have my eye on one heart in particular, it is mine and I demand you return it to me.'

Hope's eyes held a predatory gleam as, her voice low and conspiratorial she leaned forward and replied, 'The shop is always open, dear, just try the door. If you truly wish to come inside I'm sure nothing could stop you. However, take my advice, a delicate heart must be chosen with care.'

Joy bit her lip and closed her eyes, mentally counting to ten. Despite being clubbed by panic, she couldn't help being awed by the chime of tiny bells sounding in her head. Hope smiled at her confusion and discomfort while placing a cherub and violet decorated teacup in its gilt edged china saucer. Joy knew her café only stocked plain, white crockery; nothing of this delicate quality had ever risked its life in the temperamental dishwasher.

As Joy's confidence in her ability to cope with the situation began to melt away like snow in spring time she gathered the remnants of her courage and taking a deep breath said, 'Do you remember the paper hearts you asked us to make for the Friendship Tree that Christmas? You *stole* my heart. You, Hope, are nothing but a *common thief*.'

Hope's eyes flashed violet sparks as she crashed her fists down on the table. The café shook as if in the grips of a violent earthquake and the temperature plummeted as fast as an eagle swoops to hook its prey. Frost drew patterns across the shuddering table top, biting Joy's finger tips as he passed. Hope appraised her with eyes as ancient and cold as glaciers. Having reached an important decision she hissed her reply, 'You, Joy, will not insult me again.'

Joy shook with cold. 'Admit that when you vanished you stole my heart.'

Hope wanted to strike Joy for insolence. Her quiet, angry words dripped like icicles as she said, 'Yes, I took your tiny heart and kept it safe from harm for all these years. You are ungrateful.'

'I want it back.'

'Which begs the question as to why you threw it away so lightly? You were a child, but you knew it was a bad thing to do. A very bad thing indeed.'

'I don't know what you're talking about. What did I do?' Joy shivered to the point of seizure.

Hope watched unmoved as Joy suffered, her voice held razor sharp edges as she said, 'You may or may not remember, it matters not to me. You threw your infant heart away whilst I, on the other hand, have guarded and tended it. What do you suppose would happen if I handed your vulnerable heart back to one as careless as you?'

'I demand you give it back.' Hopelessness gripped Joy's insides, turning them to slush water that began to move up into her throat.

Sensing her despair, Hope's anger cooled and she applauded her saying, 'I see you possess some fire after all. However, calm yourself, don't waste your temper with me, you may need it for another.'

Joy tried begging. 'My heart, please, give me back my heart, I need to feel love.'

Hope couldn't allow herself to soften, too much was at stake, not least Joy's life, so she said, 'It isn't in my nature to simply hand your heart back to you. Something so valuable must be earned and the cost appreciated.'

Joy clenched blue lips, gritting her teeth until her jaw burnt. She pushed her rage deep. Her mouth flooded with ice water that spilled over her teeth and choked out, 'How?' vomiting gray slush onto the floor where it instantly froze. Hope scratched the stiletto heel of one silver-gray suede boot through the ice making a noise like a knife scraping on a plate. Her voice rang bright and clear as she said, 'Well, Joy, that's the fun part, nobody knows.'

Joy was no longer able to shiver or speak, but in her head she screamed, 'Oh God help me, I'm dying.'

Hearing her thoughts, Hope stroked Joy's frozen cheek and whispered, 'You should be dying, Joy, trust me, you should be. However, I won't let my Lord take you. Time for you to sleep, sweet sister.' The sickly sweet smell of Parma violet candy filled Joy's nostrils like the scent of funeral flowers, her head hit the table and she slept.

Hope returned to 'Ye Olde Gifte Shoppe' for only as long as it took to remove a childishly decorated heart from the display cabinet and wrap it in silver shadows before she swallowed it and fled the Mortal Realm.

As Joy slumbered and Hope escaped, Death rested on the bench outside the café admiring the Milky Way and the silver waves which battered the beach below like ghostly horses. He waited impatiently for Hope to obey him and return Joy's heart, anticipating the split second when his pocket watch would play its tune. Death waited, growing ever more restless and irritable, to collect Joy's long overdue soul. Two flickering dragonflies accompanied him in his vigil, their erratic flight growing livelier as the morning sun rose over the Bay, realisation dawned and Death roared,

-Hope, you will suffer for this.-

Chapter Fourteen

-I PUT A SPELL ON YOU-

Outside the Lodge in Heavensgate, Jake, his tall frame dressed in black scuffed biker leathers hop-scotched up and down the boat deck, his heavy boots landing on rough chalk squares each containing a name scrawled in childish handwriting.

As he jumped he recited under his breath:
Hated
Burnt
Killed
He was like a child, hopping back and forth between the squares until losing interest in the game he picked up a soccer ball and kicked it against the workshop wall, adding his memories to the rhythm.
Hated
Burnt
Killed
Raped
Choked
Crushed
As the demon played in his memories, the sun fell into the lake like a stone dropped down a well. Kicking the ball into the lake where it floated like a disembodied head, Jake retreated to the Lodge where he

danced around the kitchen, banging on shiny copper pans hung from hooks in the black wooden beams. He beat the makeshift drums with a cracked wooden spoon singing *'This is the Rhythm of the Night'* at the top of his voice.

It was enough to make hot blood run cold as he stopped dancing and spoke into the empty room,

Fuck you, Jacob, I'm going to get me some Joy around here, find out how well she begs and burns.

A smile crinkled the corners of his eyes as he pumped his fist in the air and whooped, *Goodbye, cocksucker.*

Jake dropped to his knees, sliding across the shining polished floor with his arms stretched wide and head thrown back as he boomed out the anthem *'I Did it My Way'*.

He stood to take a low bow to his invisible audience, and then boogied from room to room like a disco queen.

Swinging his leather clad hips like Elvis, he flicked his fingers at the lamps, at furniture, and the art on the walls. He tipped his weight forward onto the toes of his boots and with a thrust, a flourish and a grunted 'uhu' he threw silk and cashmere cushions on the floor. Gyrating his pelvis, he bounced up and down on them before kicking them into the four corners of the room.

He danced to the kitchen like John Travolta in 'Grease', pretending to slick back his hair as managing to exactly impersonate John and Olivia he sang *'You're the One That I Want'* and bashed the pans until they rocked and rolled on the ceiling.

Jake leapt from chair to chair, shaking his head and strumming his air guitar before landing heavily on the table where he partied like a disco fuelled lunatic.

A new song drifted from the living room, interrupting Jake's crazy hip hop bop. He listened carefully and abruptly changed his tune as swiftly as he could change his mood. Like a serpent hypnotised by the music he slid slowly off the table, dreamily singing the familiar words to *'Que Sera Sera'* under his breath.

'Click *be*, click *be*, click *be*, click *be*...' interrupted his reverie. Jake wandered casually over to the old record player where his dead mother's favourite EP spun around, its black vinyl scratched and the needle stuck in a groove. Doris Everydamnday continued singing, 'click *be*, click *be*, click *be*...'

Jake giggled, covering his face with his hands, peeping around through open fingers; his movements reptilian and exaggerated as he stage-whispered, *Annie, where are you? Come out, come out, wherever you are.*

Hearing no reply he lifted the record from the turn table and frisbeed it into the open fire where it popped and melted like black treacle. Satisfied that his mother's favourite tune had died a terrible death, he raced from room to room and from one object to another shouting his joy into the empty house,

Mine. Mine. This is mine and this and that. It's all mine.

Finally bored he sat in his favourite armchair and felt his sense of victory flee like a retreating army. Jake slumped in front of the fire. Resting his cheek on the palm of one hand he whispered into the flames,

Hell, Jacob, it's quiet without you, asshole.

Hot sparks spat onto the rug at his feet and Jake leapt from the chair as a chorus of voices screamed in his skull,

I'm here, and me and me too.
We are many. Let us out Jake!

Jake thrashed his hands around as if to fend off a swarm of angry bees screaming, *Fuck off!*

When the last of the voices realised Jake wasn't giving up pole position they slipped away to the dark castle in his mind. Jake followed his alter egos, locked the worst offender in the dungeon and threw the key in the moat as he left.

Heavensgate: Joy

His mind as peaceful as it was ever likely to be, he wrapped his arms around his body as if caressing a beloved partner and danced alone as he whispered, *Ah, Mary, sweet Momma Mary, quite contrary I loved how your garden grew. I miss you, Mary, I truly, deeply miss you. I wish you were here*

This was, quite probably, the worse thing he could have wished for.

Exhausted by his antics, Jake flung himself face down on the couch and slept. His dreams were real to him, as real as anything could be. His nightmares dealt out punishment.

Dream Jake was twelve years old, a tall skinny boy messing about in the backyard of his foster home. He caught an old cat and pinned it down in the warm pink dust, holding the poor creature captive under his body. The cat lay still as death, too afraid to move, it stayed silent, playing possum. Jake whispered in the ear of his furry, ginger prisoner.

The twins, Sam and Nancy, they were dead and they looked at me. They knew what I did to Mom's princess and Dad's baby boy. They're coming for me, I know they are.

I am sorry, Laz, my puss, but you must be burnt alive. I have to sacrifice you to the twins. Forgive me twins for I have sinned.

Silent tears tracked through his dusty face, dripping down onto the sleek striped fur of the petrified cat.

Jake flicked open the Zippo lighter he had stolen from the local hardware store. His thumb moved to spark the wheel against the fuel when a man's extraordinarily deep voice boomed across the yard, 'Jake. You let the cat alone. D'ya hear me kid?'

Big Al, foster parent, part-time Darth Vader impersonator and Aunty Mary's Mr Lover man, stormed over to Jake, his ruddy face flushed as he used one meaty fist to lift Jake up by the shirt collar. The cat, Lazarus, sprang to life and sprinted off to hide shivering in the hedge. Al yanked a choking Jake across the yard, dragged his victim up the porch steps and inside the house. Jake grasped his collar with both hands attempting to breathe around the improvised noose. His feet never touched the ground as he was hauled, like a squirming sack of kittens, down the hallway. Al threw open the basement door saying, 'I done told you a thousand times to stop your damn torturin' ways, Jake.'

Heedless of the drop, Al threw the struggling boy down the wooden stairway. Jake tumbled, pitched head over heels like a discarded toy. Landing hard, he lay bruised and battered, but by some miracle, unbroken on the unforgiving concrete floor. He didn't cry out because he knew no-one would help him. Al's angry voice followed Jake into the basement's profound darkness,

'I didn't save your stupid ass from that bum bandit at boardin' school just so you can run wild around my place.'

The key turned, locking Jake in with his pain and the shadows.

He curled up in a tight little ball. Grinding his teeth, he talked to himself spitting out words like a curse, *When I am grown I will kill him. I'll kill everyone and every damn thing he loves. I will grow strong and The Dark Lord will burn.*

In the dark, damp, pain of the nightmare, Jake fell silent as an angry female voice shouted shrill and demanding in the hallway above, 'Al. Al. I can't find Jake anywhere. Where's my baby boy?'

'I threw him away, Mary. I threw him out like the filthy piece of trash he is. Now come to Poppa.'

Jake heard them fighting; at first Mary screamed, 'No no no,' but it wasn't long before he heard her yelling, 'Yes, oh yes, oh yes, Daddy, harder, oh God, yes!'

In the dirty basement, burning with jealous rage, Jake forced out a personal prayer, *So help me God, I will survive this. I will grow strong and I will torture that bastard before I burn him to ashes. Mary is mine.*

Heavensgate: Joy

As the sounds in the room above grew louder and more urgent, down in the basement there was distraction. Jake listened to scratching and rustling as something large stirred in the far corner behind the dog cage. The floor to ceiling shelves shook and jars of preserves rattled against each other like loose teeth. The darkness shifted, becoming denser. Sensing the presence of deep and outraged sorrow, Jake wept. There was nothing between the approaching malevolence and the helpless boy who remained curled up tight, his teeth chattering, his bladder and bowels emptying. Jake refused to look up. No matter what crawled out of the darkness, he would never acknowledge it. Jake's instincts warned him that to face the unseen monster would mean facing death.

The scratching noise evolved into a dragging scraping screech as if someone, or something, without the use of legs struggled to heave itself toward him. Sibilant whispers danced across the damp basement floor until they reached the terrified boy and tickled his earlobes. A babyish sweet voice giggled and asked, 'Are you ready to play now, Jacky?'

The shock of a child's tickle on the nape of his neck pulled Jake awake and back into his chair mumbling, *Go away twins. I'm sorry.*
Music streamed out of the kitchen, Nina Simone was crooning *'I put a spell on you...'*
Still trembling from the nightmare and looking all around for any sign of the dead twins Jake stood and slowly approached the source of the noise. His palms damp, his breath quickened, prepared to fight an intruder.
The volume cranked up higher.
Jake's day was about to get much worse.

He stood in the kitchen, staring in disbelief and gripped the back of a chair as he struggled with the sight of a petite blonde, her back to him as her hips swayed seductively from side to side while she crooned along with old Nina.

The music stopped abruptly, the apparition turned around to fix Jake with blank eyes and said,

'I put a spell on you, Jake baby, 'cause you're mine.'

Mary. How can it be?

She sashayed across the room on silver heeled dancing shoes. Reaching her target she said, 'Didn't I ever teach you to be careful what you wish for, baby?' Mary laughed and slapped Jake hard across his cheek. With the speed of a boa constrictor she circled her arms around his neck and pulled herself up his body to wrap her fishnet stocking clad legs around his waist. Jake's hands supported her hips as she clamped a hot, wet kiss on his dry lips and he surrendered to passion.

When Mary was certain he had forgotten the slap she released him, smoothed down her skirt and said, 'Hello, baby boy.' Jake pressed a palm to the cheek that bore an angry handprint and flecks of blood where her nails had grazed the delicate skin of his old scar.

Mary stood before him panting, waiting for his reaction and feeding off the gratification gained from the sight of his eyes trained like radar on her breasts spilling out of a low cut blouse. Her voice low and throaty, her pupils dilated, her skin flushed, she finally said, 'Hey, kid, my eyes are up here.' Jake spanned her tiny waist with his hands and, with tears choking his voice, said,

Mary, oh sweet Mary, I missed you so much. I thought I'd lost you. By the great god fuck, Mary, I swear that I was all alone and dyin' but now you're here.

'Where in hell are we, lover? You seen that crazy corridor? It goes nowhere like a rich man's folly.' Mary's words broke the spell. Jake held her at arms' length giving his vision space to drink her in. He was afraid to ask how she got to the Lodge, so he replied,

That corridor comes and goes, Mary, like you. There's a crazy tower here too and an elevator sometimes, I pay them no mind.

'Is that all you have to tell me, Jake?'

Heavensgate: Joy

You haven't changed even the smallest bit, Momma, you're still as pretty as a flower in the snow. How d'ya do that? Where've you been?

Mary smiled, grasped his chin and scraped his two day stubble with deadly red talons. Fixing him with a ravenous stare she dragged her nails under his chin, over his bulging Adam's apple and down the front of his leathers. Her hand paused on its journey, hovering for a second over the muscles on his taut stomach before she clicked one talon down each single tooth of the zipper. When he felt he could bear no more, her hand slipped between his legs, cupping him in her palm to squeeze just enough to hold him still. Her voice dripped desire as she asked, 'You don't truly care where I've been. Do you darlin'?'

Momma, believe me when I say that all I care about is where your hand is goin' next, but where's Darth?

'Mr Lover Man passed over into the Light Side, honey, too many donuts and not enough fights.'

Pity. I wanted to torture and burn him.

'No need to trouble yourself, darlin', it's just you and little old me now.'

And us.

Jake's hands flew to cover his ears. His chin dropped to his chest as he gritted his teeth in pain and foamy spittle leaked between lips. He shuddered, opened his mouth wide, and wailed, *Shit, Mary, who was that? Damn voice near blew my head off.*

'Oh, Jakey baby, there's no-one here.' Mary placed her hands over his and, licking her red lips pulled him tight, hip to hip and whispered, 'Come to bed; those nasty, sweaty leathers need peeling off, right off. Real slow.' As she spoke, Jake visibly relaxed, his face becoming brighter and more youthful.

His glance at Mary was shy as he suggested, *Maybe I should shower first, momma?*

'No need, baby, you know I like you dirty.'

Chapter Fifteen

-SOUL MATES-

In the middle of the night Jake left the musky bed he shared with Mary to climb the Tower's spiral stone staircase. Arriving in the round room, he leaned heavily on an intricately carved wooden lectern and pressed his hand on the heavy tome that rested there. It groaned under his touch, its black leather cracking and chafing against the thick iron chain that bound it. Jake picked up a pair of half moon glasses and whispered to himself, *'I need you to record this Keeper. I may need to remember what our Momma has done.'* Jake breathed deeply and as he exhaled his back bent and his shoulders grew rounded, he placed the spectacles on his nose and rested his right palm on the chain ignoring the searing pain of the burn they inflicted. He spoke, IT is I, open.

The chain hissed and slithered away from the book to slip curling down the single leg of the lectern and slither sibilantly hissing to hide under a child size bed.

you called me from my sleep. Why?

Listen and write.
The Keeper placed his pen in the ink and pressed it to a fresh page as Jake dictated the words through their shared mouth.

The Keeper wrote:

Heavensgate: Joy

I miss Jacob; he was a holier than thou fuckin' pain in the ass, but now he's gone I miss him. I want him back.

You've still got us, Jake.

Be silent, I am working and will not be disturbed.

I was surprised, shocked in fact to find Mary at Heavensgate. The last time I saw her, she wasn't quite so healthy. It was a long time ago and if I need an excuse, which I do not, a lot of bad shit happened at a particular weak moment when I was young and grieving.

Anyhow, I went to visit Mary after Susie's funeral. You should have seen her, my darling girl, she was a centerfold and she was my wife, my true love, my first love, my last. I killed her; it was an accident same as when I burnt down the house and killed my whole family. I'm plagued by accidents and fuckin' idiots. Susie died in a motor accident which was not my fault. Oh man you shoulda seen her before her face got close up and personal with the giant pine tree, what a perfect girl.

I know what Jacob said about it all being straight forward afterwards. The cops and the Judge absolved him of all blame, black ice on the mountain road, tragic accident yadda, yadda, yadda. The painful truth is that Jacob, that yellow streaked cowardly piece of chicken shit, fell asleep in the ambulance and then hid behind Doc at the Rehab Centre for months afterwards. Saint Jacob went to the Land of Nod and, as usual, the motherfuckin' streak of piss left me, Jake, to clean up his shit.

I went to Court. *I* wasn't convicted and fuckin' right too. *I* spent nine months of my life waiting in a stinking cell for a not guilty verdict.

Do they give you those stolen months of your life back? Do they fuck. This upstanding judicial system don't compensate you neither.

What did Saint Jacob do while I was rotting in jail? He spent those long months with Doc 'talkin' it through'. All that yappin' didn't bring my Susie back, did it? It sure didn't make me miss her any less. I hate Jacob; he was one stupid son-of-a-bitch. But I miss him. Maybe I'm crazy.

I digress. Let's get back to Susie's accident. My moronic lawyer said I was a 'lucky guy' to get off free and clear.

Well, I felt real lucky banged up with those cretinous psychos and mindless perverts just because of a sexy moment and black ice on the road. I was real lucky to avoid a prison-made toothbrush knife in the gut and gang rape in the shower block.

I felt like a fuckin' gold medal winner every day I spent chowing down on shit not fit for dogs. I said three Hail Marys every night spent sleeping under itchy blankets too poor for fleas. It was hell on Earth in there and that's not even giving due credit to the sick-minded, Nazi-uniformed, sadistic, fuckin' screws.

Like I said, I was represented by a *lawyer*, a pathetic waste of skin, an overpaid, parasitic bird-brain. I'd like to see him locked up for nine months, then, when he won his freedom and his own belt, shoe laces and wallet back, he could call himself the 'Lucky Lawyer' and maybe he wouldn't need to chase ambulances no more.

Any which way, she was my sweet Susie. She was a sexy girl, and, like Jacob, she left me. I'm pretty much free of her. Apart from the occasional spooky shagging visit I've been more or less alone for years. I still miss her. No, I haven't forgotten Louise; she was a dope, a doormat. Lou was Jacob's bride and Susie was mine, no matter what he told you. Just like the kid, Tommy, was mine. As any right thinking person can see, I've suffered grievous losses, too many for a man to bear, but bear them I most surely do.

OK. OK. I was talking about my old fuck buddy, Mary.

The day I arrived back at her house I needed a great deal of comforting and man could Mary dole it out, she could comfort the dead, could my Mary.

I travelled on the Greyhound overnight with her key in my shoe and, as dawn was breakin' I let myself in. I wasn't quiet and Mary wasn't asleep. She was sat at the sticky, red, Formica table drinking coffee strong enough and thick enough to hold itself together without the need for a mug. The old cow was wearing a faded red silk dressing gown with a stupid dragon embroidered on the back, and not much else. She sat half-cut and half-stoned smokin' a joint and watching CNN on the old TV mounted above the doorway so she could watch her soaps and police the hallway at the same time. Fuck me, she sure was a mess. I was mortified because I'd put myself out to see this pile of shit that called itself a woman. Anyhow, I was there, so I sat down opposite her and, snatching it from her cracked lips, took a draw on her roll-up. No reaction.

OK, I thought, two can play games, and I was taught how to play by her, the queen bitch of the national bitch league of great bitches. So I stared her out. I saw her eyes flicker as she deigned to notice me, but the whore continued to act as if I wasn't there, as if it hadn't been years since she last clapped her red-rimmed eyes on me. I spat in her ugly bitch face and said,

Look at you Momma, look what happens when Jake's not around to take care of you. You're a fuckin' disgrace to womankind. Don't ignore me, Mary, I'm here to purify your soul.

Mary stubbed out the 'cigarette' on the torn linoleum and placed her empty coffee mug by the sink. Without a glance in my direction or a single fuckin' word of welcome or affection, she laid her upper body face down on the table. I walked behind her and unfastened my belt. She raised her skinny old butt in the air, spread her legs wide and braced herself.

That's more like the respect a man deserves from his Momma.

Now, before I tell you what happened next, and before you judge me, you have to understand that Mary always had the worst kind of effect on me. I couldn't help myself. I'm not to blame.

The state of her made me feel sick to my stomach. Her legs were pale, scrawny, covered in bruises and unshaven. She stank of her beloved grass, its pungent sweetness mixed with a heady perfume of stale cigarettes, gin and unwashed skin. It didn't stop me though; I had to help her see the light.

I was so hard that I struggled to unbutton my jeans. I pushed my throbbing cock into her, thrusting deep, using her warm, welcoming sheath of wetness as if it was a thing apart from her. I wanted to feel that I had come home; I wanted to feel loved and safe. What a fuckin' joke. The old bitch stayed silent and unmoving, no matter how roughly I forced myself in and out of her, no matter that I bit her neck hard enough to draw blood and pulled out a chunk of her peroxide-blonde hair. She was cruel; I wanted my momma, my playmate, my vice, my saviour. It was like screwing a corpse.

I tried my best, but I couldn't come, my dick was sore and I was tired. I pulled out of her, erect, bewildered and angry, ready to strike her for letting me down. Mary raised herself up slowly like the old woman she was and went upstairs.

I followed her thinking, 'Now the bitch'll talk to me, now she'll tell me how much she missed me and how good it was for her to have me deep inside her, fucking her again.'

I'm a reasonable man so I was expecting more, but the whore never glanced at me. She walked into the room she shared with Big Al, slammed the door in my face and locked the bolt. I sat on the top stair like I used to when I was a kid, listening just the same. When the bitch cried out for Al to do her harder and faster I wanted to hurt myself just for some release. That was the exact moment I decided to kill her but I had to cut myself first, so I went into her pristine bathroom, took a razor blade out of its wax wrapper, and, for old time's sake, I lowered my jeans and slashed at my thighs. Then I bled on her white fluffy bath mat. I felt much better.

Mary wasn't easy for me to kill. It's hard to let go of something you love and I truly loved her. I had loved her since the day she took Jacob, the others and me in when we were just a frightened little eight year old boy. I hated Mary's Mr Lover Man, Big Al, with a vengeance; I had entertaining plans for him too.

I hung around for a few days seein' as I had nowhere else to go. I needed time to grieve for my Susie and, Mary's house, full of sad, fostered kids was as good a place as any to cry my heart out.

For a week, every morning was more or less the same. Mary made breakfast for the little kids; Al asked me when I was going to piss-off outta his hair, then he drove them to the local schools. He no longer worked as Darth Vader at the Mall, he had achieved a more lucrative and professional job at the car wash, so he was out all day.

Mary continued to behave as if I wasn't there, she never spoke to me, and she made me feel invisible. I was hurt and angry and it was all down to her, just like it had been when I was a kid and she was punishing me for some minor misdemeanour or other.

Several times a day I raped her and, believe me when say I did my best to hurt her. I almost killed her on one occasion but no sound ever escaped her mouth, she just took what I dished out without struggle or complaint, keeping her eyes closed tight even when I half strangled her. When I had finished using her she carried on as if it hadn't happened. I never even saw her limp, although she musta been in a world of pain. Mary was unnatural; I knew if I sent her to the great beyond, I'd be doing the world a favour.

One morning, as I lay in my old bed planning my next steps, I heard the basement door being unbolted, followed by the stomp of hasty feet on the wooden staircase, down and then back up again before the door was rebolted. I strained to make out angry whispers exchanged between Mary and Al, but I sure heard him when he shouted, 'I warned you, girl, and if I told you once I done told you a hundred times. This time you're on your own, you faithless stupid bitch. You ain't dragging me into your shit, Mary.'

Al left, slamming the front door hard enough to bring the house down.

I dressed and went down to the kitchen where I found Mary, shaking and pouring herself a pint of gin. I pointed at her glass and said, *It's a little early even for you...*

She ignored me and swallowed half her anesthesia in one gulp, then she chain smoked pot for thirty minutes. I sat and watched. The stinkin' bitch finally spoke to me, glory fuckin' hallelujah.

'Jake, you gotta help us, son.'

Pardon me did I hear something? I spun my head around as if searching for the source of the voice. She stood and slammed her small fists on the table sending the empty gin glass crashing and the full ashtray bouncing perilously close to the edge of the table.

'Jake, enough with the games, this is a matter of life and death d'ya hear me? *My* life and death.' She was hysterical, pacing back and forth, tearing at her hair like a lunatic.

Mary, sit. Now tell me, Momma, do you still lock little kids in the basement?

'I don't see it so much as a basement, it's more like a therapy centre.' She sighed and moved her eyes away from my face.

It fuckin' scares them, Mary.

'It fuckin' ought to, Jake. Anyhow look at you, you turned out just fine.'

I'm not so sure about that. Now tell me what happened to get you so riled up this fine and sunny morning?

She told me. I wish she hadn't, but I did ask her.

He was about five years old and he wouldn't see six 'cause Mary had strangled him. I helped her bury his tiny body deep in the woods and I tell you this, it upset me. Later, Al told the Police that the kid was dropped off at school and must've run away just like he did from his previous foster home. It didn't matter, his neglectful momma wasn't gonna have to worry about taking care of him when she got out of jail.

Heavensgate: Joy

When we dropped the little body into the hole, I was shakin' like a shittin' dog. Don't misunderstand me, although it was sad I didn't shake with sadness, I'm not soft. I shook because I was using all of my self-control to deny myself the pleasure of clubbing Mary over the back of her bleached head with the spade.

I managed to resist the impulse to whack her tiny brain right out of her thick skull and we walked away from the tiny, shallow grave holding hands like lovers. First chance I got I pushed her up against a tree by the road and screwed her fuckin' senseless as the traffic rolled on by.

I had to do it, I mean, I wasn't sure which shag with her would be my last chance and that one, knowing she would soon be dead, was in my top ten, a good one to end with. Mary obviously enjoyed the 'exhibitionist out in the wild' action as much as I did which, in the end, was what finally decided me. It's always best to go out on a high if at all possible. So, when we got home, I told her I wanted to have her in the basement, on the spot where the kid had died, and Mary being the fine upstanding person that she was, thought it was an inspired notion.

I led the way down the wooden stairway. Mary followed me into the dimly lit pit. As I passed the first shelf I picked up some blue rope and told the old bitch it was part of the sex game. I bound her and gagged her with an oily rag fixed with some carpet tape. Mary was happy and waiting for me to fuck her, right up to the moment I stuffed her nose with cotton wool, which I did out of kindness and appreciation for all she had done for me. Naturally enough she struggled to breathe, so I carried her like the precious article she was and placed her, bucking away like a mad horse, inside the big dog cage she kept in the basement's far corner as a special treat for kids. I blew her a kiss as her eyes fluttered back into her head. Out of respect, I covered her final resting place with a thick old rug, giving it a friendly goodbye tap on the top before I piled a heap of old furniture and other shit in front of it.

I smashed the light bulb and locked the basement door. I picked up my overnight bag and, as I left, I threw the key in the trash.

It was a good day's work and, taking everything into consideration, it was only fair. I could have set fire to the house. I could have topped Al and left her locked in the cage to starve. I didn't do those things because Momma Mary had been good to me in the past. Hell, hers were the first titties I ever got to suck. She was the first woman to give me a blow job when I was nine. Mary taught me all of the tricks I've used to keep a string of bitches happy ever since. That's why I was kind to her in her last moments.

I think it's understandable that, after I went to all that trouble to send her off into the great unknown, I was a little surprised when she appeared at the Lodge to play house keeper and sex kitten. No worries though, as Jacob always used to say, 'beggars can't be choosers' and, by the time Mary turned up at Heavensgate, I was like a hungry dog slavering for a bone.

Jake fell silent.
The Keeper removed his spectacles and placed them on the lectern with great care alongside the pen saying, I need to sleep.
Jake looked up from the book, startled as Jim tapped him on the back and, peering over his shoulder at the beautifully written copperplate words, said, 'What the fuck are you plannin' now, Jakey boy?'

Chapter Sixteen

-SILVER DOLLAR-

In the Bay's most popular café the morning rush was over. Joy, Ruby and Gabi sat taking a break before the lunch time madness began. Ruby had magazine open on the table showing a column of circled letters and numbers. She toyed with the red felt-tip pen dangling from her mouth, her gold flecked eyes sparkled as she pretended to drag on it and blow imaginary smoke rings before announcing with glee, 'This *fabulous* quiz says that I, Ruby, am the Mata Hari of lovers; it *correctly* states that I am a *tigerrrr* in bed. What about you, Joy, have you ever been *in lurve*?' As Joy opened her mouth to reply, Gabi jumped in waving a teaspoon up and down like a baton in front of her face and, with his Spanish accent as strong as his perfume, he said, 'No, she have not; she hesitate because she no love with all her heart and soul.' Joy snapped at him, 'Who is *she*, the cat's mother? And I did not hesitate, you interrupted me. As for *lurve*, as Ruby puts it, I never get the chance. Even gorgeous Sam Black can't remember me for longer than a quickie. Nobody takes any notice of me for more than a minute.'

Gabi pressed a hand to his cashmere covered chest, his eyes wide as he exclaimed, 'Lies. I take notice.'

'Yes but you're, well...'

Ruby snorted, sending milky tea back down her nose making her sneeze. Joy and Gabi ignored her.

'What am I, senorita? You tell me, eh?' Gabi leaned closer, his chin rested on his hands, his brown eyes, highlighted with blue glittery powder, sparkled hypnotically.

Joy tore her eyes from his stare and sputtered, 'You are, well, you are, Andalusian.'

'Good save,' Ruby snuffled as she wiped her snub nose on her striped 'Joy's Café' apron.

Gabi sat up straight saying, 'Yes I am Andaluz and verrry proud. And our Ruby, you truly love her, Joy, I know this.'

'Stop fishing for affection, Gabi. I love you both.'

'But you no been *in* love my friend, this is why you no understand it.' Gabi flounced away from the table in his tiger print leggings and pink Sketchers intent on torturing a tanned youth who desired nothing more than soda and an iced finger. Gabi smiled and batted his eyelashes, saying, 'Hola guapo, you fancy something sweet?'

'Ignore the old queen,' Ruby shouted her advice across the room. Noticing her friend's blotchy face Ruby closed the magazine and asked, 'Joy, whatever is the matter? Don't go getting all emotional on me; it's just a stupid quiz.'

Joy bit her lip, fighting unexpected tears as she confided, 'Ruby, I'm madly, stupidly, and pointlessly in love with Sam Black. I do know what true love is.'

'No, Joy. I hate to agree with the great big cupcake, but Gabi is right, you don't know.'

Joy glared at Ruby, who bravely patted her hand, saying, 'Please don't be upset, it's not your fault. We think it's as if your heart wasn't meant to be broken. We worry because, despite being protected from love's pain, you're never happy.'

'That's because I can't hang onto a man for longer than it takes to have a pint, a bag of chips and a quick shag and even then I have to constantly remind the shagger that I'm in the same bloody room. I'm sick of being Sam's conquest. I want to be his lover. I'm lonely, Ruby. I feel doomed and hopeless.' Joy pulled a paper napkin from the tin holder and dabbed at her eyes.

Heavensgate: Joy

Ruby closed the space between them and kissed Joy on her forehead saying, 'Now don't be silly, my lovely. You lead a bloody charmed life here and you know it. However, you need to forget that chancer, Sam, and get a *proper* life with a *real* man in your bed who worships you for the goddess you are. Start germinating a little hope for the future, live a little; let your hair down. There must be a good man out there who'll love and remember you always. It would be too cruel otherwise.'

Joy sniffed back her tears and hissed, 'Nobody will ever love me because nobody can remember me, Ruby! You must be exhausted after dishing out that great big dollop of unwanted advice. Maybe you should go home and give the lunch shift a miss? Some friends you two are.'

Ruby ignored her friend's anger, cheerfully replying, 'Oh, I don't know, Joy, we could be the making of you yet. What do you say, Gabi, mi amigo? Si or No?'

Gabi dragged his eyes away from the youth's sugar coated lips and replied, 'Si, mi amor, si.'

Ruby glanced at her Mickey Mouse watch and played with her hair while Joy furiously brushed imaginary crumbs off her pristine apron saying, 'Well, whatever you and your sidekick say, *I* say give me that bloody stupid rubbish, it's off to the great recycling depot in the sky.' Joy snatched the offending rag out of Ruby's hands and marched over to the trash where she dumped it, rubbing her palms together, satisfied with a job well done.

'Now get your arse behind the counter, Ruby. Gabi, put your frigging lipstick away and leave the customers alone.' The tanned youth wrapped the remainder of his sweet treat in a napkin and left in a hurry. All three shouted at once, each blaming the other saying, 'Look what you did.'

'No, you look what you did.'

'Why is it always my bloody fault?'

They fell into ashamed silence when a small boy wandered into the café wearing a serious expression and wringing wet clothes. He walked directly toward Joy leaving a trail of wet footprints behind him; she glanced through the window checking for rain, but the sun shone brightly and the street was dry as a bone. Joy crouched until she was at the eye level with her young customer.

'Did you get caught in a downpour?' He refused to look at her and shook his head. 'Did you fall in some water?' He nodded, his thick brown fringe flopping over his eyes. Joy tenderly smoothed his hair back with one finger, tipped his chin up and asked, 'Where's your mummy, love?' The boy pointed outside, then at the soda fridge as he opened his hand to reveal a silver coin in his palm. Joy smiled and offered the dripping boy a choice of orange or lemonade. She passed him a dry dishcloth and led him to the nearest table saying, 'Keep your pennies, love. Sit down here and if Mummy hasn't turned up by the time you've finished your drink, we will go and find her together. What's your name, sweetheart?'

Joy saw hesitation flit across the child's eyes before, tipping his head to one side, he replied, 'I'm called Tommy and you, ma'am, you're Joy.'

Well, Tommy clever clogs, how do you know my name?' He pointed to her apron. Joy glanced down certain she wasn't wearing her name tag. When she looked up to tell him so, Tommy had gone, leaving a full can of orange soda on the table and the dishcloth in a puddle on the floor.

'Ruby. Gabi. Where did the boy go?'

'What boy? I see no boy. Ruby, you see boy? No, Joy, we no see boy.' Gabi shrugged his thin shoulders.

Ruby dragged her feet as she fetched the mop and bucket from the back room and yelled at Gabi, 'You lazy puff, get over here and clean this mess up.'

Fortunately for Ruby and Gabi, Joy chased after the child. She bumped into a crowd of holiday makers jostling at the doorway to get the best tables for lunch, and slowing her down. As she reached the road she didn't see the floor show inside begin.

Gabi waved imperiously at Ruby and said, 'You do mop. I busy, Lardy Arsy.'

Heavensgate: Joy

Ruby marched across the café and threw a glass of water over him shouting, 'Now clean this up.' The group of lunchtime tourists laughed, enjoying the free floor show.

A red nosed local, bedecked in ribbons ready for the pub's Morris Dancing event, waved his bells in the air and called out, 'Hey, guys, I bet this is more fun than the fishing museum.'

No-one disagreed as Ruby suggested, 'Put your bloody review on Trip Advisor, Mr Ding-a-Ling.'

The man smiled as he quipped, 'I love your fiery sense of humour, Ginger.' He was saved by the distraction of Gabi dropping a plate of iced buns in fear for the ribbon and bell adorned man's life.

In the street, Joy shaded her eyes as she turned in circles. The weather was scorching hot, the sunshine blinding and Tommy was nowhere to be seen. She turned to go back inside when a glint of silver caught her eye, bending down she picked up a shiny dollar. It was wet. Death was watching.

Chapter Seventeen

-THE STALKER-

After millennia of disinterest in the innumerable souls he had gathered, Death was obsessed with the one that got away. He followed Joy in many different guises, constantly checking his pocket watch, listening out for a particular tune and time. The Creator was obliged to remind him more than once that he was omnipotent.

If she noticed Death's eyes on her as she went about her business in the Bay, Joy would press her back to the nearest wall, darting her eyes left and right like a frightened animal sensing a trap. If he approached her, she inspected her chewed fingernails and hummed a random tune, refusing to acknowledge his presence. When Death pressed her with words, she ran away as if her shoes were on fire.

In the evenings, when Joy closed the café, her dedicated suitor waited on the bench outside. Sometimes he appeared as an old woman, or a coast-to-coast walker. Other times Death disguised himself as a snap happy tourist. He occasionally waited for her in the body of a sweet, red-haired, freckle faced girl.

One particularly memorable evening Death caught Joy's startled attention by presenting himself as her twin, accurate right down to the mole on her collar bone. Most often Death preferred to pose as a magnificent male in the prime of life. However, it made no difference to Joy what outer shell Death wore; she always knew who and what he was. On her brave days she would nod at her avid follower acknowledging his excellent mimicry before setting off home at a brisk walk that quickly turned into a sprint.

Joy was unobtainable and strong. Death failed over and over again to trap his quarry and capture her soul. He was as frustrated as a spurned lover; the more Joy refused to take his hand, the more she ignored his dedication and attention, the more desirable she became.

Now and again Hope risked observing this dalliance from a safe distance as she caressed Joy's glass and paper heart, tormented by the choices and obligations that fought against her nature to bring hope where there was loss and despair. Something had to change and Hope was afraid that it might be her.

Joy wondered if she would ever find peace of mind. She hated the seductive thoughts of rest and comfort that Death placed in her mind and was sickened by the salty seaweed smell that clung to her skin after one of his stalking episodes, the scent made her itch all over. She understood Death was a threat, but had no idea why he followed her without attempting to take her. Some days she wondered if he was anything more than a figment of her imagination.

Joy needed to talk to someone.

On a rainy Monday morning, when custom at the café was slow, she invited Ruby to share a slice of coffee cake and, feeling ridiculous, said, 'I'm being followed.'

'Oooh, a stalker how romantic. Who is he?'

'No, you fool, it's not a man. Not always. Not exactly. At least I don't think so.'

'In that case, my singleton friend, I'm not interested,' Ruby pouted. 'It's a good job I don't rely on you for love interest because I may as well rely on the Virgin Mary.' Ruby crossed herself and mumbled, 'I'm sorry, My Lady.'

'Ruby, please, I'm serious.'

'I'm serious too; you never can be sure if VM's real or not. She's strong on the vision scene so I'm hedging my bets. What about you?'

Joy threw up her hands asking, 'Why are you rambling when I'm confiding in you? I'm afraid of my own shadow. I'm tired all the time and this stalker scares me. I know it sounds dramatic, but I truly sense a bad moon rising.' Ruby stared blankly at a point above Joy's head.

'OK, Ruby. I'm boring you, I realise that, but please listen. I need a break from here.'

After a long pause Ruby puffed out her cheeks, blew air between her lips and said, 'Well, I suppose I could do some extra shifts. You know better than me that the café is too busy in high season for any of us to take a vacation.' Joy's shoulders slumped. Ruby swallowed hard and snapped, 'Come on. Don't play the martyr with me, Joy. We can't always get what we want when we want it. I want to go with my cousin to Shagaluf but, as Gabi loves to point out, my lardy arse won't fit in a plane seat.'

'Perhaps you should keep your next Doctor's health check appointment,' Joy suggested, giving up any attempt to have the conversation she had set out to have.

A high pitched voice squealed across the café, 'Why you no walk to Majorca, then you be thin for to fly back?' Gabi mocked Ruby as he pranced off to chat up a big, hairy, tattooed lorry driver, causing the man's mug of tea to shake in his hand and making him choke on his jam scone.

Ruby pointed at Gabi's retreating, skinny, leopard print covered back and declared, 'I hate him.'

Despite her anxiety Joy laughed. Thinking that Gabi and Ruby could probably make her smile on the gallows she said, 'No, you can't kid me, Ruby. You don't hate our sweet boy; you love him with all your heart and soul.' Ruby ignored the comment and pushed her chair back from the table saying, 'Hey ho, here we go, quiet time is over.' The women smiled at each other as a group of excited teenagers entered the café joking with one another as they jostled for space at the cake counter.

Heavensgate: Joy

Ruby left Joy to serve the happy crowd and went to the back room from where she could usually manage to spy on Gabi without being noticed, but he had vanished, leaving a much calmer truck driver alone with his scone. Something slapped Ruby on the back of the head making her cry out, 'Ouch. Gabi, you little shit.' He skipped out of her reach, wiggling his butt and holding his manicured hands out in front of him like Skippy the Kangaroo. Ruby hissed, 'Come back here you poncey little bastard, I need to talk to you.' It was too late, Gabi was already eyeing up his next victim for adoration.

Joy was unloading the industrial dishwasher when Death entered the café and tapped her on the shoulder. She swatted him off like a fly. Unconcerned, he wandered over to Ruby's hiding place. The sight of Death so close to Joy made Ruby wring her hands as pools of tears filled her eyes dousing their usual fire. Death wrapped his soul laden fingers around Ruby's, saying,

-You do see my problem with Joy, don't you, my scarlet Angel?-

As always, Ruby found Death's beauty unbearable. His normally fathomless eyes were full of sorrow that made him appear vulnerable. Even though she knew it was an illusion, Ruby wanted to kiss him, but it was far too late for all that so she asked instead, 'My Lord. How will you take Joy if Hope won't help you? After all, she still has her heart.'

-Hope will eventually see that she must do as I command.-

'She won't give Joy's heart away easily.'

-I am not concerned with Hope; she's a fool's fantasy.-

'Yes and you, My Lord Death, you are something a girl can rely on.' Ruby couldn't stop herself from reaching up to run her index finger across Death's full, icy lips. She was shocked when he sucked her finger into his cold mouth, flicking his rough, cat like tongue across the tip.

A furnace sparked in her belly and her face grew warm. She snatched her finger back and snapped, 'Thank you, my Lord, for reminding me that even I am not completely free of desire.' She stepped away from Death's temptation and pressed her guilty hands behind her back while she tried not to imagine submitting to him entirely.

Death gave a wry smile and said,

-My Lady, you are an exercise in restraint.-

He withdrew the pocket watch from his silken waistcoat. Ruby stared hypnotised as he laced the ethereal chain between long elegant fingers and used his thumb nail to flick a catch on the silver case, releasing a perfect silence which filled Ruby's soul.

-You and your Gabi knew that Hope would betray me yet you said not a word nor took any steps to ensure Joy was returned to me.-

Ruby's knees almost buckled, only pride held her upright. She was surprised to feel her heart flutter against her ribs like a trapped bird. Death knew exactly what he was doing, and it hurt.

-Can you hear that, Ruby? It is the sound of the Nothing.-

As her heart pounded faster, Ruby's mind began to wander, she pressed down rising panic as she imagined slivers of her soul falling into the void to be lost for all eternity. Anguish pressed on her chest and seemed to force its way out of her back. She saw pieces of herself float away in the Nothing, never to be reunited, never to be whole again. Forever lost.

As she trembled, and sweat poured from her body, Death cupped her face and whispered,

-Will you not help me to stop hurting you? Will you fulfill your duty and bring Joy home to me?-

Ruby's voice shook and tears tracked her cheeks as she said, 'My Lady Joy is needed here and she is deeply loved. I cannot help you my Lord and...' Death raised a hand to silence her saying,

-Joy remains in the Mortal Realm and the demon, 'Jake' remains at Heavensgate. Hope is to blame for this mess. The Creator is no doubt disappointed.-

Gabi, unable to resist to the siren call of the Nothing, dragged himself away from a promising student to join Death and Ruby in the café's tiny back room. He noted with concern the sweat on Ruby's upper lip and touched her shoulder to soothe her. Seeing his friend relax a little, he shimmied over to Death and, despite the boiling that started in his bowels, pressed pale hands on him asking, 'Can you not let this go, My Lord?'

Death stared at the pink manicured fingernails that toyed with the ruffle on his shirt.

- **I will not avoid my duty and nor will you. Remove your hands.**-

Ruby felt her anxiety ebb away as Gabi lowered first his hands and then his eyes in deference and obedience.

'Am I the only one working here today?' Joy's shout drew their attention; Death's eyes flashed starlight as he said,

-**Prepare, my Angels. Say your goodbyes. It is almost time. Do not fail me again.**-

Chapter Eighteen

-TAKE ME TO CHURCH-

Distressed by Death's visit to the café, but unable to explain the true reason for her anxiety, Ruby was making her feelings known. Her voice screeched across the café like chalk on a board saying, 'Joy, I took your bloody advice. I saw the doctor and now I have my brilliant results.' She flung herself into the nearest chair which clung to her behind like a pair of nutcrackers to a walnut. Joy pressed her hands over her ears as Ruby shouted, 'I've got to stop drinking. Here, in this godforsaken shit hole that has a pub on every corner.' A sob tickled the back of her throat as she continued, 'I can't eat either. I can't have chips or pizzas or chocolate or biscuits or cakes. I work in this bloody sugar addict's wet dream and I've got to lose loads of weight, absolutely loads. That pompous shit of a doctor looked at me over his stupid glasses and his nasty mouth said, 'Ruby, you must stop drinking and lose weight or die."

Gabi stood behind Ruby kneading her shoulders. 'That is porque he surprised to see diabetes and heart attack in surgery, wearing long red wig.' Ruby stiffened in warning under his clever hands.

'Gabi.' Joy stifled laughter for Ruby's sake.

'It true, Joy, you know it true and now she know it true too.' Gabi risked continuing the massage, saying, 'Ruby, guapa mia, you is only one human and if you eat cake you must make jogs even if they is wobbly jogs you needs them everys day.' Ruby threw Gabi's hands off her and began to rise out of the chair.

Breaking up the exchange before blood was spilled, Joy said, 'Gabi, go and clean the display fridge. Now.' He shot to the opposite side of the café giggling.

Tears slid down Ruby's nose. She sobbed loudly and slumped across the table where spilled salt and pepper surrounded her as her big shoulders heaved and she wailed out her distress in a pitch that made the village dogs howl.

Paul Smith, defrocked vicar, pulled tiny 'Joy's café' endorsed paper napkins out of a tin dispenser, encouraging Ruby to mop up the deluge while he patted her back as if she was a fat baby. Joy sat patiently waiting for the storm to pass, holding her friend's hand and hoping no customers popped in and witnessed the debacle.

Ruby's voice lowered a few decibels as she sniffed and said, 'What will I dooooo?'

Smith attempted to comfort her. 'You know, Ruby, we are never given more than we can bear, old girl.'

Ruby speared him with bloodshot eyes and, spitting fury in his face, shouted, 'I know that's a crock of shite, you sanctimonious, God bothering old fart. Is that what you told the choir boys? Is that what you said when you got your filthy dick out? 'Hold on, child, you won't be given more than you can bear."

Paul raised rheumy eyes to the ceiling, prayed for strength and pretended not to understand. Spotting Gabi he summoned his natural cheeriness and said, 'Oh look, your nice friend has brought you a lovely cup of camomile tea, dear, drink it up. Come on now, Ruby old girl, tea is the best medicine when you are beside yourself.'

Gabi's face lit up as he placed the drink on the table. 'She everywhere by herself, she so round she everywhere she go.' He skipped sideways out of Ruby's angry reach and preened his skinny self, like a toreador, in front of the counter mirror. Gabi licked one finger to smooth his brows and, taking his life in his hands, said, 'Ruby need buy two plane seats to fit her lardy bottom so she can sit by her own self.' He applauded his own reflection then hugged himself as he creased with laughter.

Ruby sufficiently recovered from drowning in misery to shout, 'Piss off, you anorexic tart.'

Gabi raised one perfect eyebrow, puffed out his pigeon chest and proudly announced, 'I no am tart. I Andalusian.'

Despite the insults directed at the ex-Vicar and his rumoured predilections, the old man sat holding tight to Ruby's left hand as he and Joy prevented her from rising up and punching Gabi. Desperate to escape the table, Ruby attempted distraction, saying, 'I'm sorry, *Vicar*.'

'You are forgiven, of course, my dear.'

Ruby smiled and sniffed back tears. As her comforters relaxed, she felt a small easing in the hands that held hers, so continued, 'I am sure you try to be a good man, even though you have a penchant for choir boys.'

Smith dropped his gaze to the floor and shook his head, mumbling, 'Ruby, must you drag up the past?'

Ruby was relentless, she felt Joy squeeze her hand in warning, but her mouth had a life of its own and she lashed out at Smith asking, 'Did you view child rape as an occupational hazard for men of the cloth?'

Joy shouted, 'Enough, Ruby. It's not his fault you need to go on a diet. Leave it.'

Joy released her hand.

Smith lessened his grip on the other as he said, 'You know, Ruby, it's unkind to hurt one who is attempting to offer you comfort in your hour of need.'

Ruby stood and screamed in his face, 'Well piss off then 'cause I, for one, am glad there are more women in the church nowadays.'

Smith had suffered worse in prison and replied, 'Sticks and stones, Ruby.'

Joy was becoming more nervous by the second. It was as if she didn't know the Ruby who attacked the old Vicar and, in an attempt to calm matters down, she said, 'Let's get this conversation back to you and how we may help you get fit and well, Ruby.'

However, Ruby wasn't so easily distracted from her prime target and, her voice full of menace, said, 'Joy won't tell you what everyone in this God forsaken shit hole of a village thinks *Vicar*, because she is far too nice, but she knows your unrepentant soul is damned.' Ruby ripped her hand from Smith's grasp and pushed him in the chest screaming, 'Now get away from me. You will never receive redemption, never!'

Gabi threw himself under the nearest table. The café's windows rattled in their frames and every fluorescent light tube dimmed a split second before blazing bright and exploding over their heads. Crockery and glass flew from the shelves and careened around the room before crashing to the floor. The Vicar rocked back in his chair and stared at his palm, expecting to find a burn where Ruby's rage had scoured his skin.

Joy sat immobile, surrounded by splinters of glass and crockery that glinted off every surface.

Ruby loomed over Smith and wiped her hand down her apron. She seemed much taller as she snarled, 'Did I upset you, *Vicar*? Please don't fret. The road to hell is long and paved with good people *exactly* like you. Maybe you will find a frozen side street along the way.' The Vicar pushed his chair away from the table, shook splinters of glass and china off his clothes and, his voice shaking, said, 'I will pray for your eternal soul, Ruby,' as he left the café, ridden by his personal devils.

'Glory Hallelujah,' Ruby shouted after his retreating back.

Gabi, sensing that there was no longer any danger from her rage, left his shelter and shook Ruby's hand as he said, 'He not look so scared since hunky policemen knock on door and take him away in black van.'

Joy found her voice, 'How did you do that, Ruby? Why were you so cruel to him? It isn't like you to lash out at people. You can do this diet, there is no need to be so angry and upset. I will help you, even that bitchy waiter over there will help you. Won't you, Gabi?'

Gabi shrugged his pink cashmere clad shoulders as Ruby pulled in a deep, shuddering breath and, seeing Joy's shocked expression, said,

'Oh, my dear friend, I'm so sorry.' Ruby dove deeper into her misery, weeping.

Joy wiped a hand across her face and through her hair, feeling for glass and finding plenty of it, as she sat surveying the mess. She stared at the doors until the locks clicked shut then continued to stare until the 'open for business' sign flipped over to the closed position. Ruby cried as Gabi swept the floor and tried to distract Joy from her questions by saying, 'Ole. Fatty bum-bum cry again, she cry me a river. I fetch Missis Mop. You need buy more tube light, mugs and plates, boss.'

Joy snapped, 'Gabi, please stop talking. Ruby, stop crying, love. Please, for heaven's sake, just ignore him.' Desperate to distract Ruby from her anguish and cheer her up she decided to leave the postmortem as to how and why for later and said, 'Gabi kick the juke box, we need some music.'

The sounds of t.A.T.u.'s '*All The Things She Said*' filled the café. Joy threw Gabi an old-fashioned look then turned back to Ruby saying, 'Listen, here's a strange thing, did I tell you about my latest fantastical experience?'

'Nooo.' Ruby blew her nose into a tiny scrap of serviette, producing the trumpeting of an angry bull elephant. She looked at her palms in disgust and pulled out a dozen more tissues from the dispenser.

'Well, what I'm about to tell you is even stranger than my usual strange stories.'

Ruby gulped. 'Stranger than when the aliens took you?'

'Far stranger. Sit up, stop sniffling and listen.'

Joy stared through the rain lashed windows and began her story.

'I couldn't sleep last night so I got dressed and walked through the lanes trying to clear my head of a pile of random, insomnia creating thoughts. I wandered with no particular destination in mind and… Now, I know this sounds crazy…' She took a deep breath and blurted out the madness, 'I could see the souls of our neighbours as if there were no walls, floors or ceilings between me and them. It was as if they floated in space. I saw Sam Black in bed with Rose, the barmaid, so it's over for me and him, the cheating bastard. The thing is, I don't care as much as I think I ought to. Anyway, I saw good people in the village, their auras strong, brightly coloured and shining like new stars. But, I also saw bad things hanging around our neighbours like thugs on street corners. I was afraid and, after what I witnessed Sam and Rose doing, I didn't want to inadvertently snoop any further, so I walked home with my eyes glued to the cobbles. I daren't undress and hid under the covers like a scared kid. Last night crashed over my head in a wave of psychic impressions. Ruby, Gabi, I kid you not, a battle between good and evil is happening, right here, right now, in the Bay.'

Gabi stared at Joy as if she had grown another head. Ruby raised herself from the table. Her wet face and neck were blotchy, her eyes pink and almost swollen closed. Despite the snot candles dripping from her nose, Ruby still had attitude and said, 'Cut it out, Joy. That's the worst attempt at diversion ever. You have no psychic powers. You were the worst tarot reader come fortune teller this great country ever had to suffer at the British seaside. You are crap at this supernatural stuff. I don't need this shit off you right now. I need a large gin and a bigger cake.'

Gabi blushed pink, upset and embarrassed by Ruby's harshness.

Joy sighed and hung her head. 'I'm telling you both that I'm afraid. I also saw the man who's following me and I'm pretty certain he is Death. My death.'

Ruby kept her expression hidden behind her long curls. Gabi crouched at Joy's feet and, crossing himself in every Catholic direction he could think of, asked, 'What he say to you, this Mr Death, eh?'

'He say, I mean he said, "My Lady, this is the last time of asking. Will you come home?"

I said, "No." I expected to be blasted into the next life there and then. Nothing so dramatic happened; he simply shrugged his shoulders as if he was disappointed. I said, "Sorry." He replied, "You will be." Then he wandered off toward the beach. His voice left me with itchy skin and a toothache that lasted all night.'

Ruby didn't react and Gabi continued to stare in a way she interpreted as disbelieving. Joy's voice grew less certain as she carried on, 'Honestly, I mean, well you should have seen him. Death is gorgeous.' She laughed at herself as Ruby and Gabi maintained a surprising level of disinterest in her other worldly experience and said, 'Any other day I may not have been able to resist him, but I got a letter yesterday from a solicitor in town, so, really, I was forced to decline his offer...'

Joy's voice trailed off as she saw Gabi make the sign of the evil eye and receive a stern look from Ruby, who snorted and wiped her nose on the back of her sleeve saying, 'And I thought Gabi was the crazy one around here. You didn't see Death, you didn't see into everyone's cottage; Sam isn't screwing Rosie; you didn't see diddlysquat, you were dreaming, Joy. But, just for fun, did you see me on your ghost walk?'

'Yes.'

'What was I doing?'

'I won't tell you, Ruby, it's too embarrassing.'

Ruby blushed to match her flaming curls, blew her nose to cover her embarrassment and said, 'Oh. OK. I'll get on with sorting the stock room.'

Gabi took Ruby's place at the table, fluttering his long eyelashes at Joy who smiled and chewed on her lip as he said, 'Now, guapa, tell me girlfriend, what was Ruby doing?'

'No way, Jose.'

'OK, that's not important, but you must explain me what lovely Mr Death look like. What he wear? How tall he is? Did he have nice bottom? Tell me everything, pleeese.'

'After work.'

'You are hard woman, Joy. You cruel to poor Gabi.'

Joy was too busy laughing to notice Ruby unlock the doors and rush outside with tears streaming down her face to stand in the middle of the village green, her hands outstretched in supplication as she pleaded with someone who wasn't there.

Chapter Nineteen

-GRABBIT AND HEDGETT-

Clutching the officious letter which has summoned her to town Joy ambled through Whithorpe's narrow lanes on her way to an appointment with a solicitor.

She loved winter weather, so when snow began to fall in June, she stuck out her tongue to catch the icy sting of the delicious flakes. Remembering the feeling of her small gloved hand held in her foster dad's larger one, she recalled his bass voice saying, 'Don't forget to always taste the rain and the snowflakes, Joy, and cherish the kiss of warm breezes and sunshine on your skin. I tell you this, my beautiful child, because when this mortal life is over, you will miss the small pleasures.'

She smiled as she recalled her reply, 'And sparkly shoes and chocolate and Barbie dolls.'

A dark gray sky that rested on shiny red tiled rooftops. Pregnant clouds obscured the ancient ruins of the clifftop Abbey and freezing mist caressed the town's red brick Victorian buildings. The sea was muffled as though its icy waves were too heavy to make more than a dull thud as they bowed their foamy heads to the brown pebble beach. It was only four o'clock on a summer afternoon but the cold, wet streets were already shrouded in darkness and almost empty of locals and tourists alike.

A biting north wind streaked along the seafront like a banshee, making Joy shiver in her cotton summer dress as she approached the glossy black door of Grabbit and Hedgetts Solicitors. She climbed three worn stone steps and tugged the old iron bell chain on the wall. The door was immediately opened by a slim, but big bosomed woman who stood at least seven foot tall; her extraordinarily long neck was topped with a face as plain as a pikestaff. Joy struggled to make eye contact with the woman's beady eyes that darted nervously under eyebrows that shone like iridescent feathers as she smoothed down a drab brown gown which reached her ankles and adjusted a lace cap which only served to highlight her baldness.

The woman strutted on pointy tiptoes for a moment, then leaned over Joy and cooed, 'Come in, please do come in out of the cold; come into the warm. Coo. Coo. Pardon me. Mr Grabbit is waiting, Miss; he is looking forward to meeting you.' As she spoke, the woman's neck slipped back and forth like a strutting pigeon's. Joy stood transfixed until her hostess crooked a wrinkled bony finger indicating that she should follow her down a dim, oak panelled hallway. They passed paintings on the walls, framed in twisted wood, depicting death scenes of fox hunts, hare coursing, cockfights and other blood sports Joy didn't recognise.

A door leading to a sumptuously decorated office stood ajar. Joy was ushered in with much fussing and cooing and delivered to a huge armchair that faced an antique desk occupied by a man with the face of an ancient baby. Ginger tufts of hair sprouted above his ears and gray wisps dangled from his many chins. He also possessed a moustache of unprecedented carroty magnificence.

Joy smiled and the solicitor moved his features in return saying, 'Thank you, Mrs Sure, please bring our client a pot of English tea.'

Joy's tongue cleaved to the roof of her mouth, she swallowed hard saying, 'I'm terribly thirsty. I would prefer a tall glass of water, please.'

'Your wish is our command,' cooed Mrs Sure who hurried out of the office.

Heavensgate: Joy

Joy heard flapping wings behind her, but fought the urge to twist around to take a look, asking instead, 'Do I have the pleasure of meeting Mr Grabbit or Mr Hedgett?'

The peculiar man squirmed in his carved wooden chair and replied, 'Yes, you do, Miss, you most certainly do have the pleasure. You are most welcome. Please and thank you kindly.'

Joy decided the man was eccentric and took a look around the office. It was difficult to avoid staring at the stuffed birds and animals which covered every available inch of space in the room. Many of the taxidermist's victims were strange and unnatural creatures due to having too many eyes, mouths, wings or limbs and possessing colours and mixtures of feathers, fur, skin and horn which she had never seen in nature.

The solicitor cleared his throat and spoke as if he had a peach stone stuck in it. 'Ah, here is your refreshment.' He indicated a spot on the desk. Joy glanced around expecting to find the tall woman, but there was no-one there. Ice frosted the sides of the glass making it irresistible.

They sat patiently looking at one another until the man sneezed, waved at the deceased trophies and announced, 'Allergies,' in a voice so high pitched it made Joy's ears ring. She was curious; the Solicitor and his assistant reeked of magic, but she couldn't divine its source. Sneezing again, he cleared his throat and spat a globule of phlegm into a silver bowl where it landed with a loud clank. Joy sat ramrod straight, holding onto the chair arms, her knuckles aching. Needing something to do she took a mouthful of freezing water and shivered with pleasure as a seductive, warm liquid glow spread through her body. The solicitor released the breath he had been holding as he watched her relax like a specimen breathing chloroform.

Joy leaned forward and in a husky voice said, 'Come on, don't keep a lady waiting.'

'Well, you see, Miss...'

She twirled a strand of hair around her finger and smiled broadly insisting, 'Joy. Please, call me Joy.'

The solicitor noisily cleared his throat again and shuffled in his chair as he announced, 'Miss Joy, you are the most fortunate recipient of a generous bequest from my client, Mr Andersen.'

'I'm flummoxed. I don't know anyone by that name, please, continue, my curiosity is piqued.' Joy giggled and pressed her hands over her mouth to hold back a squeal of delight.

'Well, no matter, my esteemed client knew you.' The man unrolled a scroll of yellowed vellum and perched purple lensed glasses on the end of his nose saying, 'He writes that you were most kind when his wife sprained her ankle on their honeymoon in the Bay. Sadly, Mrs Andersen and their son pre-deceased my client. He remembered the happiness you brought him and his bride with an impromptu tea party in your café. How wonderful.'

Joy flicked her long hair over her shoulder, glanced from side to side, bit her lip and said, 'Let me tell you a secret. With the exception of a few special people, no-one ever remembers me. Generally speaking, I may as well not exist. You, my lovely man, will forget me as soon as I leave this room. Are you sure you haven't got the wrong person?' Joy winked at him then covered her blush with both hands.

The solicitor preened his moustache and replied, 'Yes, I am certain that you, Miss er, Miss Joy, are the sole beneficiary of the last will and testament of Mr Andersen of Heavensgate, USA who appreciated your kindness when he, and his new wife, Louise, were a long way from home. Now, please read the terms of the bequest and write your signature, here.' He tapped the officious paper with an extraordinarily long, pointed black fingernail. 'Mrs Sure and I will be happy to witness your signature.'

Joy struggled against a feeling of giddiness that threatened to send her dancing around the office as she said, 'I don't recall Mr Andersen or his wife, and hence I cannot recall telling him anything about myself, so how can he remember me?'

The solicitor passed her the glass of water. 'It is a lot to take in, isn't it, Miss Joy?' Joy swallowed the rest of the sweet, clear liquid in one gulp: the solicitor watched with satisfaction, saying, 'There you go, that's much better, Miss.'

Joy smiled and nodded at the delightful man seated opposite her as she waved the empty glass in the air and burped loudly. 'Better out than in, Miss.' The Solicitor gazed at Joy with such tenderness that she swallowed a lump in her throat and wiped tears away with the back of her hand.

A pleasant coo announced Mrs Sure. She handed Joy an old feather pen and spearing her with sharp eyes, said, 'Here you are, Miss. This is *so* appropriate for signing a document of *such* great import, coo, don't you think?'

Joy accepted the quill and, before she knew what she was doing, she had dipped it in the ink well and signed on the dotted line. The solicitor snatched the paper back, scrawled his name under her own, then he opened his jacket and the document disappeared. Joy waited like a nodding dog as drool seeped out of the sides of her mouth and her eyeballs rolled back in her head.

The solicitor's unctuous voice startled her. 'Joy, wake up and listen.'

She opened her eyes and tried to focus on his words. 'In two days a car will call for you at noon. The driver will take you to the airport where you will travel by private jet to the States.'

'What's the rush?' Joy slurred, swallowing a copious amount of saliva.

'Miss, Heavensgate is isolated and deserted. You need to get out there and let folks know it has a new owner. Meet your neighbours. Visit the bank manager. Put things in order, then you can relax and decide what to do next.'

Joy nodded until her brain hurt saying, 'I see. Thank you.'

'My pleasure. Mrs Sure will see you out now. Ah, here is my partner, Mr Hedgett.'

Joy laughed, saying 'I just knew *you* were the Grabbit; where is he?' The solicitor pointed to his jacket and said, 'He is here, in my pocket.' A tiny man popped his head out and waved at her before shouting in a voice pitched high enough to break glass, 'Business over, office closed, get out. Get out. Come on, get up and bugger off.'

Mrs Sure dragged Joy out of the chair and down the hallway before unceremoniously pushing her outside.

She stood on shaking legs, alone on the worn stone doorstep, breathing in the sweet air of a balmy June evening all signs of winter having vanished while she was inside. Turning to face the door with the intention of ringing the bell to complain about being thrown out, she faltered and dropped a large manila envelope onto the cobbles.

The door had vanished and in its place was a bricked up entryway covered in disturbing graffiti. Holding her pounding head with one hand, Joy retrieved the package and clutched it to her breast like a newborn.

She was unsettled and a little tipsy as she stumbled across the road into the Chinese tea house where, after ordering something small, jasmine scented and green to sip, she got busy on her phone.

'Ruby, pick up, come on, Ruby.'

Please leave a message after the tone.

Joy stared at the offending iphone. The beep was followed by the option to leave a message. Joy shouted into the phone attracting bemused glances from the other Tea House customers.

'Oh, Ruby, wait at the café for me. I've loads to tell you. I only had water to drink at the Solicitors but I feel drunk. I can't even find the office door. I'm going to America. I've inherited a lakeside lodge and everything in it from some stranger I honestly cannot remember. Plus, I cannot believe it, Ruby, I'm a dollar millionaire. Ruby, please wait for me. I'm on my way. I'm splashing out on a taxi. Get a bottle of wine out of the fridge.'

Joy sat in the rear of the cab reading the terms of Jacob Andersen's generous bequest over and over until it sank into her conscious mind that she was, indeed, rich. Arriving at her destination, she leapt out of the cab leaving a twenty pound tip and was in the café before the stunned driver had turned the car around.

The heir to Heavensgate skipped over to the cake display. She threw the envelope on the counter and her bag onto the floor behind it. Gabi stuck his pink tongue out at her as he picked up her belongings and took them into the back room. Ruby hissed, 'OK, Joy, I can see you've been on the piss, now sober up and calm down, we have customers.'

Joy swayed on the spot as if her feet were glued to the floor flapping her hands around and insisting, 'I only drank water, it must have been spiked by that weird man with the elf in his pocket or by his giant bald housekeeper. She coos you know. Coo coo like a dove or a pigeon. Odd pair.'

Ruby shouted across the café, 'Gabi. Take over here; Madam and I are going for a walk in the fresh air.' Ruby hustled a wobbly Joy back outside. They walked arm in arm, away from the café until, after a few giggly trips and falls, they arrived at the Bay's small cemetery.

Ruby fought to control her rising dread about Joy's inheritance and said, 'Let's sit here where we won't be disturbed, seeing as it's still daylight.' The women sank onto the graveyard's recently mowed sweet scented grass. Silent at first, they turned their faces toward the light that dappled hypnotically through the new leaves of ancient yew trees and warmed their backs on the dry stone wall. Ruby broke the silence, saying, 'Well, Joy, we can enjoy the blackbird's song or you can tell me what the bloody hell happened in town today. Which is it to be?'

'Don't shout please, Ruby, my head hurts.'

'I'll bloody well shout if I want to, you piss-artist now tell me what happened!'

'Shit, Ruby, this diet is making you nasty,

girl.' Ruby turned a look on her that made Joy's bowels tremble so she said, 'OK. Keep your hair on. Do you remember an American couple called the Andersens from years back? They were honeymooners.

Barely able to control her impatience Ruby replied, 'Yes, I do, but only because the wife kept bothering other customers with her high pitched whiney voice.' Ruby mimicked Louise Andersen. 'Oh gee we just love it here, y'all as English as Yorkshire pudding.' she made me want to slap her and you said I couldn't, so yes, I remember them.'

Joy screwed up her eyes against the glare of the sun and frowned at her friend saying, 'Right. Good. Well, they came from a one horse town called St. Johns which, coincidentally, is close to Heavensgate where the Lodge is.' Joy was too self-absorbed to notice a shadow slide across her friend's already troubled face or the trembling that swept through Ruby's body as she screwed the front of her apron into her fists.

Joy continued babbling, 'Ruby, this is bloody unbelievable, but apparently I was kind to the couple when they honeymooned in the Bay and they remembered me. Now the Andersens are dead, poor things, and I'm dead rich,' Joy burped 'and I need to put my head inbetween my legs.'

Ruby peered at her friend who sat picking at the grass between her feet, and said, 'Nobody ever remembers you.'

'What?' Joy jerked up her head and groaned, 'Ruby, the Timpsons remembered me, you and Gabi remember me, old Mr Deal who owned the café remembered me.'

'Yes that's true and Mr Deal did own the café, which is now yours.'

'Hic. Pardon. The café, yes, which is now mine.'

'How is it yours?'

'You already know that. He bequeathed it to me in his will; he had no-one else to leave his business to.'

'Were you shagging him?'

Joy poked her friend hard in the ribs replying, 'No. Ruby for heaven's sake, take your mind out of the gutter.'

'So,' said Ruby, 'let's have a recap. You, Joy, are an orphan who inherited a café from her employer's death; a house and a trust fund from her foster parents' death and, now, you have a lakeside Lodge and a million dollars in the States due to the death of an unknown American.

'Well. Yes.'

'Death has been good to you.'

'I guess he has at that.'

'What year were you born, Joy?'

'Why? Do you want to throw me a birthday party?'

'Don't get shirty, I'm just asking.'

'Stop changing the subject, Ruby. I'm going stateside. Do you fancy running the café for me?' Ruby sighed, closing her eyes to hide the pain of anxiety before saying,

'Yes, well, maybe, there's just this one little thing; do I have to keep that poncey Spaniard on?'

'Ruby, of course you do. Gabi is like family, as are you.'

'OK, but only because he's the one person I know who makes me look good. Make sure you come back soon or I'm locking the café up and coming to find you. Well, I will when I've lost five stone in weight.'

Ruby covered her eyes, pretending to shield them from the sun as tears pricked the back of her eyelids and ticked her throat. She thought maybe it would be kinder if Hope gave Joy her heart back after all. Lord Death was creating impossible choices for her and Gabi, and Ruby was angry.

Joy stood, holding out a hand to help her up and said, 'Come on, Ruby, I'm not feeling so dizzy now. Let's get back and see what damage Gabi has done to my café's reputation. Thank you for helping me.' Joy gave her friend a hug and kissed the top of her head.

They heard Gabi enjoying himself long before the café came in sight. The deep voice of Mr Tom Jones boomed enthusiastically from the Juke Box and rang across the Bay, telling anyone who wanted to know, or not, that *'It's not unusual'*. Ruby and Joy entered the café to discover Gabi refilling the coffee machine and singing along at the top of his lungs jerking his skinny hips suggestively to and fro in time to the beat.

Captain Black and his crew of fishermen rocked up against one wall using salt and pepper pots as microphones and whole heartedly provided Gabi with both encouragement and backing vocals. Ruby's eyebrows flew skywards as she spotted two men delighting three mature ladies with their comically obscene hip thrusts. The café's customers appeared to be having the best alcohol-free time of their lives. Ruby pointed to the Captain who was bumping hips with Gabi and said, 'Ooh, Joy, Sam Black's in; look at those sexy moves. I bet he's a man worth coming home to.'

The smile that had been dancing across her face ran away as Joy said, 'Sam Black likes to wine me, dine me, shag me and forget me. There's no future for me in a place where no-one except a bossy red-head and an Andalusian puff can remember me.'

Ruby slapped Joy playfully, replying, 'Stop feeling sorry for yourself. A meal is a meal, wine is wine and a shag is a f...' Joy interrupted saying,

'A fun time, and you're right; Sam is really great fun and I'm not going to be the party pooper.'

Joy joined Gabi who had started singing, *'Shut Up and Dance'* to his backing group. She danced around the tables until, out of breath and laughing, she sat on Sam's lap grinning widely. Gabi winked at Ruby, waving an empty brandy bottle the contents of which had no doubt been offered free with the afternoon's tea and coffee. Ruby beamed at him from behind her scarlet curls pulling a finger across the front of her throat and mouthing, 'Don't let Joy see that.'

When the Bay's one man show had exhausted himself, and the café audience had finished their enthusiastic whistling and applause, Joy left for home intending to sleep off the effect of the solicitor's water. Sam went with her. He walked with a spring in his step because he thought it was their first date and he had got lucky. His crew whooped and gave him the thumbs up as he left with his arm around the café's owner.

An hour later, Joy looked lovingly at the handsome man sleeping beside her. Her chest constricted and she swallowed a lump in her throat to whisper in his ear, 'I loved you, Sam Black, you bloody cheat and if you could love me back I would fight for you and never let you go.'

Sam opened his eyes and misinterpreting her expression gave her a slow, sexy smile; then pretending to be shocked, he exclaimed, 'Ready to go again so soon? Woman, you will kill me.' He dove under the duvet and began to taste his way along her inner thighs and Joy almost forgot that Sam probably did the same thing to Rosie and that he wouldn't remember a thing about her tomorrow.

At closing time, Gabi and Ruby locked the doors and sat talking in the dark.

'Gabi, I know she has to go, but it's too soon and Joy's too vulnerable. She has no idea of her powers. She'll be defenseless at Heavensgate. I can't bear it.'

'Best she gets it over and done before the August rush, Amiga.'

'Oh, Gabi, you know this is not about the café, you idiot. What can we do to protect Joy?'

'I don't know, mi amor, but we have Hope.'

'She hates us because we couldn't help her save Jake, I think she loves him.'

'Don't be silly, Ruby, you know that Hope no have mortal feelings. She just being Hope is all, nothing more.'

'I pray you're right, Gabi. I'd love to believe Hope has Joy's best interests at heart, no pun intended.

'You think this is so?'

'Hope is capricious. She's a right moody cow who changes with the wind. So no, I'm not convinced we can count on her, but I'm not ready to give up.'

Ruby stared into Gabi's eyes communicating spirit to spirit as hot tears flowed down her face and his fingers gently wiped them away. When she turned away from him Gabi covered his mouth with a trembling hand, closed his eyes and sighed into his palm. He swallowed hard and shaking his head said, 'Too risky, Ruby. You know the rules.'

Ruby wiped her nose along her forearm and replied, 'Bugger the rules, Joy's our friend.'

Chapter Twenty

-FLIGHT DELAY-

A small crowd gathered to admire the shiny black chauffeured limousine that arrived at the café to collect Joy for the airport. As the driver indicated and prepared to pull away, Ruby jumped into the car with Gabi's hysterical protests ringing in her ears.

Two hours later, Joy sat, biting her nails and fidgeting, on a screwed down thinly padded airport chair that had suspicious stains on its shiny fabric. Ruby paced back and forth, twirling a copper coloured strand of disobedient hair round and round one finger and chewing on her bottom lip.

She threw herself into the seat opposite Joy, waved her arms to emphasise the hundred or so vacant seats and said, 'Don't you find it odd that this airport is empty? And what happened to the UK's new improved security and passenger harassment protocols?'

'I'm travelling on a *private* Jet, Ruby, no security necessary, this is a *private* lounge for *VIPs*.'

Ruby tapped her heel on the dirty, cracked black and white tiled floor and retorted, 'No, Joy, this isn't a *VIP* lounge. Look around, it's a dump. Please, Joy open your mind, use your eyes and take a proper look. I need to get you out of here, this is all wrong. I won't allow it.'

Heavensgate: Joy

Joy's vision blurred. She rubbed at her eyes saying, 'It's all arranged, Ruby. I must go to Heavensgate. I feel strange. Did you mix belladonna in my tea again?'

'No, I didn't. Why would you ask me that? You feel strange because this is weird. Joy, look out the window, look at the runway shrouded in mist. Wasn't it sunny and bright a moment ago?

'It's just a *sea* fret so don't *you* fret, Ruby.' Joy grinned at her friend like a loon. Ruby clicked her fingers in front of Joy's face. 'Joy, the bloody sea must be eighty miles away. Come on, we're leaving. I should never have let you come here in the first place.'

'I can't go anywhere right now; I'm going to be sick.' Joy's hair was plastered to her fevered face. Ruby pushed her forward saying, 'Stick your head between your legs and don't vomit on your shoes. As soon as you can walk, I'm taking you home. Well, well, well, would your old mother believe it? Do I know you, sir?'

Ruby tucked stray flaming curls behind her ears as she stared for a heartbeat too long at the man who appeared from nowhere. He had almost fooled her, but behind his mirrored sunglasses she could still see his starry eyes. Death wore a navy, gold and white Captain's uniform with silver wings emblazoned on the shoulders. The creases in his jacket and trousers were sharp enough to split hairs. Joy risked a nauseous glance at him and gasped as he gazed at her much like a wolf might gaze at a rabbit.

Ignoring Ruby, he removed his cap and bowed before Joy saying,

-I am Captain Lord. I will be flying you today, my Lady.-

Joy moaned and hung her head back between her legs as Ruby threw herself between them and cried, 'She is not ready. I beg you; do not take her, my Lord.'

-I can wait no longer. Hope deceived me. Joy refused to come freely. Do not interfere, you have done too much already.-

Ruby wrung her hands, pleading, 'I love her. *We* love her. We have protected her since she was a child; please don't ask us to stop now.'

-Go. If you love her as you say you do, you will not make this journey more difficult for her.-

Death took Joy's compliant arm in his and led her away.

Ruby attempted to follow but her feet sank into the cracked floor like quicksand. She shouted, 'Joy, stop! You must not go to Heavensgate with him. It isn't time!' The floor sucked her deeper in as she screamed at Death's retreating back, 'For the Creator's sake, My Lord, I beg you, don't do this!'

Pain drove stilettos into Joy's temples as Ruby's distress broke the spell. She fixed her attention on the Captain and saw his disguise waver, trembling as she felt the cold pull of his will against her own, but her concern for Ruby was greater than her fear. In a determined voice she said, 'Let go of me. I'm not going anywhere with you. You make my friend unhappy and I don't trust you not to kill me.'

Joy had denied him once again and Death had no choice but to release her from his grip.

-I cannot and would not kill you, my Lady. I only wish to guide you to your destiny.-

Bowing, he kissed the back of her hand and disappeared, leaving behind the tangy, salty, ozone smell of the sea.

The glamour faded and Joy saw the derelict airport for what it was. Retracing her steps she found Ruby collapsed on the rubbish strewn floor. Wrapping her distressed friend in her arms, she whispered, 'Home.' The empty building spun, flinging them into the Nothing which spat them out and into the Bay where they stood, embracing outside the café, with a northerly wind whipping their hair. Joy broke the hug, narrowed her eyes at Ruby and stormed inside.

It was late and the café was empty apart from Gabi, who sat painting his nails with pink glitter polish. He stared open mouthed as Ruby burst in behind Joy shouting, 'Wait, you don't understand.' She turned the door sign to 'closed' and threw a warning glance at Gabi to keep silent.

Joy rounded on her. 'What the bloody hell is going on here? Why did you call after me? Why did I let you stop me leaving with him? I need to get to Heavensgate. I *want* to go to Heavensgate. He said it is my destiny and I believe him.'

Ruby sat next to Gabi seeking moral support, and replied in a rush, 'It's impossible to explain. You wouldn't understand. We don't want you to go. It feels like a trap; it's too quick and too hasty. Please trust me, Joy. Have I ever let you down?'

Joy pulled out a chair and sat facing her only friends. She stared at each of them in turn until they blushed.

'Yes, Ruby. Yes, you have let me down. There was the time you spent the weekend in town with the butcher's boy.'

Gabi blew on his nails and said, 'Yes, I remember that too.

Ruby threw her hands in the air saying, 'OK. I said I was sorry about that, to *both* of you. I meant have I ever let you down *badly*.'

Joy crossed her arms and said, 'Oh, now I understand your question. Yes, you have let me down *badly*. Do you recall the time you got roaring drunk on vodka, collapsed in the cake counter and slagged off all the customers?'

Gabi giggled. Ruby looked down at the table and said,

'I am sorry for all of my acts and omissions up to this point, Joy, but I am *not* sorry for saving you from that man…thing… him. He was deadly.'

'Ruby, Gabi, if you value our friendship you need to start talking. So, I ask again. What's going on?'

'Humph, you tell me, Joy. I have not a single bloody clue.' Ruby pushed her chair back and flounced away into the back room.

Gabi attempted distraction by calling after her, 'What happen, arse of lardiness, did our Mistress miss her flight?'

Ruby shouted, 'How can you walk in those appalling nylon leggings without risking static shock? You look like a plucked flamingo.' Gabi blew her a kiss.

'You look like an angel to me, mi amor.'

'Shut it, puffball.'

Joy rested her elbows on the table and covered her face with her hands, saying, 'Is it asking too much for one of you to get me a mug of tea and an explanation please?'

'Joy, what you want drink, the raspberry or the nasty green?' Gabi screwed up his nose, stuck out his tongue and shuddered.

Ruby returned from sulking in the back and, taking Joy's hand in hers, said, 'I love you, Joy, and I am truly sorry you feel like I've let you down. I value your friendship more than you know. I can't explain what happened because I am not *able* to explain. Look, if you will trust me, I may have a way to show you. We need to visit the dried up old witch at Ye Olde Gifte Shoppe.'

Gabi dropped the tea.

Chapter Twenty-One

-MEMORIES-

Hope welcomed Joy but would not countenance having Ruby on her premises; a stance which led to a lively debate that Ruby lost.

Hope led Joy upstairs to a modern living room where she sat on the edge of a black leather sofa and fought a strong urge to flee. Hope switched on the wall mounted TV to a blank channel and sat beside her. Seeing how Joy trembled, she said, 'Don't be afraid. I love this modern miracle. Look, look beyond the white noise and tell me, what do you see?'

The screen flickered into life and Joy's stomach churned as she watched herself, aged eight, curled up in the cellar. Her small hands, fingernails bitten down to the quick, were pressed over her ears as she hummed, tunelessly, to cover the sounds of fury that beat down from the room above. Her pale face was streaked with snot and tears, her underwear wet as her stomach shot acid bullets to burn her throat. Watching herself from the safety of Hope's sofa, Joy felt the sting from a recent belt whipping and the sore spots on her scalp where her hair had been cruelly pulled out in clumps.

Digging her nails into her clammy palms, Joy whipped her head back and reeled away from the psychic attack of the past screaming, 'Make it stop. Why are you doing this to me? What is it?'

'It is your personal hell, Joy, the one I saved you from.'

'Oh God, there's a cesspit in my belly.' Joy leapt to her feet and ran to the kitchen where she vomited into the sink. Hope held her hair away from her face and rubbed her back until Joy's stomach was empty.

Shaking, Joy leaned against the worktop, sipping water and said, 'There are many big, blank, barren spaces in my memory, empty years where I may as well have been dead because I sure as hell can't recall being alive. So why did you choose to show me that?'

Hope's eyes glinted like polished steel as she said, 'You need to remember your childhood. There is more to see. It's important that you remember. Death wants you. Let me help.'

'I don't want your bloody help! You just made me sick to my stomach, again. Much of my life is as mysterious to me as the millennia before I existed, there must be a good reason for that and I don't want to know what it is.'

Hope's eyes flashed ice as she said, 'Calm down and listen. When you were eight years old, I saved you from a living hell and from Death. I will always do my best to protect you. Joy, you must not go to Heavensgate with that man, he is our Lord Death.'

Joy stared at Hope as if she had never seen her before and, hanging onto the only thing that made sense to her when she was around Hope, she shouted, 'Give me my heart back!'

'If I do, you will most certainly die, so I refuse.'

'You are crazy. I have to go to Heavensgate; I have to manage my inheritance. I must go and I will go.' Joy sprinted from the room taking the stairs from the apartment two at a time. Shooting past Ruby she ran into the street where she snapped her fingers and was instantly returned to her house on the hill.

Ruby screamed up to Hope from the shop below, 'What the hell have you done to her this time, you meddling bitch?'

Hope sank onto the sofa and turned off the TV ignoring the handsome man who had appeared at her side and who rested his leather booted feet on her coffee table.

-Free will, what a bastard.-

Death, laid a comforting arm across Hope's slumped shoulders.

She shrugged him away and, between gritted teeth, said, 'I understand where all this is leading. I will see you at Heavensgate. I hate you. Leave me.'

-As you wish, my Lady.-

Chapter Twenty-Two

-DEPARTURE-

The morning after her distressing experience with Hope, Joy dressed and jogged down to the beach. Remembering her foster dad's advice to enjoy life's small pleasures, she stuck her tongue out and tasted the salty breeze. Dawn's colours dressed the Bay as the North Sea crawled home on a slow tide. Filling her lungs with ozone rich air, she gave thanks for her life and ran. The wet, rich red sand waved in ripples underfoot that jarred her bones. Joy removed her Nikes to splash in the miniature oceans scattered along the beach, alarming small crabs that skittered away to hide under rocks.

She witnessed the sunlight turn plain shells to jewels and, as she gazed into the gentle ripples on a rock pool, she saw a handsome face staring out at her. Joy passed a cautious hand through the water, blurring the image that rippled in a light breeze. She wiped her wet hand on her jeans, and the man reappeared with a smile playing on his lips. She decided it was just another strange thing in a recent list of strange occurrences.

Joy knew that Ruby and Gabi spent hours speculating if she could make such an impact on the gorgeous and sexy Sam Black that he would remember her. She wondered if she would ever be noticed by another man or die a sad single. Joy let go of her hopes for Sam and her chest constricted in pain. Then she allowed herself a small smile as she recalled Ruby's advice to, 'Let your fingers do the walking, girl, they are more loyal than any man and a lot less trouble.'

'There are worse things than being alone,' she told the stranger's rippling image; he shook his head and she watched his generous mouth shape the words, 'See you soon, my love,' before the vision faded. Joy knelt beside the pool and, feeling foolish, called into the water, 'I wish.'

A light haze rolled over the beach editing the edges of reality as it shifted on a sea breeze that lifted her hair and sent annoying strands to stick on her lips. It would soon be time to open the café; Joy didn't have much longer to wallow in melancholy so she resumed her jog along the beach.

The breeze grew more insistent, dissolving the mist around her creating a tunnel of clear space. Joy stopped, transfixed by the glimmer of sunshine through the morning's swirling haze which hovered as if unwilling to cross a hidden barrier. The mist carried the scent of Parma violets, bringing memories of Ruby and Gabi sharing twists of scented candy drops on a summer lawn.

A gust of wind pressed like a hand to her back and the mist parted, revealing a gypsy caravan, its blue and yellow paint flaked and weathered as if by a thousand years of desert wind. Sand drifted around large wheels that bent at an unnatural angle giving the caravan an air of settled permanency, which was impossible as the tide should have swept it away.

A voice rang in her head, urging her on, saying, 'Come on, be curious.' The caravan waited in a pocket of sunshine, its small windows glowing with soft, pink light. With butterflies dancing in her stomach, Joy stepped on the lowest of three rickety steps that each held a small ceramic pot of violets. The sound of Eddie Grant singing, '*Give Me Hope, Jo'anna*' came from inside. The music stopped and a beautiful hippy with summer flowers woven in her long platinum hair opened the door. Startled, Joy half turned to flee, but woman reached out a hand and she allowed herself to be led inside. Joy's lips twitched as she noticed the woman's toe nails sported the same pink glitter nail polish as Gabi's.

A small bell chimed a question in her head and Joy's curiosity morphed into embarrassment.

She counted to three before saying, 'I'm sorry. I thought this place was abandoned, I mean empty. I won't intrude. I'll be on my way.' She stepped back toward the door, intending to escape across the beach which now appeared much further away than three small wooden steps.

The woman's voice rang in her ears, 'Joy. Welcome.'

'Hope, I should have known this place belonged to you. I can't stay. I have to go to work.'

Hope ignored her. 'Isn't this just perfect? We could read your crystal ball in here one day.'

'I said I need to go to work,' Joy gripped her upper arms as if afraid she might break.

'You won't be late. After all, it is your café. Please, sit down. I'll make you a drink. Relax, you look like you've seen a ghost.'

'Have I?'

'Not the last time I checked, dear.' Hope laughed and bells rang through Joy's mind like a warning knell as the door clicked closed behind her.

She looked around. A small bed, reached by a pair of pink steps and dressed in bright shiny Moroccan silks and cushions filled one narrow wall. Light filtered through pink nets that covered the tiny windows.

A red beaded light shade hung from a painted beam. A small bow legged table, covered by a delicate lace shawl, held a slim crystal decanter and two extravagantly painted goblets that fired rainbows across the floor. Hope's wagon felt safe and inviting.

Politeness forced Joy to sit in an elegant silk chair decorated with lions and unicorns that seemed to shift slightly in the cloth. The scent of Parma violets intensified. Seizing the opportunity for small talk she said, 'What is that incredible scent?'

Heavensgate: Joy

'Homemade berry wine. I picked the fruit, mixed and brewed it myself. I have a fresh decanter of one of life's greatest pleasures ready.'

Joy raised her eyebrows. 'It's rather early in the day, isn't it?'

Hope shook her head, sending a shower of tiny, purple flower petals onto the floor.

'It is never too early to experience ecstasy.'

Conceding temporary defeat Joy accepted a gold rimmed goblet of violet liquid with grace. The glass was etched with golden, pink winged cherubs, in harmony with the garish surroundings.

Her eyes darted about seeking a pot plant to inebriate but, seeing that there weren't any, she took a tentative sip and, as the nectar warmed her insides, melted into the chair which enfolded her like a loving parent's arms.

Holding the fragile goblet in both hands, she inhaled lilac vapour which reached for her nostrils in exotic tendrils and tickled the back of her throat.

The first taste had been exquisite and the second lingered in her mouth like a lover's kiss. Joy tipped her head back in pleasure and said, 'Oh, thank you, this is heavenly.'

Hope watched her as a kestrel watches a field mouse in the undergrowth. 'Please drink a little more, *enjoy* yourself, drink as much as you like.'

Joy giggled and pointed a finger at the curved ceiling. The bright yellow, rough wood beams and the painted, gilt-edged, red and green leaves were interspersed by a chain of purple and lilac violets. At each of the four corners sat a realistically depicted flaming red rose whose contained fire licked at petals and stems. Joy was mesmerized by the sight. Hope looked at the blooms and frowned.

'Hope. Who are you?'

Hope lowered her eyes. 'Didn't you read fairy tales?'

Joy's blood raced through her veins like ambrosia, she had never felt more alive, excitement spilled into her voice as she said, 'Oh don't tell me, I'll guess. You're a fairy and I'm dreaming. May I have some more wine? It's delish.'

Hope's movements were sluggish and forced as she refilled the goblet until the wine splashed over the rim and onto Joy's fingers, which she licked clean, purring out her contentment like a cat.

Hope's voice chimed in distress as she said, 'I'm not a dirty fairy, you must never use that wicked F word again. To mortals I am a dream of what may come. You know me as Hope and that is what I am. For you I am also the Keeper of precious and necessary things. Look.' Hope's eyes brimmed with tears as she pointed to a line of beautiful hearts hung from silver hooks. The hearts pulsated in sync with Joy's breathing. Each one was crafted from a different substance. Every heart unique. Joy's breath became ragged as through the drunken, lilac haze that argued against apprehension, she struggled to grasp the importance of both the display and Hope's tears that now flowed freely.

Most of the hearts emitted a soft glow but a few cradled profound darkness that stabbed the back of Joy's eyes. They all had one thing in common: each had a name, an initial or a word trapped inside. Joy glanced at Hope and received a slow nod of permission to unhook a small, clear glass heart that containing a smaller paper heart decorated with glitter and pink feathers. Her name was written in the centre. The heart sang, *'There Once Was an Ugly Duckling.'* Anxiety ripped its way across Joy's face and she began to fade until Hope placed a palm flat against her breast saying, 'Put it back. I promise your heart is safe with me.'

Joy caressed her heart before reluctantly setting the precious object on its hook to nestle amongst its companions. She turned to Hope asking, 'Am I dead?'

Hope choked back tears. 'No, no you're not dead, but, you *are* different. My Lord Death insists you go to him. I can think of no other way to spare you from his eternal grasp than to send you to Heavensgate to fight for your soul. His fury at my interference in his plans will know no bounds and I will be forced to flee into the Nothing.'

Joy clung to the chair, feeling as if she was about to shatter and disappear. 'None of this makes sense. I went for a morning jog and now I'm pissed in a gypsy wagon, staring at my own heart and talking about Death. I want to leave.'

Hope turned her face away to hide the lie and said, 'You may leave anytime you like. Have you seen my treasure chest? It is very special.'

Gold clasps, shaped like chubby baby hands, gripped the lid of a large red box appliquéd with pictures of harp strumming cherubs. Joy admired the tiny fingers as they clenched and unclenched until the chest sprang open. Her attention was captured by the escaping sounds of waves lapping a shore and the screech of an eagle diving for prey. Her nostrils filled with the scent of a thousand pine trees breathing in a summer forest. Curious, she leant over to peer inside the chest. A gust of howling wind rocked the wagon almost to tipping point and, losing her balance, Joy toppled over the edge. The lid slammed shut above her. She fell into the Nothing where she dove like a pearl seeker, swimming deeper, floating, steady and content, as she drifted away from everyone and everything she had ever known. An eternity seemed to pass in perfect peace and serenity until, coming to, she found herself being transported down a rough made forest track in a pink Cadillac driven by a chattering teenaged girl.

In Heavensgate Jake cautiously examined a flaming red Rose that blossomed on the spot where he had once optimistically planted his blood. He called into the Nothing, *'Come to me, Joy'* and bent to pluck the delicate bloom, but snatched back his hand cursing, *Fuck. You burnt me!* Then, hearing the familiar haunting sound of the Cadillac's engine, he turned tail and ran inside.

Chapter Twenty-Three

-LOST-

In Heavensgate, Jake sat beside the Lodge's crackling fire completely engrossed in a tattered blue notebook. Now and again words attacked his hands with a sting or jolted him with electric shocks. He dismissed the pain and continued to read the tidy, cursive writing.

Day 1.
This book has my name printed on it. It pretends to be an ordinary exercise book, it's not though; it's deceitful like everything here. The bloody thing stings and bites me when I pick it up and makes me struggle to open it. But I know it itches for the scratch of my pen on its pages and when it feels the press of ink to paper it sighs like a sleazy old man.

Day 2.
I'm Joy. What a misnomer.
I hope keeping a record will help me make sense of what's happening to me because, right now, it makes no sense at all.

Day 3.
My mind is clearer today. Perhaps I've been ill? I remember that I'm in 'Heavensgate' because I inherited this Lodge.
I arrived in a pink Cadillac with a 'Mom's Taxi' sticker on the windshield. A girl called Joan with bright pink and blue coloured hair drove.

Heavensgate: Joy

She was barefoot, barely dressed and suffering from a sore throat. When I climbed out of her cab she croaked, 'Now don't you go taking any shit from *him*, ya hear? That one's a wrong un.'

There's no-one here to take any kind of shit from. I wish there was.

Jake gazed fondly at the page stroking his fingertips across Joy's words. His voice shook as he said,

Your wish is my command.

Day 4.

There are others in the Lodge. I hear them in the space between the creaks of timbers and the whistle of wind that sneaks through gaps in the window frames. When I sleep they breathe in my ears and down the back of my neck. Someone watches me when I shower. I called out, begging whomever or whatever it is to leave, and they rustled like roaches in the narrow spaces between the walls and the floorboards.

Now, now Joy, that's just rude.
Ouch.

Jake dropped the notebook which flew around the room, crashing into the windows like a trapped bird. When he finally retrieved it, he had to prise the pages apart while it whipped about in his hands. He read on,

Day 5.

Or is it day six? I could have been here for a month, a year, or longer for all I know.

Day 6.

This place is expensively decorated. The modern art on the walls gives me migraines, I hate it. I'm going to sell the lot and leave.

That should be fun to watch, honeybunch.

Joy's next sentence made Jake laugh:

There's a mangy, stag's head mounted on the wall. It's probably crawling with maggots and fleas. Why would anyone want a reminder of murder staring down at them every day?

The answer is in the question, my love.

The kitchen table is massive and heavy. I know because I tried to move it outside. I don't like the table because I never feel alone when I sit at it.

Jake thought fondly of the old table saying, *It's perfect for all sorts of activities.* He turned the page which pricked his thumb and drew blood making him swear.

Day 7.
I have to leave.
The bath is deep enough to drown in and it's haunted. I use the shower room. It's not safe in there either. When I look in the mirror, a beautiful woman in a red evening dress smiles out at me.

Susie! I thought she had followed that dickwad Jacob. Oh happy day.

Day 8.
It's cold here.

Jake put the book down. Glancing lovingly at Joy, who dozed on the couch, her fair hair peeking above a heavy woollen throw, he threw a large log on the fire before settling back down to read, whispering,
We will make history, Joy. Imagine you, me and Susie together forever in Heavensgate. The thought gives me goose-bumps.

Day 9 or Entry 9
I'm losing my sense of time.
Somebody was with me in the shower this morning. I might have to try the bath after all, or take a dip in the lake.
How did you know? I was so fuckin' well behaved. I only licked you once.

Heavensgate: Joy

Entry 10.
I have no idea what day it is. I'm not sure of the season either. Whatever the date, the seemingly endless lake, mountains, and pine forest are spectacular.
I ought to leave soon.

Entry 11.
I tried to leave. I found the key to the cherry red pick-up truck and went into St Johns. I drove through the middle of town and kept straight on, following the road out of town. I ended up back here. I drove the same route, with the same result, until the sun went down. I'm desperate. If it wasn't for the dog I would jump in the lake and drown myself.

Jake sat at attention with the book thrashing about on his lap. He pressed a hand on its spine and, as it writhed and bucked under his palm, he stared at Joy. His brow furrowed.
Dog?

Entry 12.
It's snowing and I have lost my mind. The silence is deafening. The only noises are occasional gunshot cracks as the ice shifts on the lake and the tortuous screams of the wind. Last night the monotony was broken by an avalanche tearing across the frozen lake and through the pine woods. Unfortunately, it missed the Lodge and cut a dark path into the woods, revealing a solitary, giant oak amongst the bloody endless pine trees.
Mm hmm, baby, you found my tree.

The roots are taller than me, it must be ancient. A tattered blue rope hangs rotting over a high branch. It gave me an idea.
No, it won't come to that, my love. I promise you, I have other plans.

Entry 13.
I walked the dog in the woods today. The oak is practically hollow and large enough to park half a dozen trucks in. Nothing grows close by and not one leaf or acorn litters its enormous twisted roots. The trunk is a gaping, split maw of darkness worn into a kind of path that worms upwards in a spiral. I would walk up it but I hate heights. Anyway, the dog ran off and I lost my nerve.

You are so brave. Jacob never did that.

The oak smells as if it's suffered fire, but there's no sign of one. The air is thick as treacle and the clearing is always dark. It's an unsettling place, yet I want to visit the tree, sit in the shade of its glorious branches, lean my back against its roots and sleep.

Well, it's as good a place as any to enjoy the great outdoors, so why not?

Entry 14.
I'm stuck here.
Who named me Joy and why? There's nothing resembling Joy inside me. If you cut me open you'd find fear clutching my stomach and sorrow dragging my bowels. Look deeper and smell poison in my liver and hear grief strangling my throat. Dig in my head and be flooded in a swampy mush of grief. I don't remember being loved and I never will be now.

Oh, my poor sweet baby.

Jake's eyes filled with tears that fell onto the pages burning small holes where Joy's words had been. The book went wild and flew across the room to hide quivering behind the couch where Joy slept, oblivious to her diary's suffering. Jake sat and stroked her hair saying,

Joy, please open your mind to me, I am the man who chose you above all others, my Lady.

She slept on like death. Jake crawled behind the couch and startled the book. He chased it as it fluttered around the room like a large moth. Finally, having managed to stomp on it and stun it into submission, he read on,

The dog's soft brown eyes reflect my pain. I feel guilty. I wish I didn't love Fur Face. I'm going to escape this place and leave him behind.
Fur Face? The dog again. What's going on?

Entry 15.
It's spring this morning. The weather is abnormal, it could be winter by noon.
The dog is warming my feet. This puppy has had it rough; his pads are scarred as is his gentle face. He has a hole in one ear big enough to push my thumb through and one of his flanks bears the tight pink scars of burns. His broken stumpy tail should be a proud curling brush. This baby has suffered, but he trusts me. He's my furry angel, without him, I'd give up. I've named him Skylar.
Oh fuck, what kind of weird shit is this?

Entry 16
I declare myself officially missing. I check the mirrors to make sure I'm real. The woman is still in the en-suite one so that doesn't count. There is an ache inside me so vast, so immense that I'm lost in it. I cry rivers of tears, great gushing waterfalls thunder out my distress and there is no-one to help me bear it. I'm trapped in a beautiful prison.

I'm here, sweetheart. I love your pain. I worship your grief. Your tears are my nectar, your sobs sweet music. I must be in love.
Jake waved his hands in the air and Hozier's *'Take Me to Church'* filled the room. He sang along, swaying back and forth in time with the beat until he lost himself in the music and vanished from his seat before the fire.

That night Joy sat up in bed bathed in moonlight as she scribbled in the exercise book:
This place spooks me out. There's a permanent coating of ice on my bedroom window, it's heart shaped with my initial in the middle of it. I wipe it off the glass and watch it reappear.

Jake snuggled closer, his feet rubbing hers under the covers causing her to shiver and move out of the warm spot.

I am so clever, such an amusing trickster. You will adore me. Now what are you writing?

I'm miserable because if I ever was someone, I forget who. I can't find my way home if I don't know who I am or where I'm going.
I might be dead.
Well fuck me pink and call me a flamingo!

I am hopelessly lost.
I will find you, baby. I will bring you home to Daddy.

Joy threw her pen across the room.

Next morning, she leapt into wakefulness, unaware that Jake lay on the bed biting his bottom lip as he admired the way her body moved under the thin night-shirt.

Chapter Twenty-Four

-FIRST SIGHT-

Joy found an old row boat abandoned on the narrow beach and, desperate for entertainment, waded up to her waist in water and pushed it into the Lake where she clambered in and collapsed in an inelegant, soppy mess on the bottom.

She thought she heard someone laugh, but didn't see a soul.

That was me. I'm gaining strength from your sorrow and getting closer. I'll be with you soon, my love.

Joy hadn't rowed before and soon discovered that it's not as easy as it looks. She got a few yards out, then no matter how she pulled at the oars, the boat went round and round anti-clockwise. It was frustrating. She felt the sun on her face, watched fat fish jump for the day's first insects and thought, 'Heavensgate is so beautiful. If I remember who I am, maybe I could be happy here.'

Then she saw him and spluttered, 'What the hell? Do I know you? How did you get here?'

The skin crawled over her flesh and pressure built inside her head like a sneeze. There was something desperately wrong with the boy.

He checked her out and appraised her body with eyes too knowing for his years. She blushed and stared right back as he held her gaze for a heartbeat too long. Then, as if a switch had been thrown, his eyes became wide and innocent and, in a sorrowful childish voice, he replied, 'I'm always here, this is my boat. I'm looking for my Momma.'

Joy looked back to shore expecting to spot a frantic mother, but they were alone. She turned to ask the little boy where he last saw her. He was gone. Joy panicked. There hadn't been a splash so he couldn't be in the water. She could only doggy paddle, she couldn't swim, but if he had fallen in she reckoned he would have bobbed back up to the surface.

Little hands reached out from under the water. Weeping with relief, Joy grasped the cold fingers and fell into the lake.

She held her breath, waiting to hit the bottom, praying she would be able to float back to the surface. Feeling a rush of emptiness she opened her eyes and screamed until her lungs felt as if they would burst. She fell through the sky with no up and no down; there was nothing there at all. She fell until she was slammed back into the boat. Disoriented and afraid, she grabbed the oars and rowed in a perfectly straight line to the deck where she tumbled out, landing hard on her knees. She shot upright on shaking, adrenalin powered legs not knowing what to do about the child. That was when she saw the old man walking toward her. Spilling out her words out in panic Joy beckoned him over and, her voice shaking, said,

'Did you see the boy?'

'No boys around these parts o' the woods. It's a pleasure to meet you, Miss...?'

'I'm Joy, the boy, he, I don't know. Sorry. I'm pleased to meet you too, Mr...?'

'Jim. That's mah name, just Jim. Are you OK, ma'am?

'I was just, I thought I saw, oh sweet Jesus, what's happening to me?' Embarrassed, she found herself crying in front of the stranger. Feeling stupid she said,

'I don't even know why I'm here.'

Jim passed her a crumpled handkerchief and said, 'Well I heard in town as how you inherited the old place.'

'I did? Yes, I did, I inherited the Lodge but I didn't have to come.'

Heavensgate: Joy

'Are you certain sure, Missy?'

Joy sensed that Jim was amused by her and snapped,

'Well, if I did have to come here, why did I have to come?'

Jim ignored her brusqueness. He put a gentle hand on each of her shoulders and said, 'In my experience, which is long and broad, folks go places to forget or to remember. You'll know which applies to yer situation. Leave anytime you want.'

Joy shrugged him off. 'I can't leave. I can't even get through town without ending up back here.'

'Do you have a map?'

'No, and I don't have a Sat Nav either.'

'A what? Never mind, you just need to decide to go and then learn the lie of the land prior to departure. Y'need to study the roads 'round here, Miss, they can be mighty difficult for visitors.'

'If I try to drive out of town I end up right back where I started and, if I drive from town to Heavensgate I can never remember the journey.'

The old man's eyes crinkled at the corners as he said, 'Then maybe yer not ready to go, Miss.'

'Oh. I assure you I am. Shit! I forgot about the boy!'

'That one'll be fine, Miss. Tell me, what else is troublin' you?'

'The bloody weather. How can it be winter when I go to bed at night and high summer by the following morning? Explain that.'

'I can't, Miss, except to observe it's a freak of nature; Heavensgate has its own micro-climate due to its proximity to the Sierra.'

'That's another thing. No matter how far I walk, I never, ever, get any closer to those mountains.'

'Hell, they's miles away!'

'What about the invisible tower?'

'Now yer dreamin'. There ain't no tower here.'

'There is a medieval tower at the end of my hallway.

'Miss, I've been here since forever and I ain't never seen no such construction.'

'It's invisible.' Joy blushed and Jim raised his bushy eyebrows.

'OK, I know I sound crazy. So tell me, Jim, who are you?'

'I'm Heavensgate's Secret Keeper and I will keep your secrets as safe as my own.'

He smiled an almost toothless grin and turned to leave.

'Don't go. I…I…'

'Spit it out, afore it chokes you.'

'This place is driving me insane. The boy I saw, he wasn't there was he? He wasn't really out on the lake sitting in my row boat.'

'Oh, him. Take no heed, poor kid's just a sad, bad memory. The boy ain't from around these parts no more. He probably won't be here again tomorrow.'

'So he was real?'

'Who knows who's real and who isn't? I sure don't, Miss. Don't worry, take my advice, if that kid turns up in your boat again, push the little bastard over the side.'

Jim roared with amusement, bending over he doubled up slapping his thighs in merriment as tears flowed from his rheumy eyes. He choked on his own laughter. Joy patted him hard on the back and ended up face down on the decking, alone.

She rolled onto her back and lay motionless on the boards, hardly daring to breathe.

The scraggy mutt licked her face before lying beside her. Joy's voice sounded small as she whispered, 'Hi, puppy, are you feeling lost too?'

The dog whined and pricked up his pointed ears. Joy heard the diesel chug as a vehicle bounced down the lane toward the Lodge. The noise grew louder before it died with an ominous bang and a death rattle.

'I don't care who it is. I'm not moving an inch until the world is normal again,' Joy told the dog. She felt the deck spring under approaching footsteps and lay still, her head resting on her arms, feeling stupid as a pair of brown, scuffed cowboy boots came into view.

She shielded her eyes with one hand and risked a glance up a pair of long, muscular, blue jeaned legs, their owner's face hidden by the sun's glare and the shadow cast by his dusty Stetson. Heat stung her cheeks as she struggled to her feet. A large, tanned, work calloused hand reached down to help her. She looked into the man's jade green eyes, her heart fluttered and the heat that radiated from her face was matched by liquid fire in her belly.

Flustered, Joy made a show of searching for the old man and the dog, but apart from her and the striking stranger, the only thing on the deck was a long shiny black feather. She reached for it, but just as her fingers met its quill, the breeze blew it over the lake. The stranger shook her hand as he said,

Howdy, ma'am, I'm Jak… er, I'm, Jacob Andersen and I'm here to save you from terminal boredom. You must be my new boss, Joy?

She nodded; his name was familiar and caused an itch at the back of her mind that she couldn't quite scratch. The man removed his Stetson and said,

'I'm your general dogsbody around these parts. Believe me when I say, I'm mighty pleased to meet you.'

'Er, um, yes, me too. Jacob, did you say?' The man laughed, it was a deep sexy sound that caused her insides to tremble. She could tell by his eyes that he knew the effect he had on her and she prayed to disappear like the old man. He started to walk toward the Lodge saying,

Come along, Miss Joy, there's lots to talk about.

She followed, taking three steps to each of his strides. Unable to take her eyes off the rear view, she gawped, catching flies with her mouth and thought, 'This is bad, very bad.' Despite the cruel scar that ran from the outside corner of his right eye all the way down to his jaw, this tall man with short dark hair, wearing dirty jeans and a denim shirt was striking. He had presence, and, at first meeting, Joy didn't appreciate the precise nature of that presence. She was struck stupid by the heat coursing through her veins and the head to toe blush that betrayed her thoughts.

Jake stopped in the yard and spoke gently as if soothing a skittish horse. *You see the violets and buttercups springing up by the path here? Ain't they pretty? But you, ma'am, now you are beyond my simple powers of description.'*

Despite being confused and disturbed by her contact with the boy and the old man, Joy was hopelessly attracted to the stranger. He appeared charmingly harmless, so she allowed herself to be led by the hand to the Lodge. She didn't question the intimacy as he rolled his index finger in circles around her palm and she heard her blood pound in her head.

Unknown to them there was a guest in the kitchen. Mary was berating Dead Jim.

'You're the shithead tried to get my baby boy to blow his brains out in the woods, ain't you?'

'Well, ma'am, no, well yes, shit, it weren't like that.'

'And you tried to gas him in his own truck, you old bastard.

'No. I never.'

'I don't care what you say, old man. You ain't welcome. What you doin' here?'

'I'm just keepin' an eye out for the nice folk.'

'You wanna keep them rheumy ole eyes you better fuck off outta my kitchen.'

'Hey, lady, you want my eyes you come get 'em. This ain't your kitchen, never was and never will be.'

Jim made himself at home at the table grabbing two biscuits off a plate and chewing them with his mouth open, spilling crumbs down his shirt. 'Stay away. From. My. Boy. Jake.' Mary used her modus operandi and stabbed Jim in the chest with a blood red, manicured talon sharpened to a vicious point. Jim grabbed the offending finger and pulled her in closer to him, spitting biscuit in her face as he said, 'Dontcha go prodding me, you ole whore. You damn thief of innocence. I'll show you where yer kitchen is.' Jim rose from the chair and, still grasping her by one finger, he dragged Mary screeching to the open picture window.

'Shut yer filthy mouth and look. That is yer place, baby killer, and that is where you and all the other filth are headed.'

Heavensgate: Joy

The stench of sulphur attacked their senses making them choke and their eyes sting. Mary stopped struggling as she stared at a thirty yard tall, shit spouting geyser where moments before had been beauty and tranquility. In the distance a volcano spewed foul stinking rocks and dirt miles high creating a false night. Lake Disregard moved under molten black and orange lava that spread sluggishly to melt an icy shore line. As Mary clutched at her throat, sobbing for forgiveness, the sun momentarily broke through the ash cloud to paint the frozen, barren landscape red as blood. Heat baked the acrid air, unable to melt the thick, black ice that covered the land.

'This ain't happening,' whispered Mary.

'You help me get Joy away from Jake and all this will change.'

'I wanna go home.'

'You can't. You lost the game a long time ago, you and Darth. I'll be sat by the fire, *ma'am*, use the time to consider the error of yer ways, pack yer bags and high tail it outta here.'

Realising that, as Jim relaxed his hold on her, the landscape was recovering its usual beauty, Mary found the courage to say, 'Never. There's a motel in town, so fuck off, Jim, and hang your hat there.'

'I prefer to hang around and see what happens here, Mary, que sera sera.' Jim left her in the kitchen and made himself at home on the couch. She followed him shouting, 'Get out before Jake throws you out, fucker.'

He gave her his most sincere expression and asked, 'Is it because I'm too old fer you?' Mary smiled like Mona Lisa and said, 'No, Jim, it's because you're fuckin' dead.'

'I am? Oh God. Help. Help. I'm a stiff. Come over here, girl, you need a bit of good ole fashion lovin' to mellow you out.'

With Jim's mocking laughter ringing in her ears, Mary stormed back to the kitchen where she checked the view making sure that it was normal. Satisfied that Hell was no longer on the doorstep she cussed him, filling the air so full of bad words it stank.

The kitchen door swung open and Jake entered holding Joy's hand until she saw the curse spitting woman and pulled away from him.

Jake examined his palm as if he had never seen it before and said,
Come on in, Miss Joy. This is your housekeeper, Mary. She appears to be a mite upset right now. Mary! Where's your manners?

Mary ignored Joy. Balling her fists, she shouted, 'That ole bastard Jim is here, Jakey, here in the Lodge, threatening me.'

Mary I asked you before, don't use pet names in front of people, it's embarrassing and, where are your manners?

The red faced petite woman looked Joy up and down, narrowed her eyes and, through clenched teeth, said, 'Pleased to make your acquaintance, *ma'am*. Yes, I am Mary, and this here hunk of a man is mine.'

Mary's eyes were wide and full of questions as they drilled into Jake's, he pretended not to notice. She placed her hand on his shoulder and attempted a smile that revealed a set of tiny pearly teeth. Long blood red nails curved away from her pale fingers like talons on a bird of prey. Her peroxide blonde hair was set in a Marilyn Munroe style; her body cut from the same pattern, but the resemblance ended at her eyes which were dead and empty. Despite carefully applied makeup, six inch high heels and a tight black leather skirt, it was clear the housekeeper was much older than Jacob.

Joy wasn't fazed by Mary; she had been alone with the weirdness of Heavensgate for too long. She had forgotten her past and seemingly lost all sense of danger. Her thoughts were focused on the man and what his rough, calloused hands would feel like running over her skin as his weight pressed her into her bed and his thickness filled her body.

Jake tipped his head to one side and smiled at her. He pulled out a chair then poured her a tall glass of iced water from the jug on the table. Mary snorted and beat up copper pots and pans in the sink, keeping her stiff back to her new mistress. She was tense until Jacob squeezed her shoulder and said something in her ear that made her splash water at him and blush.

Jim wandered into the kitchen. He leaned over Joy, his whiskers tickling her neck, and whispered, 'What you should be wonderin' is what his rough calloused hands would feel like chokin' the life out of you.' Joy dropped her glass on the stone floor where it shattered into an impossible number of pieces spreading a puddle around her feet. Neither Jake nor Mary appeared to notice her shock at having her thoughts relayed back to her. Jake turned, and seeing Jim, exclaimed,

Heavens to fuckin' Betsy, Mary, you weren't lyin', we have us an old friend here. Jim, do me a favour, tell Mr D and that slut, Hope, that it's too late.

Jake raised Joy out of her chair and pulled her close against his side. She leant into him, her body relaxed and her eyes glazed over as her mind left the room.

Oh lookee here, Jim. Joy's losing what's left of her heart to me. They can't have her and they don't want me, so you may as well hot foot it back over to the sweet side of the Gate.

Jim eyeballed him; Jake was the first to look away as Jim said,

'I'm watchin' you, boy. Do no harm here; you won't get another chance.' Jim glared at Mary saying, 'And *you*, bitch, you child torturin', murderin' nightmare, *you* are all out of opportunities.' He tipped his Stetson and vanished into thin air.

Joy shook her head as if waking from a deep slumber and, surprised to find herself leaning against Jake, stepped away. She felt bewitched by him, over aware of her sweaty palms and the demanding sexual heat in her belly. In a voice dripping insincerity she said, 'Pleased to meet you, Mary; I never had a housekeeper before and I'm not at all sure I need one now. Let's just see how we rub along, shall we? I guess Jacob here is your son?'

'Now then, princess, let's not you and I get off on the wrong foot. *Jacob* is not my son and I am not his Momma.'

'I see,' said Joy, her voice pouring censure on the other woman as she took her place at the scarred, wooden table. Jake covered his mouth to hide a smile saying, *We'll all get along just fine and dandy, won't we, babe?*

Mary threw Jake a furious look over her shoulder as he passed behind her and squeezed her butt. Joy felt sick, heart sick.

Mary, show Joy to her room, please, the lady needs a rest.

Jake skipped outside to his workshop to find Jim waiting there as if he owned the place. He stabbed a finger in Jake's face and said, 'I warned that ole whore and I'm warning you too, leave the girl alone or be trapped here forever.'

Jake grabbed the finger and pushed Jim away from him, his eyes dancing with fire he said,

Jim, that's no threat. That's already occurred. Where've ya been, old man? Let me tell you what's going to happen here. I am going to fuckin' bind that woman to me. I am going to devour all her light and happiness and seize her joy for myself. I will chain Joy's soul to my own for all eternity and, here's the kicker, you will help me do it, Jim.

'Well, that would be a damn shame. Good luck with the plans, Jake. Now I suggest you go floss and see if you can't clear some of that shit outta yer filthy mouth,' drawled Jim, laughter sticking in his throat.

Jake towered over him and growled, *I said you will help me.*

'Oh, I heard you, son.' Jim cleared his throat and spit, his phlegm splattering Jake's boots as he turned and, with his hands thrust deep in his pockets, sauntered out of the workshop. He strolled away, admiring the fresh view from the boat deck; his tall frame cast no shadow.

Jake's voice chased after him like a persistent fly,

Joy is my ticket outta this hell hole. Ya hear me, Jim? She is my ticket outta Heavensfuckin'gate. Stand in my way and I will burn you old man. You know I never make threats I don't keep.

'Que sera, Jake, que sera,' Jim muttered, just before he jumped in the lake.

Chapter Twenty-Five

-THE SNACK-

Gravel flew from the wheels of the black and white as it skidded to a bouncing halt outside the Lodge. The engine's throaty growl was cut and a lone cop checked his reflection in the rear view mirror. He adjusted the cap on his shaved head before climbing out of the cab and strutting across the yard with his head held high and a smirk on his face.

Jake leaned on the front porch chewing a toothpick. A Stetson was pulled low on his forehead, shadowing blood-shot eyes that fixed hungrily on the law's representative, Deputy Dev.

Dev tipped the peak of his cap with his index finger. 'Morning, Jacob.'

I am not Jacob.

'Pardon me for being kinda *obtuse*, sir, but you look exactly like him.'

I do? How observant, yes, I suppose I do. In fact, I'd place a thousand dollars on most folks noticing I look exactly like him. Butt-wipe.

Dev shuffled his feet in the dust and wiped an embarrassment of sweat from his brow. Despite his resolve to prove to the squad that he could take a suspect in alone, he found himself avoiding eye contact with this one and wishing for Captain Rob's grouchy company.

Jake spat his toothpick onto one of the cop's shiny boots. Dev swallowed his offence with his Adam's apple and said, 'So, you and Jacob Andersen must be brothers.'

The best kind.

Dev recovered his courage and pointed to Jake's cheek. 'How'd you and your *brother* get the identical scar?'

It was a special gift each to the other. You ever tried cutting?

'Sick.'

Boys can be like that. How can I help the short and stupid arm of the law this fine day?

Dev's cheeks reddened, his brain began sending fight or flight messages to his body. Sticking to his training, he ignored his instincts, placed one booted foot on Jake's porch step and said, 'Let's talk inside.'

No. Let's not talk anyplace, fuckin' comprende?

'Fine,' Dev shrugged his narrow shoulders, 'no more Mr Nice Guy. I advise you, *sir*, that I'm here on official police business, investigating a suspicious death. *I* have questions *you* will answer to *my* satisfaction. We can do this here or downtown; it's your call.'

Why is your voice so high pitched? You ain't scared of me, are ya, sweet cheeks?

Dev's right hand twitched over his holster button. His instinct screamed at him to shoot or run, only pride made him stand his ground. He used his trigger happy fingers to stroke the nape of his neck, cleared his throat and said, 'I have reason to believe that *you* are *Jacob* Andersen. If you continue to insist that you are not him, I'll need to see some ID. Sir.'

Where's Rob, why're you all alone in the woods, little girl?

Dev thrust out his chin and stood taller as he said, 'The Captain is indisposed. Now, let's stop foolin' around and pass me your ID.' Dev held out a hand, waiting.

Jake ignored it, saying, *I never go to town. Who died?*

'The deceased's *full* name remains subject to ongoing investigation. *So why not say, you don't fuckin' know?*

Dev pressed on, refusing to bend under the dread that threatened to overwhelm him if the suspect made an unexpected move. He stared into the man's empty eyes and said, 'However, I can disclose that he had a note pinned to his coat which led me to your door.'

What did it say? Come on, baby, don't be shy with ole Jake.

Dev ran a finger between the starched regulation collar and his neck; he could smell the acrid stink of his sweat as he replied, 'The note said, 'Andersen did it. Avenge me.' It was signed, Jim.'

Jake slapped his thigh with glee saying, *Jim, the wily old fox.*

'Say what?'

Pardon, officer? You said the note told you that, 'Andersen did it'. So yeah, you got me, baby cop. I am the Andersen that killed Jim. Well done with the great detecting. Where's the body?'

'In the mortuary, I guess.'

You guess? You are a magnificent example of the law, d'ya know that Deputy? Truly outstanding. You guess, huh? Now listen carefully 'cause this is mighty important, is Jim in the morgue or did he get up and fuck off outta of there?

Unwanted heat rose in Dev's face and, as he felt his bowels quiver in his guts, he finally grasped that flying solo on the arrest of a suspected murderer may not have been his best idea. He began to fiddle with the radio strapped on his shoulder and felt Jake laugh at him without hearing a sound. He took a step back.

Jake put a hand between his legs and cupped his balls as he smiled down at Dev asking, *Has anyone seen the corpse since the old bastard was put on ice?*

The air filled with radio static. Dev's voice trembled, a pitch too high, as he said, 'You obviously knew the deceased, sir.'

Jake licked his lips as he stepped down onto the gravel to taste his prey. Intruding on Dev's personal space he ran a finger across the Deputy's trembling upper lip saying, *I like your moustache, it's grown some since we last met. I recall it used to be like maiden hair on a virgin.*

Dev shot back as if burnt and fumbled with disobedient fingers to release the gun from its holster. His pale skin reddened further and his eyes filled with tears of shame as he said, 'I'm not here to feed your sick fantasies. You would do well to show the law some respect. Sir.'

Jake hooked eyes with the cop, placed his finger in his mouth and sucked away the sweat gathered from Dev's upper lip, then he sighed and rolled his eyes saying, *Man you taste good. D'ya fancy a quick fuck in the back of that state provided passion wagon you rolled up in?*

Dev finally fulfilled the desire to draw his gun shouting, 'Back off you sick bastard.'

Jake advanced, forcing Dev to take another step backwards.

I take that as a refusal of my friendly advances. Listen, kid, Jacob isn't here, my name is Jake, Mr Andersen, Sir, to you. You get one last sweet chance to run away and forget about me or suffer the consequences; your call.

Dev's gun shook in his hand as a tremor ran up his arm, along his shoulder, into his throat and out of his mouth as he replied, 'I see that a total lack of respect for the uniform is a family trait, Sir. The crew down at the station house will be mighty interested to hear of your latest perversion.'

Jake hung his head and sighed before hooking his thumbs in his pockets and saying,

You, Dev, never saw me before in your pathetic life and you know diddly squat about me. Now I know I said one last chance, but I'm feeling generous so fuck off, think of me and have a wank, you know you want to.

Dev used his free hand to remove the cuffs from his belt. His voice squeaked as he said, 'You're coming in for questioning. Sir.'

No, you come here instead. I warned you, kid. You had your chance. I've waited a long time for this, Baby Cop. Faster than a reptile catches a fly Jake's tongue flew from his mouth, winding around Dev's neck, choking off his airway like a hangman's noose and reeling him in, thrashing.

A single gunshot echoed across the lake before the useless standard issue weapon melted into the ground under Dev's feet. The cop hung two feet in the air, his vertebrae shattered. Jake's denim shirt ripped as his wings broke free then, struggling to stay Earthbound, the demon slackened its lower jaw and sucked Deputy Dev's skinny body down into hell.

As the sun set on Heavensgate, the squad car imploded, its atoms consumed by a black hole that vanished leaving no sign of the evil left behind.

Chapter Twenty-Six

-TRIANGLE-

Joy stepped outside before the sun was up and almost tripped over the dog who appeared to be sleeping, his muzzle half buried in the warm circlet of his ruined tail.

She had woken with the man on her mind, again. She knew Jacob was dangerous territory, but couldn't help being interested in him. The dog stirred as she said, 'Come on, Fur Face, wake up. I need company and a walk to clear my thick head.'

The dog rose to his feet and Joy crouched down until her face was level with his saying, 'Can you keep a secret, my sweet adorable Fur Face? I've been dreaming day and night about Jacob. He heats my blood and makes me feel alive in this lonely place. Mary's too old for him. Anyway, since when did a healthy, tidy woman i.e. me, need a housekeeper, especially one who can burn water?'

Fur Face tipped his beautiful head to one side, giving Joy his undivided attention. 'Mary has to go, boy. No Mary equals endless opportunities for yours truly to get to know the sexy handyman a lot better. I need to discover if he's totally off limits or just a little bit out of bounds.'

Heavensgate: Joy

She had a plan: after walking the dog she would prepare a brown envelope and, when Mary served Joy breakfast, Joy would serve Mary with notice.

The dog tipped his head and listened as she confided, 'With an envelope stuffed full of the green stuff I don't expect she'll make too much fuss. When she's gone the coast will be clear for me to make my move and give Jacob something good to dream about. He doesn't love her, it's as plain as the nose on your face. Tell me I am brilliant, boy.' Her furry friend wagged his stumpy tail and barked.

Dawn embroidered the sky with cloudy threads of pink, purple, red and orange as Joy hesitated in the woods, unsure which rusty pine needle strewn path to take. The dog was impatient, he ran ahead, barking, encouraging her to follow him. She laughed and Skylar led his new mistress deep into the dark woods. They were headed for the Angel Oak.

She found the dog waiting patiently at the base of the ancient tree cocking his head from one side to the other as if listening attentively to someone, or something, in front of him. There was nothing to see. A rhythmic creaking noise and soft childish singing made the small hairs on the nape of her neck stand to attention. The mist parted to reveal a boy. He was swinging on an old rubber tyre that hung by a thick blue rope from a low branch. Joy recognised the kid who had disappeared from the row boat. He was wet, he was solid, he was real. A memory of a child holding out a silver dollar for a soda flashed into her mind and shot out again before making sense.

The boy at first appeared to be unaware of Joy or the dog. He sang to himself, a little out of tune, but there was no mistaking the words of *'Que Sera Sera.'*

He met Joy's eyes across the clearing and, with a bright smile said, 'That is my Grandma's favourite song, it's by Doriseverydamnday and Grandpa Jon is sick to death of it. I like it. Do you like it, Joy?'

She glanced around looking for his mother. 'Are you OK, sweetheart? I searched all over for you the other day. You frightened me, I thought you had fallen into the lake.'

The boy's voice rang in her ears and she gasped with pain, crossing her arms protectively across her chest as he said,

'But you didn't try to save me, did you?'

'I'm truly sorry, I was afraid to jump in after you because I can't swim properly. Did you find your momma?'

While they spoke, Fur Face had lain alongside in the shelter of towering, gnarled tree roots. Joy jumped when he leapt to his feet, fur bristling, snarling and showing sharp teeth. He rushed to her and, trembling, pressed his flank onto the side of her leg. The boy continued to swing on the tyre.

'Hey, pup, what's occurring? Did you hear the pesky squirrels?'

There was a sharp crack in the undergrowth behind them. Skylar stood firm, protecting Joy even though his muscles quivered with fear. Raising his muzzle to the sky, he let out a blood curdling howl which was immediately answered by a louder one, shocking the dog as much as the woman. The boy, however, swung his legs and sang his song, completely unaffected by the change in atmosphere.

Joy spun around, her heart rate accelerating, her eyes searching through the mist and half-light for the threat. There was nothing except a definite and present silence that gave her goose-flesh.

The sickening stench of rotten flesh seeped into the air. Joy dry heaved and pressed her hand to cover her nose and mouth. Skylar dropped to his haunches, a frightened mewling issuing from his throat. Joy struggled to move, her feet heavy as if wearing lead boots. The surroundings went by in slow motion as she rushed to the boy, desperate to protect him and redeem herself for her cowardliness at the lake. Seeing the alarm on her face, he clambered off the swing and into the safety of her embrace. Her arms flew up above her head as the invisible weight of their emptiness almost unbalanced her. The child had vanished and Skylar was on his haunches growling into the trees.

Someone whispered in her ear, 'Hello, bitch.' She spun round. There was no-one there.

Her tongue cleaved to the roof of her mouth. Desperation moved in as an unnatural silence pressed down. She turned in a slow circle searching for the whisperer. The voice came again, 'I am waiting, bitch.'

Loud cracks and rustling shattered the silence, heralding something large making its careless way toward her. Fear always created crazy bravado in Joy and this time was no exception, she shouted, 'Show yourself, you bloody stupid coward!'

Her voice rang flat as if it hadn't the strength to travel more than an inch from her mouth before dying away. There was no reply.

The dog's hackles were raised. Joy patted his head, wiped her sweaty palms on her thighs and said, 'Come on, boy, time to leave.' A booming voice replied, 'Stay and play, bitch toy!'

Skylar bolted, squealing like a frightened puppy. Dread had stolen Joy's ability to move. She whimpered. Acid bile rose to burn her throat, extinguishing her ability to scream. Big hands covered her eyes and her racing heart stopped dead in her chest.

Guess who?

Warm breath caressed her ear; she could smell clean earth, pine, and something indefinable that she wanted to investigate. Relief flooded her body as she lifted his hands off her eyes and turned to face him. He was too close.

'Jacob, you frightened my dog.'

And you? Did I frighten you, Joy?

She lied, 'No, nothing scares me after what happened out on the lake. Don't you ever call me a bitch again!'

I don't know what you heard Joy, but it wasn't me.

Joy searched his eyes and, finding the truth there, said, 'I must be overtired, imagining things, but the dog was scared. And I saw the boy again, here just now, he was playing on a tree swing.'

Are you sure? Jake stepped closer forcing her to step back and said, *Let's sit here a while, shall we?*

'I'd rather get out of the woods and walk at the water's edge. I need to think.'

Fine, I'll walk with you and we can think together, two heads are better than one, or so they say.

They made their way out of the woods and back down the slope, not speaking until they arrived at the narrow strip of sand and pebbles which ringed the lake.

Jim told me you saw the boy out on the lake.

'He did?'

Yes, he did. You must have the sight, not everyone can see him.

'Can you see him, Jacob?'

Hell no that would be impossible, me being me and all that.

'I don't understand.'

You don't need to understand, Joy, sometimes you just need to follow your heart and trust your instincts. His eyes held hers for long enough to make her uncomfortable; she was the first to look away.

Come on, Joy, forget about the boy and skim some stones.

'OK, if you don't want to talk about him, fine, for now, but in return for my patience I need your help with a sensitive matter.'

Jake watched his stone skip seven times before sinking.

Lucky number. He picked up another smooth pebble.

Joy took a deep breath and launched straight in, 'Jacob, I'm going to ask, actually, I'm going to tell Mary to leave.'

He dropped the stone on the beach and stared at her open mouthed.

Joy crossed her arms across her chest and said, 'Don't look at me like that. I appreciate that you two are, er, *close*. The thing is, I don't need a housekeeper and I can't ever see her and me getting along.'

Well you can try, honey, but believe me, that woman isn't easy to get rid of.

'Are you upset with me, Jacob?'

Hell no, girl. If anything, I admire you, it's always good to know what you want. Jake watched her unblinking as if weighing her up for a fight. Joy shuddered and wrapped her arms tighter around her body, pushing her hands into the sleeves of her fleece.

Heavensgate: Joy

It's getting cold, let me walk you home; you can tell me how I can help rid you of a useless housekeeper and maybe we will stumble upon that mutt of yours along the way.

Joy allowed him to rest an arm around her waist, acutely aware of the warmth and closeness of his body. After a few awkward steps she placed an arm around him and hooked her thumb into the top of his jeans' pocket as if it was the most natural thing in the world.

She didn't see the smirk that spoiled Jake's handsome face. She forgot about her terror in the woods, she forgot the vanishing boy, she forgot everything and everyone. All she had ever needed was right there walking besides her, humming that old fashioned tune, *Que Sera Sera*.

When they reached the Lodge, he walked her to her bedroom, kissed her on the tip of her nose and left her there, alone. She closed the door and threw herself face down on the bed until her heart rate slowed to normal and the heat left her face.

Joy drifted off to sleep, but was woken by the racket of clashing pots and pans.

Hearing the ruckus, Jake smiled knowingly and went to face the music. Leaning his long frame against the kitchen table and crossing his arms, he asked,

Mary, are you jealous of Joy?

'Jake, that little tramp is infatuated with you.'

No-one uses the word tramp anymore; and stop calling me Jake, we can't have her overhear it.

'I don't give a shit what that flighty little madam overhears. I saw the way she made them googly eyes at you, and you was lollygagging right back.'

If I was, so what? But she didn't and I wasn't.

'You just fucked her.'

No. She is asleep and I just got outta the shower.

'Well you *want* to fuck her.'

Hell, Mary, I want to fuck everybody. I fuck you, don't I?

'Jake, sorry, I mean, Jacob, baby, what we have is real. We don't need that slut getting in the middle of us.'

She won't, she can't, I love you, Mary, you know I do. Come over here and I'll show you how much I love you. He pointed to the growing bulge in his jeans. Mary drew closer to him, her voice calmer as she said,

'I tell you, lover, the little bitch has to go.'

If it makes my momma happy, your wish is my command, but the comings and goings around this hell hole are not generally up to the likes of you and me, honey.

Mary grasped the front of his shirt her eyes shining up at him full of crazy excitement as she said, 'You can slaughter her, baby, you'll enjoy it. I can help you. Let me help you. We can make love on her warm corpse, we can share her alive, dead, whatever way you want, baby.

'Way I understand it, I can't kill Joy in Heavensgate. Either the Gate Keepers will collect her or she'll leave when she decides and not before.

'So we'll have to make the whore want to fuck off outta here real soon.'

How?

'Let's scare her to death.'

We can scare her for sure, Mary, but it's real hard to die around these parts. I tried, they wouldn't take me. And look at you.

'What about me? Do you need to tell your momma something?'

No, not a thing, babe. What's your sexy, evil plan for our house guest?

Chapter Twenty-Seven

-SCHIZOID MAN-

Joy lay on her bed trying to sleep while images of Jacob flooded, uninvited, through her mind. She imagined how his strong hands would roam slow and warm across her body, and how she would raise her hips to meet him as he lowered his weight onto her, his hot generous lips pressing hers, his tongue exploring her mouth, her ears, her neck, moving lower, much lower.

She groaned, the anticipation was too much. Where was he? Why hadn't he made a move on her? She couldn't recall desperately wanting anyone before him and her common sense warned her to deny the attraction. However, her body wasn't good at denial and here, in her warm bed, it insisted that there couldn't be any harm in a bit of solitary fun. Her hand drifted across her nipples and down over her stomach, her fingers insisted on checking between her legs and she was too idle to disobey them.

She had just reached the part in her fantasy where he pushed himself hot and hard into her wetness, when the door opened and Jacob slipped into the room.

Excited and embarrassed in equal measure, Joy froze, shut her eyes tight and feigned sleep as he carefully slipped his arms underneath her. It had to be a dream and, after all, no-one takes responsibility for what happens in those.

At first she couldn't understand why he lifted her off the bed, but she went along with it, sleepily slipping her arms around his neck, she nuzzled under his ear. He straightened up, cradling her like a child in his arms; she felt aroused by his strength and the body heat that penetrated her night shirt.

Jacob bent to kiss Joy's forehead before laying her on a cold hard surface where he strapped down one arm. Her eyes flew open and she screamed, 'What are you doing, Jacob?' He grabbed her other arm, effortlessly strapping it down.

Joy panicked. She bucked her hips and kicked. She twisted her body painfully from side to side. Mary grabbed her feet, sticking her nails into the soft depressions behind her ankles as Jacob fastened the restraints around them, spreading her legs apart. Joy was helplessly trapped.

Unwilling to accept the reality of what was happening she began to chant, 'Wake up wake up wake up wake up!' Jacob and Mary watched her with amusement. Maybe this wasn't a dream. Joy took a deep breath and, making a gigantic effort to stay calm, said, 'OK, so I'm awake.' Mary tightened the strap around one wrist. Joy screamed, 'Ouch, Shit. Jacob, Mary, stop. You're hurting me. Bloody hell. If this is the kind of game you play I don't swing that way. Let me go.'

Mary pointed to herself then to Jacob, saying, 'Honey, me and lover boy here ain't that cosmopolitan, now don't make me gag that pretty mouth of yours, we want to hear you moan.' She scraped her nails slowly down Joy's inner thigh and laughed, saying, 'Be *patient* and follow me,' as she led the way out of the bedroom. Jacob pushed Joy, bound onto the old squeaking hospital gurney, across the hallway. Where the guest bedroom had been there was now a pair of dull gray metal, elevator doors. Jacob pressed a blue call button, above which a yellowed plastic sign advised,

ELEVATOR FOR THEATRE ONLY

Joy swallowed painfully as the green display above the doors changed from LB to B, then sent out a ping as it reached G, displaying an arrow pointed downward. The doors rattled open and an internal rusty trellised gate was quickly slid back by Mary with a screech and a crash.

Jacob pushed the gurney into the elevator. A disembodied voice said, 'Elevator going down please mind the doors.' Joy bit the inside of her cheek, desperate to discover she was dreaming and wake up. It stung and the salty tang of blood hit her tongue and ran across her teeth while everything else remained the same.

Jake held Joy's right hand; Mary snorted in disgust, pressed button B and the bottom fell out of the world. They were in free fall. The elevator plummeted and bounced once on landing. Joy trembled at the sight of two bloody handprints on the doors. She swallowed bile as panic soared like a bird in flight. There was no point in begging or screaming, there was no-one to hear.

She had to wake up. She bit down hard again, this time on her tongue and as before, she tasted blood as hot pain flared like a match in her mouth and cried out, 'Oh God, please help me.'

He ain't here, Honeybunch. In fact, I must confide that I'm beginning to doubt His existence. I mean, how could He let such tragedy befall a sweet child like you?

'Jacob, Mary, please don't hurt me. I will do anything you want. Please, I am begging you, don't hurt me.' She choked on a mixture of snot and blood, her heart banging against her chest, desperate to escape.

Calm down, my pretty. There's no more pain where you're going. Enjoy the free ride, relax.

Her head thrashed from side to side as she screamed, splattering fresh blood into the air. Jacob raised his voice singing *Locked out of Heaven* as the gurney followed Mary down a long corridor,

She hollered over her shoulder, 'Shut up, Jacob, that ain't no tune like I ever heard before. You're ruinin' the atmosphere.'

The ceiling rolled by overhead, weeping from damp patches like infected sores. Menacing shadows chased along sludge green, cracked tiled lower walls and industrial cream paint flaked off the upper section like psoriasis. The further along the corridor they travelled, the narrower the space between the crumbling walls became.

The gurney wheels grumbled on old rubber as they squeaked on, passing rusty, leaking, old fashioned radiators that hung on the walls like giant toothed iron monsters. Joy shuddered against the leather straps as icy cold water dripped from a network of ceiling pipes covered in slime and condensation. Jake shouted to Mary, *Hey, honey, what about this for a worthy tune?*

His voice echoed off the dank walls and a passable impression of Frankie Goes to Hollywood's '*Relax*' echoed around the narrow space.

He sang, working himself into a frenzy, as the nightmare corridor continued to narrow until the sides of the gurney scraped along the walls grating the skin from Joy's knuckles. Jake stooped under increasingly low ceilings. Mary, wearing a striped uniform and a small white hat on her straw-like hair kept walking, not speaking or looking back, now and again she scratched at the ceiling with sharp, red talons. Jake sounded ecstatically happy, which only added to Joy's heart pounding terror.

He leaned over Joy, his face upside down as he gazed lovingly into her eyes, then he kissed her lips and whispered, *Do you want to come, Joy? Do you want to suck?*

'Let me go, I'll do anything you want.'

You are a brave girl, such a brave girl.

Joy's voice filled with sobs as hysteria rose in her like the tide and spilled her pleadings into the nightmare. 'I'm not brave. I'm afraid and I'm a coward. Don't do this, Jacob, whatever this is, please stop. There's a million dollars in the safe. It's yours. I have the combination. Unstrap me, let me off here, we can walk back together. I'll give you both the money or, just you; you choose what to do about her. You can do anything you want, go anywhere you want. I won't tell anyone. I promise, just, please, let me go.'

Sssh, wait.

The corridor abruptly opened out into a large cave; they headed for a set of rubber doors set in the far wall on which was painted THEATER 1. The cave was a waiting area, painted sparking white and boasting bright art work on the walls. Jake asked Mary to stop. The pair moved away from Joy, whispering and throwing occasional glances her way. Hope surged as they appeared to seriously consider her proposal until, sighing, Jake returned and said,

I'm truly sorry, sweetness, it's a good offer, but there's no way back, look.

He spun the gurney around. Joy's brain baulked against the impossibility of what her eyes saw. Back the way they had travelled was nothing, nothing at all, not even a discernible up or down. The effect of total nothingness was disorientating. No longer able to hold back her horror she began to choke on a flood of vomit. Mary rushed to her side saying, 'Oh no we mustn't lose our star patient so easily, Doctor.'

She wrenched Joy's head to the left and stuck two fingers into her mouth to clear her airway, scratching the back of her throat in the process. Jake cleared the sweat from Joy's brow and licked his fingers. Narrowing her eyes at him Mary said, 'No harm done. Hurry and turn this ride back around, lover, it's not safe to linger this close to the Nothing; we've got a schedule to keep.'

Jake spun the gurney and their journey recommenced. Dizzy, sick and petrified Joy began to cry desperate, painful, heaving sobs Grinning, Jake said, *Don't fret, beautiful, we're in the operating theatre, it's state of the art. Now we can cut out those nasty infectious pieces of hope and joy. If you survive, we can live happily ever after, together. We will have us a wholesome threesome.* He raised his voice a little, *Won't we, Nurse Mary?*

'We sure will, Dr. Andersen,' she replied, leaving a tray of sharp instruments she had been admiring under the lights to join Jake and lock off the gurney wheels. Joy drew in her breath feeling her insides roll and churn as she birthed a scream that echoed across the theatre, magnified and haunting until it drifted into silence.

Mary shivered with excitement and leaned across their hysterical victim to kiss Jake long and hard as he fondled her breasts.

Joy lay panting in horror. Mary licked her ear and whispered into the wetness, 'I can't wait to cut you open, princess, and see what's inside you that my man finds so appealing.'

Joy shuddered and tugged at her restraints until she bled. Then she was travelling forward at speed as Jake and Mary ran behind the gurney. He yelled,

Go girl, go. Man she's fast. Ain't she fast, Mary?

'She must be in a hurry to get well, Doctor.'

Unchecked, Joy and the gurney crashed through the theatre doors, spinning until they came to a perfectly straight and central halt under the insectile multiple eyed glare of surgery lights.

Jake and Mary danced in behind, whooping and cheering. Mary asked, 'What's your music choice for theatre today, Doctor?'

21st Century Schizoid Man will be perfect. Nursey?

'Yes, Doctor?'

Get me the drill.

'What about anesthetic, Doctor?' Mary pouted, snapping on a pair of surgical gloves.

You're so right, Nurse, that's just what this Doctor needs.

A voice boomed in his head, 'LEAVE JOY ALONE JAKE. YOU ARE NOT THE DOCTOR!'

Jake howled and shook his head so fast it became a blur as he shouted, *Get out. Get out. Fuck me. He was weak, he's gone.*

Mary rushed to comfort him with a bottle of bourbon which Jake waved in front of Joy's terrified eyes before taking a long swig. Filling his mouth, he gurgled on the spirit. His pupils narrowed into red slits as he leaned over and, forcing his tongue between her teeth, spat alcohol down her throat making her gag and struggle for breath as she choked.

'She loves it, Doctor, give her more, give her a lot more.'

Don't mind if I fuckin' do.

Heavensgate: Joy

Jake refilled his mouth with bourbon and Joy let him kiss her. Encouraged, he slipped his hand inside her panties. Joy waited until she saw him begin to move his other hand to his zipper and bit down hard on his tongue.

Shit! The bitch bit me. He squealed as blood ran over his teeth, mixing with the alcohol and stinging like hell.

'Oh, baby, come to Nursey. Here suck on this. Momma will make it all better.'

Later, Nurse, I have a job to do here. Jake spat black blood onto the white floor making the tiles hiss and buckle.

Straining to be heard above the crash of King Crimson, he shouted in Joy's ear,

Now you're in trouble, babe. I'll use the drill on you and Nurse Mary will use the pliers.

She screwed her eyes tight and again willed herself to wake up. It was no use, she remained bound to the gurney and trapped in the nightmare with the scents of bourbon, antiseptic and death battling for supremacy.

Smiling into her eyes, Mary lifted one of Joy's hands and shouted, 'Doctor, this poor child bites her nails.'

Pull them out, Nurse. I'll remove the cancerous joy and hope which have poisoned our patient.

Jake raised a hand in command. The heavy rock music stopped. Silence descended on the theater. Mary adjusted the overhead lights blinding Joy's weeping eyes while Jake positioned a hand-drill above the bridge of her nose. Joy began to call upon her God to help her.

Her prayer was cut short as she heard Jake say, *I can't do this Nurse, this girl has a spirit, she is warm, she is a sweet person. I can't hurt her.*

Joy's heart fluttered with hope, she risked a glance at her saviour and he saw it in her eyes. Mary giggled and clamped the pliers tight onto Joy's right index finger. Jake moved as if to stop her and Joy exhaled with relief. Jake laughed like a lunatic saying, *Get ready to operate on this lost soul, Nurse, after three. One. Two ...*

Joy prayed to all the Gods of heaven and earth and every Realm inbetween.

She felt a wrench on her fingernail and the sharp point of the drill break the skin on her forehead. Her bladder released.

She stopped praying and begged for death to find her.

The drill clattered across the theatre floor.

Joy opened her eyes to see Jake lifted off his feet and barrelled into the wall by a furious, growling ball of fur that attached its mouth to Jake's throat and ripped at the soft spot where his Adam's apple bobbed.

Mary quickly recovered from the shock and grabbed a scalpel, lunging at Skylar as blood spurted a fountain from Jake's ruined throat splattering the dog's silver fur.

Joy cheered on her brave defender, then screamed in rage and horror when Mary stabbed the vicious blade between Skylar's shoulder blades. Releasing Jake in a spray of blood that flashed across the walls, the dog spun in mid-air, snarling at his attacker and clamped his heavy jaws on her hand.

Jake twitched on the floor in a spreading pool of gore, clutching the wreckage of his throat. The frenzied, wounded animal dragged Mary by her neck, out of the theatre and into the Nothing.

Joy lay shivering under the lights in a mixture of blood and urine. Trapped, unable to move and utterly lost.

Chapter Twenty-Eight

-JEALOUSY-

Joy had to get free of the gurney. She thrashed and bucked her hips and, surprised to find she could move, threw herself over the edge where she bumped against Jacob; too shocked to scream she rolled away from him, and fell out of bed. Skylar licked her face. She checked her body for injuries, there were no strap marks on her wrists or ankles. No scratch on her forehead. She breathed into her hands, they didn't stink of bourbon. Running her unbitten tongue around the inside of her mouth she found that it wasn't sore. Apart from the man snoring in her bed, everything was normal.

She got up on her knees and peeped over the quilt at Jacob, he wasn't there. Rubbing sleep from her eyes she ran her hands over the place he had slept; there wasn't a crease in the sheets or an imprint in the pillows. She sat on the end of the bed, covering her face with her hands, thinking that after such a powerful nightmare the bedding should at least have had the decency to knot her into the shroud she had been sure she was destined to wear.

Opening the curtains, she caught her breath as she watched a black eagle swoop to snatch a silver fish from the lake. As daylight flooded the room her horror receded and the last of it subsided in the shower, reshaping itself into a resolution to leave Heavensgate before any of her dreams came true.

Skylar snuffled about on her bed, making a doggy nest in the quilt. His ears pricked up when Joy entered the room towel drying her wet hair and sat beside him to stroke her fingers through his thick gray scruff.

She began to dress and said, 'We have to get out of here, boy.' The dog whined and tucked his mutilated tail between his legs. His pointy ears flattened against his head as he stretched out his long, pink tongue to lick away a trace of blood from his snout.

Joy went looking for Jacob and Mary. She averted her eyes as she passed the elevator doors and hung tenaciously onto her sanity, determined to understand what was happening.

Jacob was nowhere to be found. Mary was in the kitchen, apparently calm and content as she sang a tune Joy recognized as 'Relax'. Joy shook her head at the irony of it and swallowed her sarcasm like marbles.

'Good morning Mary,' a steaming mug of black coffee was slapped down in front of her, its contents splashing over the rim.

'Here you go. *Ma'am.*'

'Thank you. *Mary.*'

'How'd ya like yer eggs?'

'Over easy, please.'

'Easy, sure, ma'am, everything here is easy.'

The tension was palpable.

Joy took a deep breath before saying, 'Mary, why are there bloody hand prints on the elevator door?'

An egg hit the pan and angry, boiling fat spat at the cook.

'Fuck. Sorry, ma'am, but that burnt like a branding' iron at the rodeo.'

'Run cold water over your hand.' Joy turned off the heat under the frying pan and leant back against the drainer. 'Mary, I was asking you about blood on the elevator door.'

Mary faced the sink, avoiding eye contact as she ran icy water over her scalded skin and said, 'What elevator?'

'The one in the hallway, the one which goes down to the basement.'

Heavensgate: Joy

'There ain't no basement and there ain't no elevator neither, and if you think there are you had a vivid dream or you need help, *specialist* help.'

Mary turned off the water. Narrowing her eyes at Joy she dried her hands on an old striped dish cloth.

'You are lying, Mary. Tell the truth. You don't scare me.'

'Really? Then you are a bigger fool than we've had around these parts for many a long day.'

'Let's talk about the elevator.'

Mary rolled her shoulders and animosity almost played a tune on the air. 'I. Just. Done. Told. You. There. Ain't. No. Elevator,' Mary spoke slowly as if dealing with an idiot. 'There. Ain't. No. Basement. Neither.'

Joy glared at her and said, 'There is, you and Jacob took me down there last night. In the non-existent elevator.'

'Ma'am that musta been a real rough dream. This here Lodge is a single storey pretentious log cabin.' Mary sat at the table sneering at Joy through thick makeup.

Anger gave her strength. She grabbed Mary's bleached hair and dragged her out of the kitchen, pulling the smaller, struggling and cussing woman across the living room and into the elevator corridor only to find that it had morphed into the hallway. She released Mary and stood dumbfounded.

Mary, her dignity recovered, laughed as she rubbed her head. 'You should see your face. You look like an aborigine who went walkabout and fell in a snow drift. Priceless. Jacob, where are you? Come and look at Lady Di's face.'

Joy was speechless; she pressed her palms against the guest bedroom door that occupied the space where the elevator had been. Mary's voice quivered with glee as she said, 'You go into your nice room and lie down, ma'am, or better still, pack your pink case and leave us alone before trouble finds you.'

Joy ran to the kitchen and chose a long carving knife from the rack. Returning to the hallway, she ran at Mary brandishing the weapon and screaming, 'Get out of my house. Go or I swear I will kill you.'

Mary snarled and rushed her, knocking Joy backwards and sending the knife clattering across the floor. They fought their way with nails and teeth toward the weapon. Joy reached it first, but as she snatched it the blade twisted and sliced open the fleshy pad under her thumb.

'Look what you made me do!' Joy screamed, facing her housekeeper with blood dripping down her wrist.

'There's nothing to see, ma'am, so calm down.' Joy waved her hand in front of Mary's face. 'You call this nothing?' She ran to the kitchen and sank into the nearest chair, stared at her palm, wrinkled her brow and muttered, 'It's not cut.'

'No shit? You're dreamin' again.' Mary stood at the head of the table, a sneer on her face and her hands on her hips.

'I'm bloody well wide awake. The knife cut me, my hand was sliced open. I can't understand why there's no wound.'

'Oh for Christ's sake hand me the damn knife.' Unable to tear her eyes away from her uninjured hand, Joy begrudgingly passed the knife to Mary, who tested the blade for sharpness before saying,

'Now shut yer slaverin' an' watch.'

Joy screamed as Mary thrust the serrated blade deep into her own abdomen, slicing a jagged tear up between her breasts and down to her pubic bone. She smiled and opened up her insides; loops of intestines, glistening and gray, slopped like dead fish spilling from a barrel onto her blood soaked, fluffy slippered feet. Her blue eyes mocked Joy as she said, 'Right, Lady Muck, it's time to tell Aunty Mary, is this a fuckin' dream or not?'

With a wet sucking squelch she withdrew the knife from her body then bent to collect and push back her dripping entrails as if tidying a room.

A soft keening issued from Joy's mouth as Mary advanced on her waving the blood and gore stained knife. She had to fight back, she had to get away, but she couldn't move a muscle to escape the blood lust that shone in Mary's eyes. Snatching a handful of long blonde hair, Mary whipped back Joy's head to more easily slit her rival open ear to ear. The blade flashed lightening across her skin and gushing heat exploded from her throat to run down her body like molten lava.

Smiling into Joy's fading sight, Mary pushed her off the chair onto the pristine kitchen floor where she lay bleeding to death.

'Now that's what I call a cut, my Lady.' Mary kicked her victim hard in the head and spat on her body.

As Joy slipped away, she had a split second to register that the same knife used to slit her throat had left Mary unhurt and unmarked.

Chapter Twenty-Nine

-A FULL MEAL-

Mary grabbed Joy's lifeless arms, intending to hide the body and clean up the blood before Jake returned. Instead, she stood quivering with rage, her hands empty and the kitchen floor unstained as Joy vanished before her eyes. Breathing heavily, she stared out of the kitchen window where she saw Joy on the beach, gazing out across the calm lake.

Mary removed a fresh knife from the rack and ran outside determined to attack her elusive adversary. She thrust the blade into Joy's back and fell through her unmoving body, landing hard on her hands and knees in boiling, sulphuric mud. She screeched and raised her hand to fling the useless knife into the steaming lake squealing, 'Fuck,' as she realised it wasn't there.

She couldn't believe that, after she had murdered Joy so quickly and painlessly, the undeserving, man stealing bitch taunted her by behaving as if nothing Mary did made any difference.

Crawling out of the blistering filth she got to her feet and stomped back to the Lodge shouting, 'Jake, you cheating bastard, why didn't you tell me the whore has magic?' She stormed from room to room working herself into insane fury, pulsating like strobe lighting, flashing in and out of existence. Every few seconds she glanced through the window to see Joy, serene and smiling at her from the now calm and beautiful shoreline. Mary's screams of rage shook the Lodge with the violence of a storm thundering across the sierra.

Jake raced down the boat deck and into the kitchen, ducking pots, pans, vegetables and glassware, all thrown in his general direction. Every item fell short of the mark as if she didn't dare strike him. He threw a few heavy objects back just for good measure. His missiles flew straight through Mary's frazzled image and hit the walls.

Jake wasn't afraid of her, he knew what she was and thrived as he fed on her emotions. He began to pulsate until his frequency matched hers beat for beat and black lightning arced in the air that boiled between them. Stepping into the storm, Jake reached out to grasp her light, merging it to his own in shades of purple and sick yellow. Mary solidified and steadied in his embrace. He stroked her electrified hair, saying,

Sssh, momma, your baby's here. I'm always here for you. You can rely on me, Jake has what you need.

Mary beat at his chest, sobbing with jealousy and rage. Eventually, she relaxed in her lover's arms and he loosened his hold. She glanced outside and finding no sign of Joy slumped against Jake's chest with relief.

Releasing her, Jake hooked his thumbs into his belt and said, *I know what you did to her, Mary.*

'I'm sorry, OK? I can't help myself, it's the nature of *what* I am, but that's not *all* I am. I love you, Jake and I never meant to...'

Jake gripped her shoulders cutting off her words with his mouth. She returned his kiss and pressing herself against his long, muscular body, wrapped her legs around his waist and latched onto him like a black widow spider onto a fly.

As her poisonous tongue reached into his throat, Jake broke the kiss, his voice rough with warning, *No, Mary, you just made a huge mistake. I am no longer one of your fuckin' victims.*

Mary ran a hand between their bodies and demanded, 'Then screw me, baby.'

Joy wandered back to the Lodge, drawing down lungs full of warm summer air. Her skin itched and she felt twitchy, as if she should be concerned, but her mind was full of clouds. Pushing open the kitchen door she saw Jacob with Mary; his hands on her thighs, his hips grinding between hers as she writhed and moaned against him. Joy stared in fascinated disgust and horror. Jake was changing.

Her feet disobeyed the instruction to run. Her hands flew to her face as Jacob's jaw jolted and flexed as if on springs until, with a sound like strong elastic bands snapping, it opened impossibly wide. Mary was too lost in her orgasm to notice the danger. Joy was too frozen with disbelief and horror to cry out or turn away.

Jacob dropped his gaping jaw. Steaming green saliva oozed over black mirrored teeth as he slid his bottom lip to encompass Mary's chin while he continued to thrust into her. She sighed, her eyes closed in ecstasy.

Joy's blood thundered in her head, but she still heard Jake mewl deep in the back his throat, the sound was sick, needy and repulsive. She retched as he flexed his back and his shirt surrendered to the power of silky black wings that sprang free, their elegant, silver tipped feathers sweeping the floor.

Jake wrapped his magnificent plumage around Mary's quivering form, partially shielding her from view. Joy bore witness as his elongated top lip slipped over the back of Mary's head like a wet cowl, passion and rapture snuffed out as she struggled against oblivion. Jake's muscles convulsed. He bent over his prey, forcing his head down and simultaneously using his hands to push her further up his body and into his mouth. His throat swelled as he swallowed Mary whole.

The world tilted underfoot; Joy vomited and fought for the strength to run. Every free object in the kitchen flew at Jake to join a vortex that spun in a funnel of darkness around him.

The curtains ripped from shattered windows and the floor cracked as his body jerked and his wings thrashed with the effort of digesting his prey. He was the eye of a storm of utensils, knives, crockery and cloths, herbs, pans, ornaments and chairs all eager to feed the chaos. When the spell broke and the tornado fled abandoning its collection of captives to the floor, it left a stench of sulphur and burnt flesh behind it.

Jake's wings retracted. He steadied himself amongst the wreckage, waiting to regain his human form. Joy found her strength and had turned to flee when he hooked her with eyes that sparked fire and roared,

Joy, run! Run as fast as you can! I am the servant of the Beast that will destroy you!

Chapter Thirty

-RESCUE-

Hell snapped at her heels as Joy fled the winged abomination she knew as Jacob. The lake was still, an early evening mist hovered over its pebbled beach. The mountains, their peaks dressed by clouds, bore witness as she sprinted down the narrow beach and splashed into Lake Disregard. The water was freezing cold. She was pleased, thinking that death would be quicker. She thrashed her arms, desperate to swim until exhaustion claimed her, but could only doggy paddle. Her heart beat at panic speed. Twisting in the water she found that Jake wasn't in pursuit and gave herself up to the lake.

Silt slipped between her toes and mud sucked her feet. Weeds caressed and grasped at her legs like tiny hands. Gentle waves lapped at her chin and sloshed against her lips; they tasted like earth and she opened her mouth to welcome them. She began to do her pathetic doggy paddle, her movements weak and erratic as she stared ahead, praying for forgiveness. Certainty fed her the necessary courage. Jacob had deceived her, he was evil, and death was the only way to escape him, Heavensgate and herself.

The shore line receded behind her and, unable to float, Joy allowed her body to sink. She felt calm. The lake covered her head like a veil. Her eyes remained open. Sunlight didn't pierce the depths, and although it was dark, she was no longer cold. She wondered how she could be so relaxed while swallowing the water that rushed to flood her lungs. She prepared for the moment when the inevitable panic of survival instinct hit her. It never came.

Her feet hit the bottom of the lake. She waved a pale hand through silver bubbles that drifted like pearls from her open mouth. There was no doubt, she was still breathing. If Death was on schedule he should have been waiting in the dark water amongst the weeds and black mud.

Instead, a thick blue rope hung before her eyes like an invitation, its length nibbled by a school of tiny fish. Joy gave it a tug; it was secured out of sight above the water line. She clasped both hands tightly above one of the large knots that were helpfully tied at regular intervals and set her feet upon another. Unable to drown, and resigned to whatever fate had planned, she held on tight, her ears popping with the pressure change as she was slowly raised up to the light by an unseen saviour. Trembling arm muscles and cramped fingers confirmed that she was, indeed, alive.

When sunlight kissed her newborn head, Joy released the rope, hung onto the side of the boat and spluttered, 'Get away from me. You bloody evil bastard.'

Jake's eyes shone, their expression unreadable and, before she could slip back under the water, he dragged her screaming, kicking and biting into the boat. She fought every inch of the way, forcing him to sit astride her to avoid tipping them both overboard. Joy shuddered, breathless under his weight.

Gathering the bile that threatened to choke her, she spat in his face, Jake wiped it away with the back of one hand. Something unknowable swirled behind his eyes and he leaned in close, gripping her wrists until her burning skin seemed to sink into the small bones. She screamed, he released her hands and, as his jade eyes cleared, all pain left her. Warm breath flickered across her face and his tears fell as he whispered,

What are you playing at, you crazy bitch?

She coughed up earthy water before bucking under him and snapping, 'You tell me, you vile piece of shit. It can't be beyond your magical powers to read my mind, you bloody evil monster.'

Jake released her and retreated to the bench seat. He held out his hand to help her, she flinched away from his touch and scurried to sit shivering in the stern. He sniffed using his thumb to clear the wetness from his cheeks and said, *So now you know. It's not easy to die around here. Here endeth Heavensgate's first lesson.*

Joy's chest clenched and, like the times when she was a child terrified and alone in the blackness of the cellar, she swallowed her tears.

Jake attempted a weak smile and said, *But if you really want to give it a go, we can try the hanging tree tomorrow, if you'd like?*

He rowed back to the shore, pulling the oars without apparent effort, chewing his bottom lip and, although Joy attempted to burn him with her glare, he avoided meeting her eyes. The moment the boat hit the shore she scrambled out and ran to the Lodge, leaving Jacob laughing hysterically on the wooden deck.

There was nowhere to run. No escape. No help. She was trapped. Locking herself in the bathroom she beat on the mirror crying out for the auburn haired girl to come and save her. There was no-one there.

Ripping off her wet clothes as if they offended her she turned the shower on high and stepped under the spray. Opening her mouth and eyes to boiling water that washed away a sudden flood of tears and swept steam into her throat leaving her clean and, despite the scalding temperature, unhurt.

Joy scrubbed her skin with a pumice stone in a vain attempt to scour away the horror of Jacob's betrayal, crying out her frustration as she released fresh, pink skin that glowed with life under the rough treatment. Screaming, she took Jacob's cut-throat razor from the shelf and dragged it along the length and breadth of her wrist. It snapped against her skin leaving her unscathed.

She sank into the shower tray, allowed shock to overwhelm her and shook until her teeth threatened to shatter in her mouth.

Heavensgate: Joy

Jake sat in the kitchen and waited for the storm to pass.

He was reading a battered, leather bound copy of "Dante's Inferno" as mimicking Old Blue Eyes he sang, *I've Got You Under My Skin...*

Joy couldn't be bothered to feign surprise when, without remembering the journey from bathroom to kitchen, she found herself seated opposite him with a mug of steaming, hot coffee in front of her. The mug announced that she was:

'THE WORLD'S GREATEST GIRLFRIEND'

Despite her resigned acceptance of Heavensgate's strangeness she felt disorientated, nauseous and confused. She watched Jacob read and ran the past few hours over in her mind:

Jake and Mary tried to kill her in the basement theatre.

Skylar killed Jacob and Mary, but they came back to life.

The elevator disappeared.

She cut her hand. It was uninjured.

Mary ripped out her own intestines. She hadn't died.

Mary slit Joy's throat and killed her, but she was alive.

Jacob sprouted wings and swallowed Mary.

There had been a tornado in the now tidy kitchen.

She had decided to end it all, and found she could breathe underwater, like a bloody mermaid, for Christ's sake.

Jacob had rescued her from the lake and burnt her bones with his touch.

Jacob was upset.

She had taken a scalding hot shower and tried to slash her wrists with a cut-throat razor failing miserably to harm herself.

Hadn't she?

Joy put a hand to her hair, it was wet and water pooled around her bare feet. Her bath towel had vanished. Her soaked dress clung to her body and she stank of fishy, earthy mud.

Jake lifted his eyes from the book, raised his coffee mug to her in greeting and said,

Hey, beautiful, you sure put those beers away last night, drink your fresh brew and I'll fry you up some grits. You like the mug I bought you?

'I'm wet and I'm not hungry. We need to talk.' Joy choked on her coffee as a large white towel appeared in Jacob's hand and he said,

OK, let's talk, me first. Have you read Dante?' He waved the slim leather bound volume in front of her face, causing her to draw back.

'I...I... No, I don't think so, he never appealed to me.' Joy's voice matched the trembling in her body as she stared at the towel and said, 'Jacob, I need to get showered and changed first. I'm so cold that my bones hurt.'

Jake shook his head saying, *'Sit there, you can get showered soon, we are talking, remember? Back to Dante, you say you haven't read this work of literary genius, well, me neither, so there's no need to be embarrassed, shame on us both. Are you paying attention, Joy, because this is very fuckin' important?*

Her pride protested, but she arranged her expression into one of interest. Jake continued speaking, caressing the book with a look of reverence on his face.

I got this first edition from Doc, he's read a whole lot of interestin' stuff. He's a studious man. Doc thinks Mary was my anima, my soul carrier, maybe she was, or is, who knows? She surely shaped me though.'

'She did?' Joy fought to speak through chattering teeth as her mind spun in a thousand directions with a single objective: escape. Jake's expression softened and he rested a hand on top of hers. Joy closed her eyes, unable to breathe as bone-melting agony drifted through her flesh. She forced out words between clenched teeth. 'Who are you, Jacob? *What* are you?'

Jake waited until Joy's eyes began to roll back in a faint, then removing his molten touch he said, *'I was telling you about Mary. She shaped me into a man, but now here you are and I'm becoming so much more than I was. Joy, I truly believe that with you by my side I may one day be free, as old Dante said, "pure and prepared to leap up to the stars." By the way, Mary gave notice, she's not coming back so you won't need the envelope.'*

He pretended to swallow his coffee, wiped his lips with the back of his hand and looked at Joy like the cat that got the cream.

She met his eyes and steadying her voice said, 'Jacob, I need a hot shower.'

OK, we can discuss the growth of my soul another time. Off you go, darlin'.

With an unnerving sense of déjà vue she set the shower running on hot and the radio on loud. Steam filled the bathroom and she stripped off her wet clothes. Her insides were trembling and her mind confused, but for no reason she could imagine, she felt more alive than ever.

She stepped under the water and allowed the heat to soothe away the last of her physical discomfort. Her mind filled with images of Jacob: Jacob screwing Mary; Jacob swallowing Mary; Jacob with black wings and Jacob's fiery eyes.

Joy tried to hang onto the horrifying images, but his words played over and over in her head like a bad jingle: *Mary gave notice, she's not coming back.*

She soaped her body, thinking, 'Which means we are alone together. Alone, at last.'

She shampooed her hair as if she hated it, hoping to shake the other images she had in her mental album: Jacob naked; Jacob on top of her; Jacob looking into her eyes as he thrust himself hard inside her. The pictures were free falling, streaming unchecked. She allowed a small laugh to escape as the voice of Tina Arena escaped from the shower's radio crying out into the steam filled room,

'*I'm in chains...*'

Joy rinsed her hair saying, 'Speak for your bloody self, Tina.' Her voice echoed off the tiled bathroom walls. 'I am not in chains,' she reassured herself, closing her eyes against the stream of scalding water.

Jake opened the shower door and stepped in behind her. She reeled around to face him, her breasts pressed against his bare chest in the confines of the steamy cubicle. Almost choking on her words, she said, 'Get out, Jacob, you can't ambush me in here.'

Jake looked into her eyes, smiling slowly as he rested large, calloused hands on her hip bones and kneaded strong fingers into her flesh.

You want me.

'No.'

Don't lie. I heard you thinking of me.

'No.'

Pressing his lips to hers Jake growled into her lying, disgraceful, ungrateful, open mouth,

You will beg me to fuck you.

Joy breathed against his lips not daring to move in case her body called her on the lie as she said, 'I will not.'

He spun her around; her face pressed against the slippery tiles. As the shower cascaded over them, she was blinded by water and steam. His short nails raked their way down her spine. Her stomach muscles clenched and her legs grew heavy as his hardness ground into the small of her back. His thick fingers hovered over her, waiting for permission to enter.

Beg me.

'Never.'

Then I will tell you a story. When I was about seventeen, I discovered a hole in the wall between the laundry store and my foster parents' bedroom. His deep voice played like music in her ears, his teeth grazed her right lobe and, despite her resolve, her body shuddered and pushed against his hands. He waited for her trembling to subside before he continued,

I pressed my eye to the hole and saw the muscled back of a young man, his long hair flowed in black waves down his back, he was tanned, naked and his tight buttocks were moving forward, Jake pressed himself on her, *and backwards.* Jake pulled away.

I could see the soles of a woman's bare feet held, by him, on his shoulders and I could hear her moans of pleasure as he moved deep inside her.

Joy's knees buckled. She stifled a moan as his thick fingers settled between her legs and slipped into her from behind. With his long hard body pinning her helpless against the tiled wall, Jake pushed deep into her wetness, his other hand cupping her right breast as he pulled hard at her erect nipple. She gasped, afraid to move, as he said,

He thrust in and out, and in and out of her, like this. Her legs opened wider, involuntarily allowing him easier access to her body. His fingers moved more swiftly. His thumb caressed her and the second that her disloyal body began to quiver, Jake withdrew his hands. Joy waited, her thighs open, her face pressed against the tiles and whimpered in frustration as he leaned away from her and she heard him say,

Oh, baby, you taste so good. Now, beg me.

Jake began to rock, rigid against her buttocks, his fingers re-entered her and hot relief flooded her body. Jake dropped the story into her ear, his warm breath caressing every syllable,

At first the man's strokes into the woman were slow and even, like this. Joy sobbed as his other hand met above the first, sheathed in her wetness.

I watched the muscles in his back and buttocks tremble. I was erect, transfixed as I saw the sweat run down his back and his thrusts become more urgent.

Jake's fingers explored her more deeply. Waves of pleasure flooded her body and a cry of desperate need escaped her lips.

His voice was rough with desire as he said, *Joy, please for fuck's sake, beg me.*

Shaking and hardly able to breathe, she whispered, 'No, never.'

Beg me, Joy!

'I. Said. Never.'

Her hands moved to cover his, pressing him deeper as orgasm spread like liquid fire in her belly and dropped languidly to her thighs licking like sweet flames at every desperate nerve ending.

Sensing she was close, Jake withdrew his hands and stepped away from her quivering body. Joy slid down the shower wall, moaning. He turned off the water, leaned over her and said,

You say never? I will wait that long and longer for you to come crawling on your knees begging me to fill and satisfy you.

He left.

Joy huddled in the shower tray hugging her knees to her aching breasts as her skin cooled, the desire to hold him inside her so strong it caused physical pain. Goosebumps pricked her skin as the temperature in the bathroom plummeted. Standing on shaky legs, she turned on the hot water and cried out her crushing shame under its onslaught, beating at the tiles until her knuckles were bruised, her head pounded and her throat was as sore as her pride.

Susie sighed as she adjusted a lock of shining auburn hair across her ruined face and rapped hard on the other side of the mirror startling Joy out of her misery.

A word appeared in the condensation. The letters made no sense until Joy realised they were written in reverse. It said:

RUN

Chapter Thirty-One

-ALL ROADS LEAD TO HEAVENSGATE-

The following morning, after a night spent fighting the sheets behind a locked and barricaded door, Joy found Jacob skimming stones across the lake. Turning his best one hundred megawatt smile on, he wiped sandy hands on jean sheathed thighs and said,

Hello, sweetness, have you come to ask me for something?

'No, you egotistical, sadistic bastard, I bloody well have not. I'm here to tell you I'm leaving.'

I want to leave Heavensgate too, Joy, but without your help I never will.

He launched another pebble sending it bouncing over the water as he counted and said, *Did you see that? It was a niner. I'm getting better at this.*

He offered her a stone. Joy slapped his hand away and between gritted teeth, said, 'I'm going into town to find a way to book my ticket out of here. I don't know why I'm even bothering to let you know.'

His slow, sexy smile infuriated her as he drawled, *Oh, yes you do know why, Joy, you know very well why you bother with me.*

He threw her the truck keys. *Here you go; be nice to Jolene. And good luck getting that golden ticket outta here.*

'Who's Jolene?'

My pick-up truck, she's my special lady so treat her nice.

'I'd rather call Mom's taxi.'

Now, darlin', that's not a good idea and anyhow the 'phone is kaput.

He stood too close, smirking. Joy blushed under his amused gaze then, remembering that she was supposed to be leaving, she walked away saying, 'Don't wait up, tosser.'

See you soon, Honeybunch.

'Stop calling me stupid names.'

OK. I will call you Goddess, Angel, Queen of Joy, light of the heavens, great bringer of happiness.

'Bloody well fuck off.'

Now, now, that's my line, Babycakes. Jake settled his long frame down on the beach and, leaning back to rest on his elbows, stared out over the still water. Joy stormed off to the truck. He called after her, *You **will** love me, Joy.*

As she turned the key in Jolene's ignition, Joy smacked a clenched fist onto her thigh and muttered, 'I think I already do, you bloody, arrogant fool.' She stared at her astonished face in the truck's rear view mirror and saw Susie who shook her head before disappearing like perfume on the wind.

Chapter Thirty-Two

-DINA'S DINER-

Despite Joy's zealous checking of Jolene's rear and wing mirrors and an occasional glance into the rear seats, the journey into town was uneventful, the weather glorious and the music on the truck's old radio appropriate as the 1960's band, The Animals exclaimed,

'*We gotta get out of this place...*'

She broke the speed limit and channel surfed as Jolene bounced her cherry-red way down the highway. It appeared that, either the tuner was broken or, every station was playing The Boss, who insisted on informing Joy that he was 'on fire'.

Joy punched the steering wheel in frustration, missing the horn and setting the wipers swiping dust across the windshield and spreading decimated sticky insect bodies across the glass. She shouted out of the truck's open window, 'Lord and the Angels of Heaven, sweet Jesus, Holy Mother of God are you listening? Please help me escape this bloody hell-hole.'

''Tween you and me, girl, I wouldn't be so sure that God or His Holy sidekicks have anythin' to do with this place,' drawled Jim from the passenger seat.

'Shit!' The truck drifted and bounced along the grass verge until Jim pulled the wheel toward him and Jolene obediently straightened her course.

'Now listen up, Miss, your job is to drive. My job is to sit and admire the scenery. How in the name of damnation am I gonna be able to do my job with you drivin' all erratic?'

'Christ, Jim, you scared the proverbial crap out of me. How did you get in here?'

'I have absolutely no idea, girl, and it annoys the livin' hell outta me.'

Joy threw him an angry glance.

'OK. Don't you be goin' and givin' me the evil eye. If it makes you feel more at ease I *could* say I was restin' on sweet Jolene's rear seat, sleepin' off a few beers. Crazy drivin' and bad taste in music woke me up so I climbed on over to sit beside you. So calm that beatin' heart. Now, where are we headed to, exactly?'

Joy narrowed her eyes and asked,

'You were in the backseat?'

'Yup.'

'All this time?'

'Sure.'

'Asleep?'

'Yup.'

'Why?'

'Well, I reckon it might annoy the hell outta Jacob when he finds out I bin snugglin' up to ole Jolene's cream upholstery.'

'That's a good enough reason for me, Jim. Welcome to my hell.'

'Don't take it personal. Please, confide in a confused and lonely man, where *are* we headed?

'Into town, to purchase my airplane ticket home.'

'How interestin'. As a concept, that is. Where's home?'

'No idea.'

Right, and what time d'ya reckon we're gonna get to the magical travel agency for a ticket to No Idea?'

'Why the sarcasm?'

'Well, it's mighty late already and the stores are all closed.'

'Don't joke, Jim. I'm deadly serious about getting out of Heavensgate and away from that madman.'

'OK, you seen the light, noted, and please accept my congratulations. However, the sun is settin', put the sidelights on, Joy.'

'It can't be setting, I left the Lodge just a few minutes ago. It's still morning.'

'Uhuh?'

'Uhuh? Jim stop messing with me. Where's the stick for the lights? A storm must be headed our way. Where's all the traffic? Do you get tornadoes in these parts?'

Jim crossed his arms and said, 'The traffic is travellin' on the other side of the highway 'cause, like I said, the sun is settin', the stores are all closed and the townsfolk are headed home for the night. And, yes, we get all sorts of unpleasant weather in these here parts, usually all in the damn same half hour.'

'I hate this place.' Joy twisted the steering wheel too hard causing the truck to careen across both lanes, much to the fear and fury of oncoming drivers.

'Look out 'fore that hot head causes an accident. Slow yer pace. Look, Dina's Diner is a hundred yards ahead, pull in and let's get us a coffee and a chat.'

Joy pulled off the highway too fast, banging her foot repeatedly on the brake pedal and sending clouds of dust and stones flying from under Jolene's wheels. The truck screeched to a halt hard enough to send Jim shooting through the windshield. He didn't even shake in his seat.

'Glory hallelujah. We lived. Good girl, well done and thank you kindly, ma'am. I'm talkin' to Jolene not you, Joy, yer one crazy piece of work.'

Feeling much better Joy smiled and said, 'Get out of the truck, old man.'

The diner was packed to the rafters with locals. The only available booth waited at the end of a long, well observed walk to the back corner. By the time they had reached their seats Joy was shivering as if many eyes had stripped her bare. She sat with her back pressed to the wall and Jim slid in opposite her. He took off his battered Stetson and placed it lovingly on the seat beside him revealing gray wispy hair that reminded Joy of dirty candy floss.

'Now, girl, sit up and pay attention to ole Jim. D'ya see the woman over there, Dina? Her name's in lights above the door.'

'Which one is she?'

'She's the sorry excuse for a woman with butt cheeks so broad there's probably a litter of dead kittens and a couch trapped in there.'

Joy laughed and said, 'Shame on you, Jim. I can't see anyone with such an extravagantly large backside.'

'You will. Be wary around her, Joy, she's a sort.'

'What type of sort?'

'The type of sort who'll cheerfully kill you stone dead with a look and no conscience. Be careful, she wants Jake.'

'You mean Jacob? She can bloody well have him. I'll gift wrap him for her.' Jim smiled and patted her hand saying,

'I'll introduce you to the kitten squasher as my English niece.'

'Why don't we just go somewhere else?'

'Because I don't need to ride with y'all in this mood and because you need to see what nice folks are up against in this here one horse town.'

Joy played with the laminated menu and said, 'You know, Jim, I think I once worked in a place a little like this. I want to go home, I want it more than ever, but I have a major problem.'

'You still can't leave?'

'I can't. I mean, look at this place, it's dark outside and it's bloody snowing. Half an hour ago it was a sunny morning. Worse than the time and weather changes, I can't remember where my home is.' Joy's eyes grew huge, her eyebrows shot under her fringe and she gasped, 'Oh my giddy aunt.'

'Ah,' Jim shook his head as if to remove the image burned on the back of his retinas, 'here's Dina. I done told you her butt has its own zip code.'

'That's unkind,' she admonished Jim. However, when Dina bent to wipe a table four booths away, Joy could not tear her eyes away from the tremendous rear view.

Jim replied, 'Dina's not kind either. When she smiles I expect the skin to peel back off her face and poison fangs to dart outta her mouth spittin' venom. I'm certain sure she sucked up her last victim whole. You can see him squirmin' in her butt.'

'Jim, you're making me feel sick.'

'Good. Look at the poor sap, trapped and decomposin' in her stinkin' bowels. When she's had enough pleasure from his demise she'll shit him out. I plan to be up wind that day.' Jim put a finger in his throat and made a retching noise.

Joy screwed up her face and said, 'You're being disgusting, stoppit.'

'I ain't kiddin'. When she walks you can see his rottin' corpse jerkin' about in there. It's a stinkin' battle ground under that skirt.'

Dina looked up and straight at Joy, her lips set in a tight narrow line. Jim said, 'When that monster gets close, be careful.' Joy grabbed his hand and stared him into silence as Dina arrived at their booth.

Her face reminded Joy of sour dough left out to rise in the sun. Dina stared at them with expressionless pale blue eyes; her sagging jowls framed by bleached blonde frizz like an ancient Shirley Temple. A yellow tongue darted between her mean lips. She spat on a pencil stub and, in a sweet, girlish voice, said, 'Black coffee and pecan pie, Jim?'

'Yes, ma'am, every time.'

'And you?' Dina looked Joy up and down, 'Will you be wantin' a skinny latte and sugar-free carrot cake, my Lady?' Her tongue flicked in and out like forked lightning. Joy replied, 'That would be lovely. However, if it's not asking too much I would prefer it without the side dish of spite.'

'That *would be lovely*? It sure would be. Y'all hear her Highness? It *would be lovely*,' Dina mocked Joy's British accent. The diner's other customers dropped their eyes to stare at their food and drink.

'*Spite?* I see yer Ladyship cain't appreciate *backwood* talk. I'll fetch yer pie, no cream; help you lose those extra royal pounds.'

Joy was half way out of her seat, eyes blazing as she said, 'How bloody ru…' when Jim interrupted saying, 'Dina, stop teasin'; send out yer finest coffee and pecan for my *niece* and try t'remember she's a guest in yer fine *backwood* establishment.

'Oh, Jim, I'm sooo sorry; pleased to meet you, your Highness.' Dina dipped a mock curtsey, her hips bashing against tables on both sides of the aisle and called out, 'Lookee here, folks, ole Jim is related to royalty. What's yer name, Princess?'

Joy leant her chin on her thumbs and steepling her fingers said, 'Don't you have a job to do? You know, like filling orders, wiping tables or squashing kittens?' She fixed Dina with a stare powerful enough to wilt grown men while the seconds ticked by in shocked silence. Dina finally broke eye contact and replied,

'I sure do, Princess. I sure as hell do, we need more pussies for the pies.' She cackled, showing a startling set of pointed teeth and turned, pressing the gargantuan force of her right buttock against Joy's cheek, who, repulsed, shot along the bench seat and pressed herself up against the window to stare at the blizzard obscuring the highway. Jim was right, there was definitely something struggling in Dina's bowels.

Jim shook his head and said, 'Keep away from her. She lives in the woods where she sucks all the happiness outta the place and builds walls of despair. The bitch is greedy; she cain't never be satisfied. Watch yerself with that stinkin' nightmare, Joy. It might be best to cool yer smart mouth around her.'

'I am bloody well sick and tired of people telling me what I can and cannot do. I have had just about as much as I...'

Joy paused as a skinny sour faced man approached with two plates of pie balanced on one arm and carrying a scalding jug of coffee in an alcoholic's shaking hand. 'Shit,' said Jim. He put his Stetson on and slid down in his seat. 'Here comes the sister.'

'Brother.'

'No, girl, that's Lynn, the cook at this here fine eatin' establishment. Anyhow, no man with a flowery pink shirt and such extravagant eyebrows would survive more than five seconds in this town.'

'She looks...'

'Mean?' Jim offered in a low voice. 'Yup. A nasty, mean old prune is what she looks like and that is what she is. Lynn smiles in yer face while considerin' how to suck the joy out of yer life and the life out of yer joy. Pun intended.'

A plate clattered onto the table.

'Here's yer pie, fuck face,' Lynn's black eyes were empty.

'Why thank you kindly, ma'am.'

'And here's yours, Princess.' A second plate landed in front of Joy who glared as sludge textured coffee was slopped into their mugs. In a voice like chalk on a backboard Lynn said, 'Know what, yer Highness? I like the look of you. I truly do. Why don't you bring that hunk of a man, Jake, over to ours for dinner this Saturday night?'

Joy tasted her coffee and shuddered before replying, 'Jacob? Thank you kindly, but I don't go anywhere with him.'

'Then come alone. I'm certain we can entertain you, even though we never had British royalty visit before.'

'I'm polishing my crown.'

'Shame 'bout that, Majesty.' Lynn smiled, revealing tobacco stained teeth the exact colour match for her skin which was tanned like a piece of wrinkled cowhide.

Jim wafted his hands in a shooing motion saying, 'Piss off, Lynn. Allow us to eat this perfect pecan pie in peace, won't you?'

'Fine, you old fuck.' She sniffed and walked away. Joy observed that Lynn's butt was as skinny as her sister's was broad.

She pushed her pie away untouched and said, 'I hate this diner.'

'Good, now you won't come in by mistake and if you see those evil ole witches you know what to do.'

'Run?'

'Good girl. Hey, lookee here, the snow has stopped. Let's get out of this shit hole; I think I'm overdue a conversation with Jacob while you make yerself scarce and unwind with a stroll on the beach. You could maybe walk the mutt round the lake? Joy, are you listenin'?'

'The beach, Jim, I remember, I lived at the seaside.'

'Well that's just dandy, Joy. Where was that?'

'I have not a bloody clue, but I'm determined to remember and make my way home.'

Jim threw a ten dollar bill on the table and they left, ignoring Lynn who shouted, 'See ya soon, Princess. Adios, fuck face.' And Dina, who called after them, 'Yeah. See ya soon, my poor royal lamb.'

Chapter Thirty-Three

-A NOSY OLD FUCK-

While Joy took Jim's advice and walked with Skylar around the moonlit lake, Jake sat crossed legged on the floor of his tower with Jacob's Forbidden Book open and melded to his thighs like a lover. In his hand he held a red wax crayon and in his mouth he chewed on the ends of three others. Shaping letters with great care, he wrote:

I'm gonna tattoo my love on that bitch with my body.

I'll hate myself and I'll hate her more for allowing it.

I'm gonna make her feel my name in every cell of her body and lose her soul in my arms.

I'll worship her and she'll revel in my praise before she begs me to cast her away.

When Joy is lost in me and I am lost in her I will grind my foot into her spirit.

I will kill her bit by little bloody bit and make a gift of her soiled heart to Hope with my name written across it in scars.

What an exhilarating ride it will be, Joy, my love.

I cannot fuckin' wait.

The iron-studded door creaked open to reveal Jim holding his hat in his hands, his hair sticking up in a cloud and a frown on his wizened old face.

Jake spat out the crayons and exclaimed, *Jim how d'ya creep up on me like that, man?*

'It's easy when a person is as self-absorbed as you are, Jake. Whatcha writin' in Jacob's book?'

Jim wandered over to sneak a look at the multi-coloured, childish scrawl. Jake snapped the pages closed and growled,

*This is **my** book, Jim. Heavensgate and every damn thing in it belong to me. Jacob, that pathetic jerk-off crossed the Gate with his momma and poppa.*

'Yup. I done heard about that, Jake. Dontcha miss sweet Jacky boy and good ole Jacob?'

I miss 'em like I'd miss a nun in a brothel. Why d'ya ask, nosey old fuck?

'Why's everybody callin' me an old fuck today? It hurts.' Jim grimaced as he placed a hand over his heart.

Jake laughed. *Cut it out, old man, you ain't got no heart, and I haven't forgotten what you did to me in the truck or the day you blew your brains out in the woods.*

'That was just a game, Jake. You do know yer dead, dontcha?'

No, Jim, this isn't what I'd call being dead. You, on the other hand, are just a figment left over from Jacob's overactive imagination. I know the difference. For example, my sweet Susie is dead. I, on the other hand, am very much alive. Ask Joy how lively I was in the shower this morning.

'And what about the others, Jake?'

What fuckin' others?

US.

Jake leapt to his feet, sending wax crayons and the Book flying across the room, where the latter waited as its chains slid across the floor to cling to it with a wet sucking sound.

He bellowed like a wounded bull. *Fuck off before I come in there and finish you.*

'Sounds to me like they miss you, son.'

Jake began to spin like a top, his lips stretched back from his gums and he screamed, *Get outta my head. Follow Jacob. I don't need you. Get the fuck out.*

As Jake twisted and twirled in panic Jim watched, his wrinkled face impassive, and silently prayed for Jake to explode or implode or just vanish never to return to Heavensgate. He had no such luck so he shouted, 'Doc, are you in there? I need a word.'

Jake stopped whirling and quickly found his balance. His face relaxed and his features softened. He looked around the tower, brushed a hand across his hair, straightened his clothes and exhaled loudly.

His broad shoulders became stooped and rounded as if he had spent years hunched over a desk.

Jake cricked his neck and spoke in a soft cultured voice.

'Good evening, Jim.'

'Good evenin', Doc. It's mighty good to see you, son. How the hell are you doin'?'

Doc's voice was slow and steady. 'Not so good. Since Jacob left I've felt rather redundant. I tried to help Joy, but I'm afraid I failed.

Doc pressed his fingers to his temples and panic stained his glassy eyes as he said, 'I haven't got long, Jim. The others are holding Jake prisoner in the dream tower, but they are weak and he is strong, far stronger than he was before Jacob passed over.'

'Jim, you have to help Joy get away from him. Read the Forbidden Book, he's going to murder her.'

A shadow passed across Doc's weary face and was immediately replaced by Jake's wicked grin.

You almost had me there, fuck face.

Chapter Thirty-Four

-SUSIE-

Jake was rattled. Jim had summoned Doc, and the Others, those weak-willed insignificant nothings, had tried to lock him away. He was mighty pissed off. He tried to force his muscles to relax in a bath of boiling water while he waited for Joy to return, ready to appear sympathetic when she explained how, no matter what she did, she couldn't leave. Closing his eyes he imagined all the ways he could deceive and bind her to him once and for all, preferably branded, bleeding and in despair.

He stirred and opened one eye as water splashed his face. Susie, his deceased first wife, sat on the edge of the tub in full evening dress, her thick auburn hair piled carelessly on top of her head, a few stray tendrils framing half her lovely face. The other, wrecked half, was almost hidden by a long fringe that stuck untidily to the space where her eye used to be and clung to the gaping hole where, years ago on the mountain, her beauty was crushed into oblivion. Susie glided an elegant, manicured hand through the steaming water, grazing Jake's inner thigh with long red nails.

Hello, baby. He looked up at her, his smile genuine and warm. *I've missed you.*

'Never mind the soppy stuff, lover. Tell me straight, what the hell do you think you're doing with Joy?' Susie slid her hand higher, cupping his balls while fixing him with her one remaining eye.

I ain't doing any damn thing with her, Susie. I spend my time dreamin' of you, babe.

He reached out to touch her, but instead of her curves his hands found empty air. Frowning, he said, *Now, Susie, play nice. Put your body in this cleansin' water and sit down on what's waiting for you.*

Susie released him and said, 'Not 'til you tell me the truth. Let's face it, honey, your escapade with Hope bombed disastrously and now you are finger diddling her sister with a view to screwing her rigid in the very near future.'

Oh, baby, don't be jealous. You know I only ever loved you, but you went away. You entered the Gate, sweet cheeks, leaving me all alone. That's OK, it's in the past, forgotten. You're here now, so get in and straddle this.'

Susie gazed at Jake's manhood held slick and soapy in his hand and biting her bottom lip said, 'I want you to stop messing with her. Leave her alone. The Mortal Realm needs Joy more than you do, Jake.'

I'm just having fun, Susie. Why do you care? Face it, honey, if you don't want filling with this fuck machine, you're most definitely stone, cold, dead.

'If I'm as dead as you say, and Jacob entered the Gate, what does that make you, Jake?'

Horny as hell. Come on, baby, you gotta finish what you started.

'You sure you're not dead too, Jake?'

You sayin' you need more proof than this, Susie?

Jake pulled her on top of him, water splashed over the tub as he pushed her red spangled dress up to her waist while he avoided looking at her ruined face.

Susie settled astride his thighs, placed stiletto heeled feet under his buttocks and began to rock slowly back and forth as, locking her one eye with his two, she said, 'You have everything you need, Jake, right here with me. I'm in the mirrors. You can have me anytime you call.'

He placed his hands on her slim waist to slide her up and down the length of him. His voice rough, he said, *Shush, honey, I'm concentrating here.*

Susie freed her breasts and leaned forward, moving from side to side as he took one then the other in his mouth, grazing her nipples with his teeth, sucking and pulling. Jake gasped as he felt the responsive tug of her desire. Her body clenched tight around him and he bucked his hips to meet her climax.

Jake stroked her fringe away to reveal the devastation wreaked by the accident on their wedding day. He swallowed scalding tears saying, *Susie, this is most probably our afterlife, so, if you try, I'm certain you can fix your beautiful face and change out of that evening get up too.*

She climbed out of the bath, smoothing her dress to cover long slim legs and said, 'I don't have the energy to change at Heavensgate. I need all my strength to escape the mirrors. I want you to stop playing with fire. I'm allowed here to tell you that you must leave Joy alone. Jake, please, my love, my husband, do the right thing. Remember who you once were. Repent and enter the Gateway with me.'

Jake stood, steam pouring in clouds off his wet body. He flexed broad shoulders to spread his jet black wings wide and whined, *Honey, I can't do that. If I cross the Gate, Jacob will swallow me and the 'others' like crumbs.*

'You have to set Joy free, Jake, your soul is already in peril.'

I have no soul, Jacob took it. Joy's free and able to go any time she chooses, but she can't bear to leave me. Just like you.

'Jake, be honest with me; do you plan on hurting her?'

Oh come on, babe. The only woman I ever hurt was you and you know how sorry I am. Change the record. D'ya fancy another ride, Susie?

She sighed and lifted her ruined gaze to his as he pressed her against the wall where, placing his hands under her buttocks and his mouth on her breast, he speared the sheath of her cold body. Susie shuddered in his arms.

Jake cried, *No!*

Heavensgate: Joy

He was pressed up against the bathroom wall, alone, watching Susie's retreating reflection as she left through the bathroom mirror. He sank to the cold tiled floor and sobbed like a man recently bereaved.

Chapter Thirty-Five

-SCARRED-

Joy left Jim smoking a cheroot as he strolled by the lakeside. Fur Face met her on the boat deck, barking in warning as she drew closer to the kitchen door.

'What's wrong, boy?'

The dog tipped his head to one side, listening, and barked again.

'Don't fuss, Skylar, I can't be doing with even a teeny-weenie jot more of fuss today.' Joy stroked his soft head and left him slunk down on the deck, his pink and black wet nose slumped between his front paws. He whined softly as she entered the Lodge.

Jake was waiting at the kitchen table; his eyes rimmed red and his skin flushed. He wore a towel around his waist. Joy ran to him and said, 'Jacob, are you crying?'

No. I'm allergic to dogs and that sneeze makin', eye waterin' mutt has been skulkin' around out there all day.

'I see. So how come as Skylar is outside, and you are inside with the door and windows closed against the threat of even the tiniest bit of dog hair, your eyes are all watery and red?'

Maybe I got soap in them. He chuckled as if enjoying a private joke. *Come sit by me, Joy. I have something interesting to tell you.*

Joy put her hands in the air and shook her head saying, 'I'm not falling for any more of your tricks. I prefer to stand.'

OK, stay where you are. But will you listen to what I have to say?

'I have no choice since I'm stuck here. So, I will listen and after you've finished trying to con me again I want you out. Take this as your dismissal.'

No, please, Joy, you can't do that.

Joy wagged a finger, her voice brittle with unshed angry tears as she said, 'Just watch me, Jacob.'

I can't leave you and you can't leave me, Joy; we are bound together in Heavensgate for better or for worse.

'What utter crap. We are not in any way shape or bloody form bound together. You are nothing to me. You are the odd-job man and you are dismissed. This lodge is not your bloody property and neither am I.'

Jake hung his head and cracked his knuckles as he replied, *Heavensgate isn't anyone's property, not even yours, Joy, ownership is an illusion.*

'Get dressed and get out, Jacob. I'm sick of this weird place and, whatever you say or do, as soon as I can get to town, I'm leaving.'

You can't leave me, Joy, because God sent you here to save me.

'God sent me? Good Lord, Jacob I must sit down if I have to listen to the whims of a crazy man's God.'

His voice flat and dead, he whispered, *I am not like other men.*

Joy snorted and began to rise out of the chair; Jake reached out to stop her, crying, *No, don't go. Please stay and listen. Joy, I am different. I'm not whole. I'm damaged goods and I need saving before I self-destruct.*

He pointed to his cheek and said, *Look at me, Joy.*

She drew her eyes to his face and said, 'So what? You told me you got that scar in a fight, Jacob.'

Joy, will you please look at me, I mean, really look at me?

Jake held out his arms displaying the damage he had wreaked on his perfection. Joy stared open mouthed at the numerous lines of raised scar tissue that criss-crossed his beautiful skin.

The fragment of humanity left in him, the part that truly loved her, wept openly as the demon croaked, *Joy, look at my chest.*

Transfixed by the horror of old and fresh wounds tracking his torso, Joy let out a strangled so and, finding herself in front of him with no memory of crossing the room, she rested her cool palms on his burning chest, and said, 'Oh sweet heaven, Jacob, how did I not see those before?'

Fixing her with an intense tear stained stare Jake stood and the towel fell to the floor. His strong thighs were scarred with intersections of white lines some raised side by side, others crossed over with new cuts, many still raw and bleeding.

He stood before her, bleeding from his wounds like Christ on the cross and cried, *Joy, do not forsake me.*

She picked up the abandoned towel and felt her answering tears course down her cheeks as she said, 'Oh my God, Jacob, what have you done?'

Covering his nakedness she guided him to a chair like an invalid and sat beside him. His chest heaved as he sobbed great gut wrenching, breath choking tears. Joy opened her arms and he fell into her embrace like a wounded child returned to his mother.

Joy's voice cracked as she held him tight and spoke softly in his ear, 'Sssh, Jacob, I'm here, it's OK.'

Please don't leave me. I need you. I need you to love me; I can't go on like this.

'Hush.' Joy's tears fell like soothing balm onto his head as she rocked him back and forth stroking the soft hair at the nape of his neck. When his sobs subsided, she cradled his face in her hands planting soft kisses on his wet face then, taking a deep breath like a diver preparing to launch into the deep, she said, 'I won't leave you, Jacob. Whatever happens I won't leave you alone. We can work through this, whatever this is, together. I promise.' He raised his head from her breast and stood. The towel fell away for a second time. Then he walked out of the kitchen and, admiring the angel's wings tattooed on his broad back, Joy followed him.

Heavensgate: Joy

She followed him all the way to death, she just didn't know it.

Next morning Joy rolled away from her lover feeling languid, satisfied, and for the first time in her life, joyful. Jake lifted the sheet admiring her perfect skin and ran a calloused hand over her naked buttocks.
I could brand her, he thought.
Joy's breathing slowed and she drifted back to sleep.
Jake slipped out of the warm musky scented nest and, dressing in the bathroom so as not to disturb her, he sang *Que Sera Sera* under his breath. Tiptoeing to the kitchen, he poured himself a mug of coffee and carried the drink outside where, realising he couldn't actually drink it, he poured it onto the ground. Happy and singing Jake boogied along the deck, kicking the sleeping dog hard in the ribs as he passed him by.
The demon danced all the way into his workshop where he began to forge the necessary tool.

In her dream, Joy stood in a summer field, enjoying the warmth of the sun on her skin. The childhood scent of Parma violet candy drifted like memory on the warm breeze. She breathed deeply, shook out her shoulders, rolled her neck and paused mid-stretch when she heard a child's sweet voice singing the old Doris day tune, *'Que Sera...'*

She ambled across the pasture searching for the singer, parting the tall grass, enjoying the rustling noise as it closed behind her to conceal her path. When her limbs became heavy, she yawned and looked around for shade. An insect stung the back of her knee making her squeal and the day grew too humid for pleasure.

In the vast expanse of grassland, searing light abraded her pale skin raising bumps that itched and burnt. Sick of the heat, she spotted a solitary giant oak tree that sheltered a girl in the coolness beneath its glorious branches. It was the singer. Re-energised, Joy pelted through the undulating sea of grass, eager to be with the child.

Feeling that she was getting no closer wiped the beads of sweat that glistened like dew on her fevered skin and paused to look to the horizon. The oak and the singer had vanished. Fighting the panic that pursued her frantic passage across the scorching summer meadow Joy ran on, trampling wild flowers and releasing their heady perfume in her wake.

Exhausted, sun burnt and afraid she stumbled, twisting an ankle. Flapping her arms as she struggled to get back on her feet, she squinted and let her gaze drift over the meadow. To the far horizon blades of grass, tall and sweet, waved like dreamy dancers in a light breeze. The stalks behind her were serene and whole as if no-one had blasted a trail through them.

Sweat sneaked along her brow to drip into her eyes, salt stinging and blurring her vision as her dry tongue seemed to swell in her mouth and her throat tightened with an unbearable thirst. The sun beat relentlessly down on her uncovered head making her feel sick and dizzy, but having no other choice, she continued through the swaying green skirts until she stumbled into a clearing and almost tripped over the girl sitting amongst buttercups and tiny violets.

The child wore her long hair loose. It streamed down her back as fine as the lace on a bridal veil. Her shimmering lilac smock dress was embroidered with scarlet hearts. Her feet were bare, her toenails glittered pink. At her side a crystal decanter brimming with a lilac liquid waited beside an intricately carved goblet on a silver tray.

Joy ground the heels of palms into her eyes as the ground spun under her feet. When the world steadied, she risked lowering her hands and saw that the cruel sun had set. Three moons now hung in an oppressive green night sky overwhelmed by rivers of starlight.

The girl's tiny fingers weaved a long chain of violets and buttercups. Fighting the urge to steal a drink from the decanter, Joy crossed her arms over her chest and looked down at the child. The girl spread her flower chain on the ground, adjusted it into a heart shape and stepped into the middle of it.

A sweet voice chimed like a dozen small bells in Joy's head.

'Hello, Joy, do you want a drink?'

Heavensgate: Joy

Joy swallowed a hard dry lump in her throat and said, 'How do you know my name?'

The girl smiled and, in the universal gesture of secrets, tapped the side of her nose. Then she poured the lilac nectar into a goblet until it overflowed, soaking the ground. Joy snatched the drink and swallowed its sweet salvation in one long gulp. The child glanced up at Joy from under frosted silver lashes, and ignoring her visitor's rudeness, asked,

'Do you like my heart? The violets are for me. The buttercups are for you.'

Bemused, Joy nodded and bent to take a closer look.

The girl held out a fragile length of her handiwork saying, 'Do you like the piercings? See how I forced the flowers to join, they are linked in an eternal circle. Shackled.' She patted the grass at her side, her gray eyes demanding that Joy join her.

Hot and dizzy, Joy sat down, cleared her throat and said,

'Where's your momma?'

'I like you, Joy, so *I* will ask *you* a question. Do you know what would happen if I lost my heart, or a part of my heart?'

Joy shook her head, her legs felt heavy and numb, the sting itched and the salty tang of sea air rushed like hoarfrost into her lungs making her gasp. The girl stroked Joy's hand and discomfort fled her body to be replaced with a sense of anticipation of something wonderful and new.

Shards of ice seemed to move in the depth of the child's strange eyes as she said, 'If anything happened to *my* heart things wouldn't be the same, oh no, definitely not the same. *Everything* would change for *everyone*.'

Hearing menace in the chiming voice Joy's brain instructed her legs to stand and her feet to run, but they refused to obey. The girl offered her a red silk pillow embroidered with golden cherubs. Unable to refuse an unspoken command Joy placed it under her head and lay down, her eyelids grew heavy as the distant sound of pealing bells carried her to another place and time.

Freezing spray hit her face and Joy opened her eyes on a wintry beach under a leaden sky. A few feet across the cold wet sand a small girl stood screaming into huge, thundering waves that crashed and broke over her feet. Joy tried to open her mouth to shout a warning. The sea was going to snatch the careless child, she had to save her, but she was trapped in paralysis as strong as death.

The meadow child's voice pierced her terror saying, 'You must remember. You know you did a bad thing.'

Locked inside the vision Joy was forced to watch the heartbroken little girl run into the merciless sea where she was consumed by the raging foam.

The chiming voice was angry, 'Oh yes, you did a very bad thing indeed, Joy. Look what you did. See how you tried to kill your precious heart.'

Joy strained against invisible restraints until her teeth chattered in her head and every muscle trembled and twitched, but she couldn't move to save the drowning child.

'You are a bad, bad girl. You tried to murder your precious heart in the cold sea.'

Back in the meadow Joy's head thrashed from side to side, flecking the flower heart with spittle while her heels drummed on the ground.

On the beach, her captive spirit stood helpless as she relived her own death by drowning.

The voice rang louder. 'Joy, you were wicked, but you were lucky. Your heart is here,' the girl in the lilac frock pressed a small hand against her chest, 'safely nestled with mine. I have protected it for all these long years and you repay my devotion by trying to give this priceless treasure away to that demon.' Discordant bells jangled in temper, 'Wake up and look at me, Joy.'

Beating out of sync, Joy's heart trembled under her ribs. An agonising pounding hammered behind her eyes as something boomed across the meadow like cannon-fire. She heard a panicked shout, 'That abominable noise is the Nothing. Come back to me.' 'Wake up!'

Heavensgate: Joy

Reluctantly, leaving the beach Joy dragged her eye's open under the green sky. In place of the girl, a silver haired woman stared down at her with the same icy, ancient expression.

Next to her, the tall mirror of Joy's childhood shimmered into reality.

The stranger helped Joy to her feet, saying, 'Look in the mirror. Who do you see?'

Afraid, but compelled to look in its silver depths Joy gasped and asked, 'Is that me? Was that me?'

The mirror revealed her eight year old self curled up on the cellar floor, small hands pressed over her ears as she sang '*My Favourite Things*' to drive out the sound of fury beating down through the floorboards overhead.

The vision changed and Joy saw her innocent face taut with the effort of holding back tears. She winced as she watched her mother scour her only child's skin with a scrubbing brush until it was red raw. Spots of blood flecked Glenda's clothes like polka-dots bearing testimony to how hard she worked to graze her daughter clean of sin.

The mirror clouded momentarily then cleared to show Joy on her mother's lap being stroked and cosseted. Her terror filled underwear clung, stinking and wet soaking into the pretty flowered material of her mother's best dress.

Joy's reality trembled as memory twitched the curtain between present and past. The scene changed and Joy pressed a shaking hand to her head mirroring her childhood refection who touched patches of sore, pink scalp where clumps of her beautiful hair had been ripped away.

Eight year old Joy stretched out her arms pleading, 'Please mirror, let me in, please.'

Covering her face with her hands Joy reeled away from the past; she felt sick, shivers wracked her body and grief gripped her throat. Her childhood reflection thumped at the glass until her knuckles bled then the mirror disappeared leaving a disturbance of fear and sorrow on the air.

Bells tolled a funeral dirge in her head as the woman said, 'That was your personal hell. The hell *I* saved you from. You are ungrateful.'

Joy spread her arms in supplication pleading, 'No, I promise I am not ungrateful, I am simply lost, please help me find my way home.'

'How can I help when you are determined to create hell in Heavensgate while you enact this abhorrent, sick relationship with the demon you call Jacob?' The stranger spat out his name as if it offended her tongue.

Unexpected anger flooded Joy's soul and she shouted, 'Don't call him a demon, he is just a man.' The woman pushed Joy hard, making her stumble and fall. The sickly green sky loomed closer as the woman leaned over her and said, 'Stay down and listen. There are many dangerous creatures at Heavensgate, but your *Jacob* is the most dangerous of all. He frightens me. He should frighten you, too. If you want to survive that place, you must cheat the Beast in order to cheat death. You must make a pact with the demon and you must break it.'

Joy struggled to her knees and cried, 'I can't betray him. I love him.'

The woman pushed her again, sending her sprawling and cursing. With her silver hair billowing on an invisible wind, her feet left the ground until she hung over Joy and, raining down her fury with a noise like hailstones hitting a tin roof, said,

'No, you do not love him. You *cannot* love him. You have been alone too long. You are infected by the falsehoods he shows you. Your body's mortal hungers have led you astray. *Jacob* is a manifestation of evil, he is made demon by the Beast. He is Lucifer's imp and his presence in Heavensgate is an infestation of sin.' Slivers of ice flew from Hope's words piercing Joy's heart like a thousand wasps.

Her hand clutched at her throat as she fought for breath and whispered, 'What the bloody hell *are* you?'

The woman's icy eyes bore into Joy's soul, turning her guts to water, before she spat out, 'I hate that you forget me when I suffer so for you.'

'I am sorry, but I don't understand what's happening. Please, can you help me escape Heavensgate?'

'I cannot interfere further in your ridiculous life without facing terrible consequences. I have risked the hope of the world for you and you repay me with fresh scars on your heart.'

The furious stranger reached into her gown and pulled out a paper heart hung from a silver ribbon. She caressed the glitter strewn pink and green feathers that framed one childishly shaped word: 'Joy.'

Dangling it before Joy's stricken face she said, 'Do you know what this is? Do you remember me now? I am your sister, Hope. I hold your poor, damaged heart in my hands.'

Joy reached for her heart, but wasn't quick enough to snatch it away. Hope's coral pink lips grew huge, blocking out the sky and filling Joy's vision, then her mouth opened to reveal clarion bells that rang out in deafening discord saying,

'You sacrificed your heart and you shall *not* have it back. Make a pact with the demon, Joy. Make a lovers' pact to the death. Do your duty, sister, and remember who you are or die, forever. Now go.'

The world tilted swallowing Joy's consciousness and regurgitating her, spluttering and shocked, under the onslaught of her morning shower. Her return was watched by Susie whose shadow rapped ineffectually on her side of the steamed up mirror.

By the time Jake returned from fashioning his demonic branding iron, Joy's dream of hearts and her terrifying encounter with the being who claimed to be her sister were forgotten. Fear was replaced by a tune that ran around and around in her head until she joined in singing, *'Don't worry, be happy...'*

As Joy soaped her body her only thoughts were of Jacob. As if in answer to an unspoken prayer the demon reached into he shower, wrapped an arm around her waist and drew her out of the wet heat onto the contrasting cold of the tiled floor. As he covered her, Joy's nails scratched his shoulders stimulating wings that began to rise and fall under his skin, moving in time with the rhythm of their lovemaking.

'I love you, Jacob.'

How much do you love me?

'Enough to die for you.'

It isn't necessary, but if you wish to die, I will die with you.

He rolled onto his back and she sat across his thighs facing away from him, her hands reached down to gently stroke his calves as he pulled her up along his body until he found her with his mouth and she found him with hers.

Neither of them heard the commotion out on the lake as lightning hit the centre of the small island smashing the old shack there into a hundred pieces of flotsam before attacking the forest, repeatedly striking the oak tree until it writhed and smouldered as a blanket of roses blazed around its ancient trunk.

Chapter Thirty-Six

-RAINBOW'S END-

Jake was sleeping. Joy was counting sheep and glad to be distracted by the sound of Skylar whining outside. Dressing quietly in jeans and a hooded sweatshirt she crept to the kitchen and opened the door. The dog barked and wagged his stumpy tail as she tickled him between his ears and said, 'Hi, Fur Face, what can I do for you this fine night?'

Light played on the surface of the lake, but it was the quality of that light that caused the dog to chase his tail and play-bow while Joy rubbed her tired eyes, certain they must be deceiving her.

Bright colours arced out of the water, soared overhead and curved down into the pine forest.

Joy and the dog jogged to the shoreline to stare at the phenomenon as crickets sang and mosquitoes bit every inch of her exposed skin. She swatted ineffectually at the nocturnal blood suckers before conceding defeat and flopping down on the soft sand to gaze in wonder at the sky. The dog flopped down beside her, his flanks trembled. Joy's voice was gentle as she said, 'I know, boy, it's a perplexing sight. I've never seen a rainbow spanning a midnight sky before.'

They sat admiring the rainbow. Joy waited for it to disappear. It didn't.

She stood, brushed sand off her legs and said, 'Do you want to help me find the end of the rainbow, doggie? Pardon? I agree, there is almost certainly no harm in going for a look. We need a lamp.'

The dog followed her to the workshop. Inside, she saw an iron brazier filled with blacksmith tools, its outline kissed by the strange light of the rainbow, it made her shudder.

The beloved Harley sat on its stand, waiting for someone reckless to take it for a ride. Joy gave the bike a passing caress, grabbed a flashlight and left, saying, 'Come on, pup let's follow the yellow brick road.'

They entered the forest where the trees were sparse and the ground fairly level. Light bounced from tree to tree casting long shadows that appeared to follow their progress. Feeling a sudden change underfoot Joy looked down and burst into hysterical laughter, saying, 'Hey, Skylar, if this doesn't prove I'm dreaming, nothing bloody well will.'

A narrow path of tightly woven buttercups stretched ahead, shining with its own light source. She tickled the dog between his pricked ears and said, 'I'm glad I said yellow brick road and not the road to hell.'

Making the sign of the cross Joy paused, wondering if she was religious. Unable to remember, she picked a buttercup and crouched to wave it under Skylar's furry chin, saying, 'Nope you don't like butter, pup. Bloody hell, this is crazy.'

Fur Face ran ahead, leading Joy deep into the forest; she couldn't keep up, but now and again she heard his guiding bark. Whichever twisted path she took the golden flowers blossomed ahead. The flashlight couldn't compete with the buttercups' dazzling sheen and was shoved, unneeded in the front pocket of her hoodie.

Joy gazed at the sky now filled entirely by the colour radiating rainbow and intuited where the path would take her. She slowed her pace, dragging her feet, half of her wanting to turn around. Curiosity won out and she followed the path to its conclusion.

She found Fur Face rolling about with a stupid floppy tongued doggy expression. The flowers ended directly under the gigantic oak tree whose gnarled and twisted branches rippled in the darkness, dressed with swarming fire flies. Seemingly unfazed by such a miraculous event Skylar continued to play in the golden bed of flowers. His pink tongue lolled out the side of his mouth, he was smiling.

Her earlier anxiety brushed aside by his doggy delight, Joy threw herself down beside him and spreading her arms and feet apart waved them back and forth to make buttercup angels. The dog rolled with her and Joy laughed with pleasure until they bumped into something unseen. She jumped to her feet and moved away until her back hit an invisible solid barrier that knocked the breath from her lungs sending her to her knees. Skylar whined and crawled on his belly to lick her face. Joy stood on wobbly legs and tentatively pressed her hands around the space like a mime artist stuck in an imaginary box. After repeatedly being pushed back by thin air it became clear that they were imprisoned in a six foot square of emptiness. The coloured lights overhead blinked out. Joy and Skylar were trapped at the end of the rainbow.

Moonlight seeped out of the clearing, heralding in a weighty darkness that pressed down until Joy's knees buckled and Fur Face howled his distress. Plunged into blindness she spoke out loud, 'What the bloody hell?' and her voice died in the claustrophobic trap.

The dog was the first to notice a weak glow emanating from the earth at their feet. He began to dig, sensing the invisible walls moving closer, closing in to crush them. Joy joined him and scraped at the earth; making a conscious effort to slow her breathing and deny the panic beating on the door of her rational mind like a sledge hammer. They dug knowing their lives depended on it, pursuing the miniscule radiance. The cruel walls pressed against her back and Joy allowed herself a small moan of despair. Skylar barked sharply and continued to dig.

A dazzling, solid beam of light shot from the ground to pierce the night sky like a beacon of hope. The air around them began to shimmer, flex and bend like warm plastic before finally transforming into a plain wooden door at the sight of which Joy's feelings of oppression and claustrophobia flew away.

Skylar was less enthusiastic; he yelped and crawled to hide behind her. Joy gazed in anxious wonder as the miraculous light faded and disappeared, leaving behind a luminescent glow. She sat back on her heels, picking dirt from under her nails and wiping her hands on her jeans. 'Wow. What the bloody hell was that all about? Can you breathe, Fur face? I think I can breathe OK now.'

She nipped hard in the crook of her elbow and squealed causing the already terrified dog to yelp. Her voice trembled in sympathy with his shivers as she stroked him and said, 'Be brave, Pup. There's not a lot of sense being scared. Whatever's behind that door has to be faced. We have to move forward, so, here goes nothing.'

Joy tensed her muscles and tried the horn shaped handle. The door opened easily revealing steep damp steps cut into black soil and illuminated by the glow of light from somewhere far below.

She heard hysteria rise in her voice as she said, 'Come on, Skylar, we have weirdness to check out.' Fur Face lay at the threshold, his ears flat, his body shivering on the disturbed earth; Joy was on her own.

She descended the rough stairway on her butt, using her hands to steady herself against slippery root-veined walls. The deeper she went, the brighter the light became. She looked back; the shining oak tree was framed in the doorway, buttercup radiance reflected on its massive trunk illuminating the spiral path that climbed into the darkness inside it. Skylar lay with his nose hanging over the top step- whining. Tired of feeling afraid, Joy climbed to her feet and leapt, screaming, down the remaining steps into the light.

She arrived in a basement lit by dirty fluorescent tubes. A large dog cage stood in one corner with dusty carpets and blankets stacked on top of it. The walls were lined with shelves filled with enough jars of pickled goods to feed a small army. Opposite the steps, an ordinary red plastic tool box stood on an otherwise empty workbench. Joy heard a soft whimper. Skylar had found his courage.

Heavensgate: Joy

'Come here, brave boy, and take a sniff around.' The dog crept closer to huddle behind the shelter of Joy's legs. His wet nose nudged the back of her knees as if to say, 'Get on with it so we can leave.'

She fiddled with the locked lid of the tool box. She looked around the basement for something to pry it open with and was startled by Skylar's sudden bark. He had been buzzed by a pair of flickering dragonflies, one had iridescent wings shot with silver and the other shone red as blood. He leaped and snapped his jaws on empty air. Joy shuddered and watched the large insects as they hovered above the box, then she stumbled back against the dog cage as the insects flew at the locked catches and the lid popped open. She muttered Jake's favourite phrase, 'Fuck me,' and approached with caution. The dragonflies flew up the staircase to disappear into the forest.

Skylar's furious barking echoed off the walls, forcing Joy to shout, 'Cut it out. There's nothing to be afraid of. I think.'

Opening the box she lifted out an array of objects. Tension returned to her stomach and her mouth grew dry as she inspected each item with care before setting them to one side.

The box contained:

- A creased photo of a woman nursing twin babies, stood beside a man carrying a toddler and smiling down at the infants.

- A Polaroid snapshot of a boy with one arm in a plaster cast, proudly holding a bow and arrow out to the photographer.

- A Children's Bible

- A twisted, melted vinyl single with a charred label that read of Dor.. .ay 'Q.. ..ra, Se..'

- A completed Rubik cube

- Two wedding photos showing younger versions of Jacob with two different brides.

Joy stroked a finger across Susie's perfect features and felt tears prick the back of her eyes, saying, 'Bloody hell, Fur Face, I've seen this woman. She told me to run.'

With sweaty palms she continued to rummage and found:

- A torn, dirty fishnet stocking
- A small silver flask containing a drop of bourbon
- A crumpled pack of two Lucky Strikes
- A pair of crumpled, soiled, pink and black lacy panties
- A team coach's whistle
- A box of long matches

Would you like to light my fire?

Joy almost leapt out of her skin. Her voice shook as she said, 'Jacob, don't you ever sneak up on me again.' She laughed to cover her nerves.

There was no tease in Jake's voice when he said,

What are you doing in the basement, Joy? Someone could creep up on you down here and slit your pretty throat.

He picked up the family photo, smoothing out creases while hooking her with his jade eyes and reeling her in. Joy heard herself gulp. She closed her eyes, counted to three and asked, 'Why and how is there an entrance to this basement in the forest?'

Jacob shrugged, turning his attention to the matches. He struck one along the edge of the box and watched until it burnt down to his fingertips. Then he grinned at her and flicked it over his shoulder.

Joy's voice was sharp as she said, 'Fine, next question. Whose stuff is this, Jacob?'

God you're so beautiful. Why are you afraid of me, Joy?' He stroked one finger across her lips making her shiver.

This crap belonged to my brother, Jake.

'You said you had no relatives.'

Well we weren't what you would call emotionally close. In fact, he hated me. Let's put the sentimental old sap's memories back in his hiding place.

'Who are the people in the photo?'

I love your eyes, your mouth, and the way your hair falls across your face like a golden waterfall.

'Jacob!'

OK, cool down, Honeybunch. The toddler in the snap is Jacky. The pretty twin is me and the other one is Jake. I'm the sole survivor.'

He scanned Joy's face, alert for the slightest sign of disbelief. Finding no expression at all he said, *My family died in a house fire. Aren't you sad for me?*

'If Jake died in the fire how did he collect all this, Jacob?'

Aren't you the amateur detective? I never said he collected it I just said it was his stuff.

'Ridiculous. Why are you lying to me, Jacob? How old was your twin when he died? And who are the brides?

My dead wives. How'd you get in this here treasure trove?

'A door appeared in the woods, it just popped up out of nowhere.'

Joy, you know how crazy that sounds dontcha? It's the basement door, darlin'.

'Mary said the Lodge doesn't have a basement.'

Everywhere has a basement, Joy. He laughed in her face and spread his arms out at his sides. A look of scorn spoiled his face. Joy persisted, desperate for answers from the stranger who stood before her, pressing the fishnet stocking to his nose, inhaling a long lost scent while his eyes never left her face.

She fished deep for courage and said, 'Jacob, I went into the woods with the dog.' She pointed at her feet, but Skylar had abandoned her, she sighed. 'We followed the buttercup path and the rainbow until we came to the oak tree. An invisible barrier trapped us so we dug around inside it then an incredible light flashed out and the door appeared above those...' She pointed behind her and the world rocked under her feet as she witnessed dirt steps morph into a sturdy wooden staircase. Her head swam and her vision began to fade. Smiling, Jake put his arm around her waist and helped her upstairs to the Lodge.

Let's go back to bed, beautiful. I'll explain all this crap later. If after you know the full story you decide you want to leave me, well, it'll kill me but I won't stop you.

She didn't see Jake's fingers crossed childishly behind his back.

Chapter Thirty-Seven

-HANGING BY A THREAD-

The following morning, Joy sat at the kitchen table battling a panic attack that fluttered like newborn moths from her stomach to her throat. Her body threatened to choke her with its insistence that something was terribly, terrifyingly wrong. Her fists and teeth clenched as horror fought vivid memories of the passion she and Jacob had shared, the tender intimacies, the whispered words of adoration and worshipful glances. She was in love and in fear for her life.

A knock on the screen door almost sent her over the edge.

Her voice an octave too high, she said, 'Jim, come on in. I'm so glad to see you.'

Jim removed his battered Stetson and sat beside her, his rheumy eyes gentle as, taking her hand, he asked, 'What's troubling you, child?'

A strangled sob escaped her. She swallowed the torrent that threatened to follow and croaked, 'It's Jacob. I can't bear it. We spent a perfect night together, but this morning he wouldn't explain the things I found in the basement even though he had promised me he would. I got angry and he laughed at me, so I told him that love without trust is worthless and, as I had no faith in him, I was leaving.'

Jim squeezed her hand and, in a voice tinged with admiration, said, 'Well played, Joy.'

'Jim, it wasn't. I shouldn't have said it. Jake was sobbing. He was heartbroken. It was awful to see, but I can't bear lies so I stood my ground.'

'OK, and now you can leave him.'

'No, you don't understand. He kissed me goodbye and ran outside. I followed him into the forest. Oh, Jim, I was too late. I saw him hang himself from the old oak tree.'

Jim tried not to laugh and said, 'You gotta be kiddin' me?'

'It happened, Jim, I swear it did.'

Becoming serious, he asked, 'Could you cut him down?' Joy shook her head unable to find words to explain what had happened next.

'So he's still hangin' out in the woods.'

Joy moaned, 'No, no he isn't.'

Jim screwed up his face and said, 'Joy, look at me. Now breathe easy. Good girl. If the bastard ain't danglin' from a rope and you didn't cut him down, where's the body?'

He had to lean in close to hear her reply as, her eyes wide with horror, she whispered, 'He's out in the workshop polishing his pride and joy.'

Cracking a smile to hide his disappointment, Jim said, 'Which proves that the deceitful, nasty bastard didn't hang himself so, despite that being a cryin' shame, there's no need to get all riled up about it.'

'I saw him hang. It was real. Well, it looked and felt real to me.'

'Yes and it will feel real the next time and the next and the next. Each time you experience that demon's sick illusions will be worse than the last.'

'I don't understand.'

'You can't save him, Joy. He's beyond help. He's infecting yer spirit. Come away with ole Jim, leave him.'

'I cannot.'

'He's already stolen yer peace of mind. He wants yer heart. He'll lock yer soul in the basement, he'll make you walk and sleep in fear and trap you in his hell.'

Heavensgate: Joy

Joy had a coughing fit which almost left her breathless. Straining for each word, she said, 'He isn't evil, he's an ordinary man in a world of pain.'

'Joy, yer thoughts are already being censored before they get chance to reach yer mouth.'

'No, Jim, you really don't understand.' She was choking.

Jim poured a glass of water and handed it to her saying, 'Sip this and breathe slowly. Now listen to yer Uncle Jim. That man is *not* Jacob Andersen. Jacob passed over and what he left behind in Heavensgate is Jake and he ain't human. If yer mouth betrays true pain to me or any one he'll punish you because no pain is greater or more important to him than his own. You've gotta leave him.'

Joy slammed her glass on the table and cried, 'I cannot believe you would say such things. It's bloody obvious that I can't just up and leave. Have you seen what he does to himself with those razor blades? I'm here because he needs me. I was sent here by God to save him.' Joy's eyes opened wide and her hands shot to cover her mouth in an attempt to hold back the involuntary flood of words that had sprung to Jake's defense.

'Listen to yerself, you can't even speak what you know to be true. Jake, *not* Jacob, needs you like the scorpion needed the fox to cross the river. He'll take you down with him. He can't help himself, it's his nature.'

Joy spoke hesitantly, expecting her words to be censored, 'Even if you're right about him it makes no difference, I love him beyond reason and there's no way out of Heavensgate for me. It's too late. I tried to leave before; you know how hard I tried.'

Jim pressed a finger to her lips and opened the button on his shirt pocket. He took out a small notepad and pencil and wrote:

Now and again, when there's a lightning storm, a whirlpool appears in Lake Disregard in place of the small island. When you see it, get in the boat and row into it.

Joy read the note and returned it saying, 'I am hopelessly in love with him, now get out.' She shook her head to deny her words.

Jim tore the note into tiny pieces, which he ate. His old eyes danced with amusement as he whispered, 'Leave him while you still have some good feelin' for him, give him that gift. Please get ready; the change has begun in him, and in yerself. Look in a mirror, you don't look so good these days, my girl.'

Joy was silent. Jim was right, she was changing, she couldn't remember the last time she had any appetite or thirst and she looked exhausted. Jim slid a huge leather bound book across the table. She mouthed at him, 'Where did that come from?'

Jim's next words confused her. 'I found this in the Locked Room, at the top of the non-existent tower. It is the Forbidden Book. You had best read it, Joy.'

Bemused, she opened the book which used its yellow scorched pages to scratch like a wildcat until she smoothed her hands gently over its bindings, whispering words she had forgotten she possessed. The book collapsed on the table, waiting to be read. It was silent, acquiescent and definitely alive.

Joy studied the pages; some scrawled in wax crayon others written in many different inks by several hands. Now and again her breath caught in her throat and tears fell onto the words.

She read seven year old Jacky's misspelled, recollections of guilt and terror after he accidentally burnt down his family home killing his parents and the twins, Nancy and Sam.

Her hand clutched at her throat as she read scrawled words that ripped through pages covered in ink blots, expressing the pain and betrayal Jacob felt when he was hurt by his foster parents, Mary and Al; and how he was savagely raped at boarding school.

Jim watched her face as she discovered how Jake murdered Jacob's casual pick up after the Prom. It was the girl, Joan, who drove the pink Cadillac she knew as Mom's Taxi.

Joy experienced Jacob's nightmares after Susie's death and the loss of his wife, Louise and his son, Tommy.

She skipped over rudimentary wax crayon sketches of murder, rape, arson and in the case of Skylar, mutilation. She fought the burning horror in her throat as she read of Jacob's guilt as he took responsibility for every evil act Jake had relished committing.

Joy retched as she reached the entry that told of her arrival in Heavensgate, and how an excited Jake planned to trap, torture, and brand her as his own.

She read about Jake's love-hate relationship with Jim and his disgusted disdain for the other fragments that occupied his mind, including Doc.

Joy raised her eyes from the compliant book's battered pages and spoke all her questions in one word, 'How?'

The Forbidden Book vanished.

Good fuckin' day and a great big howdy do to you, Jim.

Jake slapped the old man's back and Jim's face crashed onto the table top, sending Joy's water flying.

I hope you aren't talkin' dirty to my girl here.

He laughed and straddled the chair next to Joy. She sat frozen, unable to believe that the man she had seen hanging by his neck from the oak tree and polishing his Harley Davison in his workshop, was the same man who sat beside her.

Jim straightened up and replied, 'No, Jake, I was just talkin' bad about *you*; you murderin', deviant spawn of the Devil.'

Jake's voice was happy and relaxed as he said, *That's OK. Thank you kindly for your unsolicited assistance in this private matter, but now you can leave us alone and don't come back. We don't need your sort hangin' around us lovebirds like a bad smell.*

Jim looked disgusted as Jake eyeballed him, saying, *Don't worry, old man. Joy knows I'm her pussy cat. Now, weren't you needed in the woods? I heard Dina has an appetite she needs satisfyin' with some wrinkly lovin'.*

Jim was on his feet, struggling to not betray his concern for Joy's safety. She waved him back down saying, 'No, Jim, please stay.'

He shook his head and said, 'It's OK, girl, thanks for the chat, sorry about the mess. If you need me, holler.' He winked.

Jake threw Jim his Stetson and opened the door saying, *That'll never happen. I'll walk you to the edge of the woods, old timer, and make sure you fuck right off outta here.*

The moment they left Joy seized the opportunity to escape.

She raced around the Lodge in increasing panic, sobbing with distress as she found every door and window locked tight.

There was no way out.

Chapter Thirty-Eight

-EDEN-

Having seen Jim on his way, Jake returned to find Joy shivering as she stared longingly out of the guest room window. He stepped behind her, wrapped his arms around her stiff body and whispered in her ear, *Hey, babe, what you doin' in here? You sleep with me.*

She managed to reply, 'Leave me alone; I have a migraine coming on.' She screwed up her eyes and pinched the bridge of her nose. Jake pressed against her back, his big hands massaging her rigid shoulders. Joy trembled under his touch as an uninvited molten wave of desire rushed through her traitorous veins. She grabbed the edge of the window sill to steady herself, her knuckles white as she clung on, afraid to even breathe.

Jake kissed the nape of her neck and said, *Love is painful isn't it, Joy?*

'This isn't love, Jacob, this is lust.'

You love me. You told me so.

'That was before I read the Book.'

You did? Yeah, I guess you did. Jim's one sneaky bastard. I didn't know he had it in him.

Jake pressed strong fingers deeper into Joy's knotted muscles saying, *Baby, relax, you are so tense.*

'I'll feel better if you promise you won't hurt him.'

I promise I won't hurt him. He did me a good turn; he saved hours of cryin' to you over my miserable life made hell by my twin, Jake.

'I can't live with a man like you.'

Joy, the Book is not about me, it's about Jake. I don't even know if half of what the crazy fucker wrote is true. I have immense gaps in my memory, like mini-deaths, same as you do. Please, you gotta believe me, baby, there were months, sometimes years when I wasn't around.

Joy relaxed under his hands. Leaning against him she sighed, 'I want to trust you, Jacob or Jake, whoever you are. I can't because you said Jake died in the fire and a dead man can't do those things.'

Joy, sweetheart, I was just tryin' to avoid reliving the grief he put me through. I'm sorry I lied. I'm gonna burn that treasury of misery. I'll rewrite the Book, it'll be Our Book, we can write our love story. Please, you can trust me.

Joy felt her last hope of escape leave her and said, 'I can't. You'll kill me. Then you will write *your* story in *my* blood and turn the sticky pages with a smile on your face.'

Fuck me! Joy, you made me swear. That is not true. I couldn't hurt you. I won't ever hurt you.

In a voice empty of emotion, she continued, 'Or, perhaps, you will turn the gas on, light a match and sing '*Que Sera*' as you watch me scream and burn.'

Jake's teeth nipped her ear lobe sending gooseflesh racing along her arms.

I won't burn you, I hate fire.

'Maybe you'll pick up a kitchen knife one day and gut me like a fish.'

His hands slipped to her waist. He pressed her against the tightness growing in his jeans.

Joy, feel how you turn me on. You are so fuckin' beautiful. Gut you? Never, come on, lighten up. Anyway, knives scare me.

She pushed back against his hips and said, 'You scare me, Jacob.'

You terrify me, Joy.

He turned her around and, cupping her face with both hands, said,

You've no idea what you've done to me. I didn't want to fall for you, but I did, hard. I promise you, my love, my heart, my life, my Joy, I will never hurt you.

Her eyes welled with tears as she said, 'Then you'll drive me to hurt myself.'

He kissed the tip of her nose fighting to control his lust and hide his impatience.

Perhaps, who knows what the future holds? It's too late for us to worry about infinitesimal possibilities and what ifs. Take another look outside, the Nothing is back.

'Stop trying to change the subject. You don't love me, you are obsessed with me.'

It's the same thing.

'No, it is not and we can't hide away here forever.'

Fuck, baby, this is Heavensgate, where'd you want to go? There's nothing out there for us; no-one else exists in the universe for us. Heavensgate is our Eden and it's our solemn duty to populate it with our love.

His words reignited the panic that had been dampened down by arousal.

Joy pushed him aside and ran for the front door. He followed, confident, until he heard the lock pop. Flinging the door open, Joy pelted out into a total absence of anything.

And merged with the Nothing.

Her headache was forgotten, her body missing and her soul in panic mode when Hope's disembodied voice chimed out, 'I told you to make a death pact. What went wrong? What are you waiting for?'

Joy swung around and spotting Hope's shadow struggling to find form, replied, 'I give up. I don't know what to do. Jacob says Heavensgate is our Eden.'

Hope wavered in and out of focus as her voice insisted, 'Jake, NOT Jacob has a penchant for the dramatic. Must I spell everything out for you? Sweet Creator in Heaven, help me. You cannot begin to comprehend the risks I take for you. Will you please remember that you are JOY?'

The clang of metal banging on metal reverberated in the Nothing and Hope cried, 'We must leave. We can't get stuck here. I beg you, Joy, time is short and dangerous in this place, hurry up and remember who you are.'

'I know who I am. My name is Joy.'

Hope battled her natural impatience knowing it was best not to rush the revelation. She bit her lip and her nature triumphed over caution. 'Not *exactly*, you have been blind, open your inner eye and remember. Joy is not *who* you are, Joy is *what* you are. I am HOPE and you are JOY.'

The violent clanging and scraping noise drew closer, tearing apart and shattering the last shred of nerves that Joy possessed and she pressed her hands to her ears and screamed. Hope lost all patience and, pressing her hands over Joy's, she pierced her with ancient eyes and shouted, 'Oh, for the Great Creator's sake, stop carrying on like a child. Remember before you get us both killed.'

Hope's words tore through cacophony of the Nothing to blast away the earthly dam of consciousness that trapped Joy's soul and in that instant everything changed. Finding strength and form in self-knowledge, she pulsated with blinding yellow light as a tsunami of immortal memories crested and crashed over her, washing every mortal sorrow she had suffered, decimated and meaningless, before it.

Joy's voice cut like a holy sword as she declared, 'I *am* Joy!' Aftershocks rocked the Nothing and, as if it howled in pain, metallic screeches and banging raced to consume the sisters.

Hope raised her voice to ring above the Nothing's fury saying, 'Time to go. Close your eyes, Joy, and remember the Light, think only of the Light. Well done, now open your eyes and listen.'

Looking around in amazement, Joy shook her head and said, 'First, explain where we are.'

-Home.-

Death bowed low to plant his kiss on the back of Joy's hand.

'Bloody hell.'

'No, not hell. Home,' Hope insisted.

Joy inspected Death and said, 'I know you; you've been stalking me.'

-Yet in the end you came freely.-

'I am dead.'

-Not exactly. My Lady, Joy, listen to your disobedient, heart-thief sister. Then, if you must act according to your nature, do so while I am minded to allow it.-

Death opened his silver pocket watch and smiled as discordant chords of '*Que Sera*' made Joy flinch.

He vanished. Joy stared at the spot where he had stood, drowning in questions as Hope said, 'I'm sorry, sister, there is no time to explain. You heard our Lord Death. He has granted you a reprieve. We must plan to free you from that demon. Are you ready to fulfill your immortal destiny, sister?'

Chapter Thirty-Nine

-HOT WATER-

Joy returned to Heavensgate. She had an escape plan clear in her mind and her fear of Jake was banished, if not her irritating desire. She recalled how she had fled into the Nothing in mortal terror. Now she had returned as the immortal, Joy. Lord Death had been kind, there was nothing to fear.

The sound of sobbing interrupted her thoughts. It sounded like Jake. Evil didn't cry, did it?

Jake's anguish poured from behind the bathroom door. Taking a deep breath, she entered the room and humidity flashed over her skin shooting her pores open and instantaneously drenching her in sweat.

Blinded by an enveloping cloud of scalding steam and anticipating one of Jake's tricks, she said, 'Jacob? Jake? Why are you crying?'

The seconds ticked by. His ragged, broken voice scratched at her soul as he replied, *Get out, Joy. Leave me while you still can. Go before I harm you.*

A gust of hot spray filled wind clouded around her, blocking her view. Undeterred, she approached the tub and, coughing as wetness filled her lungs, said, 'I can't leave Heavensgate and I can't leave you. I tried and here I am, back again.'

She heard panic and warning in his tone as he growled, *Don't come any closer.*

Heavensgate: Joy

A fresh noise, resembling rustling leaves in the wind, filled the space between them. She risked another step closer. The noise grew more frantic. Something was thrashing at the air and creating waves of scorching steam that rolled across the room. The noise was incredibly loud. As she tried to place the sound, a furnace blast of heat sought out her throat and wrapped its searing fingers around it. Joy staggered and wheezed, her lungs burned as if gripped in molten tongs fresh from a brazier. Blinded by curious tendrils of steam that investigated her eyes, breathless and stumbling, she grasped the washbasin and her hands cleaved to a ceramic oven. Screaming in pain and horror she snatched them back, leaving a layer of skin sizzling on the bowl.

Joy lurched, holding her bleeding palms in front of her as she fought the shock that streamed in icy rivers through her overheated body. Her throat bubbled and bled. She was choking on her own blood. Her rational mind screamed that the pain and heat were illusions, but all the while those illusions continued to kill her. Weeping, she chastised herself for believing in her burns and, in agony from her wrecked throat, she tried to speak. Her voice whistled and grated, but her meaning was clear.

'Jake, let me help you.'

More blisters formed on her face, neck, hands and in her nose and mouth. Joy was in hell. She crawled forward until her bowed head bumped the edge of the tub where Jake sat weeping and naked in boiling water. His back was bent, his forehead rested on his knees. He was as pale as death. Joy couldn't speak or catch her breath. Scolding steam continued to pour down her throat, blisters bloomed, popped and bled to be replaced by more, but still she reached out a shaking hand to help him.

Jake raised his head and looked at her with dead eyes.

I told you to go. I warned you. Whatever comes next is entirely your own fault, my Lady, Joy.

His magnificent glossy black wings spread open and pitch black feathers tipped in silver wrapped his nakedness. Silence descended.

Joy's eyes bled blind tears. It was too late; she'd seen what he was once before and now she was forced to accept it.

She collapsed. Jake leapt from the tub, steam curling away from his body. Joy lay unconscious on the bathroom floor; her body and face scalded as though it was she who had bathed in boiling water. Her skin was a canvas for bloody red, blue and yellow blisters. What had once been Joy was now a raw, bleeding mess, her breathing barely discernable as she slipped away.

Jake screamed, *NO!*

He furled his wings and raced to the kitchen where he ripped the old fashioned phone from the wall; he knew the emergency number by heart.

He screamed into the handset,

Doc, I need you. Joy needs you. Now. He left the receiver bouncing on its coiled cable and raced back to the bathroom. He was afraid to touch Joy's blistered and crusted skin so he sat nursing her head on his lap for the ten seconds it took Doc to arrive and order Jake to rest.

Doc was confused by Jake's concern for the woman. He felt both relieved and furious as he lifted Joy into the now empty tub and ran cold water over her boiled skin. His firm voice echoed off the tiled walls,

'Hope, if you can hear me, now would be a good time to play nice. Your sister needs you.'

Joy woke to find Doc and Hope staring down at her. She searched to define her emotion and came up with 'angry'. She was naked in a tub of freezing iced water, miraculously unblemished by the burns she had suffered for a ridiculous, pointless, shameful love. Her temper hot, her skin smooth and cold, she shivered uncontrollably and attempted pull herself up with numb fingers that failed to grasp the edge of the tub. A firm, calloused hand pressed her back down. The jade-eyed man in a white coat hovered over her. She watched Jacob smile at Hope who laid her palm against his cheek. It was too much to bear.

Heavensgate: Joy

The next time she woke she felt crisp, cotton sheets caressing her skin. The lighting was warm and subdued, the bed high with metal cot sides.

Joy moved her right arm. She was attached to a canula that fed clear liquid into her veins from a drip-bag hung on a silver stand. The pristine room had bars on the window. She struggled and tugged at the canula, starting a steady bleed. She had to get out of bed. She started to move, but couldn't feel her legs. Her heart thumped against her ribs, and she screamed, 'Help me!'

The door opened with an electronic beep. A familiar looking Doctor rushed to calm her with soothing words and soft touches. Joy thrashed about as she tried to fight him off. He pressed cool hands on her shoulders, and she croaked, 'Who are you? Why am I here?'

'I'm Doctor Andersen. You're here because you bathed in boiling water.'

Joy stared at the Doctor's handsome face and swallowed hard to quell the dread crawling out of her stomach. 'Jake tried to kill me.'

'I don't believe that he did. In fact it was his swift thinking that saved you. You're lucky to be alive. Don't worry, the burns were minor and the coma gave you time to recover.'

Joy pinched the skin of her inner thigh hard. She couldn't feel it and she didn't wake up, so she said, 'Coma? What bloody coma? How long have I been here? What's wrong with my legs?'

The doctor smiled, saying, 'It's just a side effect of the drugs. The numbness will wear off soon. There's absolutely no need to worry.' He patted the sheets making her flinch.

'Who are you? Where's Jacob or Jake or whatever he is?'

He grimaced and said, 'Jake is resting. For now.'

In a small scared voice, she said, 'You look exactly like him.'

Doc sighed, rubbing a thumb and finger across his eyes. Joy thought he might cry.

'You are correct, I do look like him. Of course I do.'

The sneaky prick of a needle stung the back of her hand before a total absence of being descended on her and she walked alone in the Nothing.

She tapped her foot; it made no sound although she could hear another's steady footsteps approaching. She spun around; there was no-one there.

'Why the bloody hell am I here?'

She had no voice. She raised her hands to her face to discover she had no body either. 'What am I? Oh dear God, *who* am I?'

Doc appeared, he was solid, he was real. Joy pressed her hand on his chest in relief at finding him there and squealed as it drifted through a body with no more substance than light.

His voice reached her as if from a great distance.

'In response to your questions: you are nowhere; you are nothing; you are nobody. Neither am I. Unpleasant, isn't it?'

'Why?'

'You already know one reason why.'

'I was a child. I didn't know what I was doing.'

'Yes, you were and yes you did. You knew drowning yourself was a sin.'

'It was an accident. The sea overwhelmed me. I made a stupid, childish mistake.'

'You intended to cause grief and sorrow to your mortal parents.'

'It was no greater sin than the abuse I suffered at their hands.'

'We are not debating the state of their souls, we are discussing you.'

'Who are you to preach at me?'

'I am the best part of the one you are too close to. I nurture and protect you. I heal you and comfort you. I defend you against Jake's evil. I am the one who fights for you.'

Joy shook her head as she said, 'I can't accept he is evil. Jake is a wounded child trapped in Jacob's psyche. He needs love.'

'Joy, please listen, Hope told you and Jim tried to show you, now *I* will try my best to make you comprehend that Jake, known to you as Jacob, cannot be saved by your love. He is beyond redemption.'

Heavensgate: Joy

'No soul is completely beyond help.'

'Listen to yourself, he was beyond *Hope*. How do you expect to save him with something so fleeting as *Joy*? Jake's soul is rotten; he needs to kill, to consume utterly, and he will destroy you. You must escape. Leave Heavensgate or the Nothing will imprison you alone, immortal, unable to die, unable to live, for all eternity. You are too important for that to be allowed.'

'Take me back to the hospital.'

'Heed my warning. Jake needs you to suffer and kill for him. When he has no more use for you, he will devour you.'

'Liar! He loves me.'

'You already forgotten the plans you made with Hope. You must remember or you *will* die. Jake cannot control his nature. However, I'm interested; tell me, why do you love him?'

'I love him without and beyond reason; I have no choice. I can only love him whatever may come and whatever the cost.'

'Then you have made your decision?'

'I have.'

Hope appeared at Joy's side, icy tears streamed down her lovely face as she turned to Doc and said, 'Thank you for all that you do, Doctor. I wish I could release you. I will take her back to Heavensgate.'

Chapter Forty

-THE POWER OF LOVE-

Morning sunlight streamed into the bedroom to dance with dust motes in the music of perfect silence. Sweat trickled down Joy's spine as she peered through thick icicles that hung like prison bars over the window, blocking her view. She rocked back on her heels, shocked by the vast expanse of white that blanketed the lakeside, mountains and pine forest. Yesterday, Lake Disregard had basked in high summer; today all of Heavensgate suffered deep winter and not a creature stirred in the sub-zero landscape.

Sweet Jesus! How had she got here? Yesterday she was in the hospital; today she was in the Lodge. The bedroom was too warm. Joy raised the corner of her t-shirt to wipe her hot and clammy brow then raised the window catch and pushed, but it was frozen shut. It was getting harder to breath. Even the Lodge seemed to hold its breath against a weight of emptiness. Where the hell was he? She shrugged on her dressing gown and slippers, raked fingers through crazy morning hair and made her sleep drugged way into the cool of the bathroom. Looking in the mirror she whispered, 'Good morning,' trying to ignore the anxiety written across the reflection of Susie's damaged face.

Having washed and dressed without any amorous intrusion, she went in search of breakfast determined to see things through with

Jake. She would save him. Her love was strong and her joy in her love deeper than the lake outside; she would drown him in her adoration until his sins were washed away and he was reborn. Her love would redeem him.

She entered the kitchen humming, 'The power of love.' The table was set with a plate of bacon and grits, an egg over easy, toast and coffee waiting for her. Her stomach growled its approval and she began to eat. Licking butter from her fingers, she was about to call Jacob to join her when Mary appeared announcing, 'He isn't here, your Ladyship. Eat up.'

Joy spat crumbs and spluttered, 'You? What? I?'

'My thoughts exactly, your Majesty. Now don't fuss, we need a little chat.'

Joy waved the apparition away, pretending a nonchalance that the erect hairs on the back of her neck knew she didn't feel. Her voice sounded strong in her ears as she said, 'Piss off, Mary. I have nothing to say to you. You aren't real and this isn't happening.'

Mary shrugged. 'OK. Have it your way seein' as it makes no difference. I'll do the talkin' while you listen, Princess.'

Joy poured a mug of coffee, surprised that her hands remained steady and asked, 'Are you going to slaughter yourself in front of me and slit my throat again or do you have something more shocking planned?'

Mary pressed her palms flat on the table. She noted a change in the younger woman that she couldn't pin down and didn't like. She pressed on, determined to win the round and said, 'Joy, like you, I've been in the Nothing. To be more precise, darlin', I was sent there to consider several unpalatable options. The option I chose is to save *you*.'

Joy blew out her cheeks and, frowning, said, 'I don't follow. However, I'm not afraid of the weirdness this bloody place produces anymore, so, go ahead, knock yourself out. Save me, Mary.'

Mary placed a manicured hand over her heart saying, 'I loved that boy, Jacob, Jacky, Jake. The name he goes by ain't the most important thing about him. I raised him like he was my own son, even though I knew he'd killed his entire family. Me and Big Al, we both loved him. We fed and clothed him and, when he was in trouble with the damn law, which was often, we protected him. When he murdered his first whore we sheltered him under our roof. So, Lady, how d'ya figure the poor orphan kid repaid all that sweet love and devotion? Well, Miss La De Da, you most probably already know that he fuckin' murdered me. Me, the lovin' kind woman who replaced his own momma.' Mary paused for breath that she no longer needed and waited for Joy's reaction.

'Really?' Joy slurped her coffee, staring at a point in the middle distance.

Mary pressed shaking hands to her throat and, with eyes full of tears, said, 'My boy suffocated me then stuffed me in a stinkin' dog cage in my own basement.'

'Bravo!' Joy clapped in slow applause. 'Give this woman an Oscar. Wipe your crocodile tears. Try the blessed truth on for size and tell me, Mary, did you achieve Sainthood in the Nothing? Did God all bloody mighty give you special dispensation to visit me in Heavensgate? You being so *Mother Theresa* and everything.'

Joy munched on the last slice of toast, brushing crumbs off her top as if her life depended on it. Mary pouted glossy red lips and shouted, 'Now, now, Lady Muck, that's enough of your British sassiness. I'm here to save you, so don't go gettin' all Mother Superior on me. Your legs opened just as wide as mine for that ungrateful motherfucker.'

Joy kept her voice steady and low as she said, 'The difference is, oh *Holy Mother*, that you abused him, whereas I love him.'

Mary snorted in disgust. 'There's no difference between us, *my Lady*, Joy. You're just as big a whore as I was and that evil bastard will use you and throw you away just the same.'

Joy's green eyes flashed. Her fists clenched as she fought to keep her voice calm and said, 'He will not. What Jacob and I have is different. I am different.'

Shaking her peroxide head and wagging a finger, Mary said, 'You shoulda kept yer googly eyes off my man. You followed him round like a super trooper at a rock concert. That bad boy is mine for all eternity, so get it into yer thick head, before he does to you what he already done to me.'

'You are wrong. I love Jacob and he loves me.'

Mary banged her small fists on the table sending crockery rattling as she screamed, 'He's not Jacob. Jacob passed over. You saw what Jake did to me. You saw the demonic bastard swallow me whole.'

'I saw what you wanted me to see, an illusion, a dream, a nightmare. I don't bloody care what it was. I don't even care if it *was* real. I don't need saving by a stinking murdering, child abusing witch like you. Leave or suffer the consequences when Jacob gets home.'

'Is that a threat yer makin'?'

'No way, bitch, it's something far more dangerous, it's a bloody British promise.'

Goosebumps rose on Joy's skin as the door burst open bringing in a blast of arctic air. Jake filled the doorway; he held an axe over his shoulder. Mary got to her feet, smiling her welcome. He looked her up and down and said, *Hello, Momma, what a nice surprise to see you again.*

He dropped the axe on the table and went to Mary who threw her arms around his waist. He trapped her in a bear hug and shouted to Joy, *Fetch the rope outta the workshop. Hurry.*

Without hesitation Joy ran outside and waded through knee high drifts of snow. Reaching the workshop, her breath hung in miniature frozen clouds before her numb face as she fought to free the door. that abruptly flew open and knocked her over. She struggled to her feet, brushing off snowflakes and abandoning her slippers to the drifts.

Apart from the Harley, waiting seductively on its stand, the workshop was empty and hot as Hades. The wood burner blazed with an unnatural green flame that sent Joy's shadow leaping across the floor to dance erotically up the wall. Firelight illuminated a coil of heavy duty rope. She lifted it off the hook and, stumbling under the weight, with the cold attacking her bare feet, she fought her way back.

Shocked to find Jake, shirtless and kissing Mary with his hands inside her blouse, she dropped the rope on the table. Her teeth chattered. She rubbed circulation back into her hands and fighting angry tears watched Mary run her manicured nails down Jake's back.

Joy was regretting her earlier decision to save the disloyal bastard from himself, when he lifted his mouth from Mary's and pinning her arms, said, *What are you doing? Get over her, bless the rope with a kiss and help me bind this filthy bitch.*

Mary struggled and spat in his eye. A globule of yellow puss slid down his cheek.

'Kiss the rope?'

Just do it. I can't hold onto this piece of shit forever.

Mary fought hard, spitting and scratching, kicking and biting Jake who used his weight to force her down onto the floor.

Feeling ridiculous and afraid, Joy kissed the rope and dragged it across to him. 'What are you going to do?'

I'm gonna restrain her, she's as mad as a shot bear. Help me for fuck's sake.

Hot tears of shame stung her frozen cheeks as she helped Jake tie the first slip-knot around Mary's ankles and pull it up behind her petite body. Jake dragged the rope tight around her delicate wrists. She was hog tied and screaming,

'Stop him. Save me and we can finish him together. Oh shit. You crazy bitch, he's gonna kill us both.'

Joy heard teeth and bones break as Jake's fist connected with Mary's face. He slung her unconscious body over his shoulder as if his foster mom, abuser, protector, lover and victim had even less weight than value. Revulsion crept along Joy's skin as he said, *Help me get rid of this whore once and for all. We need to chop and burn, you hear me? Chop and burn until there's nothing left of the bitch to use against us.*

Joy couldn't hide her horror. 'No, I want you to be good, *I* want to be good. We can find another way.'

Adjusting Mary's weight, Jake replied with false patience,

This motherfucker has powers. She makes me bad. I don't know how long I can resist the evil she pushes into my mind and I don't want to hurt you, my love.

Joy swallowed her repugnance and rested a hand on his forearm saying, 'You won't hurt me. I won't let you.'

Please, Joy, help me kill her. She's a paedo. The bitch is violent, her soul is sick, and you've seen what she can do. Please, please, help me. It takes good to destroy evil.

'I can't kill. I can't do it, not even for you.'

Jake's face twisted, he felt confused and shocked as he realised he felt genuine love for Joy. Battling the call of the Beast and his rising blood lust, he said,

Mary's already dead. She's been dead for years. Now I'm gonna throw this pile of shit in the workshop and when I get back we'll talk. Put a pot of coffee on to brew, darlin', I'll only be a minute or two.

He kicked open the door and disappeared into the snow with his bloody, bound burden. The moment he left, Joy's legs gave way and she dropped, shaking, into a chair where she stared in disbelief at the cold remains of a normal, everyday breakfast.

Ten long minutes later, Jake returned, shivering as he stripped off bloodstained clothes. Numb with shock, Joy watched him and whispered under her breath, 'Dear God. What have we done?'

Come to me, my love.

He led her to the rug in front of the fire and removed her clothes with a reverence never shown before. Joy's mind battled with her body as he suckled each frozen toe and blew tiny kisses along the soft inside of her thighs, the scratch of fine stubble making her quiver.

Tears blinded her to the sight of his head between her legs. Her hips bucked under his hands as his hot tongue tortured her sex. Jake rested his chin on her stomach, reached up to caress her breasts and said,

Beg me.

She placed a hand on his dark head and pressed him back down her body murmuring, 'Please, Jacob.'

His voice rough and deep, he commanded,

Beg me.

Joy closed her eyes. Tears squeezed their disloyal way between her lashes as she cried, 'I beg you. Please, I beg you.'

What are you begging me for, Joy?

He slid his body higher, planting soft kisses on her eyelids, pressing his hardness between her legs, but refusing to enter as his large hands pinned her writhing hips to the rug. Shame flooded Joy's body and soul. It was too late for regrets. She was lost. Her eyes locked with his and she said, 'I beg you, please, make love to me.'

Gazing down between their bodies they both watched him plunge into her again and again, filling her and making her scream his name until, overwhelmed and submissive, her quivering body rocked beneath his and she felt herself shatter like fragile glass.

As passion subsided, Joy caught the look of triumph in Jake's eyes causing her soul to flood with feelings of worthlessness and violation. Closing her eyes tight she fell into despair. She didn't see glossy black wings unfurl from his shoulders as he said, *You are mine, you love me, you are mine and mine alone and you will never leave me. Now rest, my Lady Joy.*

Dear Lord, why was she so weak, why had she betrayed herself and failed him?

Joy fell into the darkness.

She floated adrift in space, illuminated by a circle of flaming red roses that trapped her in their light.

Chapter Forty-One

-TOO GOOD TO BE TRUE-

Joy vaguely remembered an earnest conversation with a silver haired woman about something important. In her mind's eye she saw Mary smash her small fists onto the table top, but try as she might she couldn't hold onto any thought that didn't involve Jake making love to her.

She turned on the shower and soaped herself under the spray of warm water. Her heart fluttered as she day dreamed about Jake while her memory of the escape plan made with Hope, itself escaped into the cellar of her mind locking the door behind it like a guilty fugitive.

Joy dressed feeling an itch of anxiety that was dismissed as Ella Fitzgerald's haunting voice filled the Lodge singing, 'So in Love.'

The sound of a Skylar barking cut through the music like a knife. Joy opened the kitchen door and he ran to stand shivering outside Jacob's workshop, his ears flat against his head and his maimed tail tucked low. Following him, she crouched down to look into his soft brown eyes and ask, 'What's wrong, sweetie pie, are you scared of the nasty rats?' The dog sped off, almost knocking her over. He headed to the beach and leapt into the lake where he swam for the small island without looking back. Joy cupped her hands around her mouth and shouted, 'Come back, you crazy mutt. I'll catch the nasty ratty blighter for you.'

Skylar swam on. Joy returned to the workshop and cautiously pushed open the door to Jake's sanctuary.

He worked with his back to her, bent over the flaming coal brazier. His muscles bulged with effort as rivulets of sweat ran down his bare torso making his tattooed angel wings shimmer and shine. Red sparks flew from a huge hammer that Jake repeatedly smashed down onto a long strip of molten iron.

Unnoticed, she heard him say,
Thank you, Mary, for the bones that birthed such passionate flames. This iron is for Joy.
Jake began to sing a Christmas Carol in time to the hammer's beat. Hearing the words behind the tune, Joy felt her bowels shudder and turn to water,

Joy to the world, your Lord is come
Let Joy receive her king
Let her great heart prepare him room
And Heavensgate will swing
And Heavensgate will swing
And Hell at Heavensgate with Joy will swing

Joy grasped the door frame and, filled with righteous fury, was about to ask what the bloody hell he was doing when she was knocked outside by fifty pounds of flying wet dog. Skylar was right, this was not the time for confrontation. Recovering her wits, she sprinted back to the Lodge where she checked the hook for the truck keys, they weren't there. Frantic, she raced around the kitchen, pulling out drawers and scattering the contents of cupboards. Skylar chased her from room to room jumping on the furniture and barking. She looked everywhere. No keys.

'Shit!'

The dog howled. Joy burst into the bedroom, crying in fear and frustration as she heard Jake holler,

Heavensgate: Joy

Come to daddy
and found the dog waiting for her on a rough path that stretched away into a cool misty evening.

She turned around in time to see the Lodge swallowed up by the Nothing.

Skylar ran ahead with his ears flat and his stumpy tail tucked between his legs. Joy realised she had no choice but to step into the unknown. She refused to give in to the confusion that beat at the walls of her fragile sanity. So, instead of chasing after the dog, she took a moment to orientate herself.

On her left ran a swift sweet scented river whose waters sang, caressing smooth pebbles and rocks on the way downstream and stealing leaves from the willow trees which bent their sad heads to listen to the song.

She drew close and the river rose, spilling over the grassy bank. No longer singing, the thrash of water at her feet pounded out a warning: *go back, go back, go back.*

Mottled, spiny creatures surged over each other in the foam. They battled the current, almost hidden by the sunlight's reflected glare. Joy couldn't find a safe place to cross.

On the right of the track, tall wild flowers kissed the edge of a bright green forest. Among the blooms, something colossal and unseen ploughed, occasionally roaring like thunder and causing tremors in the ground. Small stones skittered on the path which wound up a steep hill littered with unidentifiable bones.

Feeling powerless and afraid, Joy called for Skylar. He was long gone. She walked on, shouting his name until the sun sank below the horizon and three ringed-moons rose in a green sky pregnant with unfamiliar constellations.

Lost and alone, Joy repeatedly glanced back, hoping to find a doorway. The Nothing had advanced to within two yards of the spot where she hesitated, threatening to consume her into the void and driving her forward. The temperature plummeted. She called again, her voice hoarse and weary, 'Skylar, come back and lend me your fur, you stupid mutt.'

Water splashed over her shoes making her shiver. Looking down she screeched, startled by a many toothed wet creature snapping and snarling at her feet.

She flew up the path as if propelled by a strong wind, hopping and cringing as hundreds of small skeletons crunched underfoot. Tripping over, she fell onto the bones and stayed there, too stunned to move, praying for the world to return to some semblance of normality.

A hand reached down to drag her back on her feet.

Dina snapped, 'Are you dim, your Ladyship? When my sister invited you for supper you said, "I'm polishing my crown." Now you turn up as entrees for these stupid bastard river rats. Follow me.'

'It seems I have no other choice,' replied Joy, shaken by the woman's presence.

'So it does, Your Majesty. Hurry up, I haven't got all night.'

Joy trailed behind Dina until the sight of the squirming mass in her butt cheeks revolted her to the point of sickness and she hurried to catch up and walk at her side. Dina glanced at her, saying, 'Found yer manners, Princess?'

Joy swallowed sarcasm. 'Have you seen my dog?'

'He's like as not been eaten by now, forget him, your Highness.'

'Could we drop the royal references, please?'

'Sure, Queenie.'

'I see.'

'You don't see nuthin', my Lady, you've not even seen the moons.' Dina pointed to the vermillion sky where three green-ringed moons spun a million stars around their orbits.

'I simply chose to ignore them. Nothing makes sense here. Where in the name of God am I?'

'Your God has nothing to do with it, but I'll tell you this much, your Majesty, it ain't Kansas.'

Joy swatted at the twilight biters feasting on her exposed arms and face and said, 'That's enough nonsense. I'm exhausted. We need to find a place to stop.' Sweating and trying to conceal her tremors, she crested the hill with Dina as the triple moons rose higher in the star sodden sky.

'Don't worry, my Lady, you have no further to travel. Here is where I leave you to your right royal rest.'

Joy glanced around and, despite her determination to show no weakness, her skin paled under the green moonlight.

Dina watched her reaction with a smile of satisfaction dancing across thin lips and, under her gaze, Joy felt despair wrap its arms around to hold her in its deadly embrace. Her shoulders slumped in defeat, she said,

'Go. Leave me. I don't care if this is some kind of sick test. I'm tired. Jake is deadly. I can't save him, I can't love him and I can't live without him. I don't want to carry on. Leave me here to die.'

'I see that my Lady has come to her senses. Your wish is my command, Princess.' Dina vanished. Joy shuddered at the sight of endless, bone-built walls that reached into the clouds.

Chapter Forty-Two

-ABANDON HOPE YE WHO ENTER HERE-

A black fortress blocked the horizon, its outer defenses bleeding shadows into the far distance. Joy faced a gigantic iron studded door and desolation slid through her veins like a virus. The edifice shed hopelessness in fatal doses. Misery and defeat poisoned the air that seemed to tremble around its walls.

Joy bit her cheek until it bled, but the ground beneath her sore feet, the moons and the fortress persisted in being her reality. Dina had abandoned her and she had given up on herself.

She swallowed a lump in her throat and raised a heavy, fist shaped brass knocker to announce her presence. Dropping it, she expected to hear a deafening crash. The knocker landed with a dull thud. Her arms trembled with effort as she raised it again, and a third time. There was no reply.

Sand rose from around her feet to scratch and exfoliate her skin as an angry wind howled around the walls.

She waited with her arms wrapped tight around her body. A feeling of worthlessness wormed its way into her, and she sat clutching her knees to her chest, shivering against the wall's damp stones.

A memory surfaced of a different, warmer wall at her back. She relived the sensation of light dappling through branches and summer leaves to stroke warm patterns on her skin and recalled a redheaded woman saying,

'Death has been good to you, Joy.'

Not knowing what, if any, significance the memory held she hung her head and wept, choking on snot and tears as negative thoughts flooded her mind: I can't survive this place. Terrible things keep happening to me. I loved him. I loved a monster. I *allowed* myself to be violated. I deserve to die.

'Lord Death come for me.' Joy cried out in despair to the deaf night and, waiting for Death to collect her she curled into a ball of hopelessness against the mocking walls.

As the alien moons began to give way to dawn, she heard a dull scraping noise above her head.

A small window had opened in the door allowing angry words to fly out.

'Oy. You making all the fuss and racket out there. What do you want?'

Joy tensed and shuffled her backside further into the shadows. The voice complained, 'It's taken me a week and a day to get to this door, so show yourself. I want to see your miserable face.'

Rediscovering her survival instinct Joy began to crawl along the bottom of the wall.

The voice wheedled, 'I so, so, so deserve something for all my effort. Don't I?'

Deciding that her cover had been blown when she dropped the knocker, Joy stood and stumbled on numb legs to peer into the tiny window. There was no-one there.

Sighing, she put her lips against the hole and, in a weary voice, spoke into the darkness, 'My name is Joy. I...I... I think I, I mean, I do, seek sanctuary, that is.'

The voice held a note of interest. 'Speak up.'

She shouted, 'I am Joy and I need your help.'

'Joy, you say? Here? Well I never, ever, ever expected to hear your name around these parts, my Lady.'

The window slid shut almost taking off the end of her nose.

'You did say you are Joy?' The muffled voice behind the door was uncertain. '*The* Joy?'

Joy shouted, 'Yes, I am Joy. May I come in? It's freezing out here.'

'Wait.'

The immense door protested against its hinges, opening just enough to allow Joy to squeeze through. The stench hit hard. Her stomach clenched and bile burned her throat.

A short, scrawny man stood before her wringing his hands in glee. He wore a blood stained apron and reeked of sweat and gore. His face brought to mind a blonde angel and his large blue eyes were flecked with silver and gold. He grinned slyly up at her with cupid bow lips and beckoned her further inside saying, 'We so, so, so need Joy here. Welcome, my Lady. Oh, happy day.'

Behind her the door sneaked closed inch by slow inch until, with a polite click, it locked. Panic hit Joy like an electric shock and she rushed to place her hand against the door commanding, 'Open.' The door declined to obey her order.

She struggled to speak while she tried not to breathe the putrid air, but it had to be done. So, confronting the beautifully disgusting little man she said, 'Let me out.'

He giggled. 'No can do, your Highness.'

Deciding to wait until his back was turned to make her escape, and keeping a hand pressed over her nose, she asked the question she feared the answer to, 'Where am I?'

The man danced a happy jig and replied, 'You are *not* in the Nothing. You are *not* in the Realm. You are *not* at Heavensgate soooo, you must be here. My esteemed Highness.'

He clicked his fingers and produced a red megaphone out of thin air. He bowed to an invisible audience then, with excitement stitched onto every word, he announced, 'Boys and girls, listen up, Joy is *here*. Joy has come to save us all...' his voice drifted away into emotional sobs. Green globular tears slid down his perfect nose and splashed noisily onto the filthy, straw strewn floor. The megaphone vanished and in a voice ripped with sorrow he said, 'This is *His* prison, your Majesty. We are bound here by *His* displeasure and we need you.'

Animated voices called from the cells, 'Joy! Joy! Joy!' The multitude of prisoners stamped bare feet to accompany their rhythmic chant. Metal cups set up a cacophony of familiar bangs and clangs against iron bars. Tears pricked Joy's eyes as ghostly, emaciated arms stretched beseechingly into the wide, noxious corridors that disappeared into eternal gloom.

She turned to face the sycophantic stranger and, in a voice stronger than she felt, commanded, 'Let me out. This is the wrong place.'

Her host clapped his grime encrusted hands and squealed, 'It *is* the Wrong Place, you are so clever, Highness. But I can't let you out; the door opens one way, which is this way. So, so, so sorry, my Lady.'

Keeping her sense of smell safely behind her hand Joy glared and said, 'Don't be ridiculous. I *am* leaving and you should be bloody well ashamed of keeping people locked up in these conditions.'

The man stared at the floor and sniffing back tears, said, 'I am. I am painfully ashamed, my Lady. I am tortured by shame. I truly am, tortured forever and ever.'

Receiving only a retch and a heave in response to his declaration of eternal suffering he ran round and round in circles, tearing at his ragged clothes as he lamented his anguished disgrace.

Joy reached out to touch the door and in a voice full of confidence said, 'Open.' Nothing happened. Fury at her situation spilled out and she shouted, 'I'll bloody well report you to… to someone, to anyone. This stink clings. I feel as if I've been dipped in a sewer. I swear there is shit on my tongue.'

The man stopped running and Joy vomited onto his bare feet.

He looked up with fresh tears brimming in his eyes and said, 'Oh my, oh thank you my Queen. I won't wash for another millennium. Let me show you to your room, Majesty.'

Joy's feet left the ground as two huge fur clad creatures carried her, screeching in protest down a dark hallway. With a definite spring in his step the jailer accompanied her and said, 'No point struggling,

Princess. Oh it smells so, so, so rich. Try holding your royally scented hand over your pretty nose again. Dearie me, my Lady, what a lot of fuss about nothing.'

They stopped before an open cell. Joy stared at the advice painted above the bars:

'*Abandon hope ye who enter here*'

She renewed the struggle against her captors' greasy arms shouting, 'Let me go. I demand to leave.'

The jailer held his barrel shaped stomach and rocked merrily as he said, 'My Lady Joy, *you* said you wanted to die and *you* knocked on *my* door. You should be careful what you ask for. Here you are and all is well.'

The guards shoved her into the waiting cell where she landed on her knees in the dirt.

The jailer's merriment faded as he spoke from the opposite side of the locked bars. 'Can't you read, Highness? No-one leaves here.'

The clanging and cat calling from other inmates stopped as if a switch had been thrown. Darkness descended and silence collapsed into the space around her like soil in a grave.

Joy grasped the bars and peered across the dark chasm that separated the two rows of prisoners. The cell opposite emitted a sickly green light and an elderly woman staggered from her wooden bunk, her pain carved into her once pretty features. Joy called, 'Hello?'

She watched the woman pass an emaciated, wrinkled hand across her eyes, shake her head and step onto a rickety chair. Finding her balance, she slipped her scrawny neck into a frayed noose that hung from the ceiling.

Joy stuck her head between the bars and shouted, 'Oh God, no, please take that off. Talk to me. Please don't do it. I'm Joy. I can help you. Don't give up. No!'

The old woman's neck snapped with the sound of a rifle being cracked open. She jittered and dangled, swinging back and forth. Her bladder and bowels released, her eyes bulged and her tongue popped out to loll on her chin like a yellowed piece of liver.

'Jailer!'

The man stepped out of the shadows, smiling shyly as Joy pleaded, 'Help her, please. Cut her down.'

'Calm, sweet Joy, it's just her time to play at meat pendulums, a game for all the family,' he sniggered and trotted across to the hanging woman's cell.

'You can come down now, Clara. Wakey, wakey rise and shine, sunbeam.'

The dead woman threw her jailer a soft girlish smile, removed the noose from around her bent and bruised neck, dropped to the floor and crawled into her bunk disturbing the other life forms there. Joy clung to the bars and slid to her knees weeping.

A serpent-skinned man pushed a squeaky metal trolley full of multi-coloured pills down the hallway. Dragging one useless leg behind him, he carried a length of rubber tubing coiled over one shoulder and sported a large copper funnel as headwear.

Joy heard the jailer say, 'Good evening, Nurse Thomas. Pop in to see me when you've finished your rounds.'

Joy strained to peer down the corridor that swallowed him in profound darkness. The Nurse pushed his trolley out of sight. The squeaking stopped.

The blast of a gunshot smashed her already terrorized heart against her breastbone. The serpent man hissed, 'Good one, Bob. Nice shot. See you tomorrow.'

The ringing in Joy's ears died away. The squeaky trolley moved on. It stopped again. She heard a man pleading, 'Please, Nurse, don't make me. I won't do it again. I'm sorry. I didn't really want to die. I'm sorry.

The Nurse's sibilant voice was gentle as he said, 'Don't be a cry baby, Simon. Open wide and swallow your medicine. No? Funnel time!'

Joy curled up on the floor, preferring it to the infested mattress and covered her ears against the retching and choking sounds which chased each other up the hallway and into her head.

She resolved to ignore everything around her and concentrate on escaping.

A familiar rushing, crashing, sloshing noise drew her attention.

She looked through the bars. It was too dark to see anything. The noise grew louder and she clung on tight as swift, gray, icy waves burst into her cell to trap her in a raging, suffocating, murderous column of salt water.

Joy struggled to no avail as her personal sea covered her mouth and nose, pouring in to fill her, bursting her lungs and, retreated like the tide when she dropped lifeless on a floor covered with wet sand, shells and seaweed.

The jailer's voice rang with pride. 'Open your eyes, Joy. Well done, Your Highness. Welcome to another day in paradise.'

He stood outside her cell with a bloodied meat cleaver held in his left hand and a shotgun in his right. His expression benign, he said, 'Oh I am so, so, so happy to have you here, my Queen. You've made such a difference already.'

He pointed to his curved yellow toenails, almost washed clean by the deluge and kicked a pretty shell that poked out of the sand announcing, 'Boys and girls, our Lady Joy has brought us a beach.'

The mug clanging and frantic cries of the prisoners' desire for Joy were louder and more insistent than the night before. Joy was sopping wet, alive and terrified.

The jailer gingerly placed the recently used cleaver between his rotten teeth and fired a shot into the air. Obedient silence descended. Passing the bloodied blade to Nurse, who licked it clean, and tucking the gun out of sight, he clasped his filthy hands behind his back and rocked self-importantly on his heels saying, 'I understand. You all so, so, so want a piece of Joy. You must all be patient. Who knows what gifts our royal resident will bring tomorrow.'

His eyes lit up as Nurse's tongue shot out to spear a silver skinned fish that had been flopping around with a dozen others on the sandy floor.

'I am so, so, so very much thanking you, Your Majesty. Tonight we will eat a feast of fresh fish fit for a King and, his beloved Queen. Dina will bake it in salt for our delight. You do know my chef; don't you?' He smiled revealing black, soggy rotten stumps and licked his beautiful cracked, pus weeping lips with a green and black coated tongue.

The jailer bowed to Joy, revealing a deep head wound crawling with maggots. In a voice full of cheer he winked one sparkling eye and, his voice full of hope, said, 'See you later, Princess.'

Despair's icy fingers clutched Joy's soul. She lay on the cell's sandy floor and closed her eyes. Images drifted into her mind. She saw a man holding a red hot poker on a beach covered in black, barnacle encrusted mussels. She gazed at violets in the shape of a heart padlocked by buttercups. Her eyelids fluttered. She felt the wind press her back while she paddled in icy foam as a yacht with glittering, fluttering paper heart sails floated by. The vessel's captain was a pink lycra clad man singing, 'It's not unusual'. She shielded her eyes and watched a car careen in slow motion over the cliff to crash onto the rocks below. Joy stared up at Sam Black's confused face as he made love to her; she smelt parma violet candy. She saw a gypsy caravan and touched Jacob's scarred chest as locked café doors sprang open at her touch.

Joy leapt to her feet. 'Memories,' she muttered and pressed her palms flat against the bars whispering, 'Open.' Nothing happened. She clasped her hands over her head and moaned in disappointment and frustration.

Remembering the words of doom painted above her cell inspiration struck. Joy scanned the cell for something to cut herself with. Turning the rickety wooden chair over she found a vicious looking splinter under the roughly made seat which she tore off and, taking a deep breath, stabbed it forcefully into her left palm. She stifled a scream and hopped around biting her lip until it, too, was bleeding. When the fire in her hand subsided to a dull throb, she thrust a finger in the wound and, using her blood, wrote on the wall:

Spes anchora vitae

'It took you long enough to remember me,' said Hope who appeared, pouting, on the opposite side of the bars.

Joy covered her surprise by saying, 'Stop sulking and get me out of here. I have to get back to the Lodge.'

Hope's voice was discordant. 'Do you want me to help you return to your beloved demon?'

Joy flinched and said, 'Please stop clanging, Hope, it hurts my brain. Will you help me or not?'

'Of course I will help you, but we have a problem. Look.' She pointed at the dirty angel faced man who had bounded up the hallway to gaze in awe from Hope to Joy and back again.

'Oh my. You are *both* here. How in His name is this possible? I can't believe it.' The jailer struggled with excitement that lit his incredible eyes and shook his skinny body like an epileptic fit. Getting his emotions under control he cried into the dark hallway, 'Oh, my dear friends, we must so, so, so thank the Dark Lord in His torment. People, I am delighted to announce that we have Hope in the house!'

He prostrated himself, weeping, at Hope's sandal clad feet. Holding her nose she took a dainty step back and said, 'Now, sister, you may begin to see the enormity of my problems.' She waved her elegant bell and bangle clad arms in a gesture intended to encompass the jailer and his prisoners. 'These tragic souls are here because they lost me and now they have "found" me. I cannot leave without them. It is against the rules.'

Joy privately thought that the rules stank almost as much as her captor, but said, 'OK, let me out and we will free them together.'

The jailer's slimy hands caressed Hope's ankles; she kicked him under the chin and in a discordant voice said, 'I will not warn you again. Do not touch me, Imp.'

Heavensgate: Joy

The prison resonated with the sound of people calling to each other: 'find strength', 'hang on', 'have hope' and 'oh, what a joyous day.' Joy's neighbour, out of sight, but in good voice, cried out, 'Don't give up, brothers and sisters. Be full of joy. Where there is life there is hope.'

Down the hallway a familiar voice rang out, 'Don't cry, Simon, I have swallowed your pills myself and thrown the funnel away.'

Hope screwed up her nose in disgust and said, 'See, sister, these souls now have Joy *and* Hope. We shall pay dearly for this, the Creator demands balance and the Wrong Place is not His territory.'

Joy ran her fingers through wet, knotted hair and smelt fish. Her face flushed, her jaw clenched tight and she exploded, beating at the bars and screaming, 'Hope, stop bloody well pontificating and...,' the bars disintegrated. Hope said, 'Let you out. Is that what you were about to demand?'

Joy ignored her petulant sister who once again screeched at the amorous Jailer to never, ever again dare suck her toes or touch any other part of her person.

His angelic eyes grew wide with something akin to desire mixed with fear as he watched Hope and Joy united in the endless darkness of the prison hallway. Joy barely touched the nearest sewage dripping wall and whispered, 'Open.'

The fortress trembled, the ground shook and all sound was vanquished as the prison vanished.

Hope rushed to the river to wash her feet; Joy stood on the skeleton path with her mouth open and arms outspread. She called, 'There are biters in the river.'

'Jump in the lake.'

'Pardon?'

'You need to go back to Heavensgate and jump in the lake. Unless I give you back your heart and deliver you to Death once and for all, he won't let me free you from that hell hole. I cannot do that, I will not have your death on my conscience, so you have to escape on your own. I can guide you through the Nothing and back to the Lodge, but then I must leave you.'

Joy smiled and said, 'It's OK. I had time to think in the Wrong Place. I must save Jake in order to help him cross the Gateway and join with Jacob. I believe it is my destiny to reunite them.'

'Are you crazy? Save yourself. Forget him. That demon has one hell of a deadly kiss. I tried him once and he almost killed me. Joy, are you listening? Your beloved Jake tried to kill *Hope*.'

'You aren't dead.'

'That's not the point. He didn't know it was impossible for him to kill me. You must leave him, Joy.

'It's my duty to bring him to the light. He needs me.'

'I have half a mind to leave you here and the other half wants to shatter your foolish heart into a million pieces; sticking it back together would keep you out of mischief for a very long time.'

Discordant bells pealed, forcing Joy to cover her ears and shout, 'I have *hope* that I can save Jake and myself. You and I are stuck with one another, so stop your tinny ringing and lead me back to the Lodge. Please.'

Hope took Joy's hand and neither woman spoke as the Nothing enveloped them. They fled through the void, keeping the metallic grinding and clashing noise at their backs, until they felt solid ground underfoot and snowflakes settled in their hair. Hope said, 'Welcome back to Heavensgate, Joy.'

Silver bells chimed a melancholy tune causing Joy to cry out, 'Please, Hope, don't leave me.'

Hope wrung her pale hands. 'Your suffering is my punishment for guarding your heart. Lord Death says I should not meddle. If you ask it of me, I will set aside the pain it would cause me and call him to collect you. All this will be forgotten at your reincarnation.' The immortal sisters clung together as a dam of pain and sorrow broke inside them.

Joy attempted a smile through tears that threatened to wash away her resolve and said, 'No, don't call him, he will take me soon enough. You must leave and I must free Jake alone.'

Hope shook her silver mane and Joy heard the slow chime of funeral bells.

'Hope, please don't cry. It doesn't matter if I fail, it is my destiny to try and raise Jake from sorrow. I am Joy.'

Hope sniffed and shrugged her shoulders saying, 'I tried and failed to save him. I do not think he deserves another chance at redemption.'

'Hope, try and understand that I have no choice.'

'Whatever comes, sister, I promise to guard your heart with all my strength; I will pour myself into its sweetness until it shines and guides you home.'

Hope turned to retreat into the Nothing. Her voice faded behind the swirling blizzard as she said, 'I will do everything in my power to meddle in Lord Death's quest for your soul.'

Hope was gone.

Joy's stomach clenched and her head pounded like a bass drum behind her eyes. Her throat tightened, the blood cooled in her veins and her teeth chattered in the freezing cold.

The Lodge loomed out of the snow. An icy gale force wind whipped around Joy's shivering body, picked her up as if she weighed nothing and dropped her from high onto the stone steps below. She landed face down, hearing the snap as her nose broke and the rush of hot blood gushed into the snow. Helpless and afraid she drifted in and out of consciousness as the temperature plummeted and her blood formed ruby crystals of ice around her head.

Despite Hope's promise, Joy the immortal was dying.

Chapter Forty-Three

-THE BEAST-

Two dragonflies, one flaming red and the other almost opaque, flitted around the shattered frozen body. They flew weaving gossamer strands of swirling neon light, creating a vast nebula where Joy's pure soul blinded Heaven and Earth.

The resurrected spirit threw her energy through time and space, battling Death's siren call to eternity. Joy was focused on a single objective: 'Save Jake.'

She plunged at the speed of light, bursting the veil between life and death to smash into her body and shoot to her feet. Feeling the rush of warm blood fill her veins in a tidal wave of power she opened the door with an anger fuelled touch. Bursting into the Lodge in a furious blaze of light she came face to face with a waxen faced stranger.

He was unusually tall and fair. Underneath a dirty panama hat his features were bland and forgettable. He wore a creased linen suit and a black silk shirt with a distasteful Hawaiian pattern tie. Button-up spats sat atop shiny black shoes that covered extraordinarily large and misshapen feet. Fetid steam seeped from every foul atom of his being and his milky blue eyes danced with amusement as the Beast gave Joy time to fully comprehend his nature.

She froze, totally unprepared for the malevolent creature that smiled down at her revealing rows of razor sharp mirrored teeth. Speaking in a cultured English accent it asked, 'What are *you* doing here?' His voice struck Joy like a fist in the solar plexus, driving out her new found breath. Bent double, she gasped, '*You* are not invited and will leave. *I* live here.'

The monster leaned against the wall, loosening the disgusting tie while he checked her over. He salivated, long stinking strands of puss hanging off his chin, but made no move toward her. Joy returned the stare, her heart banging in her chest like a team of racing horses, sweat beading on her upper lip and streaming in burning rivulets down her spine while her mind panicked like a rat in a trap.

The Beast licked black lips with a serpent's tongue and said, 'Your presence in Heavensgate is a trifling annoyance for me which won't last much longer.'

He pulled a Havana cigar out of thin air and lit it with a spark from a red clawed nail. The shabby suit faded away to reveal a muscular male body at least ten feet tall, with rippling shoulders half as wide. Its face distorted to give up the last vestiges of human appearance, its skin became thin and blood red, thick black veins throbbing beneath the surface in complex patterns. The stink of burning flesh rolled across the space between them.

Joy vomited on her shoes; her bladder gave way and burning shame washed over her. The Beast laughed and his words left abrasions on her skin as he sniggered, 'You are weak, exactly like your blessed virgin mother.'

He lunged and grabbed her hair, singeing it in his burning grip and adding to the overwhelming stench. Holding her dangling in midair, he stared into her eyes and sucked in a strong rancid breath that tugged at her chest. In a voice like baying hounds he howled, 'Come out and play, Lady Joy.'

Her soul fought to deny the Beast's command, her limbs twitched involuntarily and her fingers and toes cramped in spasm. Pain stabbed behind her eyes and her vision blurred as she was crushed in the monster's arms. Then, screaming with pleasure, he threw open the door and flung her outside like trash.

She landed on her back, hearing but not feeling a sharp crack as her spine smashed against the frozen ground. The Lord of Hell stood astride his victim, spitting fury into snow that hissed and turned to steam and screamed, 'Get out of that human body, you stinking whore. In the name of the Dark Messiah I command you to get out.'

Sucking in a rattling breath of freezing air, Joy tried and failed to scrabble away on the icy ground. A shot of rancid phlegm seared through her flesh to burn like acid in her shoulder. She tried to scream, 'Jake…'

A huge, pointed shoe kicked her in the temple, snapping her neck like a twig. The Beast roared his victory, 'This is what happens to fools who dare enchant our beloved warrior and destroy our glorious prison.'

Grunting, he dragged Joy's body up the steps of the Lodge, cracking her skull on all three. Back inside, he shouted, 'It takes a real *man* to do the job right. Are you listening, Jake? You infernal, useless lump of imp-shit, I need an axe. The Creator's servant won't leave this stinking flesh so we must cut her out.'

The Beast flung Joy's lifeless body onto the kitchen table and roared, 'How the hell did this whore get here?'

Jake crawled on his belly, not daring to raise his eyes. In a voice dripping with subservience he said, *My Lord, I beg your indulgence. I thought you sent her to me as a toy. She is nothing more than a plaything, an object used to pass the time spent waiting for your Holy presence to grace your Lodge.*

The Beast banked the fire in his eyes. He shook and the monster disappeared under a white scene of crime body suit covered by a striped butcher's apron. Snarling at Jake, who lay with his belly and throat exposed like a whipped dog, his master kicked him in the ribs and said, 'You dare forget me, the Vengeful One, for *this*? I am hungry and impatient for joy. Get up and fetch an axe.'

Pointing at Jake's retreating back ihe shouted, 'Ligaveris.' The word punched into Jake's spine and wrapped itself around him binding his magnificent wings to his torso with three cruel iron hoops 'Your body is mine to control, remember that, minion.'

Passing the table, Jake grabbed Joy's limp arms and threw her over his shoulder.

The Beast grunted, 'What are you doing with my prey, Imp?'

Looking into his blazing eyes, Jake felt a feral urge to drop Joy and violate her where she fell. Fighting for self-control he gritted his teeth and replied, *I'm taking it to the workshop where there are tools, My Lord. We can chain its body to a bench. We can play with the flesh and brand it. If you would rest, Mighty Lord, I will light the brazier, sharpen the axe and heat the irons in preparation for your pleasure.*

'Call me when the whore is ready for my delight. Strip it, chain it down, wake it and get its body ready and screaming for me. I will amuse myself with the stinking bitch until it begs for release. Don't take too long, Imp.'

As you command, my Lord.

Jake felt his insistent wings protest at their bindings as he ran, carrying Joy out of the kitchen and along the deck. Passing the workshop he hesitated as images of delicious torture and foul pleasure flooded his mind and stirred his loins. He fled the Beast's influence, crying with frustration, battling an overpowering desire to defile her and hurried on to the lake.

Jim and Skylar awaited him by the old row boat. As Jake approached the water, his mind rejected the foul images and longings that had attempted to possess and control him. He moved Joy from his shoulder to cradle her in his arms startled when Jim slapped her across the face shouting, 'Wake up, my Lady.'

She has gone. Her neck is broken.

A storm boomed and rolled overhead. The first fat drops of rain hit their faces and Jim shouted to be heard above the crash of thunder, 'Nonsense. Don't give up on her now, Jake. This one's special.' He slapped Joy again, harder. She groaned and raised one hand in a feeble attempt to swat him away.

Forked lightning lit the scenery flashing across the forest of swaying pines. Jake wept as he kissed her forehead. Jim screamed as the wind threatened to fling his words across the lake, 'Put her in the boat. Hurry, Jake.'

The small vessel repeatedly pulled tight against its moorings then tossed about like weightless flotsam. Soaked by the downpour, Jake lowered Joy into the bottom of the flimsy boat as if she was treasure. Skylar jumped in beside her. The storm raged more violently by the second.

Jake shouted, *Joy, wake up. There's a hole in the lake, head for it and jump in. There's no other way out.* He kissed her again and whispered, *I won't let the Beast take you too, my love.*

Woozy, and finally aware of the peril she faced, Joy tried to scramble out of the crazily bobbing craft. Pushing her back and shaking his head at her, Jim unhooked the mooring and, wading into the lake, pushed the boat away from the shore. It shuddered once then catapulted over the waves.

Jim slid beneath the water and vanished.

Joy sobbed hysterically as driving, icy rain lashed at her face and lightning hit the bow splitting the old wood. She clung to the dog as the vessel was dragged inexorably toward the vortex created by a huge whirlpool where the island used to be.

Over the cacophony of the squall and the raging boom of thunder Joy heard the Beast bellow in unholy fury. She yelled into a gale force wind that snatched at her words, 'Jake. It's coming for you, run!'

Jake stood firm and unflinching as the Beast bore down on him and as fiery arms locked him in a lethal embrace and razor teeth approached his jugular, he whispered, *I love you, Joy.*

The boat rocked and dipped violently. It was floundering, taking on water, freezing waves struck at every side and sharp, earth scented spray slapped her face.

A warm mouth tugged at her hand. Hugging the trembling dog to her side, Joy murmured, 'Skylar, my Fur Face, my sweet friend, I'm sorry.'

She sank to the bottom of the waterlogged craft and Lake Disregard collapsed into the void.

G-force trapped Skylar and Joy in the bottom of the shattered vessel as it plummeted through a cloudless sky. The wind tearing a single word from her throat, 'Jake...'

Chapter Forty-Four

-HOPE SPRINGS ETERNAL-

Skylar's hot tongue licked her face. Joy spat sand, tasted salt and opened stinging eyes to see a ceiling of thousands of fossilised shells entombed in granite. The shining tide sat at least a mile out while heat mirages shimmied like belly dancers in the sunshine.

The dog pricked his ears and cocked his head to one side as Joy said, 'Well, Fur Face, that was quite a ride. I guess we could be dead in worse places. Let's take a walk.'

Shielding her eyes from the glare she left the cool of the cavern and looked across a rock-strewn beach, deserted apart from a gypsy wagon that stood under the shelter of dark cliffs. The wagon was decaying gracefully on wheels bent and half buried in the sand, its wind weathered forget-me-not blue paint flaking away in strips and curls. Joy hurried to take a closer look as the sun squeezed steam from her wet clothes and pressed her long hair into gentle waves that mimicked the ripples in the sand.

'Bloody hell, Skylar, I remember this place.' She ran the last few yards splashing through rock pools and kicking up sand, all anxiety swept away as she leapt up three rickety steps and smacked her flat palm on a narrow door.

'Hello!' There was no reply.

Heavensgate: Joy

Skylar crawled under the wagon, tucked his nose beneath the stub of his tail and curled up as if he belonged there.

Leaving him to sleep, Joy raced to the slipway, grinning in anticipation of home as she climbed the steep cobbled road that lead to her café.

Struggling for breath, but still smiling, she read a sign in the window: 'Closed for refurbishment.' Her smile slipped. She pressed a finger to the double doors, saying, 'Open.' They remained locked. She stared at the offending digit and tried again with no success. Pressing her face to the windows, shielding reflections with her hands, she saw only empty space. She swallowed hard as tears pricked the back of her eyes and happiness drained away like water in a sandcastle moat.

A small boy observed Joy from a bench opposite the café. Streams of water flowed from his shoes and ran down the hill seeking the sea. Spotting him she shouted, 'I don't have time for your games, kid. Go away.'

The boy shrugged as if he couldn't be bothered one way or the other and vanished, leaving a puddle on the cobblestones with a shiny dollar glinting at its centre. Joy picked up the wet coin and muttered, 'Bloody annoying.'

She headed for a row of Victorian houses, almost all of them converted to Bed and Breakfast establishments. Ruby's scarlet door stood out from the rest. Joy took a deep breath, plastered a smile on her anxious face and rang the big brass bell; no-one was home. Disappointment elbowed out anticipation until, remembering Gabi, she walked with renewed optimism to the church yard and bounded up the steps to Gabi's lodgings over the Vicar's garage. Joy banged on the bright pink door with both fists but received no welcoming Andalusian kisses. However, she knew that wherever Ruby went Gabi followed, so she returned to the lower village certain of finding them together.

Her first stop was Hope's shop, but it had been replaced by a second-hand bookstore. She entered, feeling the absence of Hope's silent bell. A tall, beaky-nosed bald man with rounded shoulders sat on a high stool behind the counter. He reminded Joy of a nesting stork. Stifling a hysterical impulse to laugh, she cleared her throat and said, 'Excuse me, do you mind telling me when you took over these premises?'

The shop keeper climbed off his perch and walked on extraordinarily long skinny legs to a step ladder which he climbed unsteadily in order to peruse the upper bookshelves. Joy held the bottom of the steps and said, 'Excuse me, I'm talking to you,' he ignored her. Exasperated by his ignorance she swept out of the store slamming the door so hard that book spines trembled and pages rustled in fear.

She wandered into the Oaktree Inn expecting to find Gabi preening himself in the pub mirrors while Ruby threw back medicinal gin and tonics. They weren't there. Sighing, she approached the bar saying, 'Excuse me, have you seen Gabi and Ruby from the café today?' The nose pierced, gum chewing, blue haired barmaid ignored her. Joy raised her voice and said, 'Oy. I'm talking to you.' The girl began a conversation with an acne spattered tattooed male who was using the bar for physical support. Frustrated and angry, Joy walked out, once again slamming the door behind her. Brass horseshoes bounced off their nails and scared the young barmaid and her customers half to death with yet more evidence of a haunting.

Following her nose to the sweet shop, Joy found Rose behind the counter using antique scales to weigh out old fashioned candy into small paper bags. Eva Cassidy's sweet voice filled the air singing, *'Over the Rainbow.'*

Lost in the melody, Rose sang along. Joy waited for the song to end then said, 'Hi, Rose, have you seen Ruby or Gabi?' Rose limped to the back of the shop and settled into her old rocking chair with a cup of tea.

About to follow Rose and insist that she turn up her hearing aid, Joy gasped as she saw him reflected in the leaded glass cabinet. He opened his fob watch and the fractured notes of *'Que Sera'* assaulted her ears.

Keeping his attention on Rose he blew Joy a kiss and she whispered, 'Please, my Lord, I can't leave with you today. The Beast has Jake. I have to find a way to help him.' Death shrugged his shoulders, snapped the watch closed and replacing it in his embroidered waistcoat said,

Heavensgate: Joy

-Lady Joy, don't distress yourself. I have summoned my Lady Hope. She awaits your presence in her...beach hut.-

Joy pleaded, 'Please, allow me to save Jake and live a human life span with him.'

-You flatter me with your notion of my power.-

She swallowed the lump in her throat as Death pointed at Rose.

-If you will excuse me, my Lady, I have work.-

The watch reappeared. Joy watched in horror as Rose's sweet face slackened and her teacup fell to the floor. '*Que Sera*' filled the shop and Death waved Joy away.

-Hope is waiting. Go.-

Dragging her feet Joy retraced her steps. All sense of urgency gone. She now understood why Death was nonchalant in her presence and why no-one, apart from the wet boy, could see or hear her.

She reached the wagon and despair flooded her soul at the sight of Dina sat on the steps saying, 'In the Wrong Place again, Your Majesty?' She shook her head and the vision disappeared, but Dina's mocking voice continued to scream from the gulls wheeling overhead.

Joy beat on the door hard enough to break it. It did not open, so she sat slumped on the top step crying, 'Oh, Jake, I'm so, so sorry.' She stared across the sand as the sky and the sea merged into the horizon and vanished leaving only her and the door at her back. She had resigned herself to an invisible death in the Nothing when the scent of Parma violets crept up her nose and tickled the back of her throat making her cough.

'Come in, sister.'

Hope stood in the open doorway. Wild flowers threaded her long silver hair, her eyelashes shone with ice and snowflakes glittered on her toe and finger nails. Joy raised her eyebrows at Hope's appearance and followed her inside.

She sat without being invited and gulped wine from the fancy goblet before being offered a drink. Smoky lilac tendrils rose from the goblet to soothe her dry throat and calm her frazzled nerves. Placing a hand in front of her eyes, she swallowed tears with the wine and grief threatened to overwhelm her. Her misery was interrupted by Hope's jingling.

'I'm happy you feel at home here, *Joy.*'

'What other home have I got, *Hope?*'

'Now, now, don't be despondent, that won't do at all. It's only a matter of time, quite literally if you understand the quantum side of it all.'

'And do you? I mean, do you understand the quantum side of it all, Hope?'

'Hush your sarcasm. I don't have to understand electricity to turn on the light, little sister.' Hope patted Joy's knee. 'Come on, cheer up. Joy to the world and all that jazz, remember?'

Joy's face crumpled. 'I can remember everything. Giving Joy to the world is a big ask for me right now.'

Hope offered her sister the tarot, her voice brusque as she said, 'Stop wallowing. Pick a card.'

Joy glared at her saying, 'I don't have time for games.'

The wagon filled with the sound of a thousand percussion instruments. Joy placed her fingers in her ears and shouted, 'Stop it. Can't you communicate normally for heaven's sake?'

'I am sorry. I forget your persistent and delicate human sensibilities. I explained time to you. Do you ever listen?'

'I'm listening. Don't jingle jangle at me.'

'Joy, you and I have as much time as we will ever need. Have you learned nothing from your adventures?'

Joy sniffed. 'I learned that I don't like games.

'It's all a game, now stop feeling sorry for yourself and pick your first card.'

Joy waved the deck away saying, 'Help me return to Heavensgate. The Nothing swallowed Jake and the Beast and when I fell through Lake Disregard I saw the future. If I do not save Jake he will hang from the Angel Oak.'

Hope raised ice-covered eyebrows and said, 'Goodness me, not again, how very medieval. I once knew Jacob and his alter ego, Jake, *very* well if you get my meaning. I remind you that the demon is a lost cause. He has travelled to dark places, do not follow him.'

Joy found her glass refilled and swallowing a mouthful of the lilac nectar said, 'I don't care about his past. I can save him in the here and now.'

Hope snorted in disgust and said, 'The here and now? You are naïve. Future, past, present, they are all illusion. Don't look so crestfallen. Enough talk, pick a card.'

Joy bit her bottom lip as she unwillingly let her mind linger on the thought of Hope with Jake then said, 'Why should I do what you want when you won't help me save the man I love?'

'Don't be petulant. You should humour me because Death claimed you at Heavensgate and we need to get the best of your heart back from your beloved monster.'

Joy's eyes searched Hope's display of hearts. Her voice shook as she said, 'My heart is missing. I thought you had it.'

'So did I.' Hope screwed up her beautiful face and frowned waving the fanned out deck until Joy took a card and concealed it in her palm. Noticing her sister's tragic expression Hope decided to confide her own feelings. Her voice held an uncertain tinkle as she said, 'Joy, I think I understand how you suffer because, I am, it's as if, well I think, maybe I feel, *perplexed*?'

Joy laughed, a sad, cracked sound that made Hope bristle and snap,

'I see you find my problems amusing. This feeling is a first for me. However, in an infinite universe, it is written that everything must happen at least once.'

Joy asked, 'Do you really believe that?'

'I must, as must you. Please, pick another four cards and let's see the end game.'

Joy set four well worn tarot cards face down on the small table; Hope's voice rang with reverence as she said, 'Sister, place your first card.'

Agitated, Joy swept all five cards together and spread them out face up saying, 'Amen.'

Hope gasped. Joy slumped in the chair and covered her face with her hands.

Hope whispered, 'I will shuffle the cards.'

Joy uncovered her tear streaked face and cried, 'Don't touch them. You know nothing will change.'

Hope and Joy held hands across the table and struggled to accept the sight of five identical tarot cards each one depicting the hanging man. He swung from a golden oak tree, the rope around his neck was blue and his bloodshot jade eyes bulged from their sockets. Even in death he was handsome, despite his face being terribly scarred down one side. A circle of scarlet roses burned at his feet.

Joy stood tipping over the table, sending its contents flying over Hope and said, 'It's Jake. This is his punishment for saving me from the Beast. He will hang. His neck will snap, over and over again for all time.'

'Yes, I think you are correct, sister. I don't understand though, whose are the roses?'

'What? You have seen my love dying for all eternity like poor old Clara in the Wrong Place and you are concerned with pretty flowers depicted on the bloody cards?'

'If the man is real and the tree is real then the roses are real too, Joy, and they are neither yours nor mine. What can this mean?'

'It's not bloody important. Saving Jake is.'

Joy stepped over to the decorated chest. The cherubic hands uncurled their golden baby fingers one at a time as if reluctant. Hope's gray eyes filled with compassion and the lid popped open.

'Joy, this tarot reading may be a trick. The Lord of Darkness wants to trap you in Heavensgate. Beware all evil and may the Creator protect and bless you, dear sister.'

Joy raised a hand in farewell, leaned backwards over the edge of the chest and, like a diver leaving a boat, dropped into the Nothing.

From underneath the wagon, Skylar howled. Inside, Hope slid, sobbing to the sunshine dappled floor. Something pricked her palm. She looked at the crimson rose burning there and comprehension lit her

eyes. Stroking the flaming petals, the spirit of Hope swallowed hard and said,
   'Thank you, Faith.'

Chapter Forty-Five

-THE HANGING MAN-

Joy travelled laser straight and burning like lightening through the Nothing until her light solidified and, with a bone shaking jolt, she landed on the bed she had once shared with Jake.

Screaming, 'Where are you?' she jumped up and ran from room to room leaving footprints on the filthy floors and sending dust flying to float in the musty air.

The kitchen stank like a stagnant pool. Vicious thorns blocked the light from the window. Shadows lurked in musty corners, waiting. The Lodge was in a state of decay and decomposition as if it had been empty for a thousand years.

Choking on dirt and dust, Joy stared warily at the axe buried to its hilt in the table. Thirsty, she took a greasy glass from the worktop, polishing it on her shirt. She turned on the faucet. Rumbling shook the stone floor. Pipes groaned.

Joy screeched as the glass shattered under a flood of stinking muck that spewed into her eyes and mouth. She ran to the bathroom, half blinded, retching and spitting. Grabbing a moth-eaten towel to wipe away the noxious sludge she heard a tapping from the mirror above the sink. She rubbed a clean circle in the tarnished surface and pressed her hand against the cracked glass. Susie watched from the other side.

Joy shouted, 'Help me, I can't find...' her voice trailed away along with her memory.

The tiled floor shifted underfoot and the walls shook. Growls emanated from the drains and Joy forgot who she was and what she was doing. Susie rapped hard on her side of the mirror. Joy stood confused as the Lodge began to sway as if made of paper. Susie's remaining eye flashed panic. She placed a hand around the front of her neck and moved the other at the side of her head in a tugging motion. Joy raised her eyebrows and shook her head. Susie stuck out her tongue and dropped her ruined face to her shoulder. The tarot's hanging man flashed into Joy's mind and dashed through her trance like ice water as tiles shot from the bathroom walls like ceramic missiles.

Blowing a kiss at Susie, Joy raced back to the kitchen to grapple with the axe, but it would not shift. Giving up, she took a short, sharp knife from the block, tucked it into the back of her jeans and, as the floor rose and fell in stone waves she battled her way to the door.

'Bitch! No!' The Beast's unholy fury rattled the windows and set copper-bottomed pans rocking on the beams. Chairs leapt into the air and battered against cupboards, smashing into splinters that flew like spears. The stench of sulphur and decomposing flesh filled the lodge as the Beast's rage infected the air. Joy tried to duck under the table, recalling a different time when she had hidden in a similar place, but it reared over her like a spooked stallion. As it teetered forward Joy lurched away and leapt across the gaping, steam vomiting chasms that stood between her and safety. The windows cracked and she felt flames lick at her heels. Vicious and hungry energy blew through the rooms, grasping like sharp claws at her hair and clothes, leaving trails of blood on her cheeks and bare arms.

Reaching the locked door, she screamed as the handle burnt her hand. The roof flew off the lodge, darkness crashed in behind it and heavy snow fell into the kitchen hissing and spitting in the heat. Murderous laughter battered her ears. Heavy footsteps resounded in the hallway. Joy moaned as her skin blistered and peeled as, simultaneously, the temperature plummeted and the air began to freeze in her lungs. She whimpered, 'Open, please, open. I can't die here again.' A huge clawed hand grasped her shoulder, hot breath scorched the back of her neck like acid and a sharp tongue flicked her ear lobe. Joy dropped to her knees screaming, 'Hope! Help me sister!'

The door shattered, the walls exploded and the blast wave propelled her outside. Chased by the Beast's frustrated roar, she sprang to her feet and fled to the pine forest. She ran, pursued by a raging wind that flung whipping branches and sharp stones to scratch and bruise her body and tear at her already ragged clothes. Freezing rain churned the ground to mud that gripped like quicksand. Her breath was laboured and her throat sore as she was dragged further into the earth. The more she struggled the deeper she sank. As the ground embraced her in its deadly arms she remembered a long ago agony as her mother's hand pressed down, forcing her head under the bath water. In the eye of the storm, once again unable to breathe, panic wrapped its fingers round her throat as the mud swathed death's shroud around her. It wasn't fair, it couldn't end like this. She would not allow it.

Remembering another storm in a kinder place, Joy felt heat course from her feet to her head. Drenched, sore and bleeding from a multitude of cuts and grazes Joy harnessed her anger to her purpose. She pressed her hands into the greedy earth and screamed at the churning sky, 'Enough! Stop!'

The tempest died away in shame and silence. The ground pushed her to its surface and grew firm. Under her feet, golden buttercups sprang into life and flashed like a flame toward the clearing. With the Beast's terrible bellows beating at her eardrums like a prize-fighter, she sprinted into the serenity of the pine forest, her purpose fixed.

The Angel Oak stood silhouetted against a fiery sky, its ancient symmetry ruined. Her hand clasped the stitch in her side, Joy gasped for breath frozen by a sight that turned her blood to ice. There was no wind. Every leaf on the tree was still.

He was waiting.

Jake hung from the highest branch. A noose tight around his neck, the blue rope creaking as he swayed, his eyes bulging and bloodshot, his generous lips open and tinged with violet. Joy gazed at her lover's corpse, helplessly imprisoned by shock.

An invisible force pulled Jake back to the branch where he sat looking down at her. He was breathing, alive, resurrected. She fell to her knees, weakened by relief that surged through her body.

Jake jumped. The crack of his breaking neck echoed through the silent forest and pierced Joy's soul.

Chapter Forty-Six

-A BRIDGE TOO FAR-

Three anxious immortals waited at the bridge that led into Heavensgate. They waited for the Creator's permission to enter, they waited for sight or sound of Joy. Sunlight faded into twilight and nothing happened, nothing at all.

They sat squashed together on the wagon's narrow wooden seat. Gabi picked at his nails, Ruby stared into the middle distance, scowling and Hope's perfect face wore a tragic expression.

Something unnatural roared in the distance setting Gabi's teeth on edge. 'There's malevolence here,' he muttered earning a sarcastic glance from Ruby who said, 'You think so? I am utterly amazed by your insight and sensitivity.'

Hope complained, 'It's over. The demon stole her heart, the Beast won and the Lord of Darkness feasts on Joy's soul. We arrived too late. I knew it would end this way. It's time we left, there's no point my being here anymore, which means you two fools aren't needed either.'

Ruby sneered, 'Aren't you supposed to be *Hope*? You chime like your ugly sister.'

'Despair, you mean? I most certainly do not chime like her, that old bell is cracked. However, unlike you, *Ruby Redemption,* I have learned acceptance. Destiny always wins in the end. My sister is lost.' Icy tears coursed down her pale cheeks. Shocked to see unemotional Hope in distress Ruby also burst into tears. Gabi hugged her tight and they sobbed together, mourning the loss of their beautiful friend.

Ruby gasped, 'Oh, Gabi, what will become of the world without Joy?'

He stroked her crazy red curls and murmured, 'Do not cry, mi amor, even in despair we still have Hope.'

Hearing Gabi invoke her name, Hope rolled her eyes and tightened her grip on the reins, ready to turn the wagon around. The horse creature shuffled his hooves, sending blue sparks flying to scorch the hem of Ruby's treasured, if tatty, scarlet cloak.

Hope was about to issue a reluctant apology when Ruby broke free of Gabi's embrace. She sat at attention, her red curls buffeted by a cold wind that carried the sounds of Holy percussion across the darkening sky and said, 'Listen.'

Hope shook the reins to rouse the gigantic horse from his stupor and shouted, 'It's the Gate. Great Creator, your mercy be blessed. The Gate is opening.'

The immortals clung to the narrow seat as the wagon careened across the bridge and, leaving summer at their backs, raced into the forest.

Joy's anguish echoed across the clearing as she knelt heartbroken and helpless in the face of Jake's eternal cycle of hanging and resurrection. She was too late. There was no way to reach him. Unless…

The wagon flew through the trees in a blur of rainbow light, wheels and hooves smashing pine needles into dust on the way.

Arriving at the Angel Oak Hope reined in and all three stared, mesmerised at the sight of Jake as he fell, the noose snapping his neck, over and over again.

Ruby passed judgment, 'Serves the evil, unrepentant bastard right.'

Gabi looked at Hope asking, 'Shouldn't Joy be here?'

As her friends watched Jake hang Joy laboured up the steep walkway that wound its way to the oak's crown. Although she was shielded from the sight of Jake's torture she still felt the living tree flinch each time he dropped and heard the creak of cruel rope rubbing against the branch. She looked up the slope that spiraled hypnotically overhead and fought the desire to stop and rest for all eternity. The longing for sweet, healing sleep grew. Her steps faltered, her eyelids became heavy and, as she crossed through pale light that streamed through a hollow branch, her exhausted legs betrayed her and she collapsed.

Hope climbed onto the wagon's roof, spread her arms wide and let her true voice ring powerful and clear across the clearing,
'JOY, WHERE ARE YOU?'

The clang and chime of Hope's anxiety roused Joy from her stupor and, gathering her courage, she crawled through a gap in the trunk and onto a thick branch. Vertigo hit like a wrecking ball, flattening her to the bark where she trembled, her breathing erratic as her heart threatened to break her ribs with its timpani.

A breeze rustled the leaves and Joy felt the branch sway like a cradle under her prostrate body. Dry-mouthed she raised her head and saw Jake sat a few yards away, the noose hung loosely around his neck, his jade-green eyes adoring her.

He jumped.

She waited.

Seconds passed, marked by the pendulum swing of his body.

Shaking, Joy crawled along the branch inch by slow inch, telling herself not to look down, never look down. She planned to use the knife to cut Jake free and, as she crept trembling to his gallows, the unseen force returned him to the branch.

High above the forest floor, oblivious to the audience below, the immortal and the demon embraced in the oak's golden canopy. Jake's wings remained bound by three iron bands and his blood ran from fresh wounds. Joy's exposed skin wept from hundreds of small cuts. She was scratched and bruised, her hair wild, her face and body caked with filth, but her face held an expression of pure ecstasy as she gazed into his eyes.

Heavensgate: Joy

Down in the clearing below, a deep sense of sorrow infected the air causing Gabi to tremble and Ruby to pull her cloak tighter. The horse hung his head and large tears dripped from his strange, silver eyes. Only Hope remained unaffected by the tangible pain which sullied the cathedral of Heavensgate's forest.

Holding Jake with her gaze, being careful not to look down on the tops of the pine trees, Joy reached behind her and, with a trembling hand removed the knife from her belt. Allowing herself to hope, she began to cut the thick rope. The branch rocked in a gust of wind and she gasped, her slippery hands almost dropping the blade. Battling to keep her breathing slow and steady she pressed all her strength down on the blade.

Jake jumped almost toppling her over with him.

She waited.

He returned.

Hope called, 'Don't look down. Use your power.'

Jake's eyes transmitted his desperation and pain. Joy fought dizziness and nausea as she tried again to saw away the noose with a knife that was as useless as water. She placed it back in her belt and screamed, clinging to the branch, as Jake dropped and hung swaying beneath her feet.

Ruby turned to Gabi. 'Enough. She can't save him. She had her chance. Hurry before the demon takes her with him.'

Jake returned to the branch only to drop again, but this time Joy clung to his broken neck. They swung together. The evil force returned them to the branch and he was resurrected.

Thunder pealed, lightening illuminated the forest canopy and it began to snow.

Hope cupped her hands around her mouth and shouted, 'You're in the Wrong Place.'

Realisation struck Joy like a slap across the face.

She placed her fingertips on Jake's neck and chest and full of hope, she whispered, 'Open.'

The noose unraveled. The metal bindings disappeared and, as they plummeted toward the ground, Joy's dark angel spread his magnificent wings.

Hovering in mid-air, the lovers kissed. His hands tangled in her hair, his mouth and eyes devoured her as Joy poured herself into him. Ruby threw off her cloak and spread her fiery wings, glowing with rage at the sight of her friend in the demon's arms. Gabi trembled with fury and his terrible and glorious transformation began.

Jake tore his lips away, anguish etched in every line of his handsome face. Joy wiped away a lone tear that flowed down the path of his childhood scar.

Hope watched and waited in eager anticipation.

Cradling Joy's face, Jake whispered, *'Forgive me, my love, this is the only way we can be together. We must hide from the Beast in the next Realm. Don't be afraid, I will follow you.'*

And the forest shook with the Beast's triumphant roar. 'Bring the bitch to me, Imp!'

Resisting the urge to bolt the horse blew violet tendrils of steam from cavernous nostrils and stamped his enormous silver hooves on the forest floor, jangling the thousands of small bells on his harness. Alerted to their audience, but keeping Joy in his embrace, Jake bellowed in rage and fury. An answering roar blasted across the forest from the Beast that skulked, hiding from the immortals, waiting for its warrior and their prey. Hearing his master's siren call, Jake fought his demon and lost.

He slipped one hand around Joy's waist and the other around her slender neck.

Surrendering herself to his love and mercy Joy waited for Jake to save them.

Jake stared into her eyes and whispered, 'Be calm, beautiful.' Trusting in his adoration and her own immortality, she tried to smile, but her body panicked and she began to choke.

Ruby screamed, 'That bastard is strangling her. What is wrong with you, Hope? Gabriel, help me.' Unfurling her wings the Angel Redemption shouted, 'Joy, don't trust him. He is a demon. He *can* kill you.' Then she exploded into flight leaving a scarlet vapour trail in her wake.

Beneath Jake and his victim, fiery red roses encircled the oak. Their heady scent escaped from small avalanches of ash that fell from the inextinguishable blooms to join the blizzard.

Hope applauded and murmured, 'Nice touch. Better late than never, dear sister, Faith.'

As Faith's roses burnt like beacons of salvation, Ruby and Gabi's fury drove them to the rescue. Redemption's copper burnished wings carried her in pursuit as the Angel Gabriel illuminated the snow laden sky with searing blue flames. In a voice that could cut glaciers he commanded, 'Demon, release her.' Jake spat fire and, feeling the heat flash, Joy's faith in her lover wavered.

Jake moved his hand from her waist to join the one circling her throat. She hung helpless in his grip, her hands clutching his, fighting for a fraction in which to breathe. He flew ever higher to escape the avenging angels as dark spots spoiled her vision and unbearable pressure built behind her eyes.

Her hands grew weak, her body heavy in Jake's grasp. She felt herself drifting away on the sounds of Jake's wings thrashing the air and the rush of blood that fought, and failed, to enter her head. There was no pain, only sorrow.

She had fought the Beast and faced death for him.

She had returned to Heavensgate desperate to free his spirit with her love.

She had used her powers to save him from eternity on the evil noose.

She had not considered his betrayal.

The Beast's disembodied roar held a note of desperation as he snarled, 'Imp, obey me.'

Gabriel's voice crashed into Jake with the power of Heaven.

'Release her to me, demon.' Redemption screamed her threat to disembowel the devil's spawn in flight. The power of their Holy voices coursed through Joy's heart like sunshine in winter.

Her friends were here and their appearance as Holy Angels was a blissful revelation. Gabi and Ruby's furious love cut through Joy's death haze and she was no longer willing to die for Jake. Hope's relief pealed like wedding bells across the clearing. Joy opened her eyes and Jake saw condemnation in her stare.

The Angel Gabriel drew his sword. In a voice dripping with scorn Jake said,

Come on, come closer, Gabriel, you too, Hope, and you, Redemption. Come witness me snap this pathetic creature's neck like a twig.

Hope sat, calm and relaxed on the wagon, apparently absorbed in rearranging the silver bangles on her wrists and wholly unconcerned with the tragedy unfolding above her. The horse blew steam into the swirling snowflakes and struck his hooves against the icy ground.

Jake's master roared, 'Bring me the fucking toy, Imp.'

The voice of Lucifer's puppet lit fires of retribution in Redemption. She hungered to wipe the Beast from the face of Heavensgate, but now wasn't the time. Hovering behind Joy on her splendid wings, she reached to snatch her from Jake who dodged easily while roaring fire laden obscenities. Gabriel raised his blazing sword and the demon used Joy like a shield, shaking her like a cat would shake a mouse.

Hope leapt from the wagon and walked with casual grace to the Angel Oak.

Feeding off the Angels' Holy light, Joy found fresh strength and fumbled for the knife.

Redemption blasted Jake with searing radiance that tore silken black feathers from his wings. Joy forced herself to remain limp while Jake shot through the clouds to flee his attackers.

In the forest below, snow bent the slender heads of the pines and frost dressed the oak in silver. Hope stepped into the circle of blazing roses and picked one, admiring its beautiful resilience as it burnt in molten contrast to the whiteness all around. Her immortal voice rang into the heavens.

'Joy loves you, Jake. She returned to Heavensgate of her own free will to save you from eternal torment. Let her go.'

Hope's words weakened the tug of the Beast's desire and, above the clouds, Jake moved one hand from Joy's throat to her waist.

Redemption cried out, 'Jake, you won the love of an immortal. Repent your sins and follow us to the Gate. Jacob is waiting.'

Hearing Jacob's name, the Beast's wrath coursed like lava through Jake's being and his face twisted with hate. Joy held tight to the blade and carefully moved her hand up her side.

In a voice racked with torment, Jake screeched, *Again, Redemption? Is that all you care about, my repentance? Fuck off!*

The Angel Joy knew as Ruby hovered before Jake, forced to scream to be heard over the Beast's pursuing rage as she said, 'Your son is here to guide you.'

Jake lashed out sending Redemption spiraling out of control. She hit the ground with a sickening crack that shattered several of the oak's gigantic roots and toppled several pines. Hearing her screams of pain and fury Gabriel flew to her aid. She cried in his arms, 'We have failed the Creator. Joy is lost.'

Hope handed the rose to Tommy. Water streamed from the spirit child's nose, mouth and clothes. As the rose-circle blazed, flashing soft warmth that melted away the surrounding ice and snow, Jake returned to sit on the branch that had been his gallows and watched the scene below with Joy's body splayed across his knees. Tommy gazed up at the creature he had once known as the playful part of his father and offered him the rose, saying, 'Daddy, please let Joy go. Come home to mummy and me.'

Longing flickered across Jake's savage eyes as he stared at his only son. Seizing the moment, Hope said, 'Jake, take the gift of hope I bring. Release Joy and you may enter the Gate and become whole with Jacob.'

Resentment swept away the last dregs of his humanity. Jake spat fire and, keeping his hold on Joy, flew at Hope who threw herself to safety under an immense tree root. The Beast's mocking laughter rocked the forest creating a tornado of snow that spun around Jake and his toy.

'Jacob? Join that motherfuckin' no good piece of chicken shit? Never!'

Tommy vanished. Jake soared high above the Angel Oak with Joy's body swinging from one hand like a pendulum. Gabriel rushed him in a blinding flash of pure white light, his sword drawn and, spinning with Joy and her captor in a funnel of ice and snow, he shouted, 'I will dispatch you to the hell that spawned you.' Still recovering her strength, Ruby yelled into the swirling sky, 'You will burn for this, demon.'

The ground quaked as the Beast replete with rage, misery and terror, approached to reclaim his warrior.

Lost in his fury, Jake didn't notice Joy tighten her hold on the knife. His being was totally absorbed by the demon and his black wings cut through leaden clouds as he flew intent on delivering her body to his master. Determined to save him, Joy reached up and, with a blade sharpened by compassion, sliced open the old scar on his cheek. Pain and shock expelled the demon from his eyes and they began to fall. His grip on her failed and she grabbed at his belt, hanging on tight. They rolled and plummeted through the blizzard. Joy screamed and the unnatural wind stole her terror and fed it to the Beast. Frozen ground raced toward them, Joy closed her eyes against the bone crushing impact, Jake pressed her to his chest, twisted his body and rocketed beyond the clouds.

Heavensgate: Joy

The demon had disappeared with Joy in a blast of arctic cold. Thunder and lightning ripped the air flinging hailstones like icy bullets. Redemption wept with Gabriel. It was over.

Hope urgently picked a dozen burning roses, inhaling their glorious scent and power. Then, after tucking them behind her creature's harness, she climbed back on the wagon and called to the defeated angels, 'Come back, the Beast approaches. Hurry.'

Unable to follow their friend and her murderer, Redemption and Gabriel climbed on board, struggling under the weight of guilt and sorrow they knew would torture them for all eternity.

Hope spoke her instructions, sending the mighty sound of cathedral bells ringing with power that chased the Beast into hell. They raced back to the bridge while Gabi plucked ice out of his wings and preened Ruby's copper feathers to distract himself from the anguish that punished his gentle soul. In a small, defeated voice, Ruby asked, 'Where are we going? What's the bloody hurry?'

'Oh ye of little faith.' Hope chimed, 'Shut up and smell the roses.'

Released from the Beast's influence, Jake had fled to the Nothing where he nursed Joy. Caressing the marks on her neck, he hung his head and wept.

Joy's voice was hoarse and sore as she said, 'You deceived me.'

He smiled through his tears.

I told you it isn't easy to die around here.

'You betrayed my trust.'

I am truly sorry, my love, but I can't cross the Gate. I can't join with Jacob, not even for Tommy's sake. I am the lost fragment. I belong to the Beast. He is my Master, Lord Lucifer, and I am His to direct. His punishment for helping you escape him at Heavensgate must be taken.

'Come with me.'

I can't. I lost Hope, I almost killed you, my Joy, and now...

'What?'

I am commanded by Lucifer, Lord of Hate, to destroy Faith.

'Faith, like Hope and Joy, is stronger than the Devil. You are destined to fail.'
I must try and you must leave.

The Nothing parted to reveal a girl at the wheel of a pink Cadillac. Jake carried Joy to the car and tenderly laid her across the crushed velvet rear seat saying, *I return the best part of your heart to you, my Lady Joy. I am not worthy of such grace.*

He pressed his lips to her mouth and his hand to her chest. As she drew in a rattling breath and pink flooded her translucent skin he turned to the driver and said,

Take my love home, Joan.

The girl clenched the wheel and replied, 'Jake, I'll surely try, but I've never been able to cross that damn bridge. Oh Jake, the Gate is openin'. I'm truly scared.'

Use the Gate to cross over. Escape Heavensgate. Take Joy home, the Mortal Realm needs her.

'I can't. I'm too afraid.'

Joan, just fuck off through the Gate. Go and don't look back.

Joan turned on the radio and the Boss boomed out her anthem, 'Pink Cadillac.'

Come on, Joan, listen to Mr Springsteen singin' about your ride and drive outta here.

She pressed the pedal to the metal and the Cadillac flew out of the Nothing to land with a hard bounce outside the Lodge.

The wheels spun, struggling to gain purchase on the frozen ground. Joan gritted her teeth and drove half-blinded by the swirling blizzard.

The old car shuddered as the Boss declared that he loved her for her pink Cadillac. Reaching the main highway, she spun the old car off the rutted lane and onto slippery asphalt.

Hitting black ice the car fishtailed and the wheel spun through Joan's hands eliciting a shriek of panic before the Caddy grabbed purchase and straightened out. Fearing that her new chance at life might be cut prematurely short, Joy scrambled into the passenger seat. Joan grinned and said, 'I can't believe that psycho, Jake, let you go. *He* freed *us* from Heavensgate. It's a freakin' miracle.'

'It is, Joan. I just hope we don't need another one to escape this bloody place.'

Happy tears streaked lines of black mascara down the girl's cheeks. Gritting her teeth, she sped down the highway, not letting up until the bridge was in sight.

The Boss was just wondering what she did in the back of her Caddy when the radio died and the engine spluttered and rattled, coughing like a forty a day smoker until it shuddered to a halt. They were still on the wrong side of the bridge. As the wipers struggled to clear snow from the windshield, the other side, the side where Heavensgate ended and the Gate waited, shimmered in a heat haze like an optical illusion.

Joan punched the wheel and said, 'Shit. I can't walk, I'm bound to the Caddy and it just died on us.'

'Change places.' They clambered over each other, Joy took the wheel and tapped the ignition whispering, 'Start.'

The engine sprang to life, ticking over in neutral and sounding as fresh as the day it left the factory.

The women contemplated the distance between them and salvation. Joan shrieked, 'Look, it's Hope.'

Joy wound down the window and stuck her head out shouting, 'Hope, Ruby, Gabi!' In response, waves of blinding light flooded across the bridge forcing Joy and Joan to shield their eyes. When their vision adjusted they saw that The Gate was wide open. Shadows could be seen flitting through rainbows that clothed the place where life and death meet.

'What the hell? I'm sorry, Joy, but look at the Gate. How have I never seen it before? And who in the name of all that's Holy are those people?'

'Gabi and Ruby are my friends. The woman you know as Hope, well, she is my sister.'

Joy stared, transfixed by sights barely glimpsed through the open Gate. Heaven looked a lot like home.

Joan bounced in her seat. 'OK, so you've friends and family in high places. I gotta get outta here before the Gate closes. Please, Joy, concentrate and drive. I'll close my eyes. Joy, snap out of it. We have a need for speed.'

Joy laughed and pushed the stick into drive.

Hope climbed down from her wagon and sat cross legged in the grass making daisy chains. Gabriel and Redemption preened their tattered wings in the sunshine.

In Heavensgate the car's wiper blades shifted fresh snow off the windshield and a summer breeze wafted into the Caddy carrying scents of Parma violet candy, Earl Gray tea and sweet pastries. Joy said, 'It's summer over there.' Joan kept her eyes squeezed shut and said, 'Please shut up and drive before I lose my nerve.'

Her panic broke Joy's trance. She checked the rear view mirror; it was blowing a blizzard and, although there was blue sky ahead, the clouds behind hung low, dark and menacing.

As Joy pressed the accelerator a huge shadow battled through the snow with fire spewing from its cavernous mouth. The sweetness on the air was driven out by the stench of sulphur and rotten flesh. Trees burst into blue flames and collapsed like pillars of ash.

Risking a glance over her shoulder Joan screamed, 'What the hell is that?'

The Beast sprinted through the storm. In one gigantic leap it sprung onto the Caddy and thrust an armored hand through the roof roaring, 'I smell you, bitch!' Its other hand broke through a side window. Panic sprung Joan into the back seat where she dodged razor sharp claws that slashed the seats to shreds while she squealed like a stuck pig.

Ice water ran in Joy's veins as she twisted the steering wheel from side to side and the Cadillac streaked toward salvation. The Beast grabbed her hair, its foul breath filling the car with the stench of a thousand rotting corpses, but Joy hung on and, inbetween shrieks of terror, Joan prayed. Despite their courage the powerful Beast was winning. Jumping onto its back Joan beat ineffectually at its fiery head as it yanked Joy toward its gaping jaws. A hundred cruel teeth grazed her forehead and salty blood stung her eyes. She pressed her fingers into the monster's eyes and felt the depths of its perversion stream into her hands stripping the flesh from her bones. Joan joined her strength with Joy's, but it was over, the Gate would close without them. The Beast had one hand squeezing Joan's neck and the other gripping Joy's as he licked her face, savoring her defeat and despair. His putrid tongue had forced its way between her lips to better satisfy his unholy hunger when a sword of light flew from Gabriel's hand like a heat seeking missile. Angelic vengeance blasted through the shattered windshield riding a wave of glacier blue light to spear the Beast on its power, decimating evil and blasting it back to hell. Depraved screams of eternal fury and frustration filled the forest. Sheet lightening crashed down on the Lodge, smashing it to matchsticks.

The ruined Caddy rolled to a gentle stop behind Hope's wagon with its battle worn occupants. Gabriel yanked open a battered door and leaned inside. Redemption stood behind him. She winked at Joy, who stared at her through blood and demonic spit, too shocked to remark on her friends' angelic appearance.

Gabriel smiled shyly as he peeled Joan's burnt hands away from the terrified girl's face saying, 'Come along, sweetheart. It's time to cross the Gate.'

Joy nudged the girl who threw her arms around her whispering, 'Thank you for rescuing me.' Joy untangled herself and, encouraged by Gabriel, Joan stepped out of the Caddy for the last time.

Joy pressed her injured hands over her eyes feeling faint at the sight of the Angel's pearlescent wings shining in the Gate's strange light.

Redemption held the hand of a smiling boy. The child looked up at Joan and, in a shy voice, said, 'I'm Tommy. My *nice* daddy, Jacob, asked me to take you home.'

Barely visible in the sunlight, Death leaned nonchalantly against a spruce tree.

Joy watched, mesmerised as the Angels Gabriel and Redemption and the child she thought of as the Wet Boy, shepherded Joan through the Gate until they vanished amongst welcoming shadows, consumed like moonlight at dawn.

Leaving the car, Joy walked to where Death waited for her. She hid her surprise as he bowed low and, taking her hand in his, pressed cool lips to her burnt skin. Using a midnight silk handkerchief he tenderly cleaned her face. Holding both her painful hands in his, and dropping a kiss on her head, Death healed her wounds with his compassion. Joy shed tears of gratitude as he said,

-The Creator sends you his blessings, my Lady Joy. Do not waste them. Come, let us join your sister.-

Joy sat with Death on Hope's wagon, waiting for her friends to return from beyond the Gate and explain themselves.

Hope kissed Joy on both cheeks. Her creature snorted, pawing the ground and sending up sparks to join the dust motes dancing in the sunlight. Scarlet roses blazed along his harness.

Death pointed at the blooms and whispered in Hope's ear.

She dropped the reins.

The wagon lurched forward, almost toppling Joy over the side.

Hope's eyes opened wide in horror. With a high pitched ring, she said, 'You are joking. My Lord.'

-I never joke.-

Hope's discordant voice couldn't conceal her distress. 'Then it is not over.'

-My Lady, you and your sister have the demon, Jake's, evil heart. I must have *all* of his soul. However, there are greater forces at play.-

'I do not have his heart, Joy stole it. What do you mean?'

'I did no such thing, he gave his heart to me willingly,' Joy snapped.

Hope raised an elegant eyebrow. 'My Lord, I returned the clay heart to Jacob when he crossed over. I do, however, guard an unimportant small, hard, burnt lump of nothingness. You know this already, Lord.

-If it is unimportant, why do you guard it?-

Hope cast her eyes down.

-What is the reason for Jake's enduring presence in Heavensgate?-

Hope glanced at Joy and chimed, 'I have no idea.'

-My Lady Joy, what are your thoughts on this matter?-

'I am sorry, my Lord, this is all very strange and new to me.'

-Then I will tell you what you already know. Lucifer has commanded his demon, Jake, to test Faith.-

Hope straightened her spine and said, 'We should not worry. Jake failed to destroy me and he saved Joy from the Beast. What chance would he have against one as strong as our sister Faith?'

Death was silent. He sat, absentmindedly playing with his silver pocketwatch chain.

The pocket watch popped open and the tinny notes of 'Que Sera' filled the air.

Hope grasped her sister's hand.

Panic clutched her immortal throat.

Death is never absentminded.

Book 3 - Heavensgate - Faith

Prologue

Everybody trusted my saintly, delusional dick of an alter-ego, Jacob, who was allowed to pass through the Gate, leaving me behind to suffer and pay for his sins.

He was blind to the truth, but I learnt my torturous lessons despite the unholy interference of Hope and Joy in my spiritual growth.

I'll tell you my secrets so you may have a fighting chance of recognising these bitches if they cross your path. See? I'm not all bad after all.

You've met Hope; immortal and ancient as the stars but still playing the innocent.

You will desire her and fix your pathetic sheep-mind on her. You will waste your days and nights longing to feel the spark that only Hope can bring to ease the misery of your darkest hours.

When the time comes that you drown in grief, gasping and fighting for each breath sweet Hope will appear to show you the insurmountable beauty of life, just before she steals your heart and kills you.

Suckers.

Hope is a malignant, cancerous tramp.

You may also know the miracle that is Joy.

Joy is the balm that overshadows despair and eases sorrow. She is the blessed sunshine among life's vicious downpours.

Heavensgate: Joy

Like me, you will long for her kisses even as she squeezes the last drop of contentment from your soul and then, knowing she is lost to you, you will plead for her to bring meaning to your insignificant life.

Fleeting and difficult to recall, sweet Joy is an unfaithful, deceitful whore.

I can't wait to screw with her again.

My Lord taught me that these two stinkin' bitches take shelter with a third: Faith.

She poisons your spirit with the conviction that everything is in the Creator's plan. Faith will make you believe even whilst you burn with the loss of her sisters, Hope and Joy.

I will destroy Faith. I will deliver her to the Beast naked and reeking of despair. She will crawl on torn and bloodied knees in supplication to my Lord. He will feed on her delicate soul, as she, hopeless, joyless, bruised and forgotten in Heaven loses the will to make the Human Realm believe in love, forgiveness, redemption and salvation.

Faith, she's a damn good mindfuck.

These are the women in my life, may the Devil help me.

By the way, my name is Jake Andersen. Welcome to Heavensgate, the Realm where Hope and Joy abandoned me.

The Realm where Faith will die.

* * *

Enter the monthly Heavensgate swag competition by e-mail: Hgleokane@hotmail.com
Send me a pic of you with any Heavensgate book on your kindle or in paperback and I will enter you in the draws for a year.

If you enjoyed Jake's madness please place your review. I will be eternally grateful and Jake will find Hope, Joy and Faith!

You can find me on Facebook where you will also find news and information about the series and its beautiful fans: https://www.facebook.com/leokaneheavensgate

Please join me on Twitter: @h_gleokane

And catch up with me on my web page:
http://hgleokane.wix.com/heavensgate
  or
https://www.nextchapter.pub/authors/leo-kane

Thank you, dear friend, for choosing this book and travelling Heavensgate's strange paths with me.

Acknowledgements

My darling husband has tolerated me for more than forty years and survived to help me edit supernatural fiction. David, it is an honour to be your wife. Thank you for believing in me and for supporting me in everything I do.

I am lucky to have fantastic friends and family who checked drafts, gave sage advice and, above all, provided me with motivation and encouragement when I stumbled. Thank you all so much, you give me hope and courage.

Special thanks to the brilliant cover artist, Elayne Griffiths, whose vision is psychic in nature and whose magical work commands attention.

There is one other person to whom I owe gratitude; we have never met, but her poetry speaks to my heart and I am grateful for her contribution to Heavensgate, this wonderful poet is **Naomi Porch**, remember her name, she is a star.

Musical Acknowledgements

Music and scents combine to make the soul remember, so I am grateful to, and acknowledge, the incredible artists and musicians who continue to help me find my way around Heavensgate. I do not claim any of their fabulous work as my own, that honour is all theirs.

There Once Was an Ugly Duckling, performed by Danny Kaye, written by Frank Loesser, 1952, Frank Music Corp.

Always Look on the Bright Side of Life, performed by Eric Idle, written by Monty Python, 1979

Jingle Bells, performed by Bing Crosby, written by James S Pierpont, 1857

Angel Eyes, performed and written by Roxy Music, 1979, Polydor

Pretty in Pink, performed by The Psychedelic Furs, 1981, written by John Ashton and others, Columbia

Rhythm of the Night, performed by Corona, 1993, written by Francesco Bontempi and others, DWA

My Way, performed by Frank Sinatra, 1969, written by Paul Anka, Reprise

Heavensgate: Joy

You're the One That I Want, performed by John Travolta and Olivia Newton-John, 1978, written by John Farrar, RSO

Que Sera Sera, performed by Doris Day, 1956, written by Jay Livingston and Ray Evans, Warner Chappell Music Inc.

I Put a Spell on You, performed by Nina Simone, 1965, written by Jay Hawkins, Philips

All the Things She Said, performed by t.A.T.u., written by Trevor Horn and others, Universal/Interscope

It's Not Unusual, performed by Tom Jones, written by Les Reed and Gordon Mills, Decca UK, 1965, parrot Records (US), 1965

Shut Up and Dance, performed by Walk On The Moon, 2014, written by Walk On The Moon and others, RCA

Gimme Hope Jo'anna, performed and written by Eddie Grant, 1988, Parlophone, EMI

Take Me To Church, performed by Hozier written by Andrew Hozier-Byrne, 2013, Columbia Records, Rubyworks-Island Records-

Locked Out Of Heaven, performed by Bruno Mars, 2012, written by Bruno Mars and others, Atlantic

Relax, performed by Frankie Goes to Hollywood, written by Peter Gill and others, ZTT

21st Century Schizoid Man, performed by King Crimson, 1969, written by Peter Sinfield, Atlantic Records

I've Got You Under My Skin, performed by Frank Sinatra, 1956, written by Cole Porter, 1936, produced by Voyle Gilmore

Chains, performed by Tina Arena, 1994, written by Tina Arena and others, Columbia

We Gotta Get Outta This Place, performed by the Animals, 1965, written by Barry Mann and Cynthia Well, Columbia Gramophone (UK), MGM (US)

I'm On Fire, performed and written by Bruce Springsteen, 1985, Columbia

My Favourite Things, performed by Julie Andrews, 1965, written by Richard Rodgers and Oscar Hammerstein II, 1959

So In Love, performed by Ella Fitzgerald, 1956, written by Cole Porter

Over the Rainbow, performed by Eva Cassidy, written by Harold Arlen, 1939

Pink Cadillac, performed and written by Bruce Springsteen aka The Boss, 1984, Columbia Records

About the Author

Born and raised in the Steel City of Sheffield, England Leo has spent a lot of her life day dreaming and can't seem to outgrow the habit. Despite this she managed to raise a family of three wonderful girls, a tolerant husband and, recently, a crazy husky, somehow acquiring a career and a Master of Science degree along the way.

Leo is a qualified clinical hypnotherapist with a fascination for the human condition. When not sending people into a trance or bringing her daydreams to life on the page Leo mainly spends her time happily staring out of windows and using her husband as a guinea pig for experimental cookery which he places in the horror genre.

* * *

Leo Kane

To learn more about Leo Kane and discover more Next Chapter authors, visit our website at www.nextchapter.pub.

Joy
ISBN: 978-4-82410-860-9

Published by
Next Chapter
1-60-20 Minami-Otsuka
170-0005 Toshima-Ku, Tokyo
+818035793528
20th December 2021

CPSIA information can be obtained
at www.ICGtesting.com
Printed in the USA
LVHW011221190122
708789LV00003B/149